From bed partners . . .

Two years ago, while on assignment for the Crown, darkly handsome Garrett Burke left Lady Ivy Wentworth sleeping naked in his bed as he went in search of the missing Martello diamonds. After apprehending the dastardly thief, he intended to spend the rest of his life in the arms of the auburn-haired beauty. But when the case came to a shocking and dangerous end, Garrett was certain he'd been betrayed . . .

To partners in crime

Ivy once loved Garrett with a virtuous heart, but these days she can barely stand him. Arriving at a deserted estate on a mysterious errand, she never expected to see him again, nor feel the same ecstasy she once did at his touch. Now, joined with him in the search for the legendary jewels, she is willing to risk everything. Everything, that is, except her heart . . .

By Adele Ashworth

A NOTORIOUS PROPOSITION
THE DUKE'S INDISCRETION
DUKE OF SCANDAL
DUKE OF SIN
WHEN IT'S PERFECT
SOMEONE IRRESISTIBLE

ADELE ASHWORTH

A Notorious Proposition

An Avon Romantic Treasure

AVON
An Imprint of HarperCollinsPublishers

This is a work of fiction. Names, characters, places, and incidents are products of the author's imagination or are used fictitiously and are not to be construed as real. Any resemblance to actual events, locales, organizations, or persons, living or dead, is entirely coincidental.

AVON BOOKS
An Imprint of HarperCollins*Publishers*
10 East 53rd Street
New York, New York 10022-5299

Copyright © 2008 by Adele Budnick
ISBN 978-0-06-112858-5
www.avonromance.com

First Avon Books paperback printing: May 2008

Avon Trademark Reg. U.S. Pat. Off. and in Other Countries, Marca Registrada, Hecho en U.S.A.
HarperCollins® is a registered trademark of HarperCollins Publishers.

Printed in the U.S.A.

10 9 8 7 6 5 4 3 2 1

*This book is dedicated to several wonderful people.
First, to my magnificent agent, Denise Marcil,
who's been the greatest champion of my work
for the last ten years, and to the marvelous
editorial staff at Avon Books, who are
forever there to help and encourage me
when I struggle: Carrie Feron, Lyssa Keusch,
May Chen, and Cristine Grace.*

*To Laura Lee Guhrke, Rachel Gibson,
Elizabeth Boyle, and Julia Quinn—
because you guys just make me laugh.*

*I also offer my deepest thanks
to a wonderful author and
even greater friend, Kathryn Smith,
for always picking up the phone
and giving advice when I run out of plot ideas.
Needless to say, she's a plotting genius
and we talk a lot.*

*As always, my love goes out to
Andrew, Caroline, Ed, Bri, and Ryan
for urging me along with this book
and not getting too upset about eating
yet another night of Chinese takeout.*

*And finally, I thank all those readers
who have urged me to return to the
mythical town of Winter Garden.
Although this story stands alone,
I hope it satisfies. I could never finish a book
without all of you at my back.*

Prologue

London
January 1850

Garrett stirred and lifted his head from his pillow, trying to focus on the clock atop the mantelpiece without waking Ivy, who slept beside him in his bed.

The hands were barely discernible in dim firelight, but he thought it read almost half past ten, which meant he still had more than an hour before he had to leave for his midnight rendezvous with a thief. A good thing, since he really was too comfortable to get up and dress just yet.

Gently, he lowered his head again, trying very hard not to move his body and interrupt her peaceful slumber. After making love to her at last, after several days of a fast and powerful seduction, she'd curled her nude form up beside him, legs intertwined with his, her arm draped over his stomach, her head resting on his shoulder as her soft breath from each steady exhale brushed his skin with moist warmth. She looked beautiful, contented, and felt to him as if she had always belonged here, something he'd never experienced with any other woman in his life.

Just the sight of her made him smile, and since the moment they'd met only one week ago, he found it difficult to tear his gaze from her. She had a face and figure stunning to behold, thick auburn hair and mesmerizing honey brown eyes that captured his with a fiery longing when they were introduced. They had been drawn to each other as a magnet to iron from that very first meeting, but they had been careful. Not even her brother knew of their love affair, and it would have to remain that way for a few more hours. If all went according to plan, after the arrest of Benedict Sharon, he would confess his identity to her and marry her immediately in the event she carried his child even now. Ivy was a lady, in the truest sense of the word, and they were obviously a perfect match. She would, of course, have to forgive him for his deceit, but after what they had shared this evening, he had no doubt that she would. He refused to let himself contemplate anything else.

After another few minutes of watching her silently and contemplating the errand he was soon to undertake, he decided it was time to slowly push himself up and brave the cold floor with his bare feet. She stirred, but didn't awaken, turning over onto her stomach and stuffing her arms up under her pillow, her glorious hair spilling across her back and shoulder and covering the indentation in the mattress he'd only just left. It took everything in him not to climb back under the blankets and take her again, but alas, he had a job to do, and she knew it. With any luck he'd be back and taking her into his arms before she ever noticed him missing.

That marvelous thought in mind, he dressed quickly in plain dark clothes, pulled his hat far down on his head, and took one last glance at her still and sleeping form as he softly opened the door.

God, she stirred his blood as no woman ever had, in every imaginable way. Her appearance, a unique combination of sensuality and grace, her temperament, both charming and passionate, her smile, with seductive secrets meant only for him.

Yes, indeed, with Ivy in his bed and the Martello diamonds within his grasp, the angels were surely smiling down on him tonight.

At ten minutes past midnight, the docks along the riverfront were quiet, the air still and thick with the odor of brine and chimney smoke. The only sound came from a faraway tolling of bells and his boots on the pavement as he walked toward Aldgate High Street near St. Anne's Church. Without a moon, and through the thin layer of fog, he saw almost nothing in his path, encountered nobody, which had been his hope as he chose the small sanctuary for their meeting.

Of course he'd thanked Ivy's brother for providing the information that led him here this night, though he still felt a pang of guilt in not telling her of her twin's involvement in his quest for the Martello diamonds. But he would. He'd have to if he wanted a future with her.

The faintest sound of female laughter in the distance jarred him from his musings. He paused for a moment, taking note of his surroundings, then crossed to the other side of the street. Swiftly, he climbed the old stone steps and pulled on the unlocked door, opening it just enough to allow his body to slip inside. Only candles burned for light, their remarkably sweet odor triggering memories of his own church in Rye, though he quickly forced himself to dismiss all thoughts to concentrate on the moment at hand. It was vital he remain alert. After crossing the narthex, he entered the sanctuary and stood for a moment behind the last pew as he allowed his eyes to adjust to the dimness inside.

His heart began beating fast and hard. This was it. Soon he would be holding the priceless treasure known as the Martello diamonds in his hands. Soon Benedict Sharon would be arrested for the theft. Soon Ivy would be his—

A creak of floorboards from behind startled him. He turned, expecting to see Benedict Sharon, ready to exchange the diamonds for money. But instead, to his utter surprise, he saw the cloaked shape of a woman in the corner, her back against the far wall watching him from the shadows. Confusion flooded him for only a slice of a second—then he heard the crack against his skull before he felt it.

Garrett reeled, a sharp, intense pain shooting through him. He dropped to his knees as blackness enveloped him. In one last gasp of breath, one last thought of Ivy, he succumbed to the warmth and peace of darkness.

Chapter 1

*Southern England
January 1852*

Lady Ivy Wentworth stood motionless in the shadow of an ominous twilight, feeling the icy January wind scrape her cheeks like bits of blowing sand, thinking little of the frost in the air as she stared at the silent, lifeless house looming in the distance. The coach that brought her from the city pulled away slowly behind her, though she scarcely heard it. Nothing filled her mind now but the same trepidation that had forced her to return to the elite and scandal-ridden town of Winter Garden—and a sharp, sudden fear that she might be too late.

Drawing a deep, cold breath, she closed her eyes and lifted her face to the darkening sky, holding on to what remained of the vision that drew her to fear this moment.

Dark hair, black eyes, cold, bright crystals. Snowflakes. Snowflakes falling around her . . . And then standing on a dirt path, staring up at the figure in the window. A window from her past. A shadow of a man, or a ghost, watching her, waiting, silently begging for help, desperately needing her . . .

She strained to remember the details, the earlier and later moments, but everything else escaped her for now. She couldn't see the face, its features or expression, but she knew who it was, which made the scene so frightening she could hardly contain her emotions, and she knew that hiding them now and in the days to come would be one of the greatest difficulties of her life. Since her visions always came and went like a rolling fog, missing certain elements of importance never bothered her too much—until now. This vision was personal, and a sudden wave of apprehension seized her as she once again thought of the life at stake. She had a great deal to do, and very little time.

Grasping her valise with a gloved hand and tightening her woolen pelisse at the neck with the other, she glanced around the village square for the first time, seeing nobody, probably because it was almost dark and the streetlamps were yet to be lit. Swallowing her weariness, she began a direct stride down Farrset Lane, hearing the unmistakable sounds of music and bawdy laughter from the tavern and inn to her left, thankful she wouldn't need to stay in such a noisy place with her nerves so jumpy.

Tonight she would stay at the small cottage owned by her contacts in Winter Garden; tomorrow she would be moving into the manor house on the lake, formerly owned as a summer retreat by Richard Sharon, Baron

Rothebury, left vacant but for a handful of servants after his arrest on charges of opium smuggling two years ago. She had the key and had been invited. With her comfortable establishment in the home, she would earnestly begin piecing together the remnants of her vision and correlating it as best she could with the more vital reason that compelled her to take such a risk in coming here. But for this evening, she would meet with Thomas and Madeleine St. James, the Earl of Eastleigh and his half-French wife, to discuss the particulars and uncertainties that awaited her once she let it be known that she'd arrived in Winter Garden and was staying at the Rothebury estate. They were the only two people in the community she knew through her work for the government, and she trusted them with the unusual and rather confidential reason she'd returned.

The earl and his countess were secretly employed as spies for the British, though they were now mostly retired. Ivy had met them both in her own service for the Home Office, through their immediate superior, Sir Riley Liddle, though she'd never worked directly with them. She wasn't a spy, and her work had never involved deception. It had, in fact, been just the opposite, as her unconventional exploits in the field of smuggling and the missing and murdered usually found their way to print, for all of London to relish and discuss at parties, sometimes in excruciating detail. Nevertheless, she very much enjoyed what she did, helping investigators with details nobody could see or know save she, only mildly irritated when she'd be asked to some social gathering or another simply as an "amusement," as if she could entertain the gossips with her mere presence. Such stunts rarely came to pass, however, for although she possessed certain gifts for knowing the unknown, she was, in the end, the respectable twin sister of the Earl of Stamford, and as such, most members of the peerage simply referred to her as "colorful . . . but delightful." Still, helping the government had been her choice, and she'd not regretted it for a moment.

The winter wind swept her skirts out in front of her as she reached the gated fence that enclosed the cottage. Shivering, she lifted the latch and moved quickly along the stone path toward the front door, which remained partially hidden by a trellis dripping with winter greenery. They were expecting her. She'd sent a note a few days prior to her departure from London, only briefly explaining her reason for the trip, and she'd been invited to stay the night in the guest room. Now lights from within shone through the beveled windows, speaking silently of a warmth inside, both in feel and hospitality. She needed that now.

Removing a glove, she rapped lightly with the brass knocker. She expected a servant to greet her, but within moments the door was opened by none other than Madeleine St. James, Countess of Eastleigh herself, one of the most beautiful women Ivy had ever known and one of the few people in the world she could honestly count as a friend.

"Ivy, it's so wonderful to see you!" Madeleine said brightly, reaching for the handle on her valise and fairly pulling her inside the foyer. "Come in, come in before you catch your death. My goodness, but it's freezing," she added, closing the door tightly and bolting it.

The Frenchwoman's relaxed and congenial exuberance was contagious, and Ivy grinned. "Thank you so much for seeing me, Madeleine, especially on such short notice," she replied. The heat from the cottage hit her in a sudden rush, the scents of cinnamon and rose sweetening the air. She glanced around her, adding, "I hope I haven't interrupted anything of importance."

"Not in the least," Madeleine shot back, foregoing formalities as she grabbed Ivy's shoulders and offered her a gentle kiss on each cheek. "With Chantal in Eastleigh, the earl and I are thrilled to have the company. The cottage seems too quiet without our very busy and talkative daughter."

"I've no doubt." Lowering her valise to the floor, Ivy began to unbutton her pelisse. "Is your husband at home?"

Madeleine helped her remove her covering then hung it on a lone brass coatrack in the corner. "Not yet, but he will be soon. He's with a friend at the moment, at the inn, but he'll be home in time for a late supper. Would you like to freshen yourself before we sit?"

Ivy folded her leather gloves and stuffed them in the pockets of her hanging pelisse, sensing a trace of ambiguity in Madeleine's answer though she tried to brush her reaction off as tiredness on her part.

"I'm fine for now," she answered brightly, "but a cup of tea would be lovely."

Madeleine nodded once and gestured toward the parlor with an elegant hand. "Then please, be seated by the fire. I've been expecting you, so the tea is already steeping in the kitchen. I won't be but a moment."

Ivy did as requested, stepping into the front room as her host made her way through a swinging door, noting that the cottage looked somewhat larger inside than it appeared from the road. Long windows to her right took up most of the north wall, and all were covered with burgundy velvet drapes that fell to the polished wooden floor. Directly ahead, in the center of the room, sat a lone, brown leather sofa and an oak tea table next to a leather high-backed armchair and matching footstool, both facing a large fireplace, now lit and burning brightly. She walked toward it, rubbing her hands together, thankful for the heat it produced, though her eyes strayed to a magnificent portrait above the mantel of Madeleine and Thomas posing together in a rose garden.

They were a striking pair, she acknowledged, with a trace of envy at the closeness they had found in each other. Thomas had to be in his midforties now, and Madeleine perhaps ten years younger, but as a couple they were stunning in appearance—the earl a darkly handsome man, enormous of stature, and scarred from the Opium War; his wife a chestnut-haired, blue-eyed beauty, renowned for her exceptional elegance and appearance both here and on the Continent. How they came to find each other, she didn't know exactly, though she'd heard their love had blossomed in Winter Garden some two or three years ago when they'd been forced to work side by side. But it was all too apparent to anyone that they belonged together, a fortune very few couples could treasure.

Ivy sighed and turned away from the painting, her back to the fire, her woolen day gown beginning, finally, to absorb some of the heat.

Love had been an elusive thing for her, a feeling she'd only once begun to grasp before it had been smothered in her heart by a man who had used her for personal gain before discarding her. In the two years since she'd lost herself in the treacherous arms of the dashing, elusive Garrett Burke, a brilliant and deceitful investigator for the Home Office, she'd renounced romance where she was concerned, deciding she and a lifetime of love were not compatible. Her short time with Garrett had given them a whirlwind week of desire unmatched, lust unbridled, and in the end, for her, a humiliation that would remain until the end of her life. But at least, with their secret love affair quashed so suddenly after a disastrous end to his investigation at the time, she had managed to keep her dignity intact by staying far away from him. Nobody knew that she'd had any acquaintance at all with Garrett aside from the professional, if one could call it that. Nobody knew the depth of the passion they'd shared, how reckless they had been, how far she had allowed him to peer into her soul. The remorse she felt would never leave her, and she would always keep it to herself, though with it came a certain caution that made her stronger, a spinster who, at twenty-six, knew her place. The only times her memories made her melancholy were those spent with couples like Madeleine and Thomas, witnessing firsthand the joy they found in each other's company.

A rattling of china brought her back to the present as Madeleine entered the parlor through a swinging door, a silver tray in hand, her eyes shrewdly focused.

"So what brings you to Winter Garden on such short notice?" Madeleine asked pleasantly, walking toward her.

Ivy forced a smile and moved forward to help her host by clearing a space on the oval tea table. "A rather complicated reason, I'm afraid."

"Ah," the Frenchwoman acknowledged, placing the tray on the hard wooden surface and arranging cups, saucers, and tiny linen napkins. "I daresay there have been some rather odd goings-on here lately. Frankly, I'm not surprised to see you. The town could use your particular expertise."

That comment grabbed her attention. "Goings-on?" she repeated, sitting at last in the armchair and absentmindedly adjusting her skirts around her ankles.

Madeleine gave her a half smile and a quick glance before lifting the pot and pouring the steaming liquid. "Perhaps you should tell me why you've come first." Seconds later, she politely asked, "Milk and sugar?"

Again, Ivy sensed a veiled guardedness in the French-woman's manner, almost an evasiveness in her words. She sat back in the chair, her elbow on the armrest, eyeing her speculatively. "Two spoons of sugar, if you please."

She watched the woman measure the sweetener into a white china cup inlaid with purple tulips, then lift it with a saucer and spoon and offer it to her. Then she moved around the tea table to take a seat on the couch, quickly adjusting her own skirts before reaching forward to pour herself a cup.

"Does this have to do with one of your dreams?" she continued, her gaze on the teapot.

Ivy forced herself to relax a little, catching a whiff of jasmine in the upward swirl of steam. In truth, to anyone else, she would probably not admit the unconventional reason for returning. But Madeleine had known about the unusual work she did for the government for more than two years now, trusted her gift, and asked the question honestly, without any ridicule at all.

"There is a dream involved, at least partially," she admitted after a moment. "But there's more."

The Frenchwoman's sculpted eyebrows rose with growing interest. "Indeed. Then don't keep me in suspense." She lifted her own cup to the level of her chin, pursed her full lips, and blew gently across the brim.

Ivy glanced down at the light brown brew in her own cup. "Five days ago I received a visit from a Mr. Heathrow Clark, a London solicitor. A client of his gave him my name as a person who helps the Home Office with unusual circumstances, and due to that experience, wondered if I might be able to help him with a matter here in Winter Garden."

In a wary voice, Madeleine asked, "Who is Mr. Clark's client?"

She drew a deep breath before muttering, "The Marquess of Rye."

The Frenchwoman's brows rose along with her intrigue. For seconds she said nothing, then she gave a half smile, "The Marquess of Rye?"

She nodded.

Madeleine took a sip of her tea, watching her closely. "I suppose you're aware that the mysterious marquess recently purchased the Rothebury estate."

"Mysterious marquess?"

"That's what some of the townspeople are calling him because nobody has met him yet," she revealed contemplatively. "It's been rumored that he's been on the Continent for the last year or two, and has now returned, though we have yet to see the man."

"Which definitely adds to the mystery of why I'm here," she replied.

Madeleine took another sip of tea. "And why are you here, Ivy? What does the marquess want you to do?"

Sinking into the leather chair, she lowered her voice. "Mr. Clark gave me a package that contained three things: the key to the manor home on the estate, a substantial amount of money to cover traveling and living expenses, and a letter from Lord Rye with instructions, informing me that although he wouldn't be here, he's arranged for a new staff at the house and wants me to move in, investigate and search it."

"Investigate the house?"

Ivy smiled again. "Apparently it's haunted."

Madeleine sighed, then slowly leaned forward and placed her cup and saucer on the tea table. "Well, most people from Winter Garden have believed this for years, especially after Lord Rothebury was arrested," she said. "And you know as well as anyone that the estate is old and has numerous passageways within, as well as secret tunnels that have been used over the centuries for smuggling. I doubt that its reputation will change anytime soon."

"True," she acknowledged, sipping her tea at last, relishing the warm brew as it slid down her parched throat. Thomas and Madeleine were both aware that as a girl she had spent several summers in Winter Garden on the Rothebury estate, when her family and the late baron's were the best of friends, before the elder baron's untimely death. Nobody, however, was aware that she and her twin brother Ian were bastard children of this same Baron Rothebury, which made her a half sister by birth to Richard Sharon, Winter Garden's infamous smuggler, arrested and charged two years ago. Thankfully, this had been a well-kept secret. To her knowledge, her legal father had never learned the truth; she and Ian had only learned of it on their mother's deathbed, a confession that had stunned, even devastated, her brother, who soon after inherited the Stamford estate, but which left her only mildly surprised. Somewhere deep within she had known, perhaps from her unusual senses, perhaps only from female intuition after watching her mother's face at the baron's funeral. And aside from the handful of family who knew by necessity, it was a secret she would take to her grave.

"Honestly," she continued, brushing away the thought, "I think I'd be a bit wary of the whole affair, except that the night before Mr. Clark's visit, I had a very vivid and frightening dream wherein I saw a man standing in an upper window of the manor house, silently . . . begging for my help. Needless to say, it's left me with a strange sense of anxiety."

Madeleine's eyes widened. She leaned forward, propping her elbows on her knees, lacing her fingers together in front of her and resting her chin atop them. "Did you recognize the man?"

Ivy shook her head, feeling an inner gratefulness that the woman didn't even blink at Ivy's confidence in her own visions.

"I'm not sure," she replied, "and I don't have any more information about him. I didn't concern myself with it too much until the following day, when I was asked to return to the very same house on the Rothebury estate."

The grooves between the woman's ice-blue eyes gradually deepened as she sat silent for a moment or two.

Ivy frowned. "What is it?"

Several more seconds of silence passed before the Frenchwoman gradually sat up and replied, "I mentioned the goings-on?"

"Yes."

Madeleine rubbed her thumbs together in her lap. "About four months ago, with little fanfare, Benedict, Richard's younger brother, returned to Winter Garden and moved into the house. It caused quite a flurry of speculation, as one might imagine. He kept to himself and didn't travel with anyone, in fact, refused callers at every turn."

Ivy remained silent while Madeleine paused in thought, though she could feel her pulse quicken. Benedict Sharon was Richard's half brother from the former baron's second wife, and not related to Ian and her, but she still perceived the sudden ominous warning that sliced through her. Part of the reason she'd returned to Winter Garden was because of Benedict, though she had no intention of telling that to anyone yet.

Madeleine continued, "It almost seemed as if the man were in hiding, or . . . staying away from the village purposely. I can't say he appeared fearful exactly, just . . . suspicious of something." She paused, then added, "Or someone."

"Did Eastleigh notice this? Anyone else?" she asked quickly.

Madeleine nodded slightly. "Eastleigh, yes, though I'm not sure of others in the village. I think they were all more or less offended that he didn't socialize, despite the scandal caused by his brother." She drew a long breath and let it out slowly. "Three weeks after he arrived, he disappeared."

She blinked, and her heart sank. "Disappeared?"

"Yes, and I don't mean he just left town, he vanished without a trace, leaving his prized steed, his clothing, his valet, who has since moved to Portsmouth in search of employment, and even his jewelry. His valet claimed he retired one evening after dinner and brandy, and the next morning when the butler went to awaken him, he was gone, his bed untouched."

For a moment, she found herself speechless, her mouth opening a little as she stared at the older woman.

Left without his clothes, his jewelry . . .

Ivy shook herself mentally, and asked, "Did anyone contact the magistrate?"

Madeleine shrugged and reached for her teacup again. "Yes, at his housekeeper's request. After several days of investigation, the local authorities found no evidence of violence or even mischief, and so they were forced to conclude that Benedict Sharon left willingly without word, as any grown bachelor is free to do."

"In the middle of the night without personal belongings?" she interjected sharply. "That doesn't make sense."

"No, it doesn't, but since he'd only been here a short time and kept to himself, nobody in the village could offer a clue as to the man's habits and behavior, whether he was rash by nature, even his general demeanor. Frankly, there was little else the magistrate could do with no evidence of a crime."

She imagined that was so. Reaching for her tea again, Ivy tried to evaluate this news in light of her own memories of Benedict. She didn't really remember much about Lord Rothebury's second son, much younger than Richard, and three years her junior. It wasn't long after he was born that his father, Robert, died, and she and her family left Winter Garden for the final time, returning to their estate in Stamford, where she and Ian lived until her mother's death. Benedict Sharon couldn't have been more than three or four years old the last time she'd seen him, which to her meant she could say good day to him on the street tomorrow and not recognize him. But her memories were beside the point. All that mattered now was the house—and its contents.

"There's more, Ivy," Madeleine said, interrupting her thoughts. "About a month ago, Eastleigh got word from an associate at the Home Office that Benedict Sharon may have been involved in some nefarious dealings of his own, and it's likely this is the reason he sold the house."

"Financial reasons?"

"Possibly," Madeleine replied. "He disappeared shortly after the papers were signed."

She took a swallow of cooling tea and licked her lips. "That certainly adds flavor to the mystery."

Madeleine smiled as her eyes sparkled mischievously. "Indeed. At the Marquess of Rye's request, they've sent someone from London, clandestinely, to try to solve the mystery of the man's disappearance. Eastleigh is at the inn right now talking with him."

"I don't know," Madeleine returned without hesitation. "But I should say it is rather interesting that these particular things should happen to bring you back to Winter Garden after all these years."

"And coincidental," she added, straightening in her chair. She planted a pleasant smile on her lips. "But for now, I look for ghosts. I was told a new staff are in the house, and they're aware I'll be moving into it tomorrow—"

"Are you afraid?"

"Afraid?"

Madeleine offered her a crooked smile. "That it's haunted."

She grinned in return. "No, but I do sense a certain . . . apprehension that I can't explain. I had planned to stay no more than a week, perhaps a fortnight at most."

Madeleine reached over and gave her hand a squeeze. "It's so good to see you, Ivy, and a week or two will give us plenty of time to chat." With a graceful air, she stood and began to pick up the dishes.

Garrett Burke leaned his shoulders back against the inn's brick wall and stared up at the southern night sky, his twine coat wrapped around him like a wool blanket, in his bare hand a pipe of sweet tobacco, which he smoked to ward off the chill in his bones.

The sharp ache in his head had finally begun to dissipate, probably due to breathing fresh air, though even fresh air often didn't work when the pain was most acute. It had actually been more than two weeks since his last attack, yet he tried not to think about that too much. He could find no use in hoping that he'd begun to heal and the frequent suffering would lessen. Every moment he agonized in pain brought his greatest personal failure to the forefront. He could not allow that to happen again, and it was this determination—to catch the thief who had altered his world years ago—that brought him now to Winter Garden.

His quiet discussion with Lord Eastleigh this evening had proved more than satisfying. He and Thomas had met at the tavern just before sunset to discuss the very reason he'd come to the village—to pursue the case of Benedict Sharon, the man he suspected of stealing priceless diamonds. The trail ended here, in this sleepy village, where someone right now withheld the information he sought, either about Sharon's whereabouts or the whereabouts of the diamonds. As is, they couldn't be easily sold, and he'd heard nothing of them since the man's disappearance. But instinct alone told him that a growing threat lay ahead for him, especially when he now knew he'd once again be coming face-to-face with the intriguing Lady Ivy Wentworth, London's famous seer, who'd arrived in Winter Garden this evening.

Just hearing Thomas mention her arrival tonight brought a quick explosion of emotions to the surface, not one of them good. The week they reluctantly worked together two years ago had been fast and heated, with temperaments that both clashed and excited, though that was about all he recalled of it. The night he left her to meet his contact was the night of the attack that had nearly caused his death.

Still, the image of Ivy as a beautiful woman lingered strong and arousing to this day, and in a dark and reckless manner, he looked forward to seeing her again. She exuded a sensuousness that defied definition, and he absolutely remembered her dark auburn hair, honey brown eyes, and full, luscious lips tipped up into a secretive smile. But most everything else that happened between them was a blur; the details of their week together remained vague at best. Even the passion her name and memory provoked in him now were confusing, disturbing, and beyond his understanding. Sometimes, when the ache in his head became so severe he couldn't leave his bed, he blamed her—for his loss of perspective where she was concerned, for trusting her brother in his attempt to find the diamonds, for the assault on him that still caused him so much physical pain, and especially for haunting his dreams with mystery since their last time together. Even now he believed she'd somehow been involved, and although he remained reluctant to trust her, he needed her help.

Garrett tapped his pipe on the wooden railing to

empty it, then stuffed it back into his coat pocket. The night was getting colder, and he shivered, taking one last, long look toward the darkened cottage at the end of Farrset Lane, where Ivy now slept peacefully, unaware of his nearness, ignorant of the impending storm of intrigue and the clash of passionate wills that was about to bring them together again. Then, pulling up the collar of his coat and taking a final deep breath of frigid air, he turned and walked back into the inn.

Chapter 2

Ivy stopped at the tall, rusted, iron gate, unlocked and open, as she stared up the driveway to the manor house on the former Rothebury summer home, the property now owned by the equally elusive Marquess of Rye. The sun shone brightly this morning, and yet a freezing wind stirred bare tree branches along the edges of the property, scraping the windowpanes and dark brown brick on the sides of the old, south-facing structure.

From the front, the house looked neither frightening nor sinister, but rather just empty. Lonely, if one could say that of a home. She knew the minimal staff arranged by the marquess would be awaiting her inside, but they would probably know less about the history of the property than she did. A disadvantage in that, though she would, at least, have most of the rooms to herself. She would need it that way if she were to sense anything unusual inside.

As a whole, she didn't necessarily believe in ghosts that haunted dwellings, though she would be the first to admit there were many strange, mystical occurrences that defied rational explanation. But she had more to do here than simply investigate the house for wayward spirits. She felt a certain keen anticipation at the thought of exploring the various tunnels and secret rooms rumored to be inside, despite knowing far more was at stake, and she had a much more important thing to do.

Carrying her valise, Ivy swallowed her trepidation and drew a deep breath for confidence as she walked to the large front doors and pulled the thick rope to ring the bell inside. After only a moment, she was greeted by the portly, middle-aged butler sporting overstarched attire, thinning brown hair, and thick jowls fairly covered with dark, curly side whiskers.

"Good morning," he said rather prosaically, ushering her inside with a sweep of his hand. "Lady Ivy, I presume?"

"Indeed, I am," she replied with a light, half smile, lowering the hood of her pelisse, then handing the man her valise as he reached for it.

"Giles Newbury, at your service," he added, his voice firm, yet on the quiet side. "Mrs. Thurman, Lord Rye's housekeeper, and I have been expecting you. May I take your cloak?"

"Thank you," she said somewhat absentmindedly, removing her leather gloves by the fingers, then unbuttoning her pelisse as she gazed around the entryway of the house for the first time in years.

Although now mostly empty of furniture, it remained as she remembered it. The foyer stood two stories in height, with a large, exquisite crystal chandelier hanging from the ornately carved ceiling, lending brightness to the pale marble floor at her feet, now polished and void of decorative rugs. The walls were bare, painted an inviting apricot that contrasted becomingly with the dark oak circular staircase directly in front of her that led to the private rooms upstairs. To her left stood a magnificent peach-and-emerald stained-glass archway connecting the foyer to the grand ballroom, its far, tall windows giving a superb view of the lake directly to the north of the house. To her right, behind partially closed doors, was the parlor, followed by the baron's library, dining rooms, and finally the kitchen and servants' quarters.

Her first impression was that the house felt as cold and barren as it looked from the outside, even with the sun shining through glass all around her. Then a sudden, inexplicable wave of apprehension passed through her, and she shivered.

"It is certainly quite chilly, isn't it," Giles said matter-of-factly, folding her pelisse over one arm and taking a step back. "Perhaps you'd like to warm your hands by the fire while I ask Mrs. Thurman to serve tea for two."

That brought her back to her senses and she frowned delicately. "For two?"

"For you and the gentleman architect from London. He's waiting for you in the parlor," Giles explained without hesitation or a trace of suspicion.

Confused because she hadn't even moved into the home and met the staff, she lowered her voice to repeat, "An architect, you say?"

The butler almost smiled. "I'm sure it has to do with the age of the house and its many additions. So many people are curious. Normally we would deny him access, as per Lord Rye's request, but he did say he needed to speak with you specifically when you arrived."

"I see . . ." she muttered, almost certain this "architect" was the contact from the Home Office Lord Eastleigh had met last night.

She straightened, her good breeding overtaking her need to encourage the butler to offer details. Better all around if he thought her in charge right from the start.

With a perfunctory smile she nodded once. "Very good, Newbury. Please ask Mrs. Thurman to serve tea for two in the parlor."

"At once, my lady," he replied, as if it were her suggestion.

"And after meeting with the architect, I'd like to be shown to my private quarters," she added pleasantly.

"Certainly. Is there any other luggage?"

"My lady's maid, Jane Smith, will be arriving late this afternoon with two trunks," was her reply. She had no intention of telling him she had arrived a day earlier than planned to speak with the earl and his wife, and of course he wouldn't ask. "Thank you, Newbury."

He offered her a gentle bow and turned on his heel, heading toward the kitchen to do her bidding.

Ivy suddenly wished she had a mirror to inspect her appearance. Without one hanging in the foyer, she had no choice but simply to brush her palms along her gown, then check quickly to make sure her long, plaited hair remained in place, pinned to the back of her head. That done, she strode with confidence toward the parlor to her right.

The heat from the fire soothed her as she pushed the double doors open and walked in. And then a coldness like she had never felt before seeped into her bones, and she stopped short, staring at the man who stood before the grate, his back to her, his head down as he gazed into the low-burning flames.

"Good morning, Ivy," he drawled without turning to look at her, his voice low and gruff.

She remained paralyzed, speechless, her well-ordered world collapsing in an instant of time. Nothing could have prepared her for this moment.

Tall and broad-shouldered, he wore a morning suit in medium gray that contrasted nicely with his nearly black hair, cut much shorter than the last time she'd seen him. His hands, their backs dusted with fine black hair, clutched the mantel with arms outstretched, causing his jacket to pull tightly across his upper back, revealing his musculature and a commanding presence she could never forget.

This was her nightmare. Not the one she'd dreamed of before she'd been summoned to Winter Garden, but *her* nightmare. The one that lingered.

Garrett Burke, the scandalously handsome extraordinary liar, had moved back into her life.

No, not moved. Slithered.

Ivy couldn't find her voice. Her mouth had gone dry even as perspiration broke out on her upper lip. Her pulse began to race. He obviously perceived her incredulity, for suddenly he stood upright and dropped his arms to his sides, and for a second or two she swayed from the knowledge that he intended to turn and look into her eyes, would try to steal a glance into a soul left shaken by his betrayal two winters ago. It took all that was in her not to run.

Slowly he pivoted, keeping his gaze locked on the worn peach carpeting until he faced her at last. And then he raised his lashes and made contact.

Her chest tightened and her breath caught. Now she couldn't move if she tried.

After a timeless moment of utter silence, one corner of his wide mouth tipped upward a fraction. "I'm *sensing* from your shock that you didn't sense my presence, madam."

The dark and sensuously deep voice of the devil. He would never know how that coldly spoken, sarcastic comment enraged her. She wouldn't give him the satisfaction. Huskily, she replied, "I try to *sense* only goodness and truth, sir. In you, I've never found either."

His eyelids twitched almost imperceptibly, though his caustic smile deepened. "Should I be insulted by that remark?"

She swallowed hard. "That's for you to decide, though you know fully well I would never attempt to flatter you, Mr. Burke."

"Touché, Lady Ivy," he all but whispered.

Friction charged the air around them, and for several drawn-out seconds neither of them spoke as they assessed each other.

The man, dark, calculating, and ruthlessly handsome, still managed to take her breath away. He stood more than six feet tall, his body filling out his tailored suit to perfection, allowing only a hint of the pleasurable sight and feel of his strength beneath the fabric. He had marvelously hard features and steely blue eyes that seemed to absorb everything and reveal nothing in return, eyes that had entranced her from the moment they met. His hair, its length cropped just above the neck, still framed his face, his clean-shaven, square jaw and molded cheekbones void of side whiskers. The only thing that softened his appearance both then and now, if just a trace, was the stray lock that hung over his forehead, forcing her to recall how she'd run her fingers through it, how she'd teased him about its making him look like a schoolboy. How he'd taken her hand every time she'd touched it and brought it to his lips, lightly kissing the pads of her fingers until she shuddered with need. And that reminded her of how, during every second of their time together, he had been using her, and she had let him.

Yes, Garrett Burke remained a magnificent man in full form, charming to few, feared by many—and loathed by her for those very same things.

"You haven't changed," she finally remarked, clasping her hands behind her.

"Neither have you," he replied at once, slowly scanning her body up and down. "You're as beautiful as I remember."

That made her uncomfortable. They stood six or seven feet away from each other, in a small parlor decorated in browns and peaches and eclectic furnishings, most of them old, and suddenly she felt suffocated—by the heat of the fire, the cluttered room, his probing gaze. She shifted from one foot to the other, though she refused to look away. "Why are you here, Garrett?"

He shrugged. "I suspect I'm here for the same reason you are."

That told her nothing, and she wasn't quite sure how to respond because suddenly she knew—*knew*—that he had come for the very same reason she had. No, the very same *thing*, priceless to each of them in completely different ways. And she almost kicked herself for being so absorbed in his overbearing nature that she didn't realize it immediately. His arrival today changed everything, now leaving her with more than one reason to be scared.

"Whatever you're thinking is wrong," she countered, attempting to hide her motives by denial. "I didn't come to Winter Garden at the request of the government, sir. I was invited by the owner to search—"

"*I'm* here for the diamonds, Ivy," he said in a low, almost taunting whisper. "And our meeting like this again just seems too . . . coincidental for me to believe that *you're* here for anything else."

Hearing it put into words made her heart nearly stop beating. Her face flushed and her legs grew weak beneath her. "The Martello diamonds."

He watched her intently, then replied, "You remember."

Of course she remembered, and for him to suggest otherwise incensed her. The Martello diamonds had been stolen from a mysterious owner who had purchased them from an aristocratic royal family years ago. Garrett had been given the assignment of recovery by the Home Office, and she had been asked to help him by that very same employer. Their pairing in the matter led to the tumultuous week they had spent together, and the night she'd given him all of herself in an attempt to save his life. He'd rewarded her by gladly taking her virginity, then ignoring her warnings and nearly getting himself killed, losing the diamonds, then denouncing her help as "problematic at best, probably the reason the thief escaped." After all that had happened between them, he publicly blamed her for his failure.

But that was beside the point now. Many people had events in their pasts that they either lived to regret or rigorously defend. She would do neither. She was on a dangerous mission and had more to accomplish in Winter Garden than stroking his feathers.

Attempting to sound cheerful and unaffected, she planted a tepid smile on her face, and said tartly, "Of course I remember, and I hope you recover them, Mr.

Burke, but at this point, I really have no intention of discussing the past with you."

His brows furrowed minutely. "I haven't mentioned our past," he replied, his voice lower still.

For the first time since she'd walked into the parlor, she sensed an evasiveness in him, as if he tried very hard to hide an even deeper reason for calling on her this morning. Standing across the parlor from him now, she could tell that he'd aged more than he should have, as the tiny lines at his mouth and the corners of his eyes had deepened, his half smiles seeming forced.

Tipping her head to the side, she looked at him askance. "Then why are you here to see me specifically, Garrett? I don't know a thing about the diamonds."

He paused, and rubbed his chin with his palm, though he never looked away. "I believe you," he drawled. "At least, I believe that you don't know yet where they are. But they've been traced to Winter Garden, Ivy, and now I learn that you've just arrived as well. Don't you think that's a bit fortuitous? Would you have me believe you're here for something else?"

She cringed inside. After everything that had happened between them two years ago, after all this time apart, when she'd thought about him, cried over him, cursed him, missed him and the week they'd shared, he still only cared about the diamonds, still believed she had failed him, or worse, deceived him. His bitterness remained, a bitterness she could feel simply by his presence in the room. He didn't only want his name cleared, he wanted some sort of obscure revenge.

Standing tall, she clasped her hands behind her back and glared at him.

"Garrett," she started, her tone thick with warning, "I was invited here to investigate the house. Regardless of whatever reason you're here, you are not welcome to stay. If you have nothing more to say, please leave."

For a moment he just watched her. Then slowly he began moving toward her, his jaw tense, lids narrowed, his gaze hardening with each step. Ivy managed to stand her ground, tipping her head back defiantly as he approached, stopping only a foot or so away from her so that the tips of his shoes brushed against the hem of her gown.

"Oh, I have so much more to say," he admitted at last, smiling wryly as he glanced down at her face. He scrutinized her inch by inch, his gaze finally resting on her lips, where it lingered so long she began to shake.

"Frightened of me?" he whispered huskily.

She swallowed, unwilling to give him the satisfaction of a denial. "Only in my nightmares, sir."

He looked back into her eyes. "You are the clever one, aren't you, Ivy?"

"Offering me a compliment?" she quickly returned. "My, you have changed."

He almost laughed. Almost. Then he murmured, "More than you know."

An extremely awkward moment passed in silence. She couldn't look away, couldn't scream, couldn't breathe. Then, abruptly, she felt a strange and utter coldness envelop the room, and she glanced up instinctively as she tried to shake off a sudden uneasiness.

"I beg your pardon, Lady Ivy?"

Startled, she nearly jumped from the interruption. She'd completely forgotten that refreshments had been ordered, and it took a second or two for her to remember her place in the house.

Recovering herself quickly, she turned and took a step back, planting a smile on her lips as she brushed the back of her palm across her brow.

"Mrs. Thurman," she said pleasantly, scarcely taking notice of the woman other than to realize she was thin, graying, and completely unremarkable in appearance.

The housekeeper curtsied slightly even as she carried a silver tray topped with sundry items. "I have tea for two and scones," she said. "Will there be anything else?"

Decorum resumed as Ivy took control, ignoring the shrewd stare she felt rather than saw from Garrett, who remained unmoved.

"Nothing else now, Mrs. Thurman," she replied, stepping aside to allow the woman access to the parlor. "We'll serve ourselves."

The woman nodded, then walked straight to the center oval table that sat between two matching, peach velvet settees. After placing the tray gently on the cherrywood surface, she straightened, shot a quick glance to Garrett without expression, then looked away.

"At your convenience, my lady," she added matter-of-factly, "please ring for me, and I'll show you to your room."

Ivy felt her cheeks burning, for no conceivable reason, though she ignored the sudden flush. "Thank you, Mrs. Thurman."

Without a second glance at either of them, the house-keeper quit the room, leaving the doors to the foyer open only a crack as propriety demanded.

Ivy turned her attention to the long window to her right, staring out at the bleak winter morning, not the least bit interested in tea or scones, or even being in the same room with the man. A black fate had obviously thrown them together again, catching her with her guard down, her anger simmering just below the surface even as her body and senses reacted to his proximity in the most embarrassing manner.

At last, as if reading her mind, he said, "I've no stomach for tea and scones, so I'll be on my way."

He didn't move, and after a moment, she turned to look at him again, unable to think of a suitable reply.

He did smile then—a rich, seductive smile that she remembered vividly. And the only honest thing she could recall about him now.

"But be forewarned," he continued, dropping his voice to a near whisper, "that I'll be here watching you, tracing your every move, investigating the same people and making my own discoveries. We're here for the same thing, and I'll find it, even if we must work together once again."

She gasped, then countered, "Never."

Suddenly he reached out and touched her, drawing the back of his index finger down one hot cheek. She jerked away instinctively, and he dropped his arm.

"Never say never, darling Ivy. I'm staying at the inn in the village square should you need me."

He appalled her even as he captivated her, and the desire for him to touch her again made her angrier at herself than she'd felt in a long, long time.

"A lovely place, I'm sure," she mocked him with flashing eyes. "Good day, sir."

A trace of another smile cut across his hard mouth. Then he swiftly stepped past her and quit the room.

Ivy stood rigidly until she heard the front doors close. Then, losing her grip on her composure, she nearly collapsed as she made her way to the settee on wobbly legs, dropped herself into it, and hid her face in her palms to cover a sudden rush of tears.

Never fear, darling Garrett, I will find the diamonds first . . .

Her search for truth and lies in Winter Garden hadn't exactly started auspiciously, Ivy decided sometime later as she followed Mrs. Thurman around the living quarters of the house. Though dusted and smelling of lye soap and wax, the rooms still reeked of generations gone by and felt of souls not healed. At least that was Ivy's first impression as she climbed the creaking, wooden stairs to the second-floor landing.

Although the shock of seeing Garrett still sent her

mind reeling and made her body hot with anger, she had at last begun to calm herself and look at the situation rationally, especially in light of the fact that she was now living in the house where the diamonds were last supposed to be. She would have the time and freedom to search here first, though she doubted the Martello diamonds would just be stuck in a drawer in the master bedchamber. Still, it would be a start.

Ushering her down a long, darkened hallway, Mrs. Thurman carried her valise to the far east end of the southern wing, then stopped in front of a massive oak door.

"I thought you might be a bit uncomfortable sleeping in the mistress's suite, as it's connected to the baron's," the housekeeper informed her, reaching for the door latch and pulling it.

She didn't have to say because Benedict Sharon had occupied the adjoining room and so strangely disappeared in the middle of the night. Ivy knew that was what the woman meant.

"This is the best guest room available," she continued without pause. "It gets a lovely dose of the morning sun and has a splendid view of the southern shore of the lake."

"I'm sure it'll be perfect for my needs," Ivy replied, gazing around the room as she followed the woman inside, feeling a draft in the darkness.

"It's also the room Lord Rye suggested for you," Mrs. Thurman added as she placed the valise on the floor at the foot of the bed, then walked to the thick purple drapes that covered the windows.

A sudden thought occurred to her. "How long have you been in Lord Rye's employ?"

"For more than twenty years," the housekeeper replied without hesitation, tying the drapes on one side of the window as she spoke, squinting from a sudden gush of sunlight. "Started in the scullery back in Rye when I was a girl, then got myself trained by the first housekeeper, Mrs. Castlewaite. I've only been in Winter Garden for a month or so, but most of the small staff here came with me from the main house on his estate. We're all very loyal to the marquess and anxious to have this become his second home."

It was more information than she'd expected, or asked for, and for a second Ivy thought the answer sounded . . . rehearsed. But she tried to shrug that off.

"I see," she returned with a smile, taking in the room as Mrs. Thurman moved to tidy up the bed. It looked fluffy and comfortable, and large enough to accommodate more than one person. She noted the tall fireplace with a bronze grate to her right, a rather large lavender satin settee in front of it, and to her left beside the window, a small oak dressing table and mirror. With dark-paneled walls that matched the floorboards, the only other color in the room came from two lavender rugs and an oil painting of lilacs in a still life hanging above the bed.

"So, you're aware of why I'm here?" she prodded, walking a bit farther inside.

"Oh, yes," the housekeeper answered quickly as she fluffed the pillows under the deep bronze and purple quilted coverlet. "We're all aware of your reputation, Lady Ivy, and it's quite fascinating to have a renowned seer visit." She turned and straightened her apron. "But I haven't heard a thing that could be construed as a ghostly noise since I've been here, I'm sorry to say. Maybe your wayward spirit doesn't haunt the servants' quarters, then?"

"Let's hope not," she replied cheerfully. "I don't think I want to be left completely alone in a house this old."

Mrs. Thurman brushed that comment aside with a wave of her hand. "Nonsense. He can't scare us off. I've seen too much in my day." With a quick change of subject, she walked to the door opposite the window and opened it. "Here is the withdrawing room, and the wardrobe is inside. I'll have your trunks delivered as soon as they arrive." She turned and walked back toward the hallway entrance. "Lord Rye said to give you free rein of the property to do your investigation, so we'll be at your service, and you may call on us at any time. Jamie, my son, tends the stables, and we do have one carriage available, though you probably won't need it unless you'd like to travel outside the village. Your girl, Jane, has a room set with us below stairs, though she won't be working for anyone but you unless you choose otherwise. We'll serve breakfast and luncheon to you at your request. Dinner is served at eight, unless you'd prefer another time, and Mr. Newbury will light your fire thirty minutes before you retire. And of course there's a lock on your door here for privacy. Is there anything else?"

Ivy got the distinct impression that she was being rushed—or that Mrs. Thurman had something more engaging to attend to. But, then, so did she.

"No, that'll be all, Mrs. Thurman," she replied with a nod. As the housekeeper turned to leave, she stopped her with, "You will tell me at once, however, if there is any correspondence for me, especially from Lord Rye, or if you should happen to see or hear anything odd?"

Mrs. Thurman curtsied. "Of course, my lady. At once."

"Thank you, Mrs. Thurman."

Ivy closed the door, listening to the woman's footsteps disappear as she made her way down the hall.

Ivy walked to the window and gazed out into the late-morning sunshine. Indeed, the view was lovely from this angle as the tree line edged down to the lake on her left. She could just make out the path that wound around the southern shore, sometimes going very near the now-still water, sometimes curving to disappear into the forest. At the far end of the lake stood the Hope cottage, where Lord Eastleigh and his wife lived, though she could only see a small trail of chimney smoke rising above the brush. And to the left of the cottage, near the town square, she could just barely make out the thatched roofing of the inn where Garrett would be lodging. The thought made her nervous. She had no idea how long he intended to stay in Winter Garden, and he had never said. But he was too close for her comfort. Far too close.

She closed her eyes to the intense rush of apprehension that suddenly coursed through her and clutched the windowpane until the wood scraped her hands, until the fear passed—

Help me!

She stilled. "Ian . . ."

Help me, Ivy!

With a gasp, her eyes shot open and she jerked back from the window—though not before she'd seen Garrett watching her.

He'd been sitting on a bench across the lake, staring at the house with his piercing eyes. And he couldn't have missed her standing in front of the glass, gazing outside in bright sunshine.

. . . be forewarned . . . that I'll be here watching you, tracing your every move, investigating the same people and making my own discoveries . . .

"The devil is haunting me," she whispered aloud to nobody. Seconds later she took a step forward again and gingerly peeked out the window to the bench, now empty, as she knew it would be.

But her vision had been of Ian. That was what had startled her in the first place. Her brother was in danger, himself missing, and he was far more important than the pain felt by a ruined love affair of days gone by.

Recovering herself, she quickly moved to her valise at the foot of the bed, lifted the latch, and opened it, rummaging through the contents until she held the letter from Lord Rye in her hands.

My Lady,

I bring to you a matter that needs the attention of your particular talents . . .

A simple note asking her to investigate a house for a ghost—and the diamonds Benedict Sharon carried on his person the night he disappeared.

She had been summoned to Winter Garden for a purpose, a purpose that somehow included Garrett. And now she feared for Ian's safety, and she had no idea why, or how he might be involved. One thing she did know, however: Far more was at stake than recovering priceless jewels.

Yes, the devil might haunt her, but she would find the diamonds first.

Chapter 3

Sarah Rodney quite possibly had the loveliest home in Winter Garden, situated on the northern shores of the lake, directly across from the Rothebury estate—now called the Rye estate by a few of those getting used to the change.

Mrs. Rodney, though not a member of the peerage, counted herself as a widow blessed by the memory of a good husband who had passed her and her children a remarkable fortune along with his very respectable name. Or so she often said. Ivy didn't remember much about them from her own childhood visits, but she did vaguely remember the house as she'd been inside several times.

A two-story structure made of pale yellow stone, it was the size of a country manor yet looked like a cottage, with French doors and wrought-iron decor, numerous rooms, and a lush conservatory boasting high windows that faced the lake and allowed for a full day of the southern winter sun to shine and warm the inside.

But with the cloud cover today, Ivy was surely glad she'd decided to bring her fur-lined pelisse and match-

ing muff, for it was a rather long walk around the lake
and through the village. She didn't see a soul along the
way, probably due to the lateness of the afternoon and
the chill in the air, though once she neared the lady's
property, she caught a very good glimpse of the tall
windows that lined the magnificent ballroom of the
Rye estate on the opposite shore. Truly, the view was
lovely—and very telling, should something be amiss at
the former Rothebury home.

Now at last she sat in the lady's luxurious parlor
of emerald green and gold, gazing at the walls covered with oil paintings in gilded frames, warming her
hands by rubbing them together as she awaited Mrs.
Rodney's arrival. She'd donned her best day gown in
rich royal blue trimmed in white lace for the occasion,
and loosely braided her hair into two plaits that Jane
wrapped around her ears and pinned with pearls after
helping her dress.

Her first night in the manor home had been rather
unremarkable, though she'd slept little. Every rustle of
the trees outside her window sounded like the scratching of nails on a wooden board, which only reminded
her of the ghosts that remained, real or imagined. But
after a breakfast of tea and toast, she sent word to
Mrs. Rodney that she'd like to visit sometime today, to
which the lady replied with a quick invitation for this
afternoon. Up until the time she left the house on her
trek around the lake, she had explored a few of the various rooms, though, unfortunately, she found nothing
of importance and sensed very little in the way of su-

pernatural spirits. Yet there still remained a great deal
to see, and plenty more to investigate, something she
looked forward to doing again this evening.

She had also spent far too much time thinking of
Garrett, and his unexpected reappearance into her life.
Damn the man that she couldn't escape his dishonest
intentions! And yet her own feelings of betrayal and
anger where he was concerned were more her fault than
his. She couldn't very well blame him for her *feelings*.
But after careful reflection throughout the day, she decided it would be in her interest to keep away from him
the best that she could. She didn't trust him, and more
importantly, she didn't trust herself when she was near
him. Most perplexing was the desire either to tear his
heart out with her bare hands or hold him tenderly as
she had done once before, kissing away the tension in
his jaw and mouth . . .

Ivy shook herself from that ridiculous notion and
tried hard to concentrate on exactly what questions
she would ask Mrs. Rodney. She knew the woman had
lived in Winter Garden all her life, and as the town's
unofficial historian, possessed more information about
the former Rothebury estate, its house and owners than
anyone. And hopefully she'd know as much about the
disappearance of Benedict, even if it turned out to be
more gossip than not. In her experience, gentlemen de-
tectives didn't give nearly as much credence to gossip
and rumor between ladies as they should.

The sound of a door closing and deep male voices
in the foyer brought her back to the moment, and she

straightened in her golden velveteen chair and smoothed her skirts. Then the thought occurred to her that one of the voices might be Garret's. But that was preposterous. He wouldn't dare—

"Lady Ivy," the old and stately butler interrupted from the doorway, "may I present Mr. Burke, an architect from London who has also been invited for tea." He stepped to the side to allow him to enter. "Mrs. Rodney will be with you shortly."

She didn't even notice the butler leave as she fixed her furious gaze on the person of her heart's deceit.

"Lady Ivy," he drawled in greeting as he walked farther into the parlor, a wry smile playing across his mouth. "What a pleasant surprise."

He didn't look surprised to see her at all. Suddenly flustered, she wanted to ask how he could possibly know she'd be here, but then it was a small town, and simple reason suggested that visiting the historian would be the first place one might start to learn information about its homes and people. And yet his threat to watch her every move made it more likely that he was following her, perhaps even investigating her, though that notion seemed a bit silly. Still, she could either ignore him, which might actually bring more attention to them as individuals in Winter Garden for a devious purpose, or she could play the innocent. After a moment's hesitation, she decided she had no choice. She must play along or risk losing every advantage.

Glaring at him as he approached, she couldn't help but notice he'd recently bathed and shaved, and dressed in a fine-quality day suit of brown woolen trousers, a beige linen shirt with dark brown cravat, and matching frock coat. He looked irresistibly handsome, and she suddenly wished good manners didn't preclude her slapping the grin of satisfaction off his face. Instead, she nodded once and lifted her hand to him. "Mr. Burke," she countered with feigned sweetness, "the surprise is all mine."

His eyes flashed with a trace of amusement, and it apparently took seconds for him to decide if he should touch her. When at last he grasped her hand firmly with his own warm, strong fingers and raised her knuckles to his lips, she felt her body go hot all over and her skin flush with color that he certainly had to notice. Her reaction embarrassed and annoyed her, and she fought the urge to jerk away from the contact, however slight it might be.

"Lady Ivy, and Mr. Burke, how delightful that you both could come for tea," Mrs. Rodney interjected as she sashayed into the room.

Ivy pulled away from his probing gaze, and he quickly released her.

"Mrs. Rodney," he replied, turning around and giving the elderly lady a gentle bow, "the delight is ours, I'm sure."

Ivy almost rolled her eyes. Truly, the man feigned charm better than anyone she knew. Standing, she nodded to her white-haired, fashionably coiffed hostess, the consummate Englishwoman, late in years, who carried herself with great poise. "It is a pleasure to see you again, Mrs. Rodney. And a respite of tea is sorely needed on such a cold afternoon."

"Indeed," the older woman agreed. "Normally, I'd serve in the conservatory, so we could all enjoy the scent of plant life and flowers, but without the sun, on a day like this one, I'm afraid it would just be too chilly. I thought perhaps we could enjoy the afternoon here near the fire instead."

Without objection, Ivy lowered her body into her chair again, and Garrett, rather than choosing to sit on the green velveteen sofa next to the grate, sat on her immediate left, in a matching chair far too small for his large frame. She could only hope he felt as uncomfortable as he appeared to be, especially after catching a whiff of his mild cologne, which made her stir and lean her shoulders as far to the right as she could. The scent of him brought back sharp memories that she didn't want intruding into her thoughts at a time when paying attention to detail would be vital.

"So, what brings you to Winter Garden?" Mrs. Rodney asked cheerfully as she lowered her robust frame onto the sofa and spread her full satin skirts daintily around her ankles.

"Mr. Burke and I are here for entirely different purposes, actually," she replied, probably too quickly. They both looked at her with raised brows.

"What I mean," she amended, "is that I am here at the bidding of the new owner of the Rothebury home, and he "—she shot him a quick glance—"Mr. Burke, is here for something else." She paused, then added, "Evidently."

Feeling utterly foolish for being so disconcerted by his presence, she grew enormously thankful when, at that precise moment, the butler rapped once on the partially opened door, then moved to his side to allow two parlor maids to enter, each carrying a silver tray topped with a variety of items, which they dutifully deposited on the tea table in front of them.

"We'll serve ourselves," Mrs. Rodney informed the girls, who then each curtsied and left the room without a word. "That will be all, Layton," she added to the butler, who nodded once, then quit the parlor, closing the doors behind him.

"Now," she continued, sitting forward to survey the fare in front of her, "where were we?"

The conversation began easily enough as their hostess served plum cakes and weak but piping-hot tea. Ivy had the most difficult time listening, or rather concentrating on the exchange about the history of the town, a bit of the scandal that occurred two years ago, and how quiet it had become after Lord Rothebury's arrest. She had the distinct notion that Garrett had little trouble paying attention, however, as he nodded occasionally and asked his own question or two. She never looked directly at him, though she really didn't need to. He seemed genuinely attentive and far less affected by her presence than she was of his.

"So, are you married, Mr. Burke?"

That question certainly came from nowhere, bringing her attention back to center as if she'd been slapped. Her heart began beating hard and fast as Garrett took his time in answering. Still, she couldn't look at him, though the warmth of his body seemed to penetrate her.

"No, Mrs. Rodney," he replied at last, "my work keeps me rather too busy to consider it as yet. One day, perhaps."

"Ahh," the woman offered with a nod of understanding. "Gentlemen must settle their careers first, I suppose, before they can consider such things."

"Indeed," he agreed, taking a sip of his tea.

Uneasy, Ivy stared into the contents of her cup, scolding herself for feeling so irrationally relieved. Who would care if he was married? She certainly didn't.

"And what of you, Lady Ivy?" came the deep voice from her left. "Are you married? Betrothed?"

The fact that Garrett would ask such a question of his former lover, in front of others, startled her. He undoubtedly knew she'd never married, but she found it almost insulting that he would expect her to answer. And she had to answer. Mrs. Rodney watched her with thoughtful eyes and a curious expression.

Planting a firm smile on her mouth, she drew a long breath and turned to face him, her gaze flat as it met and held his.

"Neither," she replied, her tone cool but pleasant. "I've never had the fortune, Mr. Burke, nor the opportunity. I've yet to meet an appropriate gentleman who . . . meets my needs socially."

For the tiniest second, she could have sworn she saw a flicker of . . . something cross his features. Annoyance? Doubt? Frankly, she hoped both.

Mrs. Rodney cleared her throat, and they both looked back at their hostess. "Well, yes, as a member of the peerage, you'll need to marry someone of your station, with your brother's approval."

With Ian's approval.

"Yes, exactly."

"And where is your brother . . . Ian, isn't it?"

That guarded question came from Garrett, whose composure had hardened just the slightest.

"I believe he's still on the Continent," was her very vague reply, covering the worry in her voice as best she could. "But we expect him home in Stamford by spring."

"Then perhaps," Garrett returned at once, reaching for a second plum cake, "you'll be betrothed to someone of your preference by summer."

Her preference? Meaning someone of her class, she supposed. He goaded her purposely, she was sure, because he had to know marriage for her now was completely out of the question. Even if she could ignore the fact that he had taken her innocence through lies, she could never forget how he'd ruined her ability to trust another man with her heart, at least for any foreseeable future.

Smiling, she lifted her teacup to her lips, and said across the brim, "Although past experience has made me wise about such things, Mr. Burke, alas I fear I may be too old for marriage."

"Nonsense," Mrs. Rodney countered with a wave of a hand, adding nothing, however, as if that one word explained everything.

An uncomfortable silence followed. Ivy shot a quick glance at Garrett, who stared at his tea as if he were reading leaves and telling fortunes. Then swiftly, he swallowed the contents, placed both cup and saucer on the tea table, and inhaled a deep breath.

"As you're aware, Mrs. Rodney," he said congenially, sitting back again and tenting his fingers in front of him as he returned to the point, "I'm employed by an architectural firm in London and we're very much interested in the construction of old country estates. I'm curious about the former Rothebury estate, or should I say, the Rye estate, and was told by the Countess of Eastleigh, that you are the one resident in the village who knows the most about its history."

The older woman smiled quite proudly, bunching her shoulders as she held her cup and saucer in her lap. "Yes, I suppose that is true. The house itself is very old, some say by several hundred years. I can certainly understand why architects would be interested in the various changes that have been made to it during that time."

"What kind of changes?" Ivy asked, feeling Garrett's eyes on her and refusing to glance in his direction.

Mrs. Rodney sighed. "Well, it's been restructured and remodeled many times through the centuries. Wings were torn down and rebuilt, rooms added. I don't think the family kept a record of the changes, either, at least none that I know of. It could possibly take weeks to uncover all the vast secrets inside that house and on the property."

"On the property?" Garrett repeated. "You mean the grounds?"

"Yes, indeed," she revealed with bright eyes. "Long ago, someone from the Sharon family dug a tunnel that leads from beneath the home, or just outside of it, well into the forest, apparently for the purpose of smuggling. Although I've never seen it, and it has since been sealed, I've heard it extends nearly all the way to the docks at Portsmouth. Baron Rothebury was caught using the tunnel to smuggle untaxed opium into the country, for which he was consequently arrested nearly two years ago."

Silence ensued for an awkward moment, then Ivy said, "It sounds so very intriguing. Have you been inside the house recently?"

Mrs. Rodney shook her head lightly. "No, sadly not since the Winter Masquerade of two years ago." She raised her cup took a quick sip of tea. "It wasn't long after the ball that the authorities took Lord Rothebury to London to stand trial, and the property was locked and the regular staff discharged. As far as I know, it remained vacant until just a few weeks ago, when Benedict Sharon, Richard's younger brother, returned unexpectedly and took up residence."

Garrett's chair creaked as he readjusted his body, spreading his right leg out so that he conveniently pushed the toe of his shoe under the hem of her gown.

She didn't move, pretending ignorance lest he think to fluster her again by that somewhat intimate action.

"What did you think of his return?" Garrett asked, speculation in his tone.

The older woman delicately frowned. "Nothing really, aside from a bit of surprise. He'd been gone for so long the town had all but forgotten about him." She cleared her throat. "Of course when a member of the family is . . . detained by the police, it becomes quite a scandalous affair for everybody. But then he kept to himself. I don't think I spoke to him once in the few short weeks he was in Winter Garden."

"I suppose it didn't seem unusual for him to stay somewhat secluded," Ivy remarked, acknowledging how very brazen Benedict's return had to seem to the local gentry. A family disgraced couldn't possibly expect to entertain or accept social invitations.

"No, and since he hired only a minimal staff," Mrs. Rodney replied with pinched brows, "I got the distinct impression that he wouldn't be staying long."

"Perhaps just long enough to sell the property?" Garrett offered lightly.

Mrs. Rodney lifted her teacup and finished the contents in a swallow. "Perhaps, though his disappearance was just as mysterious as the purchase by the new owner."

"The Marquess of Rye," Garrett said.

Ivy sat forward a little, a sudden thought occurred to her. "Have you met the marquess, Mrs. Rodney?"

The older woman chuckled and shook her head.

"Good heavens, no, and what a. mystery he is," she maintained, leaning forward to place her cup and saucer on the tea table.

"A mystery?" Garrett probed. "How so?"

Mrs. Rodney patted her the corners of her mouth with her linen napkin, stalling, Ivy was certain, for effect.

"Well, it's been said in . . . circles that the man is either an invalid, or a rake of the most clever and notorious kind. It would explain why he's never appeared in public, or chosen to introduce himself to Winter Garden's polite society. It's also been rumored that he rarely visits his home in Rye, which is not so very far from here, but spends most of his time in London."

Ivy remained quiet for a moment, trying to absorb the information. But before she could respond, she felt the slightest stirring of the toe of his shoe just above her leather-booted ankle, a gentle, up-and-down caress on her stockinged calf that both surprised and horrified her. It was a shocking, despicable, sensuous movement that flooded her mind with memory and her body with heat. Quickly, as daintily as she could, she jerked her leg to the side and adjusted her bottom in the chair, her skirts over her knees and around her ankles, noting with barely contained ire that Garrett looked quite relaxed, as if he didn't even notice the discomfiture he had purposely caused.

"So why do you suppose he bought this particular property?" he asked in a low, thoughtful voice, keeping his attention squarely on their hostess.

Ivy wanted to scream and box his ears. Instead, she smiled pleasantly, folding her hands in her lap as she awaited Mrs. Rodney's reply.

"That's the greatest mystery of all," came the soft answer, the woman's tone now quite conspiratorial. "Why buy a house in Winter Garden when he doesn't live on the estate he owns, has never been here to my knowledge, and spends his time in London, either as an invalid, or . . . charming the ladies?" She paused to reach for a third plum cake with dainty fingers, then added before nibbling, "But of course everything about this gentleman is rumor."

"Perhaps, Mr. Burke, he purchased the estate because of the many rooms and hidden tunnels the house is purported to have and simply wants to amuse himself by discovering them one by one," Ivy interjected, turning a little so she looked at Garrett for the first time since they all began talking. "As an architect, it's why you're interested in it, is it not?"

If he thought her inquiry was a bold attempt to undo his remarkable composure, he didn't show it. In his usual dashing manner, he locked his gaze with hers and smiled with a mockery only she could detect.

"Naturally, that's why I'm interested in the property, Lady Ivy," he replied easily. "But if Lord Rye purchased it for the same purpose, wouldn't he be here to investigate as well?"

She had no idea how to answer that without acknowledging the obvious—that one would think so—which she didn't consider when she asked him the question.

Offering a most pleasant smile, she ignored that striking fact, and asked instead, "So how long do you intend to be in town, Mr. Burke?"

His dark eyes bored into hers. "I'm not at all certain. My employer wishes a thorough report, though, so I shall give him that."

"I see," she replied, eyeing him speculatively. "A thorough report of what, may I ask?"

His features never changed. "Of the various changes on the property. Apparently the new owner wants a complete account of them."

"So your London firm has been hired by Lord Rye?"

His chair creaked beneath him. "Apparently. Or at least that's what I assume."

He had an answer for everything, she mused with annoyance. Just as a good investigator should.

"Suppose," Mrs. Rodney interjected, "the marquess had this planned all along."

They both turned to look at their hostess, whose gaze now focused on them with a shrewdness not seen before.

Ivy feigned ignorance. "I beg your pardon?"

Garrett just watched the older woman in silence.

Mrs. Rodney tapped the tips of her fingers on the edge of her china plate. "Well, it does seem to be a rather strange sequence of events, don't you think? The house has been abandoned for nearly two years when suddenly Mr. Sharon arrives and disappears, causing a flurry of speculation in Winter Garden. Then at almost the same time, you arrive to research the property, Mr. Burke, and are soon followed by Lady Ivy, who was summoned by the marquess to investigate the house for ghosts." She paused for a moment, shaking her head negligibly, then added, "It just all seems very unusual. Almost . . . planned."

Oddly planned. Suddenly Ivy realized that Mrs. Rodney had drawn these conclusions without any knowledge of the Martello diamonds. If one considered the jewels, their being drawn together became more than a hunt for strangers, ghosts, and secret passageways within an old house. It became a dangerous game of cat and mouse, all of them used as players, including her brother, for a reason unknown. The chilling thought unnerved her.

Garrett straightened in his chair, finally pulling his leg back, his foot decently removed from beneath the hem of her gown, which he no longer seemed to notice.

"Unless it's all just coincidence," he countered with a grin and a sigh, lightening the mood.

Mrs. Rodney smiled in return. "Yes, I suppose it's been my experience that things are only as they appear." With delicate hands, she lifted the teapot. "More refreshment, anyone?"

Darkness had fallen as they left the Rodney home, and even as he made her nervous by walking beside her, she was more disconcerted by his behavior at tea. They hadn't said a word to each other since leaving, but with every crunch of their shoes on the gravel pathway, the irritation within her increased. She kept her pace steady until they reached the inn, then gradually slowed to a standstill.

"Thank you, sir, but I can walk the rest of the way by myself," she said matter-of-factly.

He gazed down at her, his hands shoved into the pockets of his twine coat. "Of course," he maintained, "but I would be remiss in allowing your wishes to overrule Mrs. Rodney's, who might then find disappointment in my gentlemanly behavior."

"Garrett—"

"Don't argue, Ivy," he grumbled. "It's dark and cold, and I have no intention of touching you in any unseemly manner."

Her mouth opened to offer a snide reply, then she shut it again. Turning away from him, she began walking once more. "Interesting to hear you say such a thing after what you did in Mrs. Rodney's home."

After a moment's pause, he repeated, "What I did?"

She cast him a fast glance. "Do not act as if you have no idea what I'm talking about."

He continued to walk a half step behind her, staring down at the footpath. "If you're referring to accidentally touching your ankle with my toe, then yes, I have an idea. But I assure you, it was completely innocent."

"You'd really have me believe that caressing me like that was accidental?" she asked in feigned sweetness.

Dropping his voice, he leaned in to whisper gruffly,

"Why wouldn't you believe me? Because I've *caressed* you like that before?"

The intimacy implied made her heart flutter and her stomach twist in knots yet the way he said it, as if what he'd done meant nothing, made her furious, if irrationally so. She simply couldn't answer him, and she wasn't certain he even expected her to.

"How did you know I'd be at Mrs. Rodney's home for tea?" she asked, changing the subject as she stopped walking once more.

She expected him to laugh and reply that he'd warned her he'd be watching and lurking, but he didn't do either. Instead, he inhaled deeply and cocked his head to the side minutely, his eyes scanning her face in the darkness.

Finally, voice lowered, he replied, "I don't suppose you'd believe we met there strictly by chance."

"No," she answered through a shiver. "If I had to guess, I'd say you paid someone at the Rye estate to inform you of my every move."

He shrugged and glanced over her head toward the lake. "If that's what you believe, then there's nothing more I can say."

She should have expected such an evasive response from him. He refused to admit that he had prior information concerning her whereabouts this afternoon, and yet they both knew he did. He had to. Garrett was an organized investigator and had a detailed plan for everything he did. She had learned that about him the first day they met.

"If you're here in Winter Garden to carry on your search for the Martello diamonds," she continued, thinking aloud, "why are you following me? You said you know I don't have them." It was a forthright question, and he didn't deny that he had an ulterior motive for doing so. She waited, rubbing her hands together in her muff, noting a certain hesitation in his demeanor.

At last, he replied, "Benedict Sharon had the diamonds when he disappeared, and now you're living in his home. You were also there when I tried to secure them in London two years ago. I find that curious."

She hadn't been anywhere near the diamonds, she had been in his *bed*, awaiting his return, which never came. But she wouldn't mention such a thing because he very well knew it.

No, he wasn't only being evasive, she realized, he was hiding something. Something important. And he wasn't keeping information to himself simply to have an upper hand in the investigation. For some very specific reason he wanted her involved, or expected her to lead him either to the diamonds or to the person who had taken them. Yet how did he know she'd be looking for them herself? If it were any other person, she'd assume he was guessing. But Garrett relied on facts. That was how he worked.

He gazed down at her again, silence surrounding them but for the breeze whistling through the trees that lined the lake. He'd grown contemplative, his handsome features barely discernible from the distant light at the inn. For a second, just the smallest second, she felt the strangest urge to confide in him, to tell him what she knew and ask him to help her. But the notion quickly passed. She simply couldn't trust him again, with anything. And with Ian in danger, his whereabouts unknown—

"I'm cold, Garrett, and would like to return to the house," she said, deflated suddenly and hoping he'd sense her reluctance to be near him, her obvious dismissal. She needed time to think.

He said nothing for a moment longer, then, "I can't let you walk around the lake and into the forest by yourself, you know that."

She couldn't summon a suitable reply.

"You walk, I'll follow," he added.

She shook her head. "Really, Garrett, it's not—"

"Necessary?" he cut in, his tone a bit lighter. "Of course it's necessary. The least I can do is offer you my gentlemanly protection for a few more minutes."

It all seemed so strange to her, to be near him like this. And for the first time since he came back into her life, she truly acknowledged how very much his presence stirred her, emotionally and physically. Accepting such a truth meant that, above all things, where Garrett Burke was concerned, she would need to remain very, very careful until they parted for a final time.

He lightly grasped her elbow, and she shivered again, this time not from cold, but from the mere innocent contact.

Be careful . . .

"Let's go, Lady Ivy," he urged through a sigh. "I, too, am anxious for the comfort of a warm fire."

Without another word, he steered her onto the path and she led the way, leaving his company only as she neared the entrance of the Rye estate, not another word spoken between them.

Chapter 4

As much as he wanted to view her intimately, asleep and undressed, even bathing, Garrett had decided not to yield to the temptation long before he specified which bedroom would be hers at the manor house. When he had finally given Trudy Thurman instructions regarding the luscious Lady Ivy, it had been nearly impossible to resist the urge to assign her the master bedchamber with the secret passage attached. In the end, he'd surrendered to his better judgment. But after scrutinizing her in the window as he watched the house from the edge of the lake, then catching a faint whiff of her sweet-smelling perfume in Mrs. Rodney's home, he regretted his decision at the very basest level. His honor might have saved him from going to hell, but he knew now that for the next days or even weeks he'd be living in it.

To say he wanted to bed her again was an understatement of the most blatant kind. In all honesty, he could only vaguely recall the time he had, though by the static charge still obvious between them and the pure ire she exuded as they stood together in his parlor two days ago, he now realized just how much he'd wronged her that first time. He knew a sexually defensive woman when he saw one, which meant he'd taken her, without the legality or promise of marriage. He didn't know what powerful persuasion would have forced him to react so indecently and forget himself in the presence of a lady of Ivy's social status, but he suspected it had much to do with the very feminine assets that lay beneath her conservative day gown and proper carriage. Men had written poetry about women like Ivy. Still, beyond the fact that a poet might describe her loveliness like morning sun on dew-dipped roses, to him she remained the most sensual woman he'd ever met—a woman created for lovemaking. When he closed his eyes and tried to envision it, he saw flashes of long, silky legs and satiny skin, and most importantly a face lit up at the moment of supreme satisfaction. Yes, they had made love, with a marvelous passion, and his greatest regret was his inability to remember each delicious detail.

Garrett despised that fact that there were pieces of his past he couldn't recall. Somehow losing segments of one's memory made a man weak, which was one of the reasons behind his decision to keep his own lapse secret from nearly everyone. If he hadn't been stupid and tried to catch a thief on his own, if he hadn't been with Ivy or believed her brother without question, he would have met Benedict Sharon in a more public place, would have been prepared, kept his thoughts on the moment at hand, and thus prevented the attack that ultimately shaped his future.

But he and Ivy were back together for unfinished business, at *his* bidding. He would no longer let others take advantage of him, use him. With the passing of his father nine months ago, he had inherited the title and lands at Rye, told his mother firmly that he would *not* be marrying the conniving Lady Margaret Dartmouth of Brighton, and once again set about trying to recover his property—the Martello diamonds—the family heirloom that had been part of his grandmother's dowry when she came from Italy, as a princess, to marry his grandfather some seventy years ago. Technically they were now *his* diamonds, not just the family's, and as sure as he knew the sun would rise tomorrow, he knew Ivy had some major role to play in retrieving them. But he wasn't a seer, and didn't believe in the nonsense. He knew this in his gut.

Of course, there was more to his decision to bring Ivy to Winter Garden to help him in his quest than the simple need to see her once more and learn what part she had played in his failure to catch the thief two years ago. They had clearly both kept secrets from each other. Yet for all his intricate planning, he hadn't been prepared for the rush of desire he felt when he laid eyes on her again. She still had the power to dazzle him to speechlessness, even after he had tried to prepare himself by saying good morning and gathering his thoughts before he turned to look at her in the parlor on the former Rothebury estate. Thank God he'd been able to hide his reaction to her beauty even though it had bewildered him that his heart started beating hard in his chest, his mouth went dry, and his body reacted as if he'd never been with a woman. Frankly, he wasn't certain how long he could contain his desire to touch her again, and that worried him. But the past was finished. They were here together, he to right wrongs regardless of the outcome, and there could be no going back.

Mrs. Thurman had sent a note to him this morning letting him know that Ivy had gone to bed early again last night, rose early this morning, and that she planned to call on Lady Eastleigh before noon. She hadn't said why, but Garrett had no intention of allowing her to retrieve clues before him, about whatever information she thought the countess might have. She'd only been in Winter Garden for three days and already Lady Ivy had a plan. Of course it differed only slightly from his own, but she couldn't know that yet.

Now, after bathing at the inn and taking a breakfast of coffee and toast in his room, he set out toward the lake, rounding the cottage where she planned to meet Madeleine and proceeding through the forest trees, hoping to catch the enchantress of his dreams on the path before she arrived. But to his utter surprise he discovered her sitting on the bench in front of the lake—the same bench on which he had sat only days before to watch her at her new bedroom window.

Stopping short, Garrett stared at her for a moment before approaching. The sun shone off the lake with a brilliance that made her squint, but she still looked lovely and tranquil as she gazed out over the still water, her dark auburn hair plaited and coiled loosely on top of her head, the black fur collar of her woolen pelisse brushing the softness of her cheek, now rosy from cold. For a moment he was taken aback by the beauty of the entire scene. Then, very gradually, the line of her lip twitched upward and he realized she knew he was here.

Slowly, he began to walk toward her, and she turned, the look on her face leaving him fairly unsettled when she set her eyes on him at last. Satisfaction, a trace of impertinence, and even a certain desire of the heart all crossed her features when she not only glanced his way but admired him up and down. He wished like hell he could remember more details of the days they had spent together, for he was certain they had been filled with lust—albeit completely quixotic and improper.

"I thought I'd make myself an easy target for you this morning," she said pleasantly, as he approached.

He shoved his gloved hands in the pockets of his twine coat. "An easy target?"

She shrugged a shoulder and turned back to the view of the lake. "I knew you'd be coming to meet me before I reached the Hope cottage, so I thought I'd wait for you."

"I see." He glanced down to the top of her head as he finally reached her side. She remained seated on the old wooden bench, relaxing her posture a little in the natural manner that encouraged discussion. "And how did you know that, Lady Ivy?"

He could almost hear her smile.

"In the usual way," she replied.

"Ah." By "usual way" he assumed she meant through her pronounced gift of foresight. Then again it could have meant simple, reasonable deduction.

"No, Garrett," she lightly scolded as if reading his mind, "I meant that after giving it more thought, I've decided to assume you're paying someone to keep you informed of my whereabouts, and I've chosen not to fight it, or you."

Fight it? He remained silent, uncertain how to take such a comment and what he could possibly say in his defense that might sound apologetic or even just reasonable. He tried to recall if he and Ivy had fought about anything when they'd been together in London, but the effort hurt his head. Probably not, since they'd only shared a few days, hopefully filled with nothing but laughter and mutual desire, feelings he suddenly longed to know if she remembered. Or regretted.

"What are you thinking?" she asked, jarring him back to the moment.

He shifted a shoe back and forth along the forest floor. "Nothing really, other than it's cold, even without a cloud in the sky."

"After I accuse you of spying on me, you're thinking about the weather?" she countered, her tone laced with amusement. "I don't believe you. The one thing I remember is how thoroughly you think about things, especially the things you find important."

What her hair would look like spread across his pillow didn't seem very important, he considered, though in reply, he casually asked, "What things?"

She shot him a fast glance over her shoulder. "That's something else I remember," she said after a few seconds. "When the topic is uncomfortable, you're very good at steering conversation away from you by answering a question with a question."

He almost laughed, remembering how his sister once told him the very same thing. "You remember this, do you?"

She offered him a full, beautiful grin, then turned her attention back to the lake. "You're despicable."

"So I've been told," he said softly.

A long silence ensued. Then through a sigh, she stood and turned to face him, her demeanor cordial but restrained.

"I suppose if you're going to be following me, you should come with me to Lady Eastleigh's cottage."

He hesitated for a moment, eyeing her carefully, noting the wariness in her voice, the stiffness in her posture. They stood only a foot away from each other, and yet formality between them had returned.

"Why are you seeing her today?" he asked, subdued.

Her eyes narrowed in calculation. "She and her husband have drawings they made of the house, inside and out. I want to see them."

A sketch of the property. Both Madeleine and her husband were inside when they had investigated Richard Sharon two years ago, and of course they knew about the tunnel and its entrance to the house.

Yes, thinking of discussing the secret entrances with them was a brilliant move on Ivy's part, and acknowledging that fact made him annoyed at himself for concentrating so much on something as ridiculous as the texture of her hair.

"Well, then, since I'm posing as an architect, I have a very good reason to see them as well," he replied with a hint of joviality.

Her brows rose, and her lips curved up in response. "They're already very much aware of your profession, sir. If you continue to follow me, they'll begin to suspect we're working together."

He just watched her for a moment, then, "Technically, I suppose we are."

She laughed a little at that absurdity. "You may be searching for diamonds, Garrett, but I assure you, my work here is far more important than shiny stones. And I do not need your help or desire your company."

"Not desiring my company I understand. But finding ghosts more important than priceless stolen jewels?" He rubbed his temple with his gloved fingers. "Explain that logic to me, Ivy?"

She shook her head in distaste, and for a few seconds, didn't reply. Finally, she murmured, "I suppose we both have our obsessions, don't we?"

A gust of wind swirled the leaves around their feet, brushing stray strands of hair across her face. He fought the urge to reach out and touch each silky strand. "Obsessions?" he repeated very softly. "Yes, I have two."

She blinked and furrowed her brows as if confused. Then her features hardened. "One you must find at all costs, and one to rid yourself of once and for all, I suppose."

"That's not what I said, or meant," he replied, his voice dark.

"Don't play me for a fool, Garrett," she whispered up to him. "I know you better than you think I do."

That statement stirred him inside, on many different levels. They stared at each other, her face pale, countenance rigid. Uncertain how much to reveal when she seemed to despise him so thoroughly, he paused in thought, rubbing his temple again.

And then suddenly her eyes began to narrow and she took a step closer to him, scanning his face slowly and carefully, with a scrutiny that unnerved him.

"What is it?"

She shook her head once as if attempting to focus on a minute detail that escaped her grasp. Then to his utter shock, she pulled a hand from her fur muff and lifted it to press the pads of three fingers on his brow.

The contact of warmth against cold, of her gentle touch to his skin, made his body come alive with its own inner heat. He didn't move.

Lingeringly, she drew her fingers down his cheek, stopping when she reached his jaw, placing her thumb on his chin, focusing on the spot. Seconds later, she quietly asked, "Are you in pain, Garrett?"

He almost stopped breathing. His head hurt, yes, though not severely today. But what he felt most at the moment was an ache of longing deep in the pit of his stomach—and a sense of anger because, as much as he wanted to, he couldn't trust it, physically or mentally.

"There will come a time, Lady Ivy," he disclosed in deep whisper, "when we will have to discuss what happened in London."

Another gust of wind, stronger this time, stirred the trees around them and rippled the water on the lake. But she never appeared to notice as she gazed intently into his eyes for a timeless moment. Then, drawing a shaky breath, she straightened and dropped her hand from his cheek, took a step back and regained her prim composure.

"The past is over," she stated huskily, pulling the collar of her pelisse up around her neck and stuffing her hand back in her muff.

He shook his head. "Perhaps over, Ivy, but not forgotten."

With a minute tilt of her chin, she replied with the question, "Not forgotten by whom?"

For a fraction of a second that startled him—until he realized she meant to be derisive.

Garrett crossed his arms over his chest. With a shrug of his shoulder, he took a step closer. "I can't believe you have no memories of us."

"I remember being used, sir," she said in a nearly inaudible voice.

He inhaled deeply. "We were all used, Ivy. I want to know why, and by whom, that's my primary concern now."

"That, and finding the Martello diamonds. Both of your obsessions to be tied up into neat little packages," she said sarcastically.

He hesitated, then admitted, "Yes, though such a characterization of my motives is a bit extreme."

She scoffed. "And you think *I* have the answers?"

"No," he admitted at once, "but *someone* does, and we're both involved whether we like it or not. That's the reason we're here together now."

The fact that she didn't immediately deny his claim gave him encouragement. She glanced out over the water, her sculpted brows pinched.

"We're not here together, Garrett," she returned at last. "And I can't offer you anything."

After several long seconds, he asked huskily, "What are you afraid of, Ivy?"

She looked back into his eyes. "I'm not afraid."

The urge to take her hand from inside her warm muff and kiss her palm in comfort was remarkably overwhelming, but his greatest fear at the moment was that touching her would only cause her to run—and he would learn nothing.

"I believe," he revealed with complete sincerity, "that you don't fear the things you should, like empty homes, voices from the dead—"

"I don't hear voices from the dead," she cut in with irritation.

He gave her a vague smile. "Perhaps not. But the little inner voice of yours that you do hear tells you to fear me, doesn't it?"

She said nothing for a moment and he waited, watching the sunlight play upon her shiny hair, the dewy frozen breath escape her full, pink lips.

At last, she acquiesced. "I despise what you did to me, but I don't fear you, Garrett, I never did." She paused, then whispered, "I fear us."

The oddest combination of deep anger and sublime tenderness pulsed through him. He'd never expected her to be so honest in her reply, but it dismayed him, and in a breath, he admitted, "I fear us, too."

She swallowed, gazing into his eyes for a long, silent moment. Then abruptly she straightened, lifted her skirts, and began to walk toward the opening in the trees that led to the cottage, brushing by him so closely he couldn't help but notice the scent of lilac she wore—a scent he remembered as lingering on his sheets, haunting him for days after she had gone.

It was clear now, regardless of her acceptance, that they needed to help each other, for every troubling reason.

But first he needed to find his diamonds.

Chapter 5

He'd shaken her badly with his disclosure, though she couldn't decide if it had been honest and from the heart, or if he simply wanted to seduce her for his own personal satisfaction as he'd done before. Now, as she sat beside him at the small kitchen table, the room comfortably warm and smelling of baked bread, staring at sketches of the Rye estate with Madeleine and Thomas, she had trouble concentrating on anything but his overwhelming form nearly touching her.

They were getting too close—in proximity, in conversation. She needed to think, to rid her mind of a past that continued to plague her, so she could focus on the task at hand. Garrett Burke had been a mistake from which she had learned too much, but there was more. She was nearly beside herself with worry about Ian, and she had no idea what caused her distress. The last she knew of his whereabouts, he'd been traveling on the Continent, exploring the possibility of purchasing property in southern Italy. But now that she considered it more closely, his being gone for nearly a year, with only minimal contact between them, seemed rather

odd. She had always been close to her brother, but
since that dreadful day when they learned they were
bastard children of the late Baron of Rothebury, he'd
changed. He'd distanced himself from her, from friends
and acquaintances. She'd tried to heal his wound by
stressing that, with the passing of their mother, nobody
would ever know the truth about their parentage, and
she would never reveal it to a soul. He trusted her, but
there was something else that continued to agitate him.
He'd inherited the estate in Stamford, could marry at
his leisure and raise a son as the earl with nobody the
wiser. He understood this on a rational level, and yet he
feared it for some reason.

    But with her gift, she knew he was in trouble, and
her being here in Winter Garden served a purpose in
helping him. She just didn't know how, or why. And
now with Garrett at her side, seemingly constantly, her
own fear had begun to increase. Certainly not a fear
of the man, but a fear that he would interfere with her
ability to help her brother, the one person in the world
she trusted.

    Madeleine sat across from her, Thomas, the wom-
an's distinguished and handsome husband, sat to his
wife's left. Garrett sat to her left, but the table was
so tiny, each time he moved in his chair his arm or
knee—seemingly unintentionally—grazed hers. Although he seemed eager enough to be with her while
searching for the jewels that had eluded him and neg-
atively affected his career, he didn't seem to be at all
interested in her again as a woman. At least she didn't

think so because, unlike two years ago, he seemed cautious, even unsure of her. He hadn't tried to kiss her, seduce her, as he'd so willingly done before, and she supposed she should feel elated about that. And yet, in a manner she couldn't understand, it rather depressed her. She knew he thought she was involved in his failure to find the diamonds in London, but she simply couldn't discuss it with him. Not yet. Still, the fact that he sat so close to her now intimidated her immensely. She could ignore him only so much, and then his pure masculinity intruded on her thoughts, disrupting her concentration. And when it came to the diamonds, she had to remember that she needed them more than he.

"Ivy?"

She blinked, sitting up a little straighter in her chair. "Pardon?"

Garrett leaned back and frowned negligibly. "You're not paying attention," he said, his voice holding a trace of amusement.

"Yes, she is," Madeleine said from across the table. "She's just not interested in old, hand-drawn maps, *oui*?"

The Frenchwoman looked at her cautiously, and Ivy had the distinct impression she knew very well what was going through her mind. Not maps. *Him.*

"I'm sorry," she confessed, "I'm just distracted I suppose. And a bit tired."

"It's the Rothebury ghosts keeping you awake all night," Thomas teased.

She laughed softly. "I only wish they would. At least I would have something to do in the house."

"Ah," Madeleine replied, gazing back to the map of the property, then turning it so one of the pages faced her. "These will surely give you something to do. However, do keep in mind that they were drawn by my hand, and I am a terrible artist." She winked at her husband. "But far better than Eastleigh."

"You are not," her husband chided good-naturedly. "You simply refused to let me draw."

Madeleine shrugged. "I don't remember it that way . . ."

"What are these small blue circles?" Garrett asked, focusing on areas not defined by a door or window but clearly marked on a few of the walls.

"Those," Thomas replied, "are hidden, or secret, doorways."

"The ones we're aware of," Madeleine added. "There are probably more of them, but we have not been able to enter to investigate further, unfortunately. After the baron's arrest, the house was locked up and sealed, including the tunnel entrance"—she turned the page sideways—"here."

"And when Benedict abruptly arrived without announcement, he refused all callers," Thomas maintained, sounding a bit annoyed. "We were hoping the new owner would allow us in, but we haven't seen Rye on the property as yet."

"Ivy could let you in," Garrett said, pulling his arm from the back of the chair and sitting forward once more.

She glanced up to see him looking not at her, but at Thomas. "I'm not sure that's a very good idea without the owner's permission. And doing so secretly could alert someone on the staff, which in itself could prove to be disastrous."

"Exactly true," Madeleine agreed. "Even if we called on you socially, the servants would obviously know, and if we moved freely around the house to investigate, gossip of our sudden interest would spread." She shook her head. "No, the exploring will be up to the two of you."

Ivy blinked. "The two of us?"

As if reading the diffidence in her mind, Garrett said lightly, "I'm the architect, remember?"

"And an excellent identity to use for looking at cracks in walls and rooms that might be oddly shaped or newly remodeled," Thomas remarked, adjusting his large frame in the tiny chair.

Ivy ignored the implication and leaned in to study the map more closely. "So, as you've outlined here, there are secret entrances in . . . the library, the master bedchamber, and the . . . what room is this?"

They all leaned their heads over the table to closely examine the spot where she pointed, Garrett's cheek so close to hers now that she could feel the warmth of his skin, smell the faintest traces of his cologne. She sat back at once.

"That's the wine cellar, I believe," Thomas answered, frowning. He placed a large palm on the sketch and pointed with his index finger. "This door here leads to the tunnel, and probably, in the opposite direction . . . here, up a hidden staircase to Rothebury's bedchamber. We know he brought women in at night, and with such indelicate intent, he needed to avoid servants and their prying eyes."

"He was bedding women by bringing them secretly into his own room?" Garrett asked incredulously.

Ivy felt a slight flush creep up her neck at his brazen mention of the former baron's indiscretions. He had to know his question would summon memories of their own indecency in *his* bed, when he'd brought her in at night and made passionate love to her by firelight. But she'd learned too much to cower now, and she refused to glance his way for fear that he would see the embarrassment in her eyes.

Madeleine sighed and slumped her shoulders a little. "The conniving Richard Sharon was a nefarious rake who seemed to enjoy, and sometimes boast about, his reputation. He even got one of the local girls with child after filling her impressionable head with fancies, then refused to marry her, or help her with the problem in any way." A trace of anger slipped into her voice as her features grew taut. "Really, the man was incredibly arrogant, and disgraceful in every regard. He deserved to die in prison."

"He died in prison?" she and Garrett asked in unison.

"So we've heard," Thomas replied through a long exhale, leaning back in his wooden chair, which creaked beneath his weight. "And it was fairly soon after his arrival. With his title and other monetary influences, he shouldn't have remained there long. Many people knew this, and so it's rumored he was murdered quickly, possibly by poison, before he had the chance to scheme or purchase his way to freedom. But the authorities never found anyone guilty and eventually dropped the matter for lack of evidence."

Murdered by poison. A horrifying thought, and Ivy shifted her legs beneath the table as she tried to shake it off.

A lingering silence ensued, then Garrett asked, "Is the girl he ruined still in town?"

Madeleine shook her head minutely. "She moved to Northumberland soon after the scandal broke. Married a gentleman friend who took responsibility for her and the child, though we have heard no news from or about poor Desdemona in the two years she's been gone."

"Very sad for her family, too," Thomas added, seconds later. "Desdemona testified at the smuggling trial, where she revealed everything she knew, and in so doing, disgraced them all. Three family members still live in Winter Garden, her mother, Penelope Bennington-Jones, and the girl's younger sisters, Hermione and Viola."

Ivy remembered the family, or more precisely, she and Ian knew the Bennington-Joneses vaguely when they lived there as children. Desdemona, the oldest could not have been more than five or six, however, when they left Winter Garden.

Thomas exhaled a long breath and continued. "Unfortunately, Desdemona's father died soon after the scandal broke, and I think most of his estate has dwindled. We don't see much of them anymore, and I don't suppose they have anywhere to go."

Ivy felt a chilling sadness for the girl, but then she fully understood the necessity to protect oneself after a failed love affair, hoping to marry and then losing that hope only to discover you were never wanted. Thank God Garrett hadn't gotten her with child.

Forcing herself to shove that thought aside, she quickly returned to the subject of the house. "Did Desdemona give the authorities details about these hidden entrances when she testified?"

"She knew of only the tunnel," Thomas replied, "and was able to show investigators how she entered—the same way, in fact, that Rothebury smuggled opium into his home." He inhaled deeply as he stretched his arm across the back of his wife's chair, wrapping a loose strand of her hair around a finger absentmindedly. "This is the reason we're fairly certain the tunnel leads both to the cellar entrance as well as the master bedchamber. There could also be other staircases, though we aren't certain of that. We do know, however, that the house is smaller on the inside than it appears on the outside, and that it's been remodeled several times through the centuries."

Ivy furrowed her brows. "How did you learn of the entry from the library?"

"Madeleine found that one."

She smiled at her husband. "During the masquerade ball Rothebury held that winter, though I never went through it. I just know it's behind this bookcase," she said, tapping the paper map with a manicured nail. "We're not sure where it leads."

Garrett reached out and ran his finger along the wall line. "Probably, if one enters here," he remarked, "it would also lead to the master bedchamber."

"Or one of the others," Ivy speculated. Without thought, she reached for his hand and lifted it by the fingers to trace a line herself. An unexpected warmth radiated from her toes to her face at the simple contact, and she immediately let go of him, concentrating on the sketches. She could feel Garrett's gaze on her but ignored it.

"It seems as if it would be relatively easy," she continued, "to connect to all the rooms on the third landing. Look here."

Slowly, she drew her finger from the library to the master bedchamber, then to a second and third, and finally to the one in which she slept. "This is the room I was given by the marquess, but I'm fairly certain there's no entrance."

"Have you looked?" Garrett asked, his voice low.

"No, but then I didn't realize there might be a secret entrance in a spare bedroom until I saw the map," she reasoned, lifting her lashes to catch his forthright gaze on her.

Eyeing her shrewdly, he said, "Then that's where we start."

"You can't possibly expect to come near my bedroom," she insisted in a fast breath. The idea of working with him—of doing *anything* with him—made her nervous, which he likely noticed because he suddenly smiled lazily at her.

"I'll go through the library entrance and see where it leads, that's all. You stand in your bedchamber and listen for me."

"No," she countered flatly, "*I'll* follow the staircase."

Madeleine cut in, "Garrett will have an excellent excuse for being there, so what harm can it do to let him come along?"

Ivy just looked at her blankly, unable to think of a suitable reply that didn't in some manner divulge her true feelings in the matter.

"Frankly," Garrett said, his eyes narrowed in speculation as he stared at the map, "if danger lurks in places not used for years, like staircases and cellars, it wouldn't be wise for *either* of us to enter alone. Safety is the central issue."

Her annoyance bubbled near the surface, but she couldn't very well argue against such sane analysis on his part.

Suddenly Thomas furrowed his brows and gazed at her thoughtfully. "You've been inside before, haven't you, Ivy? You and your brother, some years ago?"

"I didn't know you have a brother," Madeleine said in surprise.

She smiled vaguely. "A twin, seven minutes younger than I." Looking back to Thomas, she revealed, "Yes, our parents were friends of Richard Sharon's father, but

I'm afraid that was many years ago—more than twenty, actually. I frequently visited the house as a child, but I don't remember very much, and I certainly knew nothing of secret tunnels. I'm sure Ian doesn't remember anything, either. At least he's never mentioned it."

"Where is he?" Thomas asked with genuine curiosity.

She swallowed and sat up straighter in her chair. "He's been traveling on the Continent for the past year or so, intent on purchasing property in Italy. He should be returning to Stamford in the spring, though."

She cast a glance at Garrett to notice him studying her with that same perceptive and intimidating look that made her stomach twist in knots. She'd given her standard answer, the same one she'd given to Mrs. Rodney, and he looked as if he had trouble believing her explanation. Not that a standard answer wasn't practical, and of course she could be imagining a suspicion on his part.

"You must miss him very much," Madeleine said, as if reading her mind.

"I do, yes," she replied. "He's all the family I have left, and we are very close."

After an awkward moment of silence, Madeleine leaned forward and placed her forearms on the table, over the map, and grinned wryly. "Wouldn't it be grand if the Marquess of Rye held his own masquerade ball?"

"Madeleine . . ." Thomas cautioned, saying her name in a way that almost sounded like a caress. "What are you thinking?"

His wife ignored him and concentrated on Ivy, her eyes sparkling with intrigue. "You are in contact with the man, are you not?"

She frowned delicately. "With the marquess? I suppose I am, yes."

Madeleine shrugged, then sat back in her chair, glancing to all of them one at a time. "Then why not send him a note and suggest it? He doesn't have to attend, of course, but you could imply that it would be a marvelous way to bring the community together, to welcome the new owner, or just honor him in his absence. It would also put us all into that house again. With so many people attending, one would hardly notice a person or two sneaking away to investigate."

"Investigate what?" Thomas asked sardonically.

Madeleine peered at him sideways through her lashes. "A missing person, ghosts, and stolen, priceless diamonds, darling."

"Ah," her husband replied as if she'd explained it all.

The idea was quite logical, and Ivy felt only a moment's trepidation at the thought. Madeleine and Thomas knew of Garrett's assignment to find the Martello diamonds, and they knew she was here to look for ghosts at the marquess's request. But nobody knew that she needed the jewels, or that her brother's life was in danger. Garrett suspected she had other intentions, but that's all it was—pure speculation.

If Benedict Sharon had the diamonds when he disappeared, and his last-known whereabouts were in the house, then they would all, in essence, be searching for the very same thing, and she would, by necessity, need to be overly cautious with every single move. Still, all the planning in the world could be for naught if the elusive Marquess of Rye refused to give his consent.

Garrett remained unnaturally silent, Thomas in deep thought. But then they were men and not so inclined to participate in the planning of a party, especially one as large as a masquerade ball.

"I think it's a good idea," she agreed, her eagerness growing despite her worries. "Of course the marquess might have objections we can't foresee, though if I explain that the house has hidden tunnels he's not aware of, perhaps he'll be inclined to consent to a ball simply to draw out those who might know something about structure or its history." She bit the side of her lip. "But I don't think I can ask him to pay for it, especially if he's not inclined to attend."

"I think we should pay for it," Madeleine stated matter-of-factly.

Thomas groaned; Garrett chuckled and rubbed his eyes with his fingers.

"It was my suggestion, Eastleigh."

"Yes," he replied directly to his wife, "but what you're proposing is highly impractical under the circumstances."

"What circumstances?" she persisted, crossing her arms over her breasts.

"Too numerous to name," he said, his voice sounding as if he'd already accepted defeat in the argument.

Ivy glanced at Garrett, who simply sat with his eyes closed, shaking his head, a fraction of a smile on his lips.

"Perhaps I should write him first," she said, squashing the enthusiasm for a moment. "He may simply not want people on the estate for reasons we can't know, or the fact that a person disappeared there."

"It is all rather chilling to contemplate, isn't it?" Madeleine said, subdued. "And yet the marquess may surprise us all with his answer."

At that, Garrett exhaled deeply, placed his palms on the table, and pushed himself up. "I think Lord Eastleigh and his wife have been generous enough for one day." He looked at Ivy. "I'll walk you to the house. It's time to get a closer look inside."

Ivy didn't respond to his assertion but stood as the others did. She would need to confront Garrett on her own.

"Can we keep these?" she asked, lifting the three sheets of paper.

"Please do," Madeleine replied. "And I don't need them returned. I only drew them in case someone wanted to investigate as you two are doing now."

"I still don't understand why the authorities didn't find all the hidden entrances when Rothebury was arrested," she said, the thought just occurring to her.

"I'm not sure they thought to look into passageways to other rooms, or that they cared about them," Thomas answered as he moved around the table, his limp from a prior war injury pronounced. "They knew of the large tunnel that extends from the property and into the forest, and they knew it led from the cellar to the Rothebury's bedroom because Desdemona informed them of her entry that way. Madeleine and I told them of the doorway behind the bookcase in the library, but as it didn't influence the smuggling charge, they weren't all that interested. They'd probably been built strictly for Rothebury's ancestors to spy on their servants."

"The authorities then sealed the tunnel," Madeleine added, "and Rothebury, or his brother, had the house locked up until he returned months ago. Whether Benedict knew of all the hidden passageways or not is anyone's guess."

"It certainly has quite a history," Ivy said with a smile. "No wonder the marquess thinks it's haunted."

Madeleine moved from around the table, grasped Ivy's shoulders, and kissed both of her cheeks lightly. "I only wish I could join in the excitement."

"But we can't, sweetheart," Thomas quickly said, his tone more forceful than his words.

"Yes, our daughter is waiting for our return in Eastleigh, so we'll be leaving in a few days." Madeleine grinned slyly at her husband. "But do not worry. We will certainly be back in time for the ball."

Garrett chuckled and lightly grasped her elbow.

"Let's go, Lady Ivy. Before you plan anything else that costs a fortune."

After final good-byes, they donned their wraps, opened the door, and walked outside into the frigid winter air.

Chapter 6

To stifle any rumors they might stir within Lord Rye's small staff, she got Garrett to agree to meet her at the house at four for tea rather than walk her home and enter with her after they left the Hope cottage. At least, for the sake of propriety, that looked more appropriate on the surface. It did nothing for her nerves however. She skipped luncheon altogether, instead deciding to begin the search on her own by attempting to move the bookcase in the library herself. As her luck tended to run these days, it didn't budge. She would need Garrett to help her, she supposed, since she couldn't very well ask anyone working on the estate.

She needed Garrett. The idea alone made her laugh at the absurdities in life. If only she had never met him. If only she had been more cautious. If only her feelings for him hadn't ruined her perspective regarding two or three gentlemen callers she'd had in the last two years. Her brother had expected her to marry well, especially considering her large dowry and respectable title. But he had left on his own strange mission, leaving her alone with just the comfort of their estate and a few friends. And for the most part she had been happy with that—and her work for the Crown, even if only a few trusted her visions. But that hardly mattered. *She* trusted her visions, her dreams, and instinctively knew when something was wrong.

As she did now.

Something was wrong inside Garrett. That she could sense. He kept information from her, true, but there was more. Something troubled him deeply, or hurt him, though whether physical or emotional she couldn't guess. But it made her angry that she cared. She should hate him for leaving her as he did, for not trusting her, and yet she couldn't find it in herself to do so. Even stranger, she wanted to discover his secrets, if only to put them aside and move on. She didn't want to be here, didn't want his presence at her side, and certainly did not want his help because deep down she knew the answers she sought involved him.

Now, as she paced the floor of the parlor waiting for his arrival, she couldn't help but glance at the clock every few minutes, and she positively had to fight her desire to watch for him from the window. She'd changed into an older day gown of soft gray linen because she didn't want to spoil a good new one with dirt and dust. But it also fit snugly at the bust and hips, a little annoyance that Garrett would likely notice. And she absolutely didn't want him noticing—at least that's what she told herself.

"Lady Ivy, Mr. Burke is here to see the property. Shall I show him in?"

Startled by the interruption, she turned around to see Newbury standing in the doorway, his face prosaic, posture stiff and formal. If he knew he scared her with his silent entrance, he didn't show it.

"Yes, please do, Newbury," she replied, recovering her composure even as her pulse began to race.

As soon as he departed, she quickly licked her lips and fluffed out her skirts, smoothing her waist with her palms and hoping she didn't look too expectant.

Seconds later the butler returned, followed by Garrett, who'd also changed into less than formal attire, an ecru linen shirt and trousers in dark brown. Suitable, she supposed, and no less spectacular in appearance as they hugged his masculine form in all the right places.

"Lady Ivy," he said in greeting, bowing a little before moving toward her.

She forced a smile. "Mr. Burke, so nice to see you again."

His eyes narrowed as he took in her appearance, his gaze traveling slowly up and down her body. "Indeed, it is."

She clasped her hands in front of her in a gesture of modesty. "I'll be showing Mr. Burke the estate, Newbury," she said in dismissal, "after which we may take tea. I'll call on you when we're ready."

"Of course, my lady," the man replied with a respectful nod, then quit the room.

Garrett walked closer as he continued to assess her from head to foot. "I see you've changed," he fairly drawled.

She smiled wryly, trying very hard to ignore the rapid beating of her heart as he approached. "As have you."

He stopped about two feet away from her and cocked his head to the side. "Can you move comfortably in that gown?"

She pulled back a little. "I beg your pardon?"

He shrugged a shoulder, then crossed his arms over his chest. "It's awfully . . . snug in the bodice."

She swallowed a gasp at his insolence. "That's really none of your business, sir."

He nodded. "Perhaps not. But if you can't move very well in small spaces because your movements are constricted, our work might be hampered."

She hadn't thought of that, and suddenly felt a bit let down that he hadn't mentioned, or even seemed to be impressed, by her curves. But worrying about such a thing was ludicrous and a waste of time. Cheeks flushing at her own idiocy, she disregarded the comment, lifted her skirts and walked past him. "This way, Garrett."

He followed without a word as she led him through the foyer and down the long corridor toward the closed library door. After a quick glance over her shoulder and down the hall, she opened it quickly, moved to usher him inside, then closed it softly behind them.

Garrett took control at that point and strode directly toward the first of two bookcases placed on opposite ends of the east wall. Each was about six feet long and ten feet tall, the shelves holding nary a book, but trinkets and sundry knickknacks, none of them valuable by her estimation.

"I tried to move both of them earlier," she finally confessed, as Garrett began studying the corners and sides of the first one, "but neither would budge no matter how hard I pushed."

"I assumed as much," he replied, almost absent-mindedly.

She stood behind him, crossing her arms over her breasts. "You did?"

He shot her a fast glance. "Of course. You wanted to get inside first, though I knew you wouldn't be able to move it alone. If I thought you could have, I wouldn't have waited three blessed hours to try it myself."

Ivy didn't know whether to be offended that he'd guessed her intentions or proud that he anticipated her initiative in the matter. Instead of questioning him about his amazing ability as a seer, she asked instead, "Why this bookcase and not the other?"

Without looking at her, he replied, "The other is closest to a window; this one is more centralized inside the house, which makes it a likelier choice by logic."

"How astute of you," she commented wryly.

"I thought so."

Garrett began to run his fingers very slowly down the left side of the bookcase, where the edge met the wall, from as far up as he could reach to the bottom of the wooden floor.

"Do you think we'll need a candle?"

"Probably," he replied after a moment. "Go get one, Ivy."

She hesitated for a second or two, then stated firmly, "If you manage to open it, do not think to enter without me."

He didn't look at her, but the side of his mouth twitched up in amusement. "No, I wouldn't dream of entering without you."

She turned and scanned the sparse library, seeing nothing but a sofa and end table with a large lamp sitting atop. No candles to speak of, but she now had a better idea. Quickly, she walked to the door and exited, heading toward the parlor, where she'd seen a small oil lamp on the mantelpiece, a steady brightness that would work much better with less risk of its extinguishing to leave them in total darkness. After retrieving and lighting it, she hastily made her way back to the library before Newbury or Mrs. Thurman noticed her.

She entered quietly, closed the door softly once more, and turned. "How about this—"

Mouth dropped open in amazement, she stared at the right side of the bookcase Garrett had been examining, now opened about a foot or two, his body hidden behind it so that she could only see one of his legs sticking out from the side.

"How did you do that?" she asked in awe as she rushed to his side.

"There's a—latch," he replied, pulling back to look at her, a wide grin on his face, "at the top."

She smiled in return. "A latch at the top of the bookcase?"

"Behind it, actually." He dusted his palms off as he added, "I knew there had to be something holding it tightly in place; otherwise, the staff might have moved the bookcase and discovered the entrance when cleaning."

"That's why you knew I couldn't move it myself," she retorted with feigned sweetness.

He shrugged. "I did no more than guess."

She almost snorted as she moved to his side. "Can you see in there?"

He turned back to the entrance. "Not very well, but the air reeks."

Scrunching her nose, she said, "Yes, I smell it, too."

"Probably dead rats," he concluded, taking the lamp from her hands without asking for it.

She pressed against him, with her palms to his wide shoulders, attempting to see around him. "I can manage the smell of dead rats, now let's go in."

He looked down at her face, only inches from his, the corner of his mouth curving up a fraction. "If you only knew what I was thinking at this moment," he said softly.

That took her aback, and she straightened a little, her nerves suddenly jarred by their closeness, her breasts grazing the back of his shirt. Recovering herself, she replied nonchalantly, "The diamonds?"

His grin deepened, a sparkle lit his eyes, and he whispered, "Always the diamonds—and that *I'm* going in first."

His obsession with the diamonds tempted him beyond anything else, as it had been before. Ivy struggled to make sense of him, of the manner in which he seemed to ignore her closeness, her femininity. As if he had no memory whatsoever of how much they'd shared in those few days together, how she'd been nude and willing beneath him, how she'd gasped and cried out in pleasure when he'd taken her intimately. And the worst part was that she couldn't sense his feelings toward her, couldn't tell if he felt as physically and emotionally unsettled as she did to be near him again. If she wasn't careful, such thoughts and worries would become *her* obsession.

Trying not to appear irritated, she grabbed the lamp from his hands and countered boldly, "No, *I'm* going in first."

He didn't argue, didn't look surprised. In fact, he stood back a little so that she could squeeze past him.

"Lead the way, Lady Ivy," he murmured, his warm breath on her cheek.

Drawing her last full breath of clean air, she seized the moment and began pushing her body through the small entrance, her back and bottom unavoidably brushing the front of his body, which she completely disregarded.

The second she stepped into the tight enclosure, the smell of dust, mold, and decay became almost overbearing though she could breath without much effort. The air was stale, but the lamp glowed brightly. She immediately noticed the staircase to her left, steep, and perhaps only a foot and a half wide. To her right, the landing disappeared into the darkness.

"Which way?" she asked over her shoulder.

"Take the stairs. The path to the right may only lead around the side of the house."

"Or down to the cellar and the tunnel," she rebutted mildly.

"We can go in that direction later," he said as a whisper in her ear. "For now, let's start with the stairs."

One way was as good as another, she supposed. "Should we close the bookcase in case someone looks for us in the library?"

"No," he replied at once. "Better to have someone find the entrance than risk getting locked in. I'm sure there's a latch somewhere, but if I can't find it, I don't want to get trapped for who knows how long before we're rescued. And the walls are thick," he added as an afterthought.

Meaning, she mused, that the hidden staircase might be fairly soundproof. Ivy shivered at the thought. Getting trapped in a dank and dusty place nobody knew about would be positively horrifying.

"It's cold in here," she said, hugging the lamp in front of her. "And there are cobwebs everywhere."

"Probably only in corners. Ignore it and let's go, Ivy," he returned, nudging her lower back with his hand.

She stepped onto the first wooden stair with care, uncertain if it would hold, but found it sturdy enough to support her weight. Garrett closed in behind her, blocking the light from the library with his body.

Holding the lamp out in front of her a little, she began to climb the stairs, slowly at first, testing each step for strength, pausing only when one of them creaked beneath her. By the time she reached the fourth, the light from the library had all but vanished, and she and Garrett were now enclosed in total darkness save for the dim glow of the flickering lamp.

"This is very steep," she whispered just loud enough for him to hear. "Anyone who came through here regularly would have to be careful not to trip for fear of breaking his neck."

"I'll catch you if you fall," he asserted in a voice just as quiet.

"I'm not planning to fall, Garrett."

"Afraid of landing in my arms?" he asked in a deep whisper.

She couldn't believe he said such a thing, but she brushed over the comment. "A banister would be nice. I'm afraid to touch the walls."

"The smell is intensifying," he said.

She took anther step. "You don't think we'll find a dead body up here, do you?"

He chuckled. "You're the seer. Do you feel a presence?"

"No," she snapped. "The staircase is curving to the right— how far have we climbed?"

"I'd say about ten feet."

The air had become still and stifling, though it remained cold. Ivy tried breathing through her mouth, to avoid the stench and to keep from sneezing. Garrett climbed directly behind her, taking each step as she left it, and suddenly she felt grateful, for his warmth at her back and that she hadn't entered alone.

"I see the landing," she murmured. "I think it's part of the second floor."

"So if we're to the east of the library," he conjectured, "and climbing while facing north, what room are we below?"

She thought about that for a second. "I'm not entirely sure, but I'd bet it's a bedchamber. Not the master bedchamber, but likely one next to mine, or between the two."

She stepped onto the landing and shined the lamp around her. "The passageway splits in two directions. Right or left?"

"Right," he replied. "Let's see if anyone can get to your room."

Dryly, she said, "I don't think I want to know the answer to that question."

"I think perhaps you should," he maintained with honesty.

She groaned. "Yes, perhaps I should."

She turned to the right, and as soon as she took a step, Garrett climbed up beside her, ducking a bit as the ceiling lowered.

The makeshift corridor, just slightly taller and wider than a crawlway remained black as night save for the lamp in her hand. Even she had to hunch over a bit to move forward, which she did with increasing anticipation. Suddenly she stopped short, and Garrett bumped into her.

"What is it?" he asked, sounding only barely irritated.

"There's something on the floor."

"Probably the source of the smell," he said, gazing down over her shoulder.

She lowered her body a little and moved the oil lamp toward the floor to better see.

"It's not a rat," she whispered. "It's—I think it's a cat."

"How the devil did a cat get in here?"

"At least I think it's a cat," she amended. "It's hard to tell because it's badly decomposed."

"So it's been in here a while," he mused. "Let's keep going."

The floorboards creaked beneath her as she righted herself the best she could and stepped over the animal's remains. Gingerly, she continued walking, her pace slow, the lamp raised, feeling the cold, trying in earnest to avoid touching anything, though she knew her gown and hair were probably already covered with dust. To her dismay, after only eight or nine feet, she came to a wall.

"This passageway doesn't go anywhere," she said with a trace of frustration.

He pulled up behind her. "No, it's got to be a door. Nobody would go to the trouble of building it otherwise."

She lifted the lamp up to the corners, then down the sides, searching for a latch. Suddenly, low and to her left, she noticed an odd notch in the wood.

"Wait, there's something here." She knelt a little, and for the first time, bravely reached out with a finger—and stuck it into a thick, sticky web.

Ivy shrieked and jumped back, bumping into Garrett, breathing erratically, feeling a slice of pure terror cut through her for the first time in ages.

"What is it?" he asked, keeping his voice low, holding her against him as he wrapped one arm around her and across her shoulders.

She immediately turned to face him, pressing the lamp into his hand before she dropped it.

"Spiders," she muttered through a shudder of revulsion.

As if dumfounded by her response to such a trivial thing, it took him seconds to respond.

"Spiders?" he repeated.

"Yes, *spiders,*" she seethed in a whisper, clutching his shirt with both hands.

"You hunt for ghosts in daring places," he said rather than asked, "and you're afraid of spiders."

"Yes. And so? I have no fear of snakes, Garrett, or dead animals, or ghosts," she said with emphasis, "but I am *deathly* afraid of spiders."

He exhaled a breath. "Ivy, this entire tunnel is filled with cobwebs."

"Cobwebs are mostly dust in corners." She relaxed her grip on him a little. "But the notch in that wood contains a strong web, which means it also contains at least one spider."

For a moment, she thought he might laugh. Instead, he sighed and grabbed one of her shoulders in an attempt to move around her.

"Get behind me."

She scooted to her side, noting only briefly that her breasts rubbed hard against his arm.

"What were you looking at?" he asked, lowering himself as much as he could to peer at the side wall.

"I think there might be a latch in that . . . notch right there," she answered. "But I only felt the web."

"I'll try."

"It might bite, Garrett."

He did laugh softly at that. "I'm certain I'll be fine."

She couldn't imagine anyone purposely sticking a finger into a spiderweb, but her interest in unlocking a secret door quickly overtook her concern.

Within seconds she heard a click. "Something happened."

"I know. There's a latch inside," he replied, attempting to stand again.

"Did you feel it?"

He turned to face her as he held the lamp at his side. "The latch or the spider?"

She smacked him lightly on the chest. "You weren't bitten were you."

He watched her closely, a trace of a smile on his partially illuminated face. "No, but I am fairly thankful that you care."

She sucked in a breath of stale air. "I'm thankful that you're not convulsing from the poison. I couldn't possibly carry you down those stairs all by myself."

"Ah," was his only reply.

She huffed. "So I heard the latch click, let's see if there's a door here."

She scooted up in front of him again, her bottom grazing the front of his trousers as she passed him in the tight enclosure. It disconcerted her that she hadn't considered they might constantly have to touch, though she would never mention it to him.

She began pressing her fingers against the door, gently at first, then harder still. "It won't budge."

"Let me try," he said seconds later.

She expected him to go around her, but instead, he handed her the lamp, then rested the front of his body over the back of hers, his hands pressing against the door on either side of her shoulders, his chest against her back. She could even feel his long, strong legs through her gown as he steadied them next to the outsides of hers.

"Garrett," she whispered.

"Yes?"

"You're too close."

He stopped pushing against the door but didn't break contact with her. "Can't you breathe?"

Embarrassment flooded her as she turned her head to look up at his face. The small, golden flame of lamplight revealed very little of his expression, though she could tell he watched her closely. And he wasn't smiling anymore.

"No, I—I can't breathe," she repeated.

For a long moment he said nothing, though she could feel his heart beating a strong, steady rhythm at her back, his body still pressed to hers from shoulders to feet. Then very gradually his lids narrowed and he dropped his gaze to her lips.

"Garrett—"

"I don't want to move," he revealed, his voice low and gruff.

She swallowed, her mouth going dry from the intimate contact, the implication in his words.

"We're this close, Ivy," he continued seconds later, "and I want to find out what's behind this door."

She felt as if he'd struck her. Could he possibly be so unaffected by her presence that even as they touched body to body he felt nothing? Not a stir of . . . something? She would never take him as a lover again, but she was adult enough to know her attraction to him remained as intense as ever. In fact, she wished desperately, just for this second in time, that he would kiss her, if only to know that two years ago she hadn't imagined everything.

"Hold on to me," he breathed, his eyes never leaving hers.

She pinched her brows in confusion. "What?"

"Hold on."

She grabbed the arm of his shirt with her free hand, and as she did, he pushed with a grunt and the door slipped open a crack.

A *whoosh* of warm, clean air rushed in, and immediately Ivy realized why he wanted her to hold on as the urge to fall forward made her trip.

Garrett pushed a little harder twice more, and the door opened about two feet, just enough for them to squeeze through.

"This room is adjacent to the master bedchamber; I think it's the lady's withdrawing room because we came through a wardrobe closet," she said as she released him, keeping her voice lower still now that they were in the open. "I know where we are now, but we've been turned around."

"Probably when the staircase curved," he replied.

"This is utterly fascinating," she declared in amazement, taking another step and looking around her.

"Yes, it is." He grasped her by the forearm. "But don't go any farther. We need to go back down and out the way we came."

She glanced to his face, noting a streak of grime on one cheek, a trace of dust in his hair. "To close the bookcase, I suppose."

"And because we don't want the staff thinking we're walking out of a bedroom together on the second floor," he added in a very practical tone.

God, he'd flustered her so much she hadn't given a thought to decorum. She was starting to feel claustrophobic, not from the hidden passageway, but from his nearness.

"Then there's nothing more to see here," she said as

she squeezed into the crawl space after him. She pulled on the door with her free hand, but heavy as it was, she couldn't maintain her grip.

"I'll do it," he said, hugging her body close as he reached down and yanked.

The door jerked once, then closed with a creak, followed by a click from the wall to their left, where the latch fastened inside the notch, enveloping them once more in near darkness.

He backed up a little and turned. "Let's go."

"Which tunnel are we going to follow next?" she asked, fighting the urge to grab on to the back of his shirt. "Since you're leading the way now, I'll let you decide."

"We need to get back to the library," he answered after a moment. "Better not to have anyone find out we were in here."

She supposed he was right, and yet she couldn't help but feel a little subdued. "When are we going to investigate the others?"

"Probably at night."

"At night?"

"When we're less likely to be discov—"

He stopped so abruptly she ran into him.

"What is it?"

"It's the cat," he murmured over his shoulder.

"So, I'm afraid of spiders and you're afraid of dead cats," she said lightly.

"Ivy . . ." he drawled in a way that sounded intimate. "There's something else here."

She crouched down as he did. "Something else?"

Since she couldn't see around him, he shifted his form to one side, leaning his shoulder against the wall. "Look at that."

He lowered the lamp as she grasped his shoulder and arm, peering around him to view the carcass. A tiny sliver of silver shone brightly in the dimness.

"It's a chain around its neck, I think," Garrett said as if reading the question in her mind.

He reached down and she squeezed a muscled shoulder. "Don't touch it."

He looked at her. "I have to if we're going to see it."

She couldn't argue that logic. "Just— be careful."

Without reply, he stared at it for a few seconds, then slowly lowered his left hand, the lamp in his right. Reaching out with a nimble finger, he curved it around the thin band of silver and gently pulled. Though the body of the cat had to have been nearly decomposed, it still took him two tugs to loosen it from the neck. With a final yank, it came off with a snap, and he lifted it to the lamplight.

"There's a pendant attached," Ivy whispered, her excitement building.

"It's old, too," he added, dangling the necklace by one finger. In the shape of a heart, the small pendant twirled faintly beside the flickering light. "It has an inscription." He squinted and read, *"Mine Only, B.S."*

She slumped a little. "Who's B S? Benedict Sharon? And why on earth was it around a cat's neck, in here of all places?"

He shook his head and replied, "I've absolutely no idea. But it could be a generation or two old."

"Well, the cat certainly hasn't been here for two generations."

"No," he agreed with a smile. He started to stand, and Ivy held to him for balance until they'd righted themselves again. "The cat is probably insignificant, but this is most assuredly not. We'll have to have a closer look in brighter light."

As she released his arm, he stepped over the remains, the chain in one hand, the lamp in the other.

"I'm going to come back in here tonight," she announced matter-of-factly.

He stopped short and turned. She nearly ran into him again.

"No," he stated, his tone firm. "You don't do this alone, Ivy."

His stubbornness irritated her because she knew deep within that his concern stemmed not from caring for her safety but from the fact that she might find something, or learn something, before he did.

"I have free rein of the property—"

"I'm sure the Marquess of Rye had no intention of allowing you to wander through hidden tunnels alone when he made that provision."

She put her hands on her hips and stared at him defiantly.

"Besides," he added, dropping the pendant into his left trouser pocket, "the air is bad, and there are no doubt spiders everywhere. You'll need someone unafraid to crush them for you."

She didn't know whether to laugh or continue arguing. Instead, she asserted, "I don't need anything from you, Mr. Burke, least of all your permission."

He was silent for a moment, and then he took a step toward her, so close they were nearly touching.

"I'd prefer it if you'd cease in calling me Mr. Burke," he said with quiet insistence.

She held her ground as he towered over her beneath the low ceiling, the lamp to his side keeping his face in shadow, his features distorted. She couldn't read him, but she could feel a particular tension blanketing them. She had no idea what to say.

"Nobody," he continued, "who spends half an hour alone with a man in a darkened tunnel should remain so formal when addressing him."

She raised her chin a little. "We haven't done anything improper."

He tipped his head slightly to the side, his dark eyes scanning her face. "But you thought about it, didn't you?"

She sucked in a breath through her teeth, uncertain if he meant that she feared others would find their being together like this improper, or that she had improper thoughts about him.

"I—I'm concerned, yes," she admitted in vague reply.

The side of his mouth twitched up a hair. "I'm very glad." Then abruptly he turned and began walking once again, the matter apparently closed. She had no choice but to follow or lose the light.

"I want to wash this pendant and have a closer look," he whispered, as they reached the stairs. "Tomorrow night we'll try a different passageway."

"I'm certainly glad you're making all my plans for me," she grumbled from behind him. "Lord knows I don't have a social calendar worth mentioning."

He chuckled as he ordered, "Hold on to my shoulders."

She hesitated.

"I don't want you losing your balance, Ivy," he explained as he took the first step down. "This is steep and narrow, and if you tripped and fell into me, we'd tumble down and find ourselves with broken necks."

"No need for broken necks," she said through a sigh, raising her arms to do as he asked, trying not to think about just how many times she'd touched him in the last half hour. He didn't seem to notice anyway.

Within a minute, they'd reached the bottom, the light from the library a lovely beacon that seared her with relief.

Garrett slipped through the opening first, then reached out for her hand, which she offered without thought. Seconds later, he gave the bookcase a shove, then another, and it finally swung back into place with a click from the latch.

"Let's see the pendant," she said at once, brushing her hands down her dust-covered skirts.

He turned to face her, shaking his head. "I'm going to clean it first."

Her eyes widened as she gazed up at him. "You're not taking it from this property. It was found here, and it belongs to the marquess."

Drawing a deep breath, he crossed his arms over his chest and began walking toward her.

"Very well," he submitted in a low, husky voice, "but you'll have to reach into my pocket and retrieve it. I found it, and I'm not giving it to you willingly, Lady Ivy."

It took a long time, she decided, for her to completely understand what he was asking her to do. And then she felt a rising heat within, more from rage at such a suggestion than from the humiliation he certainly expected her to feel. At least that's what she told herself. For him to call her a lady, then, in the same breath, ask her to reach into a trouser pocket, so close to his—

No, the idea was simply outrageous. And yet suddenly she was filled with a confidence she'd never felt before. He'd teased her, acted as if he didn't notice her as a woman, then asked her to search in such an indelicate place for something she desperately wanted. He knew exactly what he was doing. And he knew with certainty that she would refuse.

Features hard and set with determination, she took a step toward him, then another, noting that he didn't try to move and couldn't retreat with the bookcase at his back. But his calculated gaze never strayed from hers.

She stood rigidly before him, her pulse racing, chin raised, arms to her sides. She felt hot all over and knew her face had flushed, but at this moment she didn't care.

"Did you expect me to squeal and faint at such a suggestion, Garrett?" she asked, her tone low and wickedly sly.

His jaw tightened. "I'm quite certain you never faint, madam."

Her mouth gradually curved to form a devilish grin. "You're absolutely correct," she whispered furiously. "I never faint."

With that, she lifted her right hand and placed it on the lip of his left pocket. His eyes widened a fraction in slight surprise, but he didn't move a muscle.

Drawing a deep breath, she began to insert her fingers, inch by inch, feeling his hardened hip beneath her knuckles, moving her nails along the fabric over his skin, remembering how she'd teased him there before and how his body had reacted.

"You . . . are . . ."— she found the chain and began to pull—"a *despicable* . . . man."

He stood motionless, though his eyes had narrowed and his body tensed. She never lowered her gaze from his as she very, very slowly pulled the pendant from his pocket.

"And you, Lady Ivy," he said in a gravelly whisper, "are an extraordinary woman."

It took all that was in her not to slap his face. Then with rage seeping through every pore, she turned her back to him and walked to the doorway, clutching the pendant at her waist with both hands.

"Good day, Garrett."

Without another word between them, he strode from the library.

A freezing wind slapped his face, fairly taking his breath from him as he stepped into the gloomy dusk and headed for the inn. It felt marvelous, too, since a good slap was what he deserved after asking her to reach inside his trouser pocket for a necklace. God, what had he been thinking? Probably that she'd never succumb to such a taunt, and it had certainly been a taunt on his part, provoked, no doubt, by her blatant sexuality, which mocked him every single second they spent together.

In a manner he didn't fully understand, she heated his blood beyond words—heated him with anger, frustration, and especially lust. She bewildered him, irritated him, teased him, goaded him, and yes, felt their mutual attraction as much as he did, igniting something deep within that he hadn't felt in years, and not with anyone else in his life.

He also sensed her confusion about the passion she couldn't deny, and in that regard he supposed he'd teased her as well, although to her credit she tried very hard to deny it, to fight it. And perhaps she couldn't tell, but it had taken every good quality he possessed as a gentleman not to seduce her in the stench of a tiny, dusty, hidden staircase, something he'd never dream of doing with any other woman.

He knew bringing Ivy back into his life would be dangerous, on several levels, and he'd considered it for a long time before making his decision. In truth, he wasn't sure what to expect from their meeting again, partially because he didn't know her level of involvement in his failure to find his diamonds two years ago. But more importantly because he couldn't remember what they'd felt for each other, how they had been together, and why he still couldn't get her out of his mind after all this time. He simply had to know what happened, and learning she fairly despised him cut him to the core because he couldn't recall what he did—or didn't do—to cause her such resentment.

One thing was certain: He knew he would bed her again, and she would let him. Regardless of what had happened between them in the past, their mutual desire remained intense, and it could only be held in check for so long. He knew it, and she probably did, too. Yet taking her again soon, he realized with a deep seed of worry, would almost certainly complicate every careful plan he'd made thus far. And he absolutely did not need more complications than he had already, especially where they concerned the lovely and luscious Lady Ivy Wentworth.

"Goddammit all to hell," he muttered under his breath as he neared the inn. "Goddammit all to hell . . ."

Chapter 7

*D*iamonds, cold spaces, damp earth, pendants, hazy face . . . Ian's face, distorted, reaching . . .

The nightmare awakened Ivy before dawn, startling her to a sitting position in her bed as she attempted to clear her foggy mind and remember each detail. But like most of her visions, it came to her as a twisted mass of blurry pictures, without order, possibly signifying different events and times.

Since she couldn't possibly return to sleep after such a vivid and fearful awakening, Ivy decided that surprising Garrett early, at the inn, would be the practical way to meet with him without causing a stir, and she needed to meet him. She wished she never had to see him again for the simple preservation of her emotional sanity, but for now that wish was not to be. She had a thought regarding the pendant and the image from her dream, and needed to discuss it with him before she lost her nerve. Although perhaps not wise, she also acknowledged that meeting him this morning would give her an excellent excuse to sense his thoughts about what happened yesterday, when they'd been alone in the passageway together, if only to settle her mind once and for all about his intentions.

So shortly after seven, Jane helped her don a deep purple morning gown, then plaited her hair, which she pinned loosely atop her head. After only a quick cup of tea, she headed out of the house into the cold, gray morning, toward the inn. She rarely woke hungry, and this morning she was so nervous to see him she didn't feel like eating anyway.

Uncertain if he'd still be sleeping, she decided to surprise him before he could muster his thoughts, though she wouldn't enter his room herself. The inn-keeper would call him for her, and she would be ready for a battle of wits, dressed becomingly for the day, cheeks naturally pinkened from the freezing air, and fully awake from her tea and vigorous walk around the lake.

The sky remained dark, a full cloud cover threatening rain and creating a mist in the air, which had prompted her to wear her old woolen pelisse this morning instead of her more formal fur-lined wrap. She looked practical, self-assured, and prepared for discussion.

Ivy didn't see a soul in the town square, and the inn remained quiet as she approached, though a thick swirl of chimney smoke drifted up from behind the thatched roof. With a tug on the door, she drew a deep breath and stepped inside.

It took a moment for her eyes to adjust in the dim lighting. She'd been inside an inn or two in her travels, and knew what to expect from this one. It was fairly large for a town this size, the air permeated with the obvious smell of musty ale, fried meats, and male sweat, though at least it wasn't overwhelming.

She noticed Garrett at once, sitting on a stool by the south-facing windows now blurred from years of caked grime, drinking tea as he grinned widely at something a barmaid standing next to him said. The only people inside were the innkeeper behind the bar, the woman speaking to Garrett, and two other men who sat in a corner drinking ale from large mugs, glanced her way, and went back to their own conversation. Ignoring her suddenly racing pulse, Ivy stood erect and planted a prosaic expression on her face, then bravely began walking across the dusty wooden floor toward them.

After she took only a step or two in his direction, he noticed her, his smile fading as his brows gently furrowed. The woman turned when she realized she no longer had his full attention, at first looking puzzled, then offering Ivy a glare from cold eyes before whispering something more to Garrett and fairly slinking away.

Ivy kept her gaze on him, noting he wore a good morning suit in dark blue, a white silk shirt, and blue-and-white-striped cravat. His hair looked wet, but combed, his face shaven clean, as if he'd just stepped from his bath. Obviously, he intended to call on someone today, else he'd be wearing attire better suited for exploring dark tunnels.

"Lady Ivy," he drawled as he lifted his mug.

She tipped her head toward him. "Mr. Burke."

"You're awake early," he remarked, turning a little on the stool, then standing to view her fully as she strode to his side.

She raised a brow. "I was going to say the same of you." She glanced at his table. "I'm glad to see they still serve tea at this inn, and you're not imbibing in ale this early in the day."

He swallowed the contents of his mug, then set it back down with a thud. "I don't stomach ale, and I thoroughly despise tea. It's coffee, actually."

She crinkled her nose at the thought of drinking such a vile beverage. "I've seen you drink tea, Garrett."

He leaned toward her to reply, "That doesn't mean I like it."

She pretended not to notice that his lips nearly touched hers. "Of course."

Awkwardly, she glanced around them as he stared down at her, his hands on his hips.

"I'm assuming you came here this morning to see me?" he asked at last.

She rubbed her nose with the edge of her leather glove. "No, I wanted to discuss something with you."

He almost smiled. "Isn't that the same thing?"

Forcing a sigh, she stated matter-of-factly, "Not at all. If my intention was simply about seeing you, I could see you from a safer distance well enough."

"A safer distance? You don't feel safe in my presence, madam?"

Her lips thinned. "That's not what I meant."

Amused, he continued to watch her, then said, "Let's talk outside."

"It's cold outside, Garrett," she replied, as if he had no brain, "and looks like rain."

He leaned an elbow on the high table. "Yes, but a bit of rain won't hurt you, though a lady probably should not be seen alone with a male companion of no relation, in an inn, at eight o'clock in the morning, wouldn't you agree, Lady Ivy?"

He was right, naturally, and it irritated her. "Perhaps I'm too much trouble, and you'd rather stay and chat with the barmaid," she snapped.

He smiled wryly. "She isn't nearly as witty as you are, I'm afraid. And certainly not as appealing to look at."

Feeling enormously proud of herself, she ignored the compliment as pure false charm on his part, lifted one shoulder in a shrug, and retorted, "Pity that." Then she turned on her heel, strode gracefully toward the door and out into open air, listening to him chuckle as he followed her.

She closed the collar of her pelisse tightly around her neck and moved toward the street at the center of the town square, then stopped and turned. He followed a few paces behind her, his twine coat buttoned, his hands in the pockets.

"Where were you off to this morning?" she asked, as he approached.

A mother and young daughter strolled by them at that moment, smiling as they offered their good mornings.

As they passed, Ivy took a step closer to Garrett. "I'd like a bit more privacy if you don't mind."

His brows furrowed as he studied her. "Have you learned something?"

She dropped her voice. "Let's walk by the lake."

He motioned toward it with an elbow. "Lead the way."

They didn't speak until they neared the path that wound through the trees toward the old wooden bench. Finally, she said, "I washed the pendant and chain, then scoured it with silver polish. You were right, it's old."

"That's not exactly interesting news, Ivy, since I assumed as much already," he replied.

"Perhaps so," she returned lightly. "I just thought you'd like to see what I discovered once it had been cleaned."

He slowed to a standstill. "What did you discover?"

She turned to gaze up to his face, smiling. "That part of a small scratch covered the lettering. It doesn't say *B*.S., it says *R*.S." She waited, letting his surprise settle, then added smugly, "Do you find *that* news interesting, Garrett?"

His eyes crinkled a little, and she could tell he tried very hard not to grin at her.

"Did you bring it with you?"

Her eyes widened in feigned shock. "Of course I brought it with me."

"Then perhaps we should sit so I can see it for myself," he suggested, motioning down the path to the old wooden bench, nestled in a semisecluded cluster of trees behind the Hope cottage, just barely noticeable from where they now stood.

Without argument, she began walking toward it, pulling the hood of her pelisse over her head to shield her from the cold. Upon reaching it, they both sat, Ivy scooting as far to the edge as she could and pulling her skirts in to make room for him.

"The pendant?" he requested, as soon as he'd settled himself in, stretching a leg out casually.

Ivy stuck her hand into the left pocket of her pelisse and pulled out the silver necklace, dangling it from a leather-covered finger.

He didn't take it from her, but lifted the pendant up to view the inscription. "R.S."

"I'm assuming it belonged to Richard Sharon," she concluded, "or perhaps one of his lady friends."

"Who lost it in the passageway while he brought her in or out one evening," he finished for her.

Her brows creased in speculation. "But that still doesn't explain why we found it around the neck of a dead cat."

"Well," he considered, "it's entirely possible this chain has nothing to do with the cat at all, and the animal simply found it, got curious, and then caught in it."

"And then got stuck in the passageway?"

He shrugged negligibly. "It's possible."

Fairly unlikely, in her opinion, but she didn't say so. Finding the cat could mean nothing at all to them, and yet she couldn't help but feel a significance somewhere.

"I had another . . . vision last night, Garrett," she revealed in a low voice. "Actually it was more of a dream, but I thought maybe you'd care to hear about it."

He didn't respond immediately to her abrupt change in topic, and after a few seconds, she pulled her gaze from the lake and looked at his face.

His expression had grown markedly serious as he stared out over the water, his eyes narrowed as if in deep thought, a lock of hair hanging over his forehead unnoticed.

She slumped a little into her stays and continued. "I know you don't believe in seer visions or dreams, Garrett, but I have to interpret what I feel, and know, with the things that have happened in many of mine. It's a gift I can't deny, but I won't pretend I can prove any of it to you."

He exhaled a deep breath, then acknowledged, "You think you've learned something new about your unusual mission to Winter Garden."

"Yes."

"And it must have something to do with me, or I know you wouldn't share it," he added a bit cynically.

She had expected such a reaction and sighed. "That's true as well."

He waited, offering her a sideways glance, then replied, "So you're asking me to trust you."

She hesitated in answering, wanting to phrase her thoughts in the best possible way. Finally, she murmured, "You don't have to believe in them as proof of anything. I'm asking only that you listen, without prejudice, and try to understand that although you may discard what I have to reveal, it matters to me, as all of my vivid dreams have, and that many of them have shaped my life into the person I am."

He leaned forward and placed his elbows on his knees, both of his hands clasped together in front of him.

"Why do you care what I think of them?" he asked soberly.

Annoyed by his reluctance to at the very least give her credit for being candid in her trust of him, she dropped the pendant back into her pocket and squeezed her gloved hands together in her lap.

"I don't at all like you, Garrett," she admitted, her voice low but firm, "and I will never forgive you for what you did two years ago, and the lack of respect you then showed me as a lady. But the truth is, I respect you. I've always respected you, especially your intelligence and detailed devotion to a cause. You needn't like me, either, though I would appreciate knowing that if nothing else, you respect my talents as well."

He turned his head to view her fully, his expression unreadable as his gaze scanned her face, her eyes and lips, her hair, and even her bosom, wrapped tightly beneath her pelisse. She could sense his troubled thoughts, his struggle to understand, though she truly wished she knew the depth of what he felt about their past if only to settle it in her mind.

"Tell me about the vision," he said in a soft murmur as he turned his attention back to the lake.

Acute disappointment pulsed through her. Of course, she didn't expect him to announce his sudden undying belief in her, or to apologize and ask for forgiveness for the catastrophe that had been their love affair in London. But she had hoped for something more than reluctance.

Swallowing the hurt inside, she disclosed, "It was a dream, actually, a very intense dream that woke me. I saw the pendant we found, swinging and turning in a dark space, and then a face in—in a fog, its expression distorted, calling out to me in a kind of fear or . . . desperation, probably both."

"Calling out to you specifically?" he asked, quickly glancing over his shoulder.

"I think so, but my name was never spoken. Words usually aren't since most of my dreams, or visions, are felt. This one felt cold, fearful, tense . . . urgent." She shook her head. "It's hard to explain."

At last he sat back, the bench creaking from the movement as he stretched out fully and crossed one ankle over the other. "Did you recognize the face?"

Her truthfulness at this moment would be a turning point, she decided. Her answer would be the first time she placed her trust in him after doing so to her detriment two years ago. And his reply would mean everything.

Closing her eyes, she revealed very softly, "I'm almost certain it's Ian's."

The fact that he didn't laugh, or even say anything immediately, warmed her with encouragement. After several long, lingering seconds, she lifted her lashes to find him watching her, studying her again.

When their eyes met, he stated flatly, "You think your brother is in danger."

She sat up a little. "I know he's in danger."

"And you think whatever danger he's in has something to do with the pendant?"

"I—I don't know." She turned her body a little to face him directly. "But he was part of the dream, and I *feel* his presence, Garrett, though I'm not certain if he's physically near Winter Garden or if it's more of a mystical experience because he's calling out for help."

"I thought he was in Italy," he maintained with a new intensity.

She fought the urge to fidget on the bench. "The truth is, I don't know where he is. He's supposed to be on the Continent, yes, but I haven't heard from him in months. We've always been especially close, I suppose because we're twins, but I know when he's in trouble, and my brother is in trouble."

The sky had darkened since they left the inn, and now it began to sprinkle very lightly, freezing droplets falling upon her hood and cheeks. But she ignored them as she waited.

Finally, through a long exhale, he said, "Well, if he's in trouble in Italy, you can't very well help him. The best option is to find out more information about the pendant if we can."

A huge wave of relief swept through her. He didn't have to believe in her as a seer, but to acknowledge that there could be useful information involved in her gift meant the world to her suddenly.

She shivered as the rain gathered strength, shoving her hands in her pockets. Garrett yanked up the collar of his twine coat and drew his legs in and under the bench.

"I have an idea about finding its owner," she announced through a fast breath.

The side of his mouth twitched up a fraction. "I would never doubt you have a plan, Lady Ivy."

She bit her bottom lip to keep from smiling. "I think we should call on Mrs. Bennington-Jones and her daughter. If the necklace was Desdemona's, they would probably know about it. Even if they deny it, or frankly lie, we would certainly surprise them enough to catch them unaware with the question."

"And you might be able to sense their prevarication?" he drawled.

She knew he was teasing her, but she shifted her body on the bench uncomfortably. "Perhaps," she admitted, her tone light, "though I think it might be to our advantage to return to the passageway first and follow a different tunnel, just to verify that she would have come the way of the stairs behind the bookcase in the library."

His brows rose minutely. "But she left Winter Garden almost two years ago, and the cat hasn't been dead that long. There's no reason to think she had the necklace in her possession in that particular passageway."

"True," she agreed, "but I'd like to know how she got to Rothebury's bedchamber before we talk to her sister and mother. It might help us know more about the circumstance, and I really think there has to be another entrance to the man's room aside from the cellar."

He continued to gaze at her in speculation, his eyes narrowed, jaw fixed, droplets of rain that went unnoticed clinging to his hair and cheeks. Finally, he said quietly, "I think we should go in from the outside."

"From the outside? You mean the tunnel entrance from the forest?" she maintained excitedly.

He nodded slowly. "I want to examine the location, at night, which is when she would have entered."

"The authorities sealed it," she reminded him, "though I have no idea what that means."

He lifted one corner of his mouth. "Then I'll unseal it."

"If you can," she said very skeptically.

"If I can," he repeated, amused. "If not, I'll go in through the cellar with all the spiders."

She snorted. "And I can check from the master bedchamber to find the entrance there."

"Alone?"

"Of course alone. As you so properly mentioned before, I can't very well be seen with a gentleman in a bedroom." Her eyes widened with growing anticipation. "I'll check it today, in fact, since we can't examine the tunnel until nightfall."

"But don't go in without me if you find an entrance," he warned. "The same danger applies."

She said nothing to that, then, "So what will you do while I'm investigating the house?"

He eyed her speculatively for a moment, then exhaled a long breath. "Actually, I'd planned to call on Desdemona's mother today, though I think your idea of first getting a clearer idea of the tunnel system in the house is better. I don't suppose her sister and mother will disappear in the next day or two, so there's no fear of learning nothing by waiting."

Startled, she brushed his compliment aside. "You intended to visit them without me or the necklace?"

Growing contemplative again, he lifted his arm to rest his elbow along the back of the bench. "Ivy, you were extremely angry with me yesterday," he reminded her as he lowered his voice. "I wasn't certain I'd ever see you again."

The memory of his provoking her into fumbling through his trouser pocket brought a fresh surge of mortification to the surface. She cringed inside, but decided this might be the opening she needed to discuss the subject that truly had her baffled, and, if she were honest with herself, deeply troubled.

Abruptly, she stood and walked forward a few feet so that she stood on the edge of the lake, watching raindrops spring up from the surface of the water.

"I think you know that wouldn't have happened, Garrett," she scolded softly. "We certainly would have seen each other again unless you suddenly left Winter Garden and gave up your glorious quest for the Martello diamonds."

He remained quiet for a moment, then replied, "So are you confessing your interest in them as well?"

Anger flaring, she pivoted to face him. "I implied nothing of the kind. I have no interest in anything but—"

"Ghosts, I know," he cut in caustically, features taut. "Tell me why you're really here, Ivy."

That blunt order shocked her. Her mouth dropped open a little as she stared at him, his stark gaze assessing her with intensity.

Pulling her hands from her pockets, she wrapped her arms around her belly in a manner of self-preservation. Defiantly, she countered, "If we're going to be confessing secrets to each other, I insist you start first."

His brows drew together in puzzlement, but he didn't refuse her demand. Silence lingered until finally, in a voice edged with suspicion, he submitted. "What secret do you think I'm hiding from you?"

She inhaled a shaky breath, summoned her courage and murmured, "We were lovers once, because of your very deft seduction ability. I'd like to know why you're no longer attracted to me as a woman."

She had no idea what to expect from him, how he would respond, react, but she never anticipated the sheer incredulity that crossed his face. His eyes and mouth opened wide, his features went slack, and for a second or two she thought his response might stem from her mere mention of a sexual interlude between them. But it really didn't matter. She said what she had to say, and she would wait for an answer.

Suddenly he drew a long, staggered breath and stood, shoving his hands in the pockets of his coat. For several uneasy seconds he just watched her intently, his gaze traveling up and down her figure. And then he began to stride slowly toward her.

"Perhaps, darling Ivy," he murmured, "I think the love affair started with you."

She gasped.

He continued, "Perhaps *you* were the seducer."

"That's insane," she whispered through clenched teeth. "I—I wouldn't know how—"

"To seduce a gentleman?" he cut in, voice low, eyes clouded with mistrust as he stopped in front of her and gazed down to her face. "You know a man would need nothing more than to look at you to feel desire in his veins."

She didn't know whether to laugh at such a scandalous thought, or cry out in frustration. But his comment warmed her completely. "Garrett, I am not an idiot. I know exactly what happened between us in London, then way you talked to me, made me promises, how you— "

She simply couldn't say it.

Huskily, he prompted, "How I what?"

She swallowed, feeling unbearably too near him of a sudden, unable to verbalize the heartache, unwilling to admit she had needed him.

"How I what?" he asked more forcefully, taking a step closer so that he looked down upon her, his legs brushing against the bottom of her pelisse.

She glanced around for intruders who might be listening to their most intimate conversation, knowing her cheeks flushed hotly, her stomach fluttered, and wishing they'd be interrupted by someone. But it was not to be, and standing there alone with him now she knew she couldn't begin to draw away from his commanding presence even if she wanted to.

"Look at me, Ivy," he murmured.

She hugged herself tighter as she once again raised her lashes to meet his formidable gaze. He watched her with a calculated, building awareness she sensed as a coiled web of tension and grief and a shred of resentment.

Abruptly, he clutched her jaw with his palm and pushed her head up to scrutinize her face.

"Do you think yesterday was easy for me?" he asked harshly as he towered over her, "when you walked in a gown that teased me because it hugged every curve, when your breasts rubbed my arm, and your tempting backside touched the most sensitive part of me as you moved in that passageway? Do you think it's easy for me to be here with you now, in this town, and not want to take you again, to feel you beneath me, clinging to me in passion as you did before? Do you think I don't want to remember how perfect you *felt*?" Eyes stormy, teeth clenched, he pulled back enough to lower his gaze very gradually down and up her figure, taking in every detail. Finally, in a fierce whisper, he admitted, "Oh, yes, Ivy, I notice you as a woman, and my greatest fear is that you will forever haunt my dreams."

She had no opportunity to absorb her absolute shock at his disclosure, her amazement at his candor, for as the final words left his lips she felt a jolt of something carnal from him, something erotic and far beyond anything she could ever mention to a soul—a vibrant charge of sexual energy that made her legs go weak and her heart start to race.

"I won't be your lover again, Garrett," she whispered defiantly even as she visibly began to tremble.

For a flash of a second she thought he might smile. And then his mouth clamped down hard over hers, taking the breath from her, devouring every thought with a groan of triumph deep in his throat.

He wrapped his arms around her, yanking her tightly against him as he continued his assault on her lips. She fought him for a moment, attempting to twist herself out of his embrace, pushing her hands against his chest, and yet she couldn't begin to overcome his strength and insistence with her own. He tormented her, struggled with her, and then finally ignited that part of her deep within that she had sworn always to defend.

Ivy reeled, and then gave in to the madness, clutching the sleeves of his coat, kissing him back with a fervor that defied every rational thought. His tongue violated her mouth with an aching need, and she gave as he did, moving her hands to cup his face, holding him possessively, tightly, for fear that he would vanish. The memory rushed back, of his taste, his scent, the feel of his hard body pressed against her, and she moaned in his arms, ignoring the cold, the rain as it pelted them in a fierce rhythm of its own. He clutched her bottom with one palm, her head with the other, his breath coming fast and hard, and even beneath the thickness of wool she could feel the tension in his body, knew how she affected him physically and that the passion they shared would never, ever be quenched.

And then, just as quickly as it had started, it was over.

Garrett reached up and grabbed her wrists as he tore his lips from hers. In a breath of anguish, she jerked her hands free of his grasp and squeezed her eyes shut, but even as she attempted to run, he wouldn't let her go.

He held her tightly, his arms wrapped around her as she fought in vain to pull away. Rage filled her, and she clenched her fists and struck him in the chest once, twice.

"Stop it, Ivy," he said in a heavy rasp. "Stop it."

She calmed a little, and he cupped her head in his neck. "I hate you, Garrett," she whispered breathlessly against warm, wet skin.

He inhaled deeply as he rubbed his chin across the hood of her pelisse. "I know."

She stood in his arms for a time, listening to the steady rain, to his quick-beating heart, relishing the closeness, terrified of it. Finally, he loosened his grip, and she straightened, gathering her courage and attempting to gather her thoughts as she stepped away from his powerful form.

She had no idea what to say after such a display of inappropriate and uninhibited passion. She turned her back to him, eyes closed, a palm over her mouth, feeling frustration and a fresh surge of fury bubble just below the surface at his skillful attempt at showing her just how easily he could seduce her again.

"There's a man missing, Ivy," he said huskily as he pushed his gloved hands back into his pockets. "There are diamonds to find, visions of your brother in danger, and it all revolves around this town, around us and why we're here with each other again. That's the only problem we need to solve now." He paused for a second or two, then added, "I'll be at the tunnel entrance at eleven tonight."

She had no idea what to say, but he was right, as Garrett always seemed to be. She nodded, and then, with determination, her gaze avoiding his, she stepped past him and began to walk with hurried steps toward the path that led to the safety of the house.

Chapter 8

At ten minutes past ten, Garrett left the inn. He felt only the slightest trepidation in exploring the tunnel, as he'd had the entrance unsealed secretly two weeks before he'd come to Winter Garden. Nobody had investigated it yet, as he'd given strict instructions to his staff to avoid it, and he trusted them to follow his orders as they had for years.

But he wanted to enter it with Ivy. He wanted to gauge her reaction, to get closer in learning her secrets, and in truth, to watch the excitement envelop her again.

He shouldn't have kissed her today, shouldn't have allowed her to seep into his skin and gut-punch him with her clever female wiles and firm determination never to be his lover again. She obviously had no idea what a challenge such a statement could be to a man, especially one who hadn't been with a woman in longer than he cared to admit.

It both excited and troubled him that his desire for Ivy stirred something so deep, but not close enough to a satisfying memory. Yet the moment his lips touched hers, he accepted the perfection and satisfaction he'd felt from her two years ago. He didn't remember the incident precisely, but he knew those feelings had existed.

He hadn't been all that surprised to see her standing in the inn, looking for him early in an attempt to unsettle his routine should he have one. He perceived a cleverness in her that most women in his experience didn't possess, and he enjoyed it. In truth, he enjoyed her. She was unique—intelligent, bold in tongue, and very, very beautiful to look at. He could look at Ivy all day long and not get tired of the view.

But she wasn't a painting. She was a full-grown woman who'd once experienced passion in his arms— a passion only she could recall in detail. And he had done something, said something, during that intimate time together that made her despise whatever desire she felt for him now, that she absolutely knew existed. He didn't for a minute believe that she hated him, but somehow, in some manner, he had hurt her.

Garrett groaned within as he turned the southern edge of the path and stared at his darkened house in the distance. His shoes made a faint crunching sound as he walked along the forest floor, though the night was still, quiet, the full moon darting in and out of quick-moving clouds.

He'd been prepared to tell her of his memory lapse this morning, to explain the sequence of events as he knew them, to disclose his knowledge of her dark secret— until she mentioned her brother. Just hearing his name brought the shield up again, and her explanation of a vision of him in danger left him subdued. It wasn't that he didn't believe her exactly, but that he didn't know how much might be a lie designed to bring down his guard and confess.

Garrett knew she was after the diamonds. He'd sent her the note that asked for her help in recovering them. But there was more. He sensed her anticipation, which in itself amused him. Yes, he felt a bit guilty for keeping the secret of his title from her, but until he learned the depth of her brother's involvement two years ago, it was a secret he would keep for now. He would reveal it eventually. Until then, they would both remain pawns in someone else's power, which now remained his greatest worry in Winter Garden.

The diamonds were in the house. They had to be. And yet until they knew exactly what had happened to Benedict Sharon, there could be no certainty. And since he'd vanished from the Rothebury estate, Garrett concluded he couldn't have left through the tunnel to Portsmouth, still sealed at the time, so therefore he and the diamonds were in the house, concealed or hidden, in one of the passageways. The man simply couldn't be so elusive as to disappear to the Continent without someone being the wiser.

As he reached the edge of the property he turned south, where the forest thickened and the path disappeared. The tunnel entrance was only half a mile walk or so, and he covered the distance in only a few minutes.

He'd brought a small lantern with him, though he

didn't need it as yet, the moon being enough to see by as it darted in and out of the clouds. His head had ached all day, but the fresh, cold air either helped or disguised it, and for now he felt better. He'd foregone a hat, but donned his gloves and his warmest wool clothing beneath his twine coat, thankfully dark in color. On a night like tonight, they shouldn't be noticed by anyone.

At last he reached the small clearing where the door to the tunnel remained concealed beneath twigs and dirt. After a quick glance in all directions, he dropped to his knees, placed the lamp at his side, and began to clear the area. Ivy would be arriving soon, and he wanted to have it opened beforehand.

It took almost no time to find it—a small four-foot-square door made of old natural oak. For a time the door had been nailed tightly shut and hidden beneath the brush, but it was now unsealed as he'd requested.

Garrett swept pine needles off the right edge, where a flat brass handle lay flush with the wood. It took only a moment to lift and turn it, though it took several tries before he was able to push it into position to hear the click release because of the dirt that remained inside the lock. He knew the authorities had planned to fill the tunnel with debris so that it couldn't be used again, but Benedict Sharon, Baron Rothebury, had refused since this particular entrance, as it curved down, led onto his property. As the new owner, Garrett would eventually have it filled himself, but not until he revealed himself to all in Winter Garden as the Marquess of Rye.

He almost laughed at the thought of what his mother

would think of him kneeling in the dirt and opening a secret entrance to a tunnel in the forest. Probably feign a faint and excuse herself to bed for a day, mumbling how disappointed she was in her eldest son and his refusal to adhere to duty. But then, as with many things in his life, she would never know.

A cracking of a twig in the distance brought his senses sharply back to the present. He remained motionless, knowing it was probably Ivy but uncertain enough to take precautions.

Only a few moments later he spied her through the trees as she walked into the clearing, her body draped in darkness as she apparently wore the same woolen wrap she had this morning.

"You're early," she whispered, moving quickly to his side and kneeling beside him.

"As are you," he replied just as quietly. "Not thinking of entering without me, were you?"

"Don't be ridiculous," she snapped, her voice low as she chanced a glance over her shoulder. "How is it sealed?"

She'd pulled her hood over her head completely so that he couldn't see her face, but he could tell from the quickness of her words that she felt the same excitement he did.

Grinning, he said, "It wasn't sealed, just nailed shut. I was able to pull the boards off easily enough."

She seemed to believe him because she scooted closer.

"Then let's go in."

"Back up a little," he said, motioning with a hand.

She did as he asked without question, and as soon as her feet were off the door, he tugged once, then again, harder, until he heard it give way.

There was no rush of air this time, only a gentle creak of rusty hinges as he opened the door completely and laid it flat on the ground.

From his right, he lifted the lantern and lowered it into the crawl space, holding it as far down as possible as he pulled a match from his coat pocket with his free hand and struck the tip on the door. Quickly, he lit the lamp, blew out the match, and dropped it into the darkness.

"Hold this down," he whispered, "so the light can't be seen from the forest."

"I should go—"

"No," he cut in, "this time *I'm* going in first. I don't want you falling if the ladder gives way."

"Well, I don't want *you* falling, either," she returned in soft sarcasm.

The irritation in her voice made him smile.

"Shh. Don't argue, Ivy."

She mumbled something under her breath, then did as he requested, taking the handle of the lantern from him and holding it steady a foot or so inside. Moving as fast as safely allowed, he sat on the edge of the opening and very slowly placed his weight on the first rung of the wooden ladder. As soon as he assured himself of its strength, he continued until he'd stepped on the fourth rung, then lifted the lantern from Ivy's grasp and began to descend into the dark.

"Be careful," he warned.

"Of course I'll be careful," she replied, turning so that she began to descend the ladder after him.

Counting the rungs, he began his descent, holding the light down from him, noting the dank air mixed with the smell of damp soil. The space couldn't have been more than five feet around, just enough for a person, or a trunk or package, to be lowered without hitting the sidewalls.

He'd counted to twenty-six when he saw a widening beneath him.

"We're nearing the bottom," he said, knowing she followed closely above him.

Four rungs later he stepped onto solid ground. He moved to his side and Ivy lowered herself beside him, snuggling close to him, probably without realizing it.

Garrett lifted the lantern to better view their surroundings.

The tunnel split in two directions—north, toward the house, and south, presumably toward Portsmouth, where it was rumored to connect to another entrance near the docks, though he knew the southern end had been filled and sealed off eighteen months ago.

"This way," he said, taking her hand as he began to walk carefully into the passageway, Ivy following close behind without argument.

The tunnel had been carved out of the earth fairly evenly, about six feet high and six feet wide, held up by large wooden beams placed about every four feet or so. It also stayed fairly uniform on all sides, he noted, though the smell of rotting wood and mold increased the farther inside they moved.

"This was built ages ago," she murmured up to his ear, clinging to his coat sleeve with her free hand, her voice echoing slightly.

"It's probably been here for several generations," he concurred, noting with pleasure that even though she professed to hate him, she obviously didn't fear him after their passionate kiss that morning.

For another few minutes, they continued north in silence, seeing nothing in the distance to block their path. The tunnel curved just slightly as they proceeded, probably taking them toward the back of the property nearer to the lake.

"I need to know something, Garrett," she murmured, her tone low and cautious. "Why do the Martello diamonds mean so much to you? Why are they such an obsession?"

He had expected her to ask him that one day, and he'd been prepared since he wasn't yet ready to reveal the truth.

"Men do not like to fail in their careers, Ivy," he replied with only the slightest evasion, "especially when they're being paid by the British government."

"You didn't fail, you were trapped and attacked," she countered. "That has to mean something to the Home Office."

"Yes, but why was I attacked?" he queried, holding back the disgust he felt to his bones.

She sighed. "Your intelligence in the matter had to have been incorrect—"

"Exactly," he interjected.

"—but that wasn't your fault."

He slowed to a standstill and turned to look at her face, hidden in shadow. "Why did you warn me, Ivy?"

She pulled back a little. "Warn you?"

"With your . . . gift, shall we say, you warned me not to go to the rendezvous, knowing I would anyway. Why?"

She straightened and took a step back. "If you remember correctly, I *warned* you not to go *alone*. I should have been there with you."

"For you to be attacked as well?" He shook his head. "I'm sure you know I never would have let you take part in such a dangerous mission, regardless of the outcome."

"I was not in danger," she insisted, annoyed. "And I was also working for the British government."

He stopped himself from a snide retort. Their work had been nothing alike, and she knew it already. Instead, he turned around and started walking again. After a second or two, she followed.

"Have you ever actually *seen* the Martello diamonds, Garrett?" she asked a moment later.

"I have," he admitted without prevarication.

"Describe them to me."

Her request didn't sound particularly cunning in nature, just curious. He decided to indulge her.

"They're three stones, actually, blue diamonds, each the size of . . . oh . . . a man's thumbnail. They're set in a tiara of gold, along with some very small rubies, that once belonged to the Martello royal family in Italy."

"Once belonged?"

He drew in a deep breath of moist air to reply, "The tiara was given to the former Marquess of Rye, as part of a dowry, seventy years ago or so, when he married the royal princess."

He heard her quick gasp of surprise, and he smiled in the darkness. "Yes, the Marquess of Rye, Ivy."

She grabbed his arm to stop him. "And you didn't tell me this until now?"

He shrugged. "Why do you imagine he purchased this particular home and sent you on such a wild hunt?"

She said nothing for a moment, then, "So when were they stolen?"

He thought about lying, then decided against it. "During a party two years ago."

"A *party*?" she repeated, incredulous. "During what kind of party does a family display a tiara of priceless jewels?"

He rubbed his neck, stalling. At last he revealed, "A betrothal party for the Marquess of Rye and Lady Margaret Dartmouth of Brighton."

That seemed to confuse her, as he assumed it would. He reached for her hand again, and said, "We need to keep moving."

She followed him, her mind in deep introspection,

he supposed. Finally, she whispered, "I didn't know the marquess was married."

"He's not."

"He's not? How do you know?"

"If he was, I'm sure we'd know about it, Ivy."

"True . . ." Seconds later, she said, "So I have to wonder why he didn't marry Lady Margaret?"

Because I was deceived . . . and then met you . . .

"You're talking too much," he grumbled.

She ignored that. "And how on earth did the diamonds get stolen from the party and into the hands of Benedict Sharon?"

By way of your brother . . .

Suddenly he stopped. "The air is getting colder."

"I hear a trickling of water, too," she added, pushing aside their previous discussion.

He crouched to study the dirt floor. "The ground is moist, here. We're probably nearing the lake."

"Which means the entrance to the house shouldn't be too far now." She tugged at his hand. "Let's go."

He stood upright again, and they continued in silence. Moments later the tunnel took a sharp turn to the left, and within just a few feet, it widened into a small, rounded alcove containing two sturdy, wooden benches on either side of them. And just barely visible straight ahead, about seven feet in the distance, rose a steep incline of stairs exactly like the ones behind the library.

"Those have to lead to the cellar entrance," she whispered.

He nodded as he raised the lantern high and glanced

around. "Rothebury must have used this as a collection area" he surmised, "before moving his smuggled goods in and out of the house."

"What's that?" she asked, pulling her hand from his grasp.

He turned and followed her to his right, the dim lighting casting dark shadows on the walls as he approached her.

"I think it's a well," she announced as she glanced back to him.

"Don't get too close," he murmured forcefully.

"I'll be careful," she scolded in a whisper. Placing a gloved palm on the earthen wall, she peered over the edge. "This must connect to the lake."

"Probably, though it now appears dismantled," he said, moving up beside her and looking down into the darkened hole. "I'll bet the owners used this as their water source before the last renovation, when pumps were installed."

"It's deep," she maintained. "I can hear the movement of a spring, but it's a long way down."

"It just seems that way because it's dark. I doubt it's more than twelve or fifteen feet to the bottom." He reached for her hand again and pulled her gently away from the edge. "Let's try the cellar door."

Reluctantly, she turned and followed him past the small clearing to the stairs.

"Wait at the bottom," he ordered, handing her the lantern.

Without argument, she did as directed, holding

the light up so he could see his ascent up the seven narrow steps to the door, its latch and lock clearly visible.

Garrett climbed each step cautiously until he stood at the top, then without delay he tried the latch. The door wouldn't budge.

"It's stuck," he whispered.

"Let me try," she said as she started climbing.

He turned and gave her a wry smile. "Ivy, if I can't open it, *you* certainly can't open it."

"You don't know that," she countered, reaching up to remove the hood of her pelisse.

"I'm sure it's locked from the other side," he continued, starting his descent. "We'll have to try to find the entrance in the cellar."

He reached the bottom and stood in front of her, gazing down to her face, noticing her brows pinched in speculation.

"What are you thinking?" he asked in whisper.

"I'm thinking that I don't see any other entrance to the house from here."

"So?"

"So . . ." she said through a sigh, "if through the cellar is the only way to get in, then Desdemona would have had to walk through this long tunnel, climb the steps to the cellar, then from there enter another passageway that leads to the master bedchamber." She looked into his eyes. "That's a lot of work for a lovers' tryst, don't you think?"

He lifted a shoulder negligibly. "I suppose if I were

going to bring a secret lover to my room, that's how I'd do it."

Her brows rose. "You mean make it difficult to enter, with more concealed places to hide to avoid being caught?"

"Exactly." After a long exhale, he added, "I suppose it would also depend on how much their meeting in secret meant to her," he remarked casually.

"Well, of course she loved him," she clarified at once, "or at least she thought she did, else why would she risk her future in such a way?"

"You mean by giving herself to him unmarried?" he asked, his low tone growing thoughtful.

His question made her visibly uneasy. She squirmed a little in her stays, then turned away from him. Suddenly, she raised the lantern and walked to the center of the alcove.

"I feel a draft," she whispered, meeting his gaze again with wide eyes.

He immediately moved to her side and grabbed the light from her hand. "From where?"

"I don't know . . ." She shook her head absentmindedly and took a step around him, then turned. "Something's wrong, Garrett."

He didn't feel a draft, and heard nothing but the distant trickle of the spring at the bottom of the well.

"It's probably—"

"It's *not* my imagination," she charged, pivoting to glare at him.

"I wasn't going to say that," he insisted in a whisper.

Suddenly he heard the faintest thumping noise above them. Quickly, he dimmed the lantern, grabbed her, and pulled her into the tiny crevice beneath the stairs.

"Garrett—"

"Don't move," he whispered as he clamped his palm over her mouth to cut her off. "There's someone in the cellar."

He felt her stiffen in awareness as he lowered his hand. They stood together motionless for another few seconds, and then he heard the latch click at the door above them.

Very slowly, now in total, disconcerting darkness, he wrapped his arm around her and pulled her tightly to him, her backside pressing into his hips so that they became nearly one body, as flush to the wall as possible. With a swift surge of awareness, he felt the weight of her breasts on his arm, caught the faintest scent of her silky skin, and tried very, very hard to avoid thoughts that would drive him to distraction. She didn't move, and he could barely hear her breathing, though he had to assume she also realized how closely they touched each other.

And then, with a long, faintly heard creak, the cellar door gradually opened.

For seconds nothing happened. Then directly above his head, someone stepped onto the first step, then the second, waiting, it seemed, as a flicker of candlelight bounced off the walls of the alcove.

Garrett could feel the tenseness in Ivy's body, could hear his own blood rushing through his veins as they stood together in strained silence. If they didn't move at all, they might go unnoticed. Whoever it was would have to descend every step and walk around the staircase to see them. But by choosing not to react and confront the intruder now, he might never learn who stood above them in the earthen room nobody was supposed to know existed—except for Benedict, who he believed was probably dead. The temptation to discover the truth at that moment tore at his gut, but his desire to keep Ivy from secrets revealed trumped everything. It simply wasn't time; revelation for all of them would come eventually if he remained patient.

As quickly as he made the decision to stay hidden beneath the stairs, the quiet figure above them abruptly turned and stepped back into the cellar, the candlelight extinguished as the door softly closed.

For several minutes they waited, no movement or sound between them. Finally, Ivy relaxed and took a hesitant step away from him. Before releasing her completely, he pressed a finger to her lips, and she nodded in response.

Carrying the lantern in one hand, he clasped her elbow with the other, though instead of moving to the center of the alcove, he hugged the wall until they were a few feet away from the stairs, near the tunnel entrance.

Leaning into her, he whispered in her ear, "Whoever that was didn't lock the door."

"Then let's go in," she argued just as quietly.

He wrapped his arm around her waist and pulled

her against him. With his face in her hair, he breathed, "No. We'll check it tomorrow from the other side."

She struggled to be freed. "But—"

He rubbed his nose across her ear, and she stilled.

"Whoever it was could be waiting." His lips touched her lobe, and she shivered. "It's too dangerous."

She gave him an almost imperceptible nod and pulled back from his intimate touch. He let her go, quelling a grin of triumph.

Reaching into his pocket, he retrieved another match. "Grab on to my arm," he whispered.

She groped for him in the darkness, her palm sliding down his coat until she clutched him at the elbow. Then, with caution, he entered the tunnel, his gait slow, feeling his way by gingerly touching the wall. After countless minutes they made the sharp turn to the south. He continued for several more feet, then stopped and struck the match on the bottom of his shoe, relighting the lantern without effort.

She drew a shaky breath behind him. "Let's go."

He didn't reply. As the darkness gave way to a dim view of their path, they moved swiftly to the entrance, climbed the steps to the top, and exited into the cold night air.

Chapter 9

I vy didn't sleep at all. She tried, and occasionally dozed, but the memory of being held by Garrett as an intruder nearly caught them in the underground tunnel had unnerved her beyond all thoughts.

They had left the site by moonlight, Garrett covering the forest entrance with its wooden door, pine needles, and leaves, then walking her near enough to the house to ensure her safety. She'd been careful in entering the house as well, and for the first time felt remarkably thankful for Lord Rye's small staff. As far as she was aware, nobody knew she'd left and returned.

They'd said little to each other after such a distressing experience and only vaguely discussed the possible identity of the person who'd almost caught them. Neither she nor Garrett saw or heard anything that could characterize the individual as man or woman, but together they concluded it probably had to be someone other than one of Lord Rye's employees. If Mrs. Thurman or Giles Newbury and his staff had discovered some secret entrance, the marquess would no doubt have been notified, and it wouldn't have remained a secret. They would surely tell her, as well, or she would hear it from Jane, as servants tended to talk below stairs. The curiosity would certainly overwhelm everyone.

If, in fact, the servants remained ignorant of the tunnel system behind the various walls of the house, they likely didn't know that the main tunnel in the forest was still accessible. Most troubling to her, then, became the apparent certainty that another individual was entering the house at will, someone not employed by Lord Rye, and if that was the case, there had to be another entrance into the house from the outside—an entrance of which everyone remained unaware, including Thomas, Madeleine, and the authorities. Garrett's last words to her before departing were to remind her to lock her bedroom door as soon as she retired, something she would have done anyway.

Before leaving him last night, she'd made plans to meet him at ten in the village square, then walk together to Penelope Bennington-Jones's home on the northern edge of town. After her lack of a good night's sleep, she felt restless in waiting until even midmorning.

Jane plaited her hair and coiled it loosely at the back of her head, then helped her dress in a modest day gown of sea green with three-quarter sleeves and rounded neckline, after which she promptly donned her good, fur-lined pelisse and left the house for her trek around the lake. She noticed Garrett at once, waiting for her in front of the inn, once again wearing his good morning suit of dark brown beneath his unbuttoned twine coat. The air was perhaps a trifle warmer than it had been in recent days, but the sky remained hidden behind thick clouds as together they traversed Sedgewick Lane to the northernmost end of town, where they'd learned Penelope lived with her two remaining daughters.

They said little more than pleasantries to each other along the way. But after spending so much time in his company of late, Ivy had begun to feel a new and unusual attachment to him, coupled with a growing annoyance at being so *aware*—of his large and muscled form, his skillful hands and handsome face, his beautiful, dark eyes as they gazed at her with a kind of unfocused confusion and a trace of deception. And for the first time in ages, she allowed herself to remember what he'd looked like next to her in bed as he'd made love to her two years ago. She had touched him intimately and reveled in his marvelously male body, yet suddenly she wished that particular memory would simply disappear from her mind forever. If nothing else, forgetting the past would allow her to work with Garrett on terms of civility for the remainder of their stay in Winter Garden. Except she knew that each time he looked at her he also drew on the memory of her, undressed and willing and needful in his bed. And knowing he no doubt thought of her in such a way each time he looked at her kept her rather embarrassed in his presence, especially each time she found herself so physically close to him as they'd been in the tunnel last night. Really, she couldn't find the diamonds soon enough. Time was getting desperately short.

As they neared the property, it became apparent that

the Bennington-Jones cottage home, although once obviously cared for, now showed signs of neglect, as dried brush hadn't been cleared in quite some time. Window boxes were empty and hanging loosely, and scratches and splinters could be seen on the shutters. Garrett held open the waist-high fenced gate, and she entered in front of him, walking swiftly down the cobblestone path to the front door. It took nearly a full minute after he rapped with the brass knocker for the door to open a crack. A girl of no more than fifteen peeked out, eyeing them curiously.

"Mr. Garrett Burke and Lady Ivy Wentworth to see Mrs. Bennington-Jones and her daughters, if you please," he said in his most charming voice as he handed her his card.

The girl looked at the card, then surveyed their appearance. "Sorry, Mrs. Bennington-Jones isn't receiving callers," she informed them hesitantly, "and I'm not sure if Miss Hermione or Miss Viola is at home."

"Of course," Garrett replied with a gentle nod. "It's no trouble. Would you then please inform them at your convenience that we have information regarding property of theirs found on the former Rothebury estate?"

The girl's brows rose almost imperceptibly. "Perhaps I'll check on Miss Hermione's whereabouts. Wait here."

Ivy smiled. "Thank you."

She closed the door on them for a few moments, then reopened it, this time wide enough for them to enter. "Please come in," she said meekly.

They walked into a small foyer, a dark enclosure smelling oddly of boiled onions and furniture polish. The house was uncommonly warm for this time of year as well, feeling stuffy and . . . lifeless, she decided. Remarkably sad. A home of social outcasts without the means to relocate to another community where they'd be less noticed, or known.

The maid who had answered the door promptly walked to her left and guided them to a small parlor.

"Please be seated," she directed. "Miss Hermione will be with you momentarily."

Without a word between them, she and Garrett did as requested, sitting in matching wing chairs of faded peach brocade, both facing a velveteen settee of the same color. With their backs to the low fire in the grate, she felt perspiration break out on her neck and wished she'd been given the option of removing her pelisse. Apparently the Bennington-Joneses no longer had a butler, or the maid had been told to allow them to enter with the unspoken understanding that they would not be welcome long. In either case, she felt uncomfortable, and assumed Garrett did as well, although he'd loosened his twine coat before adjusting his body in his chair.

They waited in silence as they'd already decided he would take the lead in questions, and she would remain especially observant. Already she'd come to the conclusion that the Bennington-Joneses had little money remaining and didn't receive guests on any regular basis. The parlor, as with most families of modest means, would no doubt be their best room in the home, allowing visitors to believe them wealthier by appearance. In this case, Ivy noted small areas of peeling wallpaper, little artwork on display, and a wooden floor that hadn't been refinished in years. Rugs, furniture, and decorations were sparse, and even the draperies, drawn across every window, had faded from years of use. The house was similar in style to Mrs. Rodney's, though not quite as large, and not nearly as well-appointed or filled with quality items. For a moment she wondered if they would be offered refreshment, then decided probably not. Even tea could be considered a luxury.

A minute or two later she heard the quick tapping of heels on the foyer floor. With a quick glance at Garrett, she sat straighter in her chair, her hands folded neatly on top of the muff in her lap as Hermione Bennington-Jones swept in with an air of confidence Ivy didn't sense in her at all.

A tall and sturdy woman, she wore a day gown of plum satin, probably her best attire, cut in an attempt to hide a thick middle and widening hips, though white lace at the long sleeves, neckline, and bottom of the skirt only managed to address them. She had fine, blond hair swept high on her head, small blue eyes, and a rather undefined round face that one could only describe as homely. Ivy's first thought was that if she had been lovelier, she might have attracted a husband regardless of her social standing or lack thereof. Without a sizable dowry, and with her somewhat unappealing appearance, she could only hope for spinsterhood now that her family had been disgraced. And just that knowledge left her feeling dismayed and filled with an uncommon sadness for someone who might only be twenty years of age and had little joy in life to look forward to.

Garrett stood at her entrance. "Good morning, Miss Bennington-Jones," he said courteously, a pleasant smile on his mouth. "Thank you for taking the time to welcome us on such short notice."

The woman tossed a quick glance at Ivy, then turned her gaze directly on him, her eyes narrowed shrewdly as she continued toward them.

"I enjoy callers in the morning," she replied, "though I suppose Millie informed you Viola isn't home and Mother isn't well."

"She did," he acknowledged, "so we'll only take a few minutes of your time. I hope she'll be feeling better soon."

Hermione said nothing to that standard response as she lowered her body gracefully on the settee, then spread her skirts out daintily around her legs as good breeding dictated. Garrett returned to his chair.

For a moment an awkward silence filled the room as Hermione shifted her gaze to Ivy, candidly taking in her full appearance, her brows drawing together negligibly.

"You're the seer, aren't you?"

The blunt question caught her a little off guard, though she hid it well, smiling satisfactorily. "I am, yes," she replied. "I have been asked by the Marquess of Rye, the new owner of the Rothebury estate, to investigate it for unusual occurrences."

The woman didn't even blink. "How very interesting."

Hermione continued to gaze at her shrewdly, though her voice, Ivy noticed, seemed very small coming from a person of such a large stature. And she didn't sound interested at all, she sounded bored. Detached.

Hermione turned her attention back to Garrett. "So what may I do for you, Mr. . . . ?"

"Burke," he informed her. "I'm an architect from the city, Miss Bennington-Jones, and as such, my employer has asked me to investigate the former Rothebury home and catalog the various structural changes that have been made to it through the years." He paused, then lowered his tone to add, "Including the tunnel system."

If Hermione was shocked by his disclosure, she didn't show it, though the tiny smile she'd feigned beforehand seemed to fade.

"I'm not at all clear what a smuggler's tunnel has to do with me," she said seconds later.

Ivy sat forward a little in her chair. "I'm sure you understand we would never be indiscreet—"

"Of course you wouldn't," the woman cut in matter-of-factly.

She's clever.

Ivy offered her most understanding smile. "We are not unaware of the scandal in Winter Garden two years ago, Miss Bennington-Jones, and under normal circumstances, it wouldn't be mentioned in your good company."

The younger woman said nothing, just continued to look at her candidly, though Ivy detected a tiny twitch of her upper lip—and the slightest shift in mood within the parlor.

"However," she continued, "as Mr. Burke and I have both been employed to investigate the house—under completely different circumstances, of course—we've chanced to come upon something peculiar and thought to bring it to your attention."

Hermione's thin blond brows rose negligibly. "Again, I'm not sure what anything found on or near the Rothe-bury estate has to do with me."

It become obvious that Hermione had chosen to remain particularly vague, and yet Ivy sensed an intensity in the woman, a resentment or inner turmoil that simmered just below the surface, held in check by rigid etiquette she'd probably been taught since birth.

Suddenly, Garrett asked, "Have you been on the property lately?"

"No," she answered at once, looking back at him. "When Lord Rothebury returned several months ago, he took no callers. I did hear that a few villag-ers of quality attempted to welcome him back to the community, but he was rather inhospitable to all of them."

"How so?" Garrett asked, as if surprised by the news.

Hermione rubbed her thick thumbs together in her

lap. "Apparently he accepted no invitations and refused callers at every turn. I heard . . . somewhere, that he preferred solitude, and the company of only his cats."

"His cats?" Garrett repeated.

"Evidently he had several of them." She shivered. "Nasty creatures."

"You don't like cats?" Ivy asked innocently.

The young woman looked at her frankly. "Nor do I like dogs. Animals smell, and Mother has always reminded us that nobody of quality should own them as pets, allowing them to wander through a clean household where they leave their fur and droppings indiscriminately." She drew a long breath and sat up straighter on the settee. "All animals belong on farms."

Meaning, she supposed, that people of quality don't live on farms.

Garrett chuckled. "At least on farms they'd be useful in catching the rats."

Hermione almost smiled. "Exactly, Mr. Burke."

Ivy had to give him credit for his ability to engage her, a woman she suspected had never experienced attention from any man as handsome as Garrett.

"Were you surprised to hear that Benedict Sharon had disappeared?" Ivy asked, returning to the subject at hand.

Hermione tipped her head slightly to the right and stared at her blankly. "No, not particularly. But then I stay rather busy taking care of Mother's needs, so I haven't given his arrival or disappearance much thought."

"I'm sure every task is daunting when a family member is under the weather," Garrett said sympathetically.

Hermione smiled faintly and nodded once. "Indeed."

Ivy wished she could actually meet Penelope Bennington-Jones but didn't broach the subject. Now didn't appear to be the time. She suspected the lady was listening in to their conversation from behind a closed door anyway.

Finally, Garrett adjusted his body in the small chair, sitting up a little as he reached into his jacket pocket.

"The reason we've called on you today, Miss Bennington-Jones, is because we found something interesting, and of value, in one of the passages on the property." He pulled the necklace out slowly. "We wondered if perhaps you know if it belonged to your sister."

Ivy watched the woman closely. Although he'd not said her name aloud, just the vague mention of Desdemona brought a change to the woman. Hermione's face seemed to harden very slightly, her eyes grew cold and flat, and she even bristled in her seat almost imperceptibly.

Garrett held the pendant out in front of them by only his index finger, watching it dangle above the small oval tea table between the settee and wing chairs. It spun very slowly, the polished silver reflecting the light from the fire.

Hermione stared at it, unmoving at first. Then, as if to avoid speculation of any kind, she exhaled in exasperation and leaned over, reaching for it with a plump hand.

"I'm sure I've never seen this before," she confessed at last, as the heart lay flat in her palm, "and I'm certain it didn't belong to any member of my family."

Ivy noticed an edge in her small voice, a note of anger she could no longer repress. "You'll notice the initials on one side—R.S. We're assuming it belonged to the baron, but strangely, we found it in the tunnel," she revealed quietly, purposely neglecting to mention that it had been found in a smaller passageway in the house itself. "We know your sister had been inside at one time—"

"That is a fact we have chosen to forget, madam," Hermione interjected, her tone and expression frosty as she released the pendant and sat back once more. "And you'll note these are not Desdemona's initials. I'm quite certain Lord Rothebury had numerous paramours enter his home in such a disgraceful manner, and it could have belonged to any of them. He was a very deceitful man who took advantage of two or three of Winter Garden's finest young ladies."

A long and awkward silence ensued. Then Garrett returned to the subject at hand as he dropped the necklace back into his pocket. "Would you have any idea who the pendant might belong to if not to your sister?" he asked ruefully.

"No," she replied at once. "But I will say it would be unusual for Lord Rothebury to give gifts to anyone while he lived in that house. The man hoarded his possessions and looked upon ladies as playthings." She raised her chin a fraction to add, "I have my doubts that the man would purchase *anything* for a mistress."

"I see," Garrett remarked. "Then I suppose there's nothing more we can do here. I'm sure at some point its owner will come forward or it will remain as Lord Rye's property as it rightfully is now, I suppose."

Hermione's lips curled. "No doubt." Suddenly her gaze shifted to Ivy. "Have you found the ghost, madam?"

She blinked, caught off guard by the question. "I beg your pardon?"

Hermione's eyes narrowed. "Of course I've heard the rumor of why London's renowned seer is back in Winter Garden after all these years away."

Ivy offered the woman a light smile, which was not returned. "As yet, no, I haven't seen or heard anything remotely like a spirit presence. But I'll continue investigating the house if it's Lord Rye's wish that I do so."

"And do you find such work satisfying, Lady Ivy?" she asked coolly.

Ivy suddenly didn't know how to read the woman. For all the sincerity in her words, her voice, low and soft, revealed more than a shade of contempt.

Sighing, she said, "It can be. Are you aware of any other ghostly sightings in town? Unusual occurrences or strangers who seem out of place?"

Without hesitation, Hermione replied, "Many people

come from the north for the winter months, and each year they differ. As far as ghosts are concerned, I don't believe in such nonsense." She stood abruptly, effectively dismissing them. "Now if you'll excuse me, I'm certain Mother needs me."

"Then please don't let us keep you," Garrett said good-naturedly as he stood and offered the woman a gentle bow.

Ivy stood as well. "Thank you for your time, Miss Bennington-Jones."

Hermione glanced from one to the other, then smiled faintly. "Millie will show you out. Good day."

"One more thing?"

Hermione turned and looked her up and down. "Yes?"

"I am in contact with the new owner of the property, Lord Rye, and I believe he's planning another Winter Masquerade," she revealed with a pleasant smile. "Naturally, we'd like to extend an invitation to you, your sister, and your mother."

For the first time, Hermione exhibited an honest expression. Her eyes opened wide as her mouth dropped open in a shock she couldn't hide. Then placing a palm on her stomach, she blinked quickly and glanced around the room as if unsure how to respond to what would surely be the only invitation she'd received in two years.

At last, her voice tight and low, she replied, "I—I'm certain we'd enjoy that, Lady Ivy." Recovering herself, she straightened, and added, "If, of course, Mother is feeling up to attending the ball."

"Of course I understand," she replied.

Hermione nodded once, her cool demeanor returned. "Now, forgive me, but I must attend to duties."

With that, she turned and walked from the parlor, leaving Ivy both confused and somewhat annoyed by a frank if not rude dismissal and a gathering of information that told them almost nothing. Except for the fact that Ivy sensed the woman's prevarication.

She was hiding something, and at that moment Ivy shivered, feeling the perspiration on her neck and between her breasts turn to ice.

Without a word between them, she and Garrett stepped from the house into the cold gray morning.

"She's lying," Garrett said, after they'd walked through the village square toward the lake.

Ivy squeezed her hands together in her muff and lifted it to warm her nose. "I'm not so sure she's lying but rather evading, or . . . hiding something specific she knows."

"Mmmm."

"What does that mean?" she asked with caution.

He chuckled. "Nothing insulting, I assure you."

"Do you think she knew Benedict more than she admitted? She did seem to know of his cats."

He shrugged lightly. "I've no idea. I can't imagine why she would want to do him harm, though. He'd been gone for years and had nothing to do with the ruining of her sister."

"True . . ." She waited, then braved the question, "So what do we do now?"

He paused for a moment, then said, "What do *we* do now? So I suppose we're actually working together?"

She huffed. "There you go answering a question with a question again. And you know that if I had a choice, I'd rather not be in your company."

They both stopped walking at the same time, standing in front of the inn, and he turned to her.

"I admit it's uncomfortable," he said at last. "For both of us."

It dawned on her suddenly that she'd never considered his feelings in the matter, that perhaps his being near her brought back his own bad memories of their week together, the night he'd taken her, and then his attack. She'd felt his physical pain, knew something of that night still lingered as a dark force within him. She just hadn't taken into account how difficult his life might have been these last two years.

Before she gave thought to her actions, she leaned up and lightly kissed his cheek, noting only briefly how warm his clean-shaven skin felt against her lips.

He did nothing, didn't move or say a word at her brazen action. And then she took a step away from him and glanced to the Rye estate in the distance.

"I suggest you come to the house for tea this afternoon," she said in a wistful voice. "We'll take that opportunity to finally check the cellar."

"After tea?"

She glanced up at his face, studying the hard planes, the lock of hair that fell across his forehead unnoticed, his dark eyes hiding feelings she couldn't read.

With a smile, she amended, "I'll serve coffee just for you, Garrett."

One side of his lips curved upward.

And then she turned on her heel and left him, heading back quickly to the house of many secrets.

Chapter 10

Ivy spent the better part of the day walking through various rooms on the second and third floors, looking for hidden entrances behind bookcases and wardrobe closets in a few of the rooms, only to be disappointed in the end. The master bedchamber hadn't been used or changed since Benedict's disappearance, though it had been cleaned by the new staff. She realized a passageway entrance had to be behind one of the walls in the large suite, but to her dismay it was obviously well hidden, as she had yet to find it.

At one o'clock she took a luncheon of bread, cheese, and fruit alone in the dining room, sifting through the little correspondence that had been delivered to the estate since her arrival, noting nothing of importance. She'd written the Marquess of Rye, through his solicitor in London but had yet to receive a reply to her request for hosting a Winter Masquerade on his estate.

Finally, Garrett arrived at exactly half past three. He'd changed into the same casual attire he'd worn when they entered the passageway from the library, as had she. The day had grown darker, and the air smelled like rain, so the inside of the house already seemed gloomy and particularly cold.

After announcing to Newbury that she would be escorting Mr. Burke to the wine cellar so that he might note the additions done in that part of the house, she requested tea and coffee be served at five in the parlor. Then lifting her skirts, she led the way down the darkened hall toward the kitchen at the back of the house, Garrett following without comment.

As they walked inside the hot enclosure that had been modernized and clearly remodeled in the last few years, neither the marquess's cook nor the two servant girls peeling potatoes near a sideboard gave them more than a quick curious glance as they passed through and headed toward the rear servants' entrance.

Just before reaching the door, Ivy turned to her left and began to descend a long staircase.

"There's a lamp for use at the bottom," she said before he asked. She'd only been in this part of the house once, finding it neither frightening nor particularly intriguing as an old wine cellar—until last night when they'd found the entrance from the tunnel. But her anticipation in inspecting it had been building all day, so that she now had trouble restraining herself from rushing to get within the dank walls. Garrett followed closely behind her, though he still hadn't said a word. As she reached the bottom of the stairs, she stopped and turned so quickly he ran into her, though the quick action of wrapping his arm around her waist kept her from falling backward.

"Don't *do* that," she whispered.

"Do what?" he asked, releasing her slowly.

She wanted to admit how uncomfortable she felt each time he held her in his arms, how it managed to make her remember the times she longed to forget, but she wouldn't. Instead, she said, "Nothing. Just . . . be careful. You almost knocked me over."

She caught the slightest smirk on his face, but he didn't comment as she turned quickly away from him.

"This is a storage room that contains canned goods, oil, sacks of flour and potatoes—"

"I know what a kitchen storage room contains, Ivy," he said wryly. "Where's the wine cellar?"

She ignored him and raised her left hand, locating the oil lamp and matches on the shelf above her, always kept at the foot of the stairs for just such usage. Swiftly, she lit the lamp and held it out in front of her.

"I think that's the cellar door straight ahead," she said, motioning with her free hand as she began to move toward it.

His stride was faster, and he reached it first. "Give me the lamp."

"No."

He turned and looked down at her. "No?"

Her brows rose as she stared him straight in the eye. "It's my turn to go in first."

He almost snorted. Then, with an exaggerated swing of his arm, he said, "Be my guest, madam."

Her lips curled up in triumph as she grabbed the door handle and pushed down on the latch. "I believe you are *my* guest, sir," she whispered.

With a quickness that startled, he raised his arm and clamped his palm against the back of her neck, yanking her to him.

"You are far too saucy for a lady," he breathed. Then he lowered his mouth to capture hers.

For seconds she was so stunned she couldn't react. He apparently feared she might drop the lamp, for she felt it slide from her grasp as he took it from her.

Ivy closed her eyes. His lips felt warm and soft, so inviting. He teased them with his own, flicking his tongue across the top so that she opened for him.

He deepened the kiss, holding her head close, his hot breath caressing her cheek, his tongue invading her gently, searching, and a feeling of helplessness descended on her, forcing her to give in completely.

And just as suddenly as it started, it was over.

She kept her eyes closed as he lifted his head though she could feel his gaze on her face. She knew he had to be feeling the same skepticism, confusion, and longing.

But he apparently recovered himself long before she did.

The latch on the cellar door clicked, and without delay, he began to swing it open.

She drew a deep breath and raised her lashes, intent on giving him a resounding earful. But he only grinned at her, and that made her mad.

"Stop kissing me, sir," she seethed in whisper.

"You must admit," he stated very casually, "that kissing you cuts down on the chatter."

She fairly grabbed the lamp from him. "You forget that I despise you."

"Yes, that's very apparent," he replied with a wry grin. "Let's go."

She dropped the topic for the moment, deciding it best to ignore his inane behavior. But at least he allowed her to enter first, so in a sense, she felt she had won this particular annoying moment with him.

With the door to the wine cellar opened completely, she very slowly walked inside, holding the lamp out in front of her.

There were six steps to the left that went down to the wooden floor, and she descended without incident, seeing nothing out of the ordinary—just bottles of wine stacked on racks as they should be. The room smelled of damp earth, though the air seemed stale to her and colder than the rest of the house.

"Where do we start?" she asked as she moved farther into the room.

He strode past her toward the far end of the cellar. "If I'm not turned around, this should be the east wall, putting it in line with the end of the tunnel."

She moved to his side, scanning the racks for any indication of a door behind them. "We shouldn't have to move the bottles," she said, thinking aloud. "Whoever left a doorway to the old well would expect to be able to move an entire rack; otherwise, it would have been sealed completely. Or left obvious."

"I agree," he said simply.

She glanced up to his face, noting how lamplight made his strong features look chiseled to perfection, his eyes dark and full of mystery. And as he glanced down to meet her gaze, a soft surge of awareness passed between them, sending a jolt of heat through her body.

His gaze lingered on her for another moment or two, his brows drawn together as if he were attempting to fit pieces of a puzzle into place. And for the smallest second, she feared with an unusually desperate desire that he might kiss her again.

"Let's start looking," he insisted in a husky timbre.

She swallowed and nodded. With that, he turned his attention to the first set of racks at the southern end of the east wall.

For several minutes they found nothing beyond the ordinary as each rack of wine bottles seemed bolted to either the floor or the wall. Ivy held the lamp behind him, doing more observing as he attempted to push and pull to no avail. Then suddenly, as they neared the northern wall, she stilled.

"I feel a draft again," she whispered. "Coming from down here."

She lowered her body, and he crouched beside her.

"Near the floor?" he murmured, stretching his palm out to feel for himself.

The warmth of his breath on her ear made her shiver, and she fought the urge to rub it on her sleeve.

"No, a little higher . . . Here."

He clutched the rack in front of her with both hands. "It's loose, but unmovable. There must be a latch here as well."

Ivy stood again and stepped back as Garrett began looking for a hook or latch to release the entire case from the back wall.

Then she heard a click.

"I found it," he whispered, his tone now edged with anticipation. "Stand back."

She did as he ordered, holding the lamp up for him to see better.

"I think the whole rack moves," he said through a grunt. "The wine bottles, too."

And then, with a faint creak, the rack seemed to crawl open on its own, just as the bookcase in the library had done.

"Amazing," she whispered, noting how the bottles filled with wine didn't even rattle.

"Indeed," he agreed. "Whoever built these passageways took extraordinary care to assure they stayed sturdy and well hidden."

"It's just wooden paneling," she muttered as she drew her fingers along the back wall.

He started pushing against it as well, and almost at once half of the panel, from the floor to nearly waist height, moved to the side about four feet.

Garrett took the lamp from her outstretched hand and crouched to look inside. "It's another room . . . or passageway."

Incredulous, she replied, "Do you see the door to the main tunnel?"

He was silent for a moment. "I think so."

As he began to enter what appeared to be a crawl space, Ivy whispered, "Be careful."

He didn't reply as he disappeared inside. Ivy followed, ducking to maneuver her body through the opening. As soon as she was through, she stood next to Garrett, brushing her skirts out as she surveyed the area. She noticed the door to the main tunnel at once, straight ahead about three feet. With nothing but a wall to the left, Garrett moved past her to peer into the darkness on their right.

"I think it's another passageway," he whispered. "Probably the one that leads to the bedchambers."

"But that's got to be up at least five flights of stairs," she added with a trace of amazement in her tone.

He began to walk cautiously forward. "Let's find out."

She followed him, staying as close as possible, her palm clutching his elbow, as he began to traverse the passageway that wound first toward the southeast part of the house, almost certainly underground, then gradually began to slope upward. The tunnel seemed to be as small an enclosure as the first they'd encountered behind the library, but with cobwebs and dust, it felt much smaller, and Ivy fought the urge to cushion her face in his back, between his shoulder blades, and let him lead her blindly.

For at least ten minutes they moved steadily onward

in silence, cautiously climbing two sets of stairs and making a number of sharp turns, disorienting them more with each curve as they had yet to come upon a door or something else to indicate an entrance into the main house. Then, suddenly, Garrett slowed to a halt.

"What is it?" she murmured, unable to see anything around his large frame, which nearly filled the passageway.

"I think we're at the library," he said over his shoulder.

"Where we entered the first time? How do you know?"

He stepped forward another few feet. "I think we're coming up from the south, heading north. The door we came through is on the left, and straight ahead are the stairs we climbed."

She thought about that for a moment. "So, when we get to the top of the stairs, instead of going right, as we did before, this time we go left."

"Exactly," he agreed in a gruff whisper. "That rotten smell is getting stronger, too."

She caught a whiff of it and shuddered.

They remained silent as they passed the library entrance and began to climb the familiar staircase. Once at the top, Garrett turned to his left and started down the passageway opposite the one they'd taken two days before.

"So there really is only one tunnel that's built between rooms and traverses the entire house," she said, thinking aloud.

"Possibly," he replied. "Then again there could be another that's entirely separate."

"It's cold in here."

"I know," he replied in a whisper. "Just keep moving."

"I'm presuming," she carried on, "that the various servants through the years have heard footsteps, and perhaps even creaking noises of the doors being opened and shut, and that's where the rumors of ghosts have come from."

He didn't comment.

"And it's likely even one or two of them saw a figure disappear into—"

"Ivy, stop talking or they'll hear your voice and start shrieking," he admonished softly.

She smacked him lightly on the arm but decided he was probably right.

For several minutes they walked in silence, then he slowed again and turned a little to whisper, "I see another door."

She clung to his elbow as he neared it, then replied, "You look for the lock, I'll hold the lamp."

He handed it to her cautiously, then began to run his fingers over the edges as before, almost at once finding the same type of latch as the other entrances.

She heard the faint click, and with a gentle push, the door slid to the side about two feet, just enough for a person to squeeze through.

Garrett peered inside. "This is paneling behind a vanity table," he murmured. "The one in the withdrawing room for another bedchamber."

"That's why I couldn't find an entrance," she said, annoyed. "I was looking for a door."

"The various room entrances were all probably built at different times," he mused.

She glanced around her for a moment, thinking. "We must be above the ballroom, or the eastern end of it. We've come farther than I thought."

He pulled the door closed. "Well at least we have that answer."

True, she thought. This was how Desdemona, and possibly others, entered the lion's lair.

"Let's keep going and see if this passageway leads to other rooms."

"I'm sure it does because it continues, but we can't be gone any longer, Ivy," he maintained as he closed the paneled wall with a faint tug. "We have to return, or the staff will start to become suspicious."

He was right again, naturally. The cook and kitchen help had seen them, and tea would be served soon in the parlor.

"Then I'm—"

"No, you're not," he insisted, turning to face her, his look stern. "Promise me now that you'll not enter the main tunnel or these passageways without me, at any time."

She glared at him, hoping he noticed her annoyance in such faint light.

"We've discussed this more than once," he continued, his low voice carrying a trace of softness. "It's not safe."

Biting down a snide retort, she said instead, "What we should do is see if we can find entrances from inside the house. There have to be several."

His brows rose just enough to know she'd surprised him by not arguing.

She grinned wryly. "And of course you can't help, Garrett, as we've already decided it would be highly inappropriate for us to be seen together in private quarters."

Crossing his arms over his chest, he seemed to grow thoughtful. "The problem," he said after a moment, "is that we're not really learning anything by walking hidden corridors. I can't imagine we'll find Benedict or the diamonds just sitting in the middle of the passage."

She knew that, of course, and yet hearing him verbalize it distressed her a little.

"What are you thinking?" she asked cautiously.

He rubbed a palm down his face. "That we're going about this little investigation of ours the wrong way."

She shook her head, confused. "What wrong way? What do you mean?"

"I'm not sure . . ." He took her arm and turned her. "Let's go back, and we'll discuss it outside, where nobody can hear."

"We're whispering, Garrett. Nobody can hear—"

He put two fingers on her lips to silence her, then motioned to her with a nod to get going. Exasperated, she turned, held the lamp out to guide their way, did as he directed.

It took them only about half the time to retrace their steps and return to the small entry area behind the wine cellar. As soon as they neared the short entrance, she stopped short.

"It's been closed," she whispered, feeling her heartbeat quicken.

"That's what I feared," he said, passing her to look at the paneling firsthand. He pushed against it to no avail, then attempted to find a latch. "Someone was in here."

Ivy turned in all directions, feeling a panic rising. "After we came through?"

He stood tall and looked at her directly. "Someone, probably the same person who nearly caught us by the well, is making use of these passageways regularly. And he or she knows we've discovered them."

"We're locked in," she breathed.

He wrapped an arm around her waist and pulled her close. "No, we can get out through one of the bedrooms, I'm not worried about that."

"Well, it worries me," she murmured in agitation. "Let's get out of here before whoever it is locks us in for good."

Immediately, he took the lamp from her and snuggled close to pass her, putting him in front. Over his shoulder, he said, "Stay close to me."

He sounded calm and very much in control, she decided, but she could tell by his quick walk that although he might not be as frightened by the prospect of being trapped forever in an enclosure without exit, he couldn't hide his own concern.

At last they reached the library entrance.

"Hold the lamp," he said, fairly shoving it into her hands.

She raised it for better light while he inspected the corners above for a hidden latch. His nimble fingers inched along the top then down the left side.

"I found it."

She sighed with relief when she heard a click. He pushed on the door—and nothing happened.

"I think it's been locked from the other side," he said through a grunt as he tried a shove with his shoulder. It didn't budge.

"Garrett?"

He stood upright again and combed his fingers through his hair. "It's all right. I'll get us out of here."

She shivered, feeling icy sweat cling to her neck. "We could take the main tunnel to the forest, I suppose."

He shook his head. "That's sealed from the outside as well."

"Oh, my God," she whispered, closing her eyes.

Immediately, he pulled the lamp from her fingertips and wrapped his arm protectively around her shoulders, hugging her close.

"At least you smell better than that damned cat," she said, feeling an immense comfort in just his presence alone.

He chuckled softly. "A lady should not use profanity," he breathed into her hair.

She groaned and rubbed her cheek across his chest. "And she should never find herself alone in a hidden tunnel with a man who is not her husband," she added.

He exhaled a long breath, then dropped a gentle kiss to the top of her head. "Let's go back to the door of the master bedchamber. At least we know that one opened. I can't imagine anyone being able to lock it quickly without our noticing or hearing something."

"I can," she grumbled, glancing up to his face.

He gave her a wicked smile. "Always the optimist, you are." He rubbed her back, then gave her a nudge. "Let's go."

He carried the lamp, and she led the way, climbing the steep stairs quickly, then turning down the left passageway when they reached the top. Holding her skirts up to her ankles to avoid tripping, she swiftly walked to the door, Garrett following closely behind.

Without a word, he reached for the latch and unlocked the door. Ivy attempted to push it in, but it stood firm.

"It's locked, too," she shrieked in a whisper.

He grabbed her jaw with his hard hand. "Don't panic. Someone is playing with us, Ivy, and he wouldn't leave us in here like this without reason." He inhaled deeply and rubbed the pad of his thumb across her lips. "Trust me?"

She blinked back tears as she nodded minutely.

"Good." He glanced up and down the dusty enclosure, thinking of options, then grabbed her hand, clutching it tightly as he continued to move down the passageway. For several moments they walked forward in silence, slower than before as they were in an unfamiliar area of the house.

The small tunnel curved to the right, then turned again sharply to the left. Garrett stopped. "Where are we? Can you tell?"

She rubbed her nose with her free hand. "Well, if that was Benedict Sharon's bedchamber, then . . ." She glanced back, calculating. "We've probably passed the adjoining room, and we're—we should now be near the one Lord Rye assigned to me."

"Good," he said with a trace of relief. "I suspect whoever locked us in here knows that."

"What are you saying?" she asked very slowly, her eyes widening with concern.

He squeezed her hand faintly. "That we're being steered there for a reason. So let's find the door."

"If there is one," she groaned.

He walked a few steps farther, then murmured, "The passageway is narrowing."

"We're nearing the end?"

"I think so, but—I see a shift in the wood up ahead."

Instead of picking up the pace, he slowed his stride with caution. "Stay behind me," he whispered over his shoulder.

She nodded.

Gingerly, he strode to the end and held the light up to survey the wall. She couldn't see a door in the dimness, but it reminded her of the exit they had found the day they entered from the library.

Brushing a spiderweb aside, Garrett pressed his palm to the wall. Without effort, or even a click of a lock, it opened just enough for them to slide into Ivy's withdrawing room.

She almost threw herself into his arms with her relief, but he stopped her by squeezing her fingers again in warning.

She swallowed as he pushed the wardrobe closet door to the side and stepped into the room, then pulled her inside with him before releasing her.

"There's nobody here," he said seconds later. He walked into the bedroom proper and strode at once to the window, scanning the area below and toward the lake. "And nothing unusual outside, though it's dark, and I can barely see the shoreline." He turned and looked at her, his brows creased in frown. "And I'll wager the door to the hallway is locked from this side, too."

Ivy felt a wave of nausea course through her as she considered how someone had the knowledge to come and go from her bedchamber at will, could watch her while she slept or dressed, even bathed.

And then from the corner of her eye she caught a glimpse of something odd sitting flat on the bed. Something out of place, white against the purple quilting.

Very slowly, she moved toward it, suddenly overwhelmed by a sharp sensation of terror, a foreboding unlike any she had ever felt before.

Her mouth went dry as she felt the blood drain from her face.

"What's wrong?" Garrett asked, pushing himself away from the window to walk toward her.

She couldn't speak. With her thumb and index finger, she reached for the piece of white paper, folded neatly in two, her Christian name written in very tiny letters on top.

He grabbed her wrist. "Don't touch it."

"I have to," she replied coldly without looking at him.

With her insistence, he relaxed his grip. Nimbly, she lifted the paper, and as she did so, the bottom half opened, and from it fell a small lock of hair that landed softly on the quilt—just like hers in color, texture, tied with a small blue ribbon. In a flash she saw Ian's face, distorted and reaching . . . .

Garrett pulled the sheet of paper from her grasp and glanced at it. "It doesn't say anything."

"It doesn't have to," she breathed, and within seconds she began to tremble violently.

"Is this lock of hair yours?" he charged.

"It's Ian's . . ."

Suddenly he took action. He reached for her hand and fairly dragged her to the hallway door. Then after peeking out to make sure all was clear, he turned to her, and whispered, "We're going outside where the walls don't have ears, and you're going to tell me everything."

She shook her head as tears began to stream down her face.

"Stop it!" he demanded in a quiet voice of concern, giving her a quick jostle. "Don't let the servants see you upset. It'll alert them that something is very wrong."

Attempting to recover herself, she drew in a long, unsteady breath and nodded.

He reached up and gently wiped his fingers across her cheeks. "You can cry on my shoulder at the lake."

Then, acting swiftly, he opened the door and they left her bedchamber, walking as fast as they could without causing a commotion, thankfully seeing no one as they made their way to the foyer, grabbed their wraps from the bronze coat rack, and stepped out into the fresh air.

Chapter 11

Garrett knew he had to think quickly. If this had been just a week ago, he would have believed Ivy had set him up with such trickery to make him succumb to her emotions, to give in and trust her without question. But he knew fear when he saw it, and Ivy was afraid. She had been afraid in the tunnel, and she seemed positively terrified now. Suddenly he knew that everything had changed between them, and probably more so in him. She might have been involved in tricking him two years ago, but she wasn't involved now.

He waited until they were well away from the house before he considered talking. Instead of walking all the way to the bench that overlooked the lake from the back of the Hope cottage, he decided to lead her toward a more secluded area nearer the house, though away from prying eyes.

They didn't speak until he turned off the forest path and pushed through a bit of brush, walking downward toward a clearing by the water.

At last he motioned to an overturned log, directing

her to sit. She did as ordered, noting she still clutched the lock of hair in the palm of one hand.

"Tell me what's going on, Ivy," he insisted in a tone a bit more subdued than he felt.

She shook her head as she gazed out over the water. "I don't know."

"I don't believe you," he said matter-of-factly, lifting a leg to plant his foot on the wood next to her hip. "At least," he amended, "I know there's something you're not telling me and that it has to do with your brother."

For a lingering minute she just stared past him, across the lake, and he waited, with a patience that defied his irritation at her for being so evasive at a time when there wasn't anyone else in Winter Garden she could trust.

Finally, she turned her face skyward, keeping her eyes closed. "I told you my brother was in danger."

"Yes," he replied, avoiding the fact that he hadn't exactly believed her.

Her lashes fluttered open, and she looked at him at last, her smooth skin pale, her eyes filled with trepidation. "I don't know who to trust . . ."

In a sudden melting of will, he felt his heart swell with tenderness at her honest disclosure. And it took an endless moment, he thought, to comprehend exactly what her words implied, how even now she reached out for him in a longing she probably didn't understand. He also realized with a bit of rationality, that to tell her she could trust him with anything would cause her to deny him, perhaps even reerect that barrier that had slowly crumbled between them in the last few days. That event would cause more harm than good, and lead him further away from his own search for the truth. If he were to gain her trust, he would need to trust her.

Garrett pulled his foot from the log, and with a gradual acceptance and a slow organization of his thoughts, lowered his body to sit beside her. To his relief, she scooted a little to the side to give him room.

"Ivy, if you'll let me help you, I'll trust you with something, a . . . secret of sorts, that I've kept to myself for two years."

She turned to look at him, her eyes vibrant and sparkling with tears she attempted to hold back from his view.

"This is not about us, Garrett," she said in a forced whisper. "This is far more important than us."

He tried not to let that statement, uttered in fear, slice into his gut. Instead, he replied, "This is about me, Ivy."

Her brows creased gently as her gaze scanned his face. "It's about the pain in your head, isn't it?"

He almost smiled. "There's a bit more to it than that."

A cold wind stirred the leaves at his feet, and blew strands of loose hair around her pale face as she gazed unblinking at the water just a few yards away.

"Two years ago, when I was attacked in St. Anne's Church," he began softly, "I was supposed to meet an informant who'd arranged for Benedict Sharon to be there in his attempt to exchange cash for the stolen

Martello diamonds." He paused, then admitted quietly, "That informant was your brother."

It took a long time, it seemed, for her to comprehend his disclosure. For seconds she just sat there, staring, and then very, very slowly her brows drew together and she turned to stare at him.

"That's impossible," she breathed in a voice barely heard.

He rubbed his hands together in front of him to keep them warm. "Not impossible, Ivy. True."

She began to shake her head. "He had no reason to be involved, Garrett. He's not an investigator—he didn't even know you." She swallowed harshly, then added, "You're lying."

He noted how she nearly spat the words at him, but her confusion in the matter seemed to overcome her anger. He just didn't know how much to reveal, not without knowing how deeply her brother was involved in the deception from the beginning.

With a quick exhale through his teeth, he continued. "I . . . was brought into the case when Ian went to the Marquess of Rye to inform the man that he was being blackmailed into stealing the Martello diamonds during his forthcoming betrothal ball—"

She cut him off with a bitter laugh. "Ian blackmailed? That's insane. By whom? *Why?*"

He remained silent for a moment or two, then murmured, "By Benedict Sharon."

Caustically, she replied, "I don't believe you."

Although he still hadn't looked at her, he could feel

her icy gaze on his face, and noted that she sounded less convinced of his deception, probably because she was attempting to piece together the puzzle with the information she possessed herself. He did realize, however, that she wouldn't be able to do so without his revealing more.

Abruptly, she shook herself and stood, wrapping her arms around her waist in a defensive gesture, and walked forward to the edge of the lake.

He stared at her back, deciding to continue with his disclosure whether she chose to believe him or not in the end.

"According to your brother," he said, "Benedict Sharon knew of the Martello diamonds, as did many of the aristocracy, but he was more impressed by their value as individual stones. He intended to remove them from the tiara, sell them illegally, and use the funds to buy his brother's release from prison. Or at least that's what he told Ian. I have my doubts about that after learning Lord Rothebury died only weeks after his arrest, but without proof, I'm not sure what to think other than that Benedict wanted the money for himself. And being such a reclusive individual, I suspect he thought to disappear from England for good without anyone knowing his whereabouts, or for that matter even caring."

He watched her, remaining on the log to give her space to come to terms with the information. Daylight was fading, and the looming darkness fit his mood, his worry. Finally, she turned to him, her eyes meeting his directly, cast in a shadow of hurt and bewilderment.

"Ian has always been an honorable man, Garrett," she said, her voice carrying just above the wind. "He would never give in to blackmail, for anything or anyone."

He cocked his head to the side a little. "For you, perhaps?"

She pulled back a little, her features growing hard, lids narrowing. In a breath of warning, she asked, "What are you saying?"

Inhaling deeply, he revealed, "Benedict Sharon told Ian that if Ian refused to steal the diamonds, Benedict would disclose, to all concerned, the nature of your parentage."

For seconds she did nothing. Then he saw her lashes flutter, her lips begin to quiver, and he knew she understood.

In a second he was upon her, grabbing her around the waist before her legs gave out and she faltered. "Sharon is a shrewd and evil man, Ivy—"

"No!"

She shoved her hands hard against his chest, and he released her. She stumbled back, hugging herself, gulping for air. And then in a rage she turned to him, her breath coming fast and hard, her eyes flashing, her posture ramrod stiff.

"This is impossible!" she shouted in whisper. "Where *is* he? What has happened to my *brother*, Garrett?"

He felt gut-punched by her pain, the tears in her

eyes, her confusion and fury as she continued to clutch the lock of hair in her palm.

"I don't know, Ivy," he said, his tone gravelly. "I don't know where he is or what happened that night. But I do know he did the *honorable* thing by going to the marquess and informing the man that Sharon was blackmailing him into stealing his diamonds. That had to have been an enormously difficult thing for him to do, especially in disclosing the reason why."

She ignored that, wiping her eyes with her fingertips. "That's why you don't trust him. You think he arranged, with Benedict, to set you up for *attack* that night? Why?"

He swallowed hard. To deny it would be an outright lie, and yet he knew there was far more involved.

He raked his finger through his hair, then said quietly, "I don't honestly know, Ivy."

"What do you mean you don't know?" she cried out. She took a step toward him, pointing at his chest. "You left me—*me*—in your bed that night while you went to meet my brother? Can you imagine how knowing this now makes me *feel*?"

"Yes, I do," he insisted darkly. "But you weren't the only person hurt that night." He paused for a moment, watching his words register, then lowered his voice to continue. "I trusted him, Ivy. He didn't want you to know the details of the blackmail, and for good reason. The fact that the authorities brought you in as their beloved seer to help was beside the point. All they knew was that the Martello diamonds were missing. Your help wasn't pertinent to the plan your brother had set in motion, which was why I told you nothing at the time. It was supposed to be an easy arrest, but the fact remains that when I arrived at that church, Ian wasn't there."

That disclosure seemed to calm her a little. Then shrewdly, she asked, "If the authorities didn't know about the blackmail, how is it possible that you do?"

He hadn't thought of that, and without a better idea of what was happening now in Winter Garden, with Sharon and the diamonds still missing, her brother's lock of hair still clutched in her hand, he simply couldn't divulge everything. He needed more time—more time with Ivy, and more time to uncover the truth.

Crossing his arms over his chest, he replied, "Your brother came to me personally and asked for my help in preventing the theft of the diamonds."

She shook her head, confused. "So . . . you're telling me my brother went to the Marquess of Rye, divulging this blackmail scheme, and the diamonds were stolen anyway?" She furrowed her brows. "That doesn't even make sense."

"It's complicated—"

"Yes, it is."

He eyed her thoughtfully. "A week before the betrothal ball, your brother and I, with the marquess's good wishes apparently, made a plan to confront Benedict soon after the party and have him arrested while explaining that the marquess was fully aware of the blackmail scheme and there were no diamonds to give him in exchange for his silence." He rubbed his jaw with his fingers. "Instead, the diamonds were stolen at the betrothal party *anyway,* and how, or why, or where they are, nobody really knows. Days later Ian sent word from London that he had been following Benedict, had confronted the man, and that Sharon said he'd exchange the tiara for money, since apparently he'd come to realize he wouldn't be able to sell the diamonds quickly as they were. The Home Office knew about the theft by then, which was why you were brought in. Our intent was to confront Sharon at the church and have him arrested, hopefully with the diamonds in hand, or at least a confession as to where they might be. But the authorities were never called, never waiting at the church. After I was attacked, the only conclusion *I* could arrive at was that your brother was involved in everything from the beginning."

"You used me," she whispered, her lips curled, gaze filled with vehemence.

"No," he countered at once. "What took place between you and me was never about your brother or the diamonds, you know that, Ivy."

She faltered a little in an attempt to believe him, he supposed.

"What happened at the church, Garrett?"

She'd asked him that so softly that he barely heard the words. But he knew she was attempting to piece together her own version of what occurred that night with all this new information.

"You have to trust what I'm going to tell you," he replied, his voice low and grave.

She sniffed and shook herself, though her gaze never wavered. "I'll decide that after you explain it to me."

He almost smiled. "Very well," he agreed as he moved back to the log.

Lowering his body, he placed his elbows on his knees, his hands clasped together in front of him as he dropped his gaze to the forest floor.

"Your brother arranged the meeting place, and I suppose he chose a church because it was quiet, dark, and Sharon wouldn't question the solitude of the place," he revealed softly. "I arrived early to meet Ian, but he wasn't there, and neither was Benedict—or at least I never saw or heard him. I do recall seeing . . . someone . . . a woman, I think, standing in the shadow." He inhaled deeply and closed his eyes. "And then I was struck on the back of the head. I remember nothing else about that night. For weeks I remained in a hazy dream, in intense pain, uncertain of time and what had happened." He lifted his lashes and looked up, locking his gaze with hers. "My memory has been damaged, Ivy. Much of it has slowly returned, but—but I don't remember exactly what happened in the hours before I was struck. I don't remember the details of being with you."

The mixture of shock and anguish to cross her features in that instant nearly took his breath. Within seconds she'd gone from fury and confusion about her brother to disbelief and utter pain.

"Ivy—"

"Stop it. Just stop lying, Garrett," she seethed in

a whisper, eyes closed as she brought her fists to her mouth.

Slowly he stood, but he didn't move toward her. For a full minute or more he just watched her, not knowing what to expect as she attempted to come to terms with all she'd just learned from him. He understood the ache she felt within, but he couldn't allow her to wallow in her own pain when so much was still at stake.

Finally, he said, "I admit I've held back many facts from you, Ivy, but I haven't lied. I've never lied to you."

Suddenly her eyes flew open, and she laughed, a bitter aching laugh that tore through him. She threw her arms out wide and glared at him.

"And this is what has become of my well-ordered life," she blurted, her voice filled with amazement.

He shook his head and replied, "Your life was never all that well-ordered. What I've told you today will at least enlighten you as to the facts, that's all."

She gaped at him. "You remember nothing of me? Of the night you seduced me?" She chuckled again and turned away from him. "How very convenient for you, Garrett."

"It hasn't been convenient for me at all," he retorted, trying to control his own inner turmoil. "Don't forget that I was also a victim in this distorted, evil plan. And I have absolutely no idea who set me up to fail."

For a long moment she said nothing. Then, in a tone of great sorrow, she maintained, "The difference is that you've spent all these months attempting to remember what happened that night, to try to find reason in why you were attacked and by whom, distrusting me in your vain attempt to retrieve those precious diamonds." Over her shoulder, she whispered, "For me, Garrett, I've spent the entire time trying to rid my thoughts of you."

He sucked in a breath as her honesty hit home. In a low, grave voice, he replied, "And in my quest to find the diamonds, all *I've* been able to do is think about you."

Slowly, she turned to look into his eyes, the breeze blowing loose tendrils of hair into her face, tendrils that went unnoticed.

He took a step toward her, shoving his hands in the pockets of his twine coat, never dropping his gaze from hers.

"I don't remember details, Ivy, but I remember softness," he admitted in a deep whisper. "I remember that I felt . . . enchanted by you, and that I desired you from the first moment we met. I remember a scent of lilacs and the sheen of long, auburn hair. I remember a face of exquisite beauty and a gentle laugh." He bit down hard to contain a whirlwind of emotions he couldn't identify in himself. "I now remember that we made love, that it happened, but so help me God, I don't remember how it felt, how you felt to the touch, if you enjoyed our time together, and if I pleased you in bed." He drew in a shaky breath and closed his eyes. "And right now, even more than I've ever wanted to find the Martello diamonds, Ivy, I want to remember every single second I spent with you intimately.

I would trade everything for that one detailed memory of you lying naked in my arms."

He had no idea what to expect from her after such a heart-wrenching admission on his part. For seconds he remained still, his eyes closed as he thought of his bed in his rented town house in London, of how she must have looked between the sheets, of how he had deceived her and how she must have wanted him as much to risk her future for one night with him. It was all there in his mind, waiting to be retrieved, but edged in a blackness that eluded him.

"I won't be your lover again, Garrett."

The words, barely heard, crashed down on him, awakening him to the reality of the present, though he noted she'd said them with far less conviction than the last time.

He opened his eyes as he straightened his posture, his heart sinking into a river of ice as he locked his gaze with hers. She'd grown aloof, her expression flat, and he had to wonder for a moment how she could remain so unaffected by his honesty.

"What did I do, or say, that hurt you so much two years ago, Ivy?"

Her eyes widened just enough for him to realize he'd surprised her with the question. She hadn't considered that by not remembering the specifics of their lovemaking he also didn't recall much else that happened between them on that night. And right now, for the first time, he realized there had been more involved between them than simply taking her virginity.

Suddenly she dropped her eyes and hugged herself again. "It's getting colder. I need to get back to the house."

"Answer me first," he insisted, trying like hell not to sound desperate.

"It doesn't matter—"

"Yes. It *does*."

She eyed him candidly, her shoulders squared, features hidden now in a fading twilight. Then she inhaled deeply, and said, "You asked me to marry you, Garrett. You teased me, made love to me, and then asked me to marry you before leaving me alone and uncertain if I carried your child. I waited for you to return, worried beyond reason. I had nobody to turn to, and when I finally discovered days later that you were in hospital, instead of embracing me, or apologizing, or even just allowing me to help you recover, you *accused* me of being part of the scheme that got you injured."

Nothing she could have said would have startled him more. He took a staggered step back, his mind a blank, his head reeling. "Ivy . . . I—I didn't—"

"You didn't know because you don't remember," she interjected in a harsh murmur. "Whether that's true or not, I will probably never know. But I remember, Garrett. I remember *every* detail. And now you've returned to my life expecting me not to hate you? To understand what *you* went through? To forgive you and help you find the precious diamonds?"

"I'm sorry . . ." he breathed.

She reached up to close the neck of her pelisse tighter around her throat. "I'm sorry, too. I'm sorry for what happened to you two years ago, and I'm sorry that you can't let go of the past." She straightened with determination. "But for right now my only concern is for my brother. Someone here in this small village knows something of him, and he is in danger." She walked forward until she stood directly in front of him, her expression set with fortitude. "And now I'm going to tell you a secret, Garrett. Someone is blackmailing *me*."

For a second or two, he thought he'd misheard her. And then as her words sunk in, all self-pity and remorse evaporated. "What did you say?"

She gave a caustic laugh. "Can you believe it? I'm being blackmailed for the Martello diamonds, Garrett. And wouldn't it be funny if you were the culprit—"

He grabbed her by the shoulders and yanked her to him. "I would never threaten you with anything, Ivy, you know that. So tell me exactly what's going on. Now."

She seemed a bit unsettled by his sudden, forceful demand. "Let me go."

"Tell me first," he muttered in anger.

Her lips thinned with complete indignation. "Before I arrived, I received a note from the Marquess of Rye, through his London solicitor, asking for my assistance in finding the jewels. He didn't want me to look for ghosts, Garrett, he wanted me to find the Martello diamonds, using my ability as a seer as a false pretense for being here." She looked him up and down, then with a smirk said, "I know you're laughing inside, and you can stop it now."

"I'm not laughing. Go on."

She squirmed in his hands, and he let her go.

"When I arrived," she continued through a shiver, "I received a second note, this time sent by post directly to me at the house, stating that in exchange for the Martello diamonds, I can guarantee Ian's safety. I—I didn't know what to think of it at first, but then . . ." She raised the lock of hair, still sitting in her palm. "Then I find this, and I'm starting to think the Marquess of Rye is involved in all of it—everything. He's the only person we have yet to see or meet in this sordid tale between us, Garrett. He's the only one who knows my reason for being in the house." In a drawn-out murmur, she maintained, "And now, according to you, I learn he also knows you, and Ian."

If her revelation about his marriage proposal hadn't astonished him so much, left him so troubled, he might have been able to summon a plausible excuse for her flawed reasoning. But in all truth, it wasn't flawed. He'd sent her the original note, of course, to get her to come to Winter Garden in the first place, but never would he stoop to threats or blackmail. And under normal circumstances she might believe that—but this wasn't a normal circumstance at all. If he disclosed his identity now, not only would she despise him forever, she would probably trust him less than ever, especially as he attempted to explain.

But she was right. The most important thing at the

moment was the fact that someone knew something about her brother, and after discovering the lock of hair, he was beginning to believe the man might truly be in danger, regardless of his involvement or lack thereof in stealing the diamonds two years ago. Details could be worked out later.

Yet beneath it all, nagging him in the far recesses of his mind, he still had to wonder if Ivy and her brother were actually playing him for a fool. He just didn't know what to believe—her explanations about their past, his proposal of marriage, or his sparse memory of two years ago, which really told him little and filled him with suspicion.

One thing was certain: He would make love to her again. He'd known it from the first moment he'd laid eyes on her in Winter Garden. Now she knew it, too, deep down. Desire was something *he* could sense in Ivy. She would never be able to deceive him in bed, and getting her to succumb to him again might be the only way to ensure her forgiveness for everything when he finally revealed the truth.

"I'm staying at the house from this night forward," he said matter-of-factly.

She snorted. "You absolutely are not."

He dragged a palm down his face. "Ivy, someone has access to your bedroom, someone who may not hesitate to hurt you. Leaving a lock of your brother's hair wasn't simply to scare you. It's a message letting you, and maybe even me, know we're being watched, and that whoever it is can get to you. Someone is toying with us, and regardless of what happened in the past, I simply cannot allow you to stay in your room at night alone."

She shook her head vehemently. "I'm not alone. Mrs. Thurman—"

"—and everyone else is below stairs. They probably wouldn't even hear you scream."

She seemed to waver with that remark, biting her lower lip and casting a swift glance toward the house, now shadowed in darkness.

"No," she tried again, sounding less convinced, "you simply cannot stay in the house, Garrett. It would cause a scandal, and I'd be ruined."

"Not if nobody knows I'm there."

Confusion lit her brown eyes. "How—" And then it dawned on her. "You plan to enter through the tunnel?"

He smiled satisfactorily. "Indeed. Through the tunnel."

She hesitated just long enough for him to know he'd won the argument. In a softer tone, he amended, "You'll have the privacy you need, but I'm taking control from this moment forward. From now on we are working together to solve this mystery."

She sighed. "Garrett, I don't trust you, and I don't like you."

"Yes, I know," he replied nonchalantly. Then with little fanfare, he inhaled a breath for confidence and strode forward to place his palms on her cheeks. Startled, she could do nothing but stand there and stare into his eyes.

With a trace of a smile on his lips, he leaned over

and kissed her, gently at first, then deeply, with a passion built from years of frustration and desire for the return of every memory they'd shared. And she responded, wrapping her arms around his neck as she gave in to the need, as she heated his blood with the softness of her mouth and a whimper of longing that pleaded for more.

His cold thumbs caressed the warm skin of her cheeks as he cradled her head. Her breasts, hidden beneath layers of clothing, teased his chest and struck him suddenly with a vague image of silky skin and hardened, rosy nipples he ached to taste once more. Just one more time . . .

Very gradually, before he lost control of what sanity he still possessed, he pulled back from the kiss and rested his forehead against hers. For moments they said nothing, their breath mingling in the icy air. And then he felt a tear on his thumb, and it seared him inside.

"You can't fight destiny, Ivy," he whispered.

She shook her head quickly in tiny movements. "I won't be your lover again."

He kissed her forehead. "Let's solve one problem at a time."

She didn't reply, but allowed him to take her hand as they made their way back onto the path and headed toward the house.

Chapter 12

Ivy was restless, and growing more worried by the day. It had been a week since Garrett's decision to invade her privacy and sleep in her bedchamber with her each night. Thankfully, true to his word, he'd been a gentleman about the entire thing, leaving his day clothes on and sleeping on the small settee beside the grate. He couldn't possibly be comfortable, but then his comfort remained the least of her worries.

He arrived each night after Newbury lit her fire, and left each morning before Jane awakened her with her tea and bath. He'd kept to his word about allowing her privacy by staying away from her withdrawing room while she attended to personal needs. She'd also chosen to wear her most discreet nightgown to bed along with her lightweight robe, which she refused to remove. He'd teased her about it the first night, though he hadn't mentioned it since.

Tonight she had news for him, and in waiting impatiently for his appearance through the secret entrance, she paced the floor.

The more he stayed by her side day by day, the more he troubled her. She couldn't decide if he'd been truthful about his memory loss or if he was deceiving her because of his involvement in Ian's disappearance. The problem, she decided, was her memory of him.

She'd only known him for a week, but during that time she had trusted him implicitly. Part of her knew it was because of her gift and her ability to detect deceit in others. But there was something else involved where Garrett was concerned. Even now she had trouble defining her feelings for him, though she knew they comprised a mixture of grief, annoyance, desire, and probably what love remained from two years ago when she had fallen for him in a shamefully lust-filled passion. But she didn't hate him, and he knew it, which was likely why he insisted on remaining by her side regardless of her intentions to keep their association practical and proper. Nothing had ever been practical or proper between them, and it bothered her immensely that she couldn't keep her impractical feelings in check.

She did acknowledge, however, that she couldn't yet forgive him for the damage he'd done to her heart two years ago because she knew—positively *knew*—he was still hiding secrets from her. She sensed a reluctance in him to tell her everything about that night, his past, his desires, and, admittedly, she understood it. In that regard, she decided neither of them could trust the other until they discovered the truth behind the disappearance of the Martello diamonds. And her mission, now, centered on finding Ian.

The click of the latch in her withdrawing room brought her attention to the present. Garrett had arrived.

Quickly, she walked in to see him enter, her heartbeat quickening at just the sight of his broad shoulders squeezing through the opening.

"You're late," she said.

He grinned wryly at her as he closed the paneling. "It's so good to know you care about my arrival time each night, Lady Ivy."

She turned her back on him and returned to her bedroom. "I have news."

He shook off whatever dust he'd collected from his journey through the tunnel, removed his coat and gloves, which he tossed on the settee, then walked close to the fire to warm his hands.

"What news might that be?" he asked at last.

"I received a note from Lord Rye," she replied at once. "He gave his permission for the Winter Masquerade."

Without glancing at her, he said, "And you've probably already sent word to Lady Madeleine."

She shrugged. "Of course."

"I'm sure her husband is thanking you even now."

Grinning, she added, "The marquess has also promised to finance the entire event, and even mentioned he might attend himself."

Garrett drew in a long breath and turned to face her, arms folded across his chest, his expression skeptical.

"Now I'm *certain* her husband is thanking you," he drawled.

She grew sober as she eyed him candidly. "You haven't asked me what I think about it."

His brows drew together. "What you think about it? I should think you're happy."

She rolled her eyes. "Garrett sometimes you can be such . . . a man."

"Thank you."

She groaned and walked to her bed, the covers already lowered by Jane when she had helped Ivy undress, and sat upon the edge, watching him. "I meant, that I'm very surprised to learn the marquess might appear. It gives credence to the notion that he's more involved in this mess than I first suspected."

He ran his fingers through his hair and sat heavily on the settee, lifting a leg over one arm of the furniture and relaxing against the other. "Ivy, that's pure speculation."

She ignored that. "He suggested holding the masquerade in two weeks."

His brows shot up. "Two weeks? Can you plan a party of that size in such a short time?"

Confidently, she replied, "Of course I can. And really, the sooner the better. It will be the first time in two years everybody in Winter Garden will be inside this house. I think it could be very telling."

"Indeed," he murmured.

She sighed, drawing her legs up and crossing her arms over her knees. "I don't know what else to do, Garrett. We've searched the tunnel system, there have been no more clues left regarding Ian's whereabouts, and I have no idea where the diamonds or Benedict Sharon might be. You don't either, or you'd be gone by now."

He tipped his head to the side a little. "Gone by now? You think I'd pack my bags and leave you if I found the jewels myself?"

She squirmed a little on the bed, then lowered her legs and gazed at him frankly. "Would you?"

He stared at her for a second or two, then grumbled something under his breath and leaned his head back on a small lavender pillow, lifting his arm to rest it across his closed eyes. Aloud, he said, "No, I wouldn't leave you, but then, I shouldn't need to tell you that."

That simplistic answer annoyed her. "Why do you say that?"

He was quiet for a moment, them muttered, "Turn the light out, Ivy."

"Why?"

"I'm tired, that's why."

"I want an answer to my question, first," she insisted stubbornly.

Seconds later, he conceded, "Turn the light out, and I'll give you one."

She hesitated, uncertain of his mood, and his intention. "You'll stay there?"

He chuckled. "Ivy, it's late. Unless ghosts attack in the middle of the night, I'm not moving till morning."

Curiosity overcoming her misgiving, she leaned to her right and extinguished the oil lamp at her side so that all that remained was flickering light from the low-burning fire.

She snuggled down under her blankets and waited for him to begin since she refused to beg, and he probably knew it.

Finally, in a near whisper, he said, "I shouldn't need to tell you because of what happened between us two years ago."

Intrigued, Ivy turned on her side and propped her arm up on her pillow, her cheek in her palm. "I don't understand."

He remained silent for a long moment, then murmured, "I may not remember the details, Ivy, but you do. And I know what I'm like, and what I like in a woman. Tell me how I treated you."

Part of her couldn't believe he asked her that, and the other part remembered that such an intimate question might have come from his lips two years ago, too. She understood his question, his desire to let her find the answer herself, but it also unsettled her to have to be reminded by verbalizing her feelings of *him* during their week together.

Relaxing against her pillow, she stared at the fire in the grate. "You . . . were warm. Kind. Your smile engaged me first, then your good humor."

She paused, and when he said nothing, she continued. "You treated me like a princess, Garrett," she divulged in a low voice. "I liked you at once."

"I remember your voice," he murmured gruffly from

the settee. "I remember you laughing about something I said."

She smiled in the darkness. "What else?"

"You don't want to know."

"Yes, I do," she charged. "What are you afraid to tell me?"

"I remember your breasts—"

"You're right," she cut in, "I don't want to know."

He laughed very softly. "You asked. And I'm the one with memory loss."

Ivy smiled to herself and hugged her pillow. "So you say."

A long silence lingered, the comfort of his presence and the warmth of the fire making her drowsy. "Did you tell my brother about us?"

"No, I'm sure I didn't," he answered without pause.

Her relief was enormous. "Anyone?"

He sighed. "Honestly, Ivy, I don't remember. But I know myself as a gentleman. I wouldn't ruin your reputation like that. Secondly, if I'd asked you to marry me, I'm certain I thought I'd be asking Ian to court you formally when the quest for the jewels was over."

"You—you said you knew the secret of my parentage." With an inner turmoil, she asked, "Weren't you concerned that I was the bastard daughter of Robert Sharon?"

"No," he said at once. "At least, I'm assuming I wasn't concerned then. I'm not now."

"But you're not planning to marry me now."

She made that statement before considering her words, yet once uttered she had no choice but to wait anxiously for him to agree with her. Instead, she heard him turn again on the settee.

"Did I hurt you?" he asked very softly.

The question took her aback. "Did you hurt me?"

"Physically," he clarified. "When I made love to you."

His boldness coupled with such a depth of sincerity, both stunned her intellect and melted her heart. And it didn't take her long to decide he asked because he needed to know.

"No, it didn't hurt, at least not more than I expected. You . . . you were a marvelous lover."

She heard the settee creak again under his weight, and for a second or two, she feared he might be rising to come to her anyway, despite his promise. Then in a gruff, faraway voice, she heard him ask, "Now I'm glad to know I'm the one who seduced you. I clearly knew what I was doing."

She almost giggled. "Garrett, if I am to have only one lover in my life, and I suspect that's true, I'm certainly glad I was seduced by you."

He chuckled softly. "Somehow I *know* that's a compliment coming from you."

"Rest assured, sir, I would never speak of such a thing to anyone else." She paused, then added, "And yes, you may consider it a compliment."

"So tell me how it happened," he murmured.

Snuggling down deeper into the warmth of her blankets, she replied, "How what happened?"

"My incredible seduction of you, Lady Ivy."

If it had been any other time, in any other circumstance or place, she would have been thoroughly embarrassed by such an intimate question. But right now, in a locked room lit by firelight, with Garrett both near at hand and yet at a distance, she felt wonderfully safe. Warm and safe, as she had felt in his arms two years ago.

"You gave me roses," she replied.

After a long pause, he grumbled, "That's it?"

Grinning in the darkness, she said through an exaggerated sigh, "Even if you have no memory of the experience with me, Mr. Burke, you must remember how you've done it before."

"I've never done it before."

She had no idea how to respond to that quick statement. Guardedly, she said, "You've never seduced any woman but me?"

"I have no memory of it," he said matter-of-factly.

"You're a cad," she muttered, fluffing her pillow with a fist.

He chuckled again. "Lady Ivy, you are far too easy to tease."

A long silence lingered, and then she whispered huskily, "That's how you seduced me."

Through a yawn, he asked, "How?"

Closing her eyes to the memory, she confessed, "You charmed me, Garrett, by teasing me. You teased me about seeing into your future, and when I teased you in return by telling you how sad you'd be after I was gone, how alone you'd feel, you moved very close to me and told me you were going to kiss me." She inhaled deeply. "I told you I didn't see any kisses between us in your future, and you said *that* made you sad. And then you kissed me anyway."

"I remember kissing you, Ivy," he said in a gruff, sleepy voice. "Or I should say it's a vague remembrance. I can still see your lips, and if I close my eyes and let the pieces come together on their own, I can remember how it felt."

She had to ask. "How did it feel?"

He waited, as if gathering his thoughts, then replied, "It felt like heaven."

It took a long time for his words to sink in, but she sensed the honesty in them. She swallowed back tears of a lingering happiness coupled with frustration, of sorrow and regret and even a certain peace in knowing she hadn't imagined the emotions she witnessed from him at the time.

"You know I'm going to kiss you again," he whispered.

She didn't say anything to that, though very deep inside she longed for the time, the hour when he would hold her in his arms once more.

"Good night, Garrett," she whispered.

Through a sigh of contentment, he replied, "Good night, sweet Ivy."

Chapter 13

Penelope Bennington-Jones and Mrs. Catherine Mossley had been friends for thirty-seven years. Both now widows, they met for tea at least once a week, sometimes for nothing more than to discuss their good fortune at being rid of the tediousness of taking care of a husband.

Today was different, however. Penelope had important news, and although she preferred not to gossip, she simply couldn't resist. Catherine always listened attentively anyway, and she knew more of the details regarding Penelope's daughter Desdemona's shameful past than anyone. It helped, Penelope supposed, that Catherine wasn't an actual lady by birth, but by marriage, as her late husband had made a fortune in the gas-lighting industry before his untimely demise, leaving his wife comfortably settled for the balance of her life. If only she had been so fortunate. Still, Catherine remained the only friendly person in Winter Garden, and the only lady to graciously offer invitations now that her daughter had disgraced them all. For that reason alone,

Penelope would always count the woman a friend, even if her manners were a trifle inappropriate. As of course they were now.

Sitting across from her in Catherine's small country home, decorated deplorably in bright greens and yellows, and eclectic furniture that didn't at all embrace any style or match anything else in her parlor, she sipped surprisingly good tea and listened as her hostess rambled on about the weather. Or some such nonsense.

After dressing in her best day gown of sunshine yellow silk and donning her most expensive jewelry and fur-lined mantle, Penelope set out for Catherine's home. Since her own manners were impeccable, Penelope hadn't immediately chimed in with her reason for calling today, but allowed her friend to make pleasantries first. Yet the wait to tell all thus far had been grating her nerves. To her good fortune, Catherine brought the subject up first.

"So tell me, Penelope," the corpulent woman fairly demanded as she munched on a watercress sandwich, "what have you heard about the mysterious Lord Rye?"

Penelope took a long sip of her tea, then placed her cup and saucer on the table in front of her. "Actually, I've heard little about him personally, but the woman staying at his house certainly has become the talk of the village."

Catherine's brows rose sharply. "Indeed. I have yet to meet her, but she is rather . . . famous, is she not?"

Hiding her annoyance, Penelope smiled flatly, and replied, "She's a seer, Catherine."

"Yes, but isn't that fascinating?"

One thing that had repeatedly bothered Penelope was Catherine's manner in finding enjoyment in everything, even when there wasn't any to find. Life wasn't about joyful gratification, it was about manners, good breeding, enriching one's interests by meeting people of quality. But then her friend hadn't been raised in the good home she had.

"I suppose," she answered after fluffing her skirts. "I do find it odd that she's also a lady, the sister of the Earl of Stamford."

"Odd? How so?"

She gave an exaggerated sigh. "If you'll remember correctly," she chided with a smile, "the former earl and his wife, Lady Ivy's parents, lived in Winter Garden for a time when she was a child."

Of course such information wasn't exactly odd, or newsworthy, but that was beside the point. Catherine wouldn't think about that anyway.

"I think I recall them now that you mention it," Catherine said, her thick brows pinched in thought. "The earl's wife was lovely."

"Perhaps," she agreed vaguely. "It's interesting, isn't it, that the daughter is back in the house?"

Catherine reached for another sandwich. "I don't know. I suppose." She took a large bite and talked while she chewed. "It doesn't belong to Lord Rothebury anymore so—what's she staying there for anyway?"

This was the opening Penelope had hoped for. Eyes wide with feigned excitement, she lowered her voice to reply, "*Supposedly*, she's been invited by the new owner, the Marquess of Rye, to hunt for ghosts."

Catherine gasped, then reached for her tea to wash down a mouthful of bread. "You think the ghost of Richard is haunting his own home?" she fairly whispered.

Penelope almost rolled her eyes but had the good manners to refrain. "Naturally, I wouldn't know. But since Benedict disappeared while living there, I suppose there's a good chance she's investigating the house for the ghosts of both brothers." She paused for effect, then added in murmur, "Or so that's the story she's giving."

Thankfully, Penelope didn't need to resort to greater clarity as Catherine seemed to grasp her intent. She watched her friend's eyes widen to saucers and her mouth drop open a little as she absorbed the gossip as factual information.

"Well, do tell, Penelope, why else would she be living in such a frightening place?" She lifted the teapot to refill their cups. "Since she's a seer, it makes perfect sense that she'd be hunting for ghosts."

"Indeed, it does, which is why I find it highly suspicious," Penelope agreed at once, her tone conspiratorial.

"Ahhh . . ." Catherine cast her a sideways glance. "You think there's something else, something more involved?"

She lifted her cup and took a sip of hot tea. "Well, there's that architect she's been seen with on occasion."

Catherine sat back, fairly slumping in her chair. "Mr. Burke. Yes, I met him. Handsome man, too," she said, and winked. "My granddaughter Elizabeth has caught his eye, I think."

Penelope ignored her friend's very common disposition and carried on. Some people, even if considered a friend by those of good breeding, never seemed to change. And to think that very ordinary Elizabeth, who lived on the other side of the village with a family as their governess, and found herself nearly on the shelf at twenty-four, would catch the eye of a man like the architect was simply too much to imagine.

Ignoring the comment to get to the reason for her unexpected visit, she replied, "They stopped in to visit with Hermione last week."

Catherine's brows rose in surprise. "Indeed. What happened?"

Penelope skipped over the part about the pendant; she refused to consider the facts behind her family's disgrace as they mattered little now. What was done was done. She'd washed her hands of the shameful offspring, who'd thankfully left town, and now concentrated on finding husbands, if still possible, for Hermione and Viola. It was her only hope for a good future, for them and her. And finally, at the point where she'd all but decided she would die in a poorhouse, her prayers had been answered. At least that was her hope.

"Catherine . . ." she began, lowering her still-full cup to the table with dainty fingers, "have you heard news of the upcoming Winter Masquerade?"

Her friend's mouth dropped open again. "No, I haven't. You mean just like the one at the Rothebury estate?"

She smiled, replying matter-of-factly, "It's the Rye estate now, and yes, Lady Ivy mentioned that the new owner, the Marquess of Rye, is planning on hosting the event once again and will, naturally, invite all good members of society in the area to attend."

Catherine clapped her hands together in her lap. "How marvelous!"

"Indeed it is," she agreed, letting that statement linger before adding proudly, "and Lady Ivy said Hermione, Viola, and I will be extended invitations."

Penelope almost laughed as she watched her friend react in stupefaction. It wasn't every day that she could make Catherine speechless.

Suddenly, the woman shook herself and leaned forward to ask in a whisper, "Do you think it's a good idea for you to accept? You could very well be snubbed, Penelope, and that wouldn't be good for you or your girls."

Penelope wanted to slap her for being so indelicate, and to make certain she didn't act on her feelings, she clutched her hands together in her lap. Of *course* they could be given the cut direct, but it didn't have to be mentioned, and that wasn't the point anyway. What mattered now was having a grand opportunity to bring

Hermione and Viola out, as it were, to let society meet them and note how very gracious and well-mannered they were despite the fact that a sibling of theirs had disgraced the family name. That was two years ago anyway, and the Marquess of Rye surely didn't know a thing about it else they'd not have been invited at all. And if the marquess was a bachelor, all the better. Of course the hope that one of her daughters might catch his eye was a trifle slight, but it didn't hurt to aspire, and plan ahead.

Straightening in her chair, she said brusquely, "We'll all be attending, Catherine. I hope you will as well."

The woman blinked, then nodded. "Certainly, I'll go. I'll chaperone Elizabeth." Frowning a bit, she added soberly, "She simply does not get out enough to meet eligible gentlemen, especially since there hasn't been a masquerade ball in what . . . two years now?"

Penelope held her tongue from a snide retort. Elizabeth wasn't any more of a lady than Catherine was, though to be kind, the girl at least spoke to her own daughters more than anyone in town. Girls needed acquaintances, too, and persons with whom they could take tea and gossip. At least Catherine and Elizabeth had given them that.

"Do you know when the ball is to be held?" the woman asked seconds later.

"Soon," she said, not wanting to admit she had absolutely no idea. "Invitations will be arriving shortly, I expect."

Catherine smiled, eyes twinkling. "I'll have to consider new gowns for both of us . . ."

The night was colder than usual, and it took her longer than expected to reach the dungeon—or at least that's what she chose to call it—to give her guest medicine and let him know about the upcoming party.

She smiled to herself. *Her guest.* What an odd thing to call him, but then she'd always been clever. Just not clever enough to find the fortune in diamonds on her own. And that was the mark of a true lady, she decided—knowing when to be humble. If she had learned nothing in her life, it was how to be humble with her abilities or lack thereof, and of course patient in any life quest.

Quietly, she unlatched the lock and swung the heavy metal door open, allowing stale, odious air to escape a little before she ventured inside and down the short staircase. It had to have been centuries since it had been cleaned, but then she was not a servant and had no intention of taking a broom to any floor.

She carried a small lantern with her and held it up to view her path as she stepped carefully across old, dust-covered stones. If she tripped and injured herself, and God forbid couldn't move, she'd no doubt die for lack of food and water in a place unknown to all but her. The thought made her shudder.

As quick as safety allowed, she walked to the middle of the three chambers. Then, reaching into the pocket of her mantle, she retrieved the long, brass key and stuck it into the lock. As soon as she heard the tumblers move, she pushed the door open, shivering from the scratching of metal on stone and the foul smell within.

He was lying on the threadbare cot, exactly as they'd left him, one hand chained to a thick metal ring attached to the wall. Almost every time he saw her he attempted to pull himself free, but the medicine she gave him kept him too subdued to do much harm or speak very coherently. He tried, and sometimes managed to stand, but she never let too many hours go by without giving him another dose. And there was always the tiny bit she diluted into his cold broth every night that he wasn't aware of, just in case.

Tonight, he was sleeping, a good thing. She would empty his chamber pot into the center of the main room where a drain had been installed for just that purpose. Or so she supposed. It didn't matter. Frankly, it wasn't a job for a lady, but then if she allowed it to accumulate, she'd not be able to stand the smell and take care of him. She needed him alive, at least for now.

As usual, she brought a large pouch filled with a small loaf of bread, jugs of both water and beef broth, and set them on the stand beside his cot, just within his reach. He stirred as he heard her, and so she decided to give him the medicine first, before she cleaned his mess.

Pulling the small bottle and an old wooden spoon from her pocket, she poured the amber liquid to the full amount needed for his large body, then pushed in his cheeks to open his mouth. He fought her at first, as he usually did, but he hadn't the strength to interfere before she clamped his chin shut until he swallowed.

"Good boy," she whispered, replacing the medicine until next time.

That task finished, she dumped the chamber pot and returned it, then glanced over his dazed form to make sure all was well until tomorrow.

"There's going to be a party," she said, lifting the small blanket she'd given him over his body and tucking it under his shoulders. "A masquerade ball, and I'm going to be there to surprise everybody, even your sister. When she gives me the diamonds, dear Ian, I'll let you go to her."

He mumbled something she couldn't understand, and she smiled. "Be hopeful. It won't be long now."

With that, she lifted her lantern and empty pouch, locked the door, and hid the key in her mantle with the medicine. Then, after a quick glance to make sure all was well, she hurried from the dungeon, stopping a moment to gulp the fresh air as she stepped into the black of night.

Chapter 14

The scratching roused him from deep sleep. At first Garrett thought he heard the sound as part of a dream, but it was the subsequent *thump* against her withdrawing room wall that made him come awake with a start.

Ivy had heard it, too, for she was already sitting alert in bed, the covers lowered to her waist. They couldn't have been sleeping long, either, as the fire still burned low in the grate at his side.

Immediately, he was on his feet, his fingers to his mouth to warn her to stay quiet. She nodded, though after a moment of waiting, they heard nothing else.

She crawled out of bed and moved to his side, wrapping her robe more closely around her and tying it at the waist. Then the two of them silently walked into her withdrawing room, he leading the way toward the tunnel entrance.

They stood in front of the panel for two to three minutes, hearing nothing more. He ran his hands through his tousled hair, tempted to enter, but he didn't have a light, or a weapon handy should he need one; he wasn't even wearing his shirt.

Finally, he turned to her. "Go back to bed," he whispered.

She shook her head firmly.

"Now, Ivy."

"Are you going in there?" she mouthed.

He scratched his jaw and glanced back at the wall. "Not unless I hear something else."

Suddenly he glanced around the withdrawing room, then walked back into her bedchamber to retrieve her small vanity chair.

"What are you doing?"

"Shhh . . ."

He carried the chair with one hand, then propped it against the wall entrance to the passageway, nearly shoving it against the paneling. If someone tried to enter, it would fall, alerting them. He stood back to survey it, tested it for sturdiness, then, satisfied it would hold, took her hand to lead her back to the bedroom.

"Go back to bed," he whispered again as he let her go.

"I can't," she replied just as quietly. "I'm too awake now to contemplate sleeping."

He waited for a moment, hands on hips, then said, "Sit with me by the fire."

She didn't hesitate to do as he suggested, walking around the settee and lowering her body onto one end, resting her head against a side pillow. He followed, relaxing as best he could in a space too small for him to begin with.

He watched her by firelight, her long hair braided

down her back, her skin glowing and soft, her gaze troubled as she stared into the grate.

"What are you thinking?" he asked softly.

She shook her head and smiled faintly. "I'm wondering why you're not wearing a shirt. It's positively indecent."

He grinned. "I was hot sleeping next to the fire. And it's not any more indecent than you sitting here next to me in your nightdress and robe."

"I suppose not," she conceded with a smile.

He dropped his voice to a husky whisper. "What are you really thinking, Ivy?"

She looked at him then, her honey brown eyes wide, her features guarded. "I'm scared, Garrett."

"I know."

His heart ached for her at that moment. She looked so small beside him, a woman of inner strength who'd suddenly found herself chased by her own demons, just as his chased him. In that regard, he supposed they had much in common, both uncertain of their futures, both afraid of losing something precious.

"Can I ask you a question?"

"Of course," she said softly.

He drew in a long breath and folded his arms across his bare chest. "When I asked you to marry me before, two years ago, what was your answer?"

For a second or two she seemed perplexed, then her lips curled up into a wry smile. "I'm beginning to think your memory loss is also convenient for me."

He cocked his head a little. "If you don't reply to that

simple question, darling Ivy, I'll be forced to ask you something more intimate."

"More intimate?"

He lifted a shoulder negligibly. "About the passion we shared."

She shot him a sideways glance through her lashes. "Well, since I wouldn't want to force you to mention something indelicate, the answer is I didn't."

"You didn't what?"

She smiled at him crookedly. "I didn't answer you."

He hadn't expected that response at all, but he had to admit it was brilliant, whether she toyed with him or it truly happened that way.

He grinned wickedly. "My goodness, but my pride must have been severely damaged, Lady Ivy."

"I imagine so," she replied through a much-exaggerated sigh.

She scooted down a bit more into the pillows on the settee so that she faced him squarely, her legs wrapped under her nightgown and robe, her hands folded across her belly. He followed suit, shifting so that his bare back rested against a pillow, his legs stretched out on the floor, one ankle crossed over the other.

"I'll be honest with you," she said after a moment. "The one thing I remember most is how very much I enjoyed you, Garrett. You never failed to make me laugh, make me comfortable." Her smile faded a little as she added, "I'll always miss that."

He felt a tightening in his chest and suddenly the desire to make love to her now gripped him hard, not only for the physical satisfaction he so desperately craved but for the closeness he suspected he'd never found with anyone but her.

"I think I've missed you every day," he whispered.

That admission distressed her a little. He watched her lashes flicker and her brow gently crease before she turned her attention once more to the fire.

They sat together in silence for a long moment. Then finally he asked, "Why didn't you answer me when I proposed?"

Without hesitation, or a glance at his face, she wistfully replied, "You told me not to, until you returned with the diamonds."

He felt as if she'd struck him, sickened by the notion that a future together had been predicated on finding his precious jewels. No wonder she'd hated him for so long. He'd seduced her, kept things from her, denied her, and because of his lack of knowledge about the details of that night, never told her the truth of his identity. Logically, he probably thought to have her wait to respond to a marriage proposal because she might have turned him down knowing her brother would want to choose someone more appropriate for her title. He couldn't tell her who he was until after the arrest of Benedict Sharon.

But had he loved her? The notion that he might have confessed to loving her, then walked away and later accused her of being part of the great scheme to steal the Martello diamonds, left him numb. And he couldn't ask her now. Regardless of how she might answer, he wouldn't know the truth because her self-preservation might play a role in her decision to lie or evade the question altogether.

Garrett decided at that moment that not only did he admire and respect her, he believed her. After all that had happened between them this last month in Winter Garden, he just could not reconcile the Ivy he'd come to know all over again with a scheming seductress he had envisioned for two long years. He didn't possess any extraordinary gift, but he sensed the goodness in her, and it made him realize exactly why he had gone mad for her so quickly in London. And why he'd never been able to forget her completely.

"Ivy," he admitted at last, "if you never believe another word I say, believe this: I would give all of my wealth, all that I am as a man, to go back to the night I made you mine, to sear it forever in my memory." He swallowed hard. Then lowering his voice to a husky whisper of loneliness, he revealed, "You are the greatest treasure I've ever lost."

He had no idea what to expect from her after such a disclosure, and for seconds he didn't think he could breathe. When at last she turned her head to gaze at him once more, he felt an outpouring of feelings that matched his own, of desire and apprehension, sadness and longing. For a timeless moment she just looked into his eyes, her body still, the silence deafening.

And then, very slowly, she sat up, and after only the slightest hesitation, placed her palm on his cheek.

Bewildered by the action, he remained perfectly motionless, uncertain if she expected him to touch her in return, afraid of making a mistake that would cost him everything he suddenly valued above all else.

"Ivy—"

"Shhh . . ."

His breath began to quicken as she very gradually started tracing his lips with her thumb, studying them intently, as if she were the one trying to remember every minute detail. She explored the lines on his face, her fingertips skimming his cheek and jaw, her knuckles brushing the hair from his forehead. Finally, she locked her gaze with his, and whispered, "I want to give you back the memory."

Garrett felt his chest tighten, his throat constrict with emotions he couldn't begin to understand. He'd never expected this reaction from her, not now, when so much else was at stake. For a second he considered holding back—until she began to draw her fingers down his neck as her free hand moved to untie the sash at her waist. That's when he knew he was lost.

Holding her gaze, he clasped his large palm around her fingers at his neck and drew them to his mouth, grazing his lips against the pads, then kissing her palm lightly. Slowly, he raised himself to sit to they faced each other, their sides to the lingering fire.

She closed her eyes, and he cupped her face, then leaned in to kiss her lashes, her brow, her cheeks, and finally her lips. He heard her sigh at the contact, and he took his time, reveling in the moment to make it last, wanting her to know how he valued the gift she was giving him.

As she lifted her hands to his shoulders, he reached behind her neck and pulled her long braid forward, loosening the ribbon at the tip and gently pulling her hair free with his fingers. That done, he began to deepen the kiss, caressing her mouth with his own, flicking his tongue across her top lip, then exploring within.

She leaned closer, her breath coming faster, mingling with his. He placed a palm on the back of her head, the other at her neck as he skimmed the soft, warm skin with his fingertips. She did the same, growing bolder with her touch as she pushed her fingers up into his hair to hold him.

He ached to move faster, his desire raging of a sudden, but for him, for now, this would remain his first time with Ivy, and he intended to lengthen each second for memory.

He felt her tongue tease his as her actions grew bolder, as her breathing quickened to match his own, as she pulled him tighter against her. He lowered his hand and pushed his fingers under her robe, sliding it smoothly off her shoulders in an action she didn't seem to notice.

With one hand at the back of her head to hold her steady, he swiftly untied her nightgown at the neck, pulling the thin strings out, then placing his fingers on her collarbone, caressing her warm skin in small circles until he pulled one sleeve from her shoulder.

And then he released her mouth and began a long trail of tiny kisses along the line of her jaw, down her neck to the base of her throat. She responded in kind, leaning her head back to give him access to her throat, her fingers threaded through his hair as she clutched him.

Garrett felt his heart pounding hard in his chest, heard the rushing of blood through his veins, entranced by her sudden, aching show of desire as she whimpered and attempted to pull his head lower.

He gave as she begged, feeling a wondrous tightening within as he lowered his hand, turned it, and skimmed her breast with his knuckles, back and forth across her nipple, feeling it harden at once beneath the soft cotton.

She fell back against the pillows, and he followed, leaning over her as he gently kissed her neck and throat, finally placing his large palm over her breast and caressing. And then, as he caught her mouth with his once more, moving deeper, growing more forceful, he pushed his hand inside her nightgown to touch the skin he craved.

Her nipple felt warm, hard, and as he gently squeezed it, she moaned and arched her back, begging with her body for more.

With a quickness that defied the action, Garrett released her and knelt beside her, allowing her to stretch out on the settee, gazing down to her beautiful face, her half-closed eyes glazed with passion, her silky hair spread out across the pillow.

He touched her lips with his fingers, and she kissed them, reaching for his chest to caress him lightly with her own.

"Take me to bed, Garrett," she ordered in a fast breath of longing.

He inhaled deeply to calm the building passion inside him. "Not yet. I can see you better by the fire."

She smiled a little. He lowered his hand and placed it on her ankle, then slowly he began to draw his fingers up her leg. She squirmed as he pushed her nightgown upward, ever farther, until his fingers reached her inner thigh.

He paused to stroke her there with delicate movements, and she opened her knees a bit to give him access to the most intimate part of her. But he waited, watching her, knowing he'd once seen her face just like this, her lips moist from his kiss, her skin flushed with a building tension, her gaze melding with his, pleading with him silently to give her the release she craved.

He smiled, and whispered, "You need this as much as I do."

She nodded minutely, then lifted her hips to urge him forward. He pulled his fingers back down a little, teasing her to distraction. She whimpered in frustration, and he quickly raised the bottom of her nightdress and pushed it up nearly to the apex of her thighs.

Leaning over, he kissed her mouth quickly, then lowered his head to her neck and chest, leaving tiny pecks of pleasure, one hand threaded through her hair, the other resting on the side of her hip. And just as he placed his lips on the tender skin above her breasts and laid his cheek between them, he raised his hand to cup the mound of curls at the center of her.

He moaned as she gasped from the contact, staying perfectly still, his eyes closing as he relished the moment, the feel of her femininity and the sound of her quick-beating heart. For seconds he did nothing, and then very, very slowly, he pressed a finger up into her folds to find the sweet nub of her desire, wet and ready for him.

Garrett drew a shaky breath as he stroked her once, twice, listening to her whimper of pleasure as she clutched his head to her chest. She coated his finger, enveloping him within her soft, heated flesh, and in that instant a powerfully sweet image struck him hard—of her scent, her feel, the sound she made as she climaxed in his arms two years ago.

The slight memory had returned with such force that his breath caught in his chest, and he choked back a roar of pure joy.

In one swift action, he grabbed her nightgown with both hands and pulled it up over her body. She raised her head to help him, and in seconds she lay nude before him.

He faltered as he gazed down upon her by firelight, giving himself a new impression of her radiance. And then he dropped his mouth to hers once more and gave in to the sensual pleasure that threatened to undo him.

Then he closed his mouth over her breast and he teased it gently, sucking her nipple and kissing it, skimming it with his lips.

A soft moan escaped her as he pushed her thighs apart with his fingers, then touched her intimately once more, stroking her softly, readying her. When he moved his head lower, the heat between them building, the tiny sounds from her throat nearly caused him to lose himself too soon.

He skimmed her belly with his lips, then lowered himself to the center of her femininity, inhaling deeply the scent of absolute beauty. He stroked her breasts with the fingers of one hand, the nub of her cleft with the other, kissing her thighs, her small mound of curls.

She gave herself over to the pleasure, eyes squeezed shut, her hips and legs moving involuntarily as he brought her nearer to the peak of release.

Her slick wetness drove him wild, her scent to madness, as her soft moans begged for her fulfillment.

At last he pulled his hand from her breast and reached for the buttons of his trousers, loosening them swiftly and removing them in one smooth action.

Lifting his body, he placed his knee between her legs, moved his hands to the sides of her hips, and lowered his mouth to the center of her desire.

She sucked in a breath through her teeth as he opened her cleft and began to stroke her with his tongue.

She gasped, her head falling back as she threaded her fingers through his hair and clutched him against her.

Immediately, he found his rhythm, and she followed the movement, pressing into him with each stroke of pleasure he gave. He marveled at her sweet taste of desire for him, at the depth of her longing, and within seconds he knew she was nearing her crest.

She whimpered softly, her breath coming fast and hard, and just as she whispered his name at the peak of abandonment, he pressed a finger inside of her to feel what she felt, to know the extent of her pleasure. And at that moment she came.

She arched her back and pushed into him, a long, soft moan escaping her throat, her muscles within pulsing with their own rhythm of release as she gave in to his demand. She held him tightly as he continued his glorious assault, second by second, until she relaxed and shuddered beneath him.

Before she returned to sanity, could say or do anything, he raised himself over her and kissed her hard on the mouth as he lifted her into his arms and carried her to the bed.

She stretched out willingly across the sheets and within seconds he hovered over her, his fingers once again between her legs, caressing her, needing her, and unable to wait much longer to discover the riches she offered.

Quickly, he lifted one of her knees with one arm, holding himself above her with the other hand flat on the bed. Then, to his surprise she reached for him, lightly grasping his erection, gliding her thumb through the beading moisture at the tip and circling it slowly.

He squeezed his eyes shut to stay his release from her simple touch, attempting to draw a full breath, basking in the feel of her fingers on his most sensitive part. This reality was better than his dreams, than his fantasies of her, as she gave him all of herself without restraint or hesitation. For seconds he stilled his body, prolonging the wait, wanting to imagine for a final time what she might have felt like as he'd entered her two years ago, knowing without any doubt that this time he would savor the gift.

"Garrett . . ."

He raised his lashes to look down at her face, clenching his jaw as he reeled from an awareness that passed between them. And then, with her sweet guidance, he placed himself at the center of her, caressing her wet cleft with the tip of him until at last he felt himself slip inside her moist heat.

She stiffened a little from the tightness, and he paused, giving her a few seconds to adjust before he began to glide slowly, deeply inside of her. She kept her gaze locked with his, licking her lips as she pressed her palms to his chest, beckoning him with a gentle lift of her hips until she encased him completely.

He stilled as he came to rest deeply within her, forcing himself to control his breathing, his pounding heart, until he was absolutely ready to surrender. She reached up and touched his face, and with that he lowered his mouth to hers, kissing her fully, passionately, his tongue gliding across her lips, then delving inside in search of hers.

She began to move beneath him, and he lost his resolve. He lowered his head to her breast, running his tongue across her nipple until it hardened. Immediately, she moaned, and he took it into his mouth as he started to gently circle his hips against hers, finding a rhythm that would bring her to orgasm once more.

It didn't take her long. She squirmed beneath him as he lightly sucked the taut peak, her breath quickening, body arching into his. Then he lifted himself just enough to reach down and press his fingers between them, stroking her slowly at first, then faster, enticing her along.

He gritted his teeth, watching her from above. She kept her pleading gaze locked with his, whimpering softly, her palms on his shoulders, moving her bare leg up and down along his with each smooth thrust of his hips.

"Please—"

And then her eyes widened, and she ground her nails into his skin.

"Oh, God, Ivy, yes," he coaxed her through a rasp. "Let me feel you—"

She cried out, gripping his arms, her hips rocking into his of their own accord. He moved faster, feeling each wave that coursed through her, each pulse of her pleasure, and in seconds he reached the brink of insanity.

Groaning low in his chest he came hard, spilling himself deeply inside of her in an explosion of ecstasy that surpassed its promise, clinging to each surge of satisfaction in an effort to make the oneness last, to capture the passion forever.

She held him close and he wrapped his arms around her as he stilled the movements of his body, as his breathing slowed, and he relaxed against her at last. Then without words between them, he rolled onto his back and drew her into him, pulling the sheets and quilt over them both as they snuggled down into the pillows.

She nestled her head beneath his chin, curling one leg over his hip as he stroked her hair with gentle fingertips and rested his lips on her forehead.

She had given him more than he could have imagined, more than a repeat of a memory. She had given him back his life.

Chapter 15

Lady Margaret Dartmouth had been in love with Benedict Sharon since her coming out three summers ago. They'd met at a cotillion at her home in Brighton, and the moment she accepted his offer to dance, her heart had been lost.

A ruggedly handsome man with sandy hair and sharp features, his dark eyes had drawn her to him upon first notice, and he had been just as taken with her. She was a lady of the finest kind, properly bred, lovely in appearance, discreet when she should be, pleasant to every acquaintance, and yet she had a free spirit and a penchant for getting into trouble that most gentlemen found annoying in a gently bred lady. Not so with Benedict. His troubled youth drew him to her, leading him to frequently say that in her he'd found freedom—freedom to relax and be adventurous, and freedom to enjoy himself with a woman.

He'd asked her to marry him not two months after their initial dance, and she had accepted, though knowing her parents would be more than a trifle irritated that she would choose the second son of a baron over

Paul Garrett Faringdon-Burke, Lord Rye, a man older
than Benedict by several years, who would one day in-
herit a far better title, she and Benedict had kept their
love affair secret from everybody. She knew in the end
her parents would relent because as far as they were
concerned, as the youngest daughter of four, she usually got what she wanted. And more than anything on
earth, she had wanted Benedict Sharon.

Yet that was only weeks before his older brother
Richard, Baron Rothebury, had been arrested and
charged with opium smuggling. Her parents were
horrified, as were all the gentry, by the scandal. And it
left her with nothing but the shock of knowing the one
man she loved most in the world had now been tainted
by society and would never be able to formally ask for
her hand.

She'd been devastated, all but deciding to remain a
spinster, or perhaps run away with Benedict, if only she
could see him one more time, if only he'd ask. And then
a miracle happened. Soon after the scandal broke, he
appeared at her side after church, secretly passing her
a note. Just before dawn the next day, she sneaked out
her bedroom window and met him in the garden. Not
only did he tell her he loved her still, he asked her to
marry him regardless of the scandal, confessing a plan
that, although dangerous in many respects, if carefully
accomplished, would forever seal their fates, allowing
them to be together, and in the process providing them
with a fortune. For her part, all she had to do was accept
Lord Rye's proposal; Benedict would do the rest.

It took her all of ten minutes to decide. The hardest part, admittedly, was pretending to be happily betrothed to Paul, a rather quiet man not particularly amused by her audacious ways. Oh, she found him marvelously handsome, but rather dull, and, frankly, they had little of interest to discuss between them. Margaret had learned early on that his mother had coerced him into asking for her hand, out of duty, she supposed, but since he spent much of his time in London, she didn't have to see or converse with him frequently. All the better, as she'd needed to plan for the start of a fabulous life in southern France with Benedict, just as Paul assumed she was planning for their very dull future and tedious wedding back in Brighton.

Yet, in the end, everything went wrong.

The night of their betrothal party had been the end of happiness for her. Benedict's great plan to steal the Martello tiara had succeeded because she had worn it, even against Paul's wishes, simply by charming his mother into allowing it. But when Ian Wentworth, the Earl of Stamford, had arrived and questioned her even as he attempted to captivate her with his magnificent charm and perfectly handsome face, she knew there was more involved than her simply stealing the diamonds for Benedict. Stamford seemed to be wherever she was, watching her from a distance as if she were the only woman at the ball. And it took her no time at all to realize that he couldn't have cared any less about her, he wanted the diamond tiara for himself.

Ian Wentworth ruined her life that night. She had been able to drop the tiara down into Benedict's hands from an upstairs window before dawn, but with the Earl of Stamford keeping such a close eye on her, he'd made her own escape impossible. She had no choice but to remain in the house for the night, under heavy chaperone, and hope Benedict would send word for her the following morning.

Two days later, he sent a note, and she met with him secretly. He would attempt to remove the diamonds and sell them separately, then meet with Paul in London to exchange what was left of the tiara, the rubies and gold, for a price. And he was certain Paul would meet him because he'd sent word and made the arrangements pretending to be Ian. But Benedict had gotten greedy, deciding to attack Paul and take whatever money he had on his person that night. And then he had promised her, with a love she understood to the depth of her soul, that once he sold the diamonds he would come for her, and until that time she would carry on with the lie that was her betrothal to the Marquess of Rye.

She never heard from Benedict again.

For a time she tried to assess her love affair with Benedict, wondering if she had misjudged him, if he had used her all along to retrieve his diamonds. But in the end, she rejected that notion. Their love had been real, and he had asked her to marry him before his brother's downfall, before he needed her support to secure their future by helping him steal the Martello treasure.

It was almost two years later when she learned that Benedict had disappeared after returning to Winter Garden. He'd never told her of his need to return to the town of his birth, and she only learned about it after discovering that Paul had purchased the Rothebury winter estate through Benedict's solicitor in London. In the end, she decided Benedict was planning to leave for the Continent with her after securing funds by selling everything. But then, as if overnight, he was just . . . gone.

Margaret held back unshed tears as she thought about her plan. Fortunately for her, she had family in Winter Garden. Distant family, true, but even so, her great-aunt, Lady Isadora Birmingham, had been happy to receive her. And given Aunt Isadora's fading memory, she thought it a splendid idea to keep her niece's visit a secret so she could surprise everybody at the masquerade ball.

The diamonds—and the secret to Benedict's disappearance—were in the house. She knew it, which was the only reason Paul and Ian's sister were here, the only reason Paul would have purchased the Rothebury estate. Since Benedict had told her about every secret the house possessed, she probably knew more than they did. And if luck smiled upon her, she would finally learn the truth.

He'd grown used to the darkness and the cold, even the smell, but he could never get used to being chained like an animal. And yet he was drugged so much of the time, he had no idea what day or even what year it was anymore, or even how long he'd been living in hell.

The woman who attended to him every day had just left, dropping his bread and broth on the table and forcing the laudanum down his throat. He tried to fight her, but had grown so weak with the passing of days that his mind had become numb. He didn't think he knew her personally, and although he could never see her fully because of the cloak she wore in candlelight, something about her seemed vaguely familiar, like someone he might have met years ago, another lifetime. She said very little, and she wasted no time in completing her tasks each day. He wished he could kill her, but even if he could gather the physical strength, doing so would likely leave him to starve to death, chained to a wall. The only thing that seemed to revive him was her arrival each day to bring him food and water, which told him only that she kept him alive for a reason.

Ian shivered and tried to sit up, but his head remained foggy and his body ached from weeks of being stranded on a tiny cot. At least it felt like weeks. His last remembrance was discovering Benedict Sharon unconscious on the floor in his home—and then he found himself here. Wherever here was.

Moving very slowly, he took the jug of broth and gingerly lifted it to his mouth, afraid the hot brew would burn him if he swallowed too fast. But as he tasted it he realized it was icy cold, perhaps having been sitting on the small table chilling for hours. Again, as it was yesterday, although it seemed like only minutes ago, he really had no idea when she had left it.

He drank it quickly, as he always did, ignoring its bitter flavor and heavy spices. But he left the bread to savor, knowing she might not return for hours, even days if something changed in her routine. At least he didn't have to fight the rats for it. Wherever she kept him, he was locked in where nothing entered and not even sound could escape.

He started feeling tired again, his head aching. He lay back on the cot and tried to cover himself with the small blanket, his mind once again growing hazy, his thoughts only of Ivy, the one person he trusted. They had a special connection, and if anyone could save him, she could.

He knew his capture had to do with diamonds. The woman had mentioned them, though he couldn't quite remember why diamonds were important. And she'd said something about a masquerade ball, where he would see his sister. But he wasn't dressed for a ball . . .

In his dreams he called to her, begging her to help him, find him. As he did again now. As blackness enveloped him once more.

Chapter 16

Ivy was growing desperate—desperate for news of her brother, desperate for the ball to begin only two hours from now, and most of all, desperate for answers, not only from the house and its mysteries, but from Garrett.

She'd given in to the passion, her need to be with him, and she had no regrets—at least not of any serious nature. She'd been his lover for nearly two weeks, and although they'd been careful, she'd begun to grow rather worried that if they continued as they were, he would leave her with his child. He hadn't mentioned marriage to her again, and she hadn't approached the subject because she simply wouldn't know what to say, especially with so much still at stake in Winter Garden. For his part, Garrett seemed to be waiting, and in that she sensed his reluctance to discuss anything but finding the cause of Benedict Sharon's disappearance. He seemed on edge, telling her all would be revealed on the night of the ball. How he knew that, exactly, she couldn't guess, but she knew he continued to withhold information from her, and that troubled her.

It had annoyed her a little that Garrett wouldn't let her go to authorities with the lock of hair she'd found, but then she knew it wasn't much of a clue of any wrongdoing. She really had no proof that Ian was in danger except dreams and feelings, both of which tended to be ignored by practical men. In the end, she decided that abiding by Garrett's decision to wait for the ball might be the only thing she could do for a time.

Ivy stared at her reflection in the mirror. She'd bathed early, then sat at her vanity table as Jane curled her hair with a hot iron, wound a string of pearls through it, and pinned it loosely to her head. When Jane left to press Ivy's gown below stairs, Ivy donned her corset and stockings, then wrapped herself in her robe to await her return.

She was ready for tonight. The marquess had given her and Lady Madeleine full control of the planning and a large sum to purchase the best of everything. Even now the twelve-piece orchestra they'd hired from London would be arriving to take their places, and by eight o'clock tonight, the finest food would be served, and champagne of the highest quality would be overflowing. Thankfully, the marquess had sent additional staff from his estate in Rye, and they had been here all week preparing for what would no doubt be the grandest party Winter Garden had seen in years.

And yet she felt anxious, not certain why she should think the events of this night would tell her anything about Ian, the diamonds, or the missing Benedict Sharon. What she could be sure of, however, was that the entire village was abuzz, and everyone who was anybody would be in attendance, if for no other reason than to meet the mysterious marquess, the new owner of the estate, who, it was rumored, would make a grand appearance of his own.

She hadn't spoken to Garrett since he left her in bed this morning, and she wasn't expecting to see him again until he arrived for the ball. And just that notion alone left her feeling a bit uneasy. She wanted him to escort her, and yet she knew that couldn't happen without speculation of a dangerous kind. But she would dance with him, and later, hopefully, make love to him once again. She couldn't think about a future beyond tomorrow.

Ivy sighed and rose from her vanity table, and just as she turned, she heard him enter into the withdrawing room from the passageway. She quickly checked to make certain the sash on her robe remained closed, almost smiling at the ridiculousness of it.

"Lady Ivy," he drawled as he stepped into her bedroom and leaned his shoulder against the doorframe, his arms folded over his chest.

"Mr. Burke," she returned with a gentle nod. "Why are you here?"

He raised a brow. "You're not happy to see me?"

With a wry lift of her lips, she countered, "I'm always happy to see you, but that didn't answer my question. And you can't stay. Jane will be back shortly with my gown."

"I hope you locked the door," he said, amused.

"I always lock the door." She began to saunter toward him. "One never knows when a ghost of one's past might appear."

"Indeed." He straightened when she neared him, his gaze traveling over her curves, hidden only barely beneath soft silk. "Then perhaps I should get to the point of my visit."

"Perhaps you should," she agreed.

"I have something for you," he disclosed, his voice lowered. "A gift."

That certainly surprised her. "A gift? Why?"

He grinned, but instead of answering, he moved closer to grab the sash at her waist and yank her against him. "It's in my trouser pocket, Lady Ivy."

"You're despicable," she whispered, dragging her finger down the front of his shirt. "I can't imagine what kind of gift a despicable man like you would have for a lady like me that would fit inside a trouser pocket."

"Perhaps you should reach in and find out," he suggested, pulling very, very slowly at her sash.

With a quick glance to his face through her lashes, she did as he asked, slipping three fingers inside, taking her time in an effort to drive him crazy. She felt velvet almost at once, and her heart began to race.

With a delicate grip, she pulled the small, black pouch from his pocket and held it in front of them.

"I couldn't possibly accept this, sir," she teased with a half smile.

He dropped a soft kiss to her lips and whispered against them, "You don't even know what it is."

She paused when his mouth lingered on hers, and he pulled back a little. "No more kissing until you open it."

"You certainly are demanding," she said through a sigh, noting how he'd expertly untied the sash at her waist without her complete awareness. She ignored his overture and nimbly untied her gift to peer inside the velvet pouch.

Teardrop-shaped earrings, made of shimmering, brilliant emeralds, took her breath away.

"Garrett . . ."

"Wear them tonight," he insisted quietly.

Dazed, she looked up. He met her gaze, his eyes smoldering with heat and anticipation, and the satisfaction of triumph.

"They're magnificent," she whispered. "Beautiful."

"Made for a magnificent, beautiful woman." He smiled faintly. "You deserve more than I could ever give you, Ivy. This is only the beginning."

The complex emotions stirring within her that moment became nearly overwhelming. "Garrett, I don't think—"

He cut her off with a finger to her lips. "Don't worry. I stole them."

She fairly giggled. Then in one swift movement, she wrapped her arms around his neck and hugged him close. "You're very fortunate they match my gown."

He dropped little kisses on her neck. "You're wearing green?"

"White," she murmured, leaning her head back slightly to give him better access. "I didn't know what kind of jewels you'd be giving me, so I chose to wear something in a rather neutral shade. I wouldn't want you to think you'd blundered."

He chuckled, his mouth at the base of her throat. "That was very thoughtful, Lady Ivy."

"I always try to be thoughtful," she purred.

He inhaled deeply. "God, you smell good."

She ran her fingers through his hair. "It's the very ordinary scent of lilac bath soap."

"It smells like you," he breathed into her ear.

She shivered, noting with a tingle of gratification that he'd grown hard against her belly.

"You can't stay," she whispered, pulling back a little to look into his eyes. "Jane will be here soon with my neutral-colored ball gown."

He grinned devilishly, his gaze hot with desire. "I want you first."

"You can't have me," she teased wistfully. "My hair is already dressed and lying in bed would ruin—"

He cut her off by wrapping his arms around her waist and lifting her a foot off the floor.

"Let me show you how to make love without touching a curl," he said softly against her mouth.

"Impossible," she whispered.

Without reply, he began walking toward the settee, carrying her as he took her mouth in a slow, lingering kiss, caressing her lips with a masterful touch that weakened her resolve.

He sat on the soft cushion, pulling her along with expertise as she climbed on top of him.

"How did you learn to make love sitting on a settee?" she asked in a whisper against him.

"I'm a man . . ."

Curious, she pulled back to look at him. "What does that mean?"

He grinned wryly. "We know these things at birth."

She ran her fingers through his hair, smiling. "You have an endless supply of answers at the ready, don't you?"

"Of course. And again, having answers at the ready for our ladies is instinctively male," he drawled, stroking her back over the smoothness of her silk robe and stays. "I have no other explanation."

She sighed. "Garrett, I adore you."

His eyes lit up a fraction. "Not half as much as I adore you, Lady Ivy."

Her smile faded as she brought her fingers to his lips. He kissed the pads of them, one by one, his gaze of simmering desire never wavering from hers.

And then, with expert hands, he placed his palms on her chest and pushed them into her silk wrap, lowering it over her shoulders.

He sucked in a breath when he saw her corset, her breasts lifted high, her nipples already roused into peaks.

"Stand up," he said thickly.

Silently, she did as directed, understanding the growing heat in his eyes, the need to look at her, and suddenly wanting to taunt him with a sensuality she knew would please him to distraction.

He spread his knees a little as she stood between them. Then with care, very gradually, she pulled her arms from her robe and dropped it to the rug at her feet.

Through a long exhale, he leaned his head back to rest on the settee, his arms to his sides as he stared at her.

"You're absolutely breathtaking," he said in a gruff whisper, his voice filled with wonder.

Her pulse began to race from his words, the admiration he gave her. She'd chosen her undergarments because they complimented her gown, but suddenly she couldn't have been more thankful that she'd picked a white silk corset made to outline each curve, cut at the hips to connect to her stockings but leaving her bare at the juncture of her thighs.

For a moment he took in all of her appearance, from the top of her well-dressed head of hair to her silk-covered knees where they disappeared behind the cushion. Then his gaze found hers once more as he reached forward and placed his fingers very gingerly on the soft mound of curls between her legs.

She closed her eyes to the feel, her entire body growing weak as he began to stroke her, very slowly, expertly building the passion within her.

"Jane will be here soon," she repeated in a husky murmur.

"Jane can wait at the door and fluff your skirts," he replied, his tone now thick with lust.

She smiled to herself as he began to probe deeper with each slip of his finger, coaxing her along. His breathing had quickened to match hers, and when she softly whimpered, he pressed deeper still, her slick moisture coating his fingers, letting him know how he tantalized her.

"You're making me tingle inside," she whispered, leaning over to grasp his shoulders before she faltered.

After seconds of silence, he replied, "I want you to need me."

She raised her lashes to look into his eyes, witnessing the hunger inside of him, the yearning, the hope.

Without reservation, she revealed, "I need you, Garrett. I always have . . ."

She felt the slightest pause in his touch as her words sank in. And then his lids narrowed and he wrapped his free hand around her neck, pulling her mouth to his.

He kissed her with a longing she'd never felt from him before, or perhaps she only sensed it as his tongue teased her lips apart and plunged deeply within, searching, invading. And she gave as he asked, kissing him back in total abandonment, letting her knees relax against the edge of the settee.

Ivy felt so alive suddenly, needing him with desperation. Bracing herself with her legs, without consideration, she dropped her hands to his trousers and began fumbling with the buttons. He immediately drew his hand from her neck to help her, then swiftly lowered his clothing over his hips.

He gave a deep, throaty moan when she touched

him, skimming her fingertips along the length of his hard flesh. And as she lightly grasped him and grazed the tip of his erection with her thumb, he slipped a finger up inside of her.

Whimpering, she began to stroke him, matching his rhythm, her mouth clinging to his as their hot breaths mingled. And then suddenly he released her, grabbing her around the knees and pulling her toward him, until her legs straddled his body, his lips setting her skin on fire as he left a trail of fine kisses along her throat. Then he guided her down on top of him, and she nestled into his hardness, smothering his erection with her cleft.

She placed her palms on his cheeks as his found her breasts, caressing them through soft silk, skimming his nails back and forth across her nipples.

Moaning softly, she instinctively began to move her body as he kissed her throat and jaw, lowering his lips to her chest and shoulders when she tipped her head back to relish the pleasure.

She found her rhythm almost at once, circling her hips slowly at first, then picking up the pace as the pleasure began to build.

"I need to be inside you, sweetheart," he said through a tight rasp.

As reluctant as she was to still the movement, she lifted her hips just enough for him to reach for his erection and direct it to the center of her, the tip of him stroking her cleft, the nub of her desire until she gasped. With a groan of satisfaction from deep in his chest, he began to slide into her, gradually filling her, and she welcomed the feel of the length of him with an indescribable exhilaration as she finally came to rest against his body.

He placed his cheek between her silk-covered breasts, breathing deeply, seeming to savor the oneness of the moment as she did. And then he took her nipple into his mouth, lightly nipping it with his teeth, rubbing it with his lips, and the feel of teasing her through silk sent a fresh rush of delicious heat through her body.

She began to move once more, slowly at first, finding a pace that he soon began to match.

He leaned his head back again, his eyes closed, his jaw tight, his hands on her breasts, and she pushed her fingers through his thick, dark hair, watching him find his pleasure in her.

He teased her nipples with his fingertips, making her gasp, whimper, her breath quicken. Suddenly he dropped a thumb to the center of her and began to stroke her in small circles, moving faster with each pulse of her hips, taking her at once to the peak of satisfaction.

"Oh, yes, Ivy," he whispered, opening his eyes to meet her gaze. "Let me feel you come. Let me feel you . . ."

She rocked into him hard, nearing her crest, amazed at his beauty, captivated by his masculine form—and that he belonged to her.

"Oh, God, Garrett . . ."

He rubbed her faster. "Oh, yes, sweetheart. Take me with you . . ."

And then she was there.

Her release from the torment shattered her with exquisite pleasure. She gasped with a soft cry from deep in her throat, arching her back, feeling each small tremor that encased him, stroking him over and over as she rocked her body into his, as her wetness coated him from within, as she brought him with her to the brink.

It happened almost at once.

"Ivy—"

He grunted and squeezed his eyes shut, taking control as he wrapped his arms around her tightly and drove into her hard, twice, three times, his body tense, muscles rigid. And then he groaned low in his throat with one final deep thrust, finding his release as he left his seed deeply inside of her.

He shuddered against her, and she cradled his head to her chest, holding him close as he finally stilled his body beneath hers, as their breathing slowed, and her pulse returned to normal.

They held each other for a few long moments, until finally she kissed the top of his head and lifted her body off his.

He wiped a palm down his face and gazed at her, a playful, lingering smile curving his mouth.

"Not a curl astray, my lady," he drawled.

She reached for her robe at her feet. "You obviously have talent, sir. Or experience."

He inhaled a full breath as he reached down for his trousers, then stood beside her to dress. "I'm a man, Ivy."

She glanced up to his face to see him grinning beautifully at her.

She scoffed, tying the sash at her waist. "Meaning making love without mussing a lady's hair is given to a man by birthright?"

He grabbed her at the shoulders and yanked her against him. "Precisely," he whispered, his lips teasing hers. "But the truth you should know, my darling, is that you are the only woman who has ever held my heart in her hands."

She grinned against his mouth and wrapped her arms around his neck. "Then I'll try very hard not to drop you . . ."

"Ever?" he breathed, skimming her lips back and forth with his own.

She shrugged negligibly. "Perhaps."

"That's an awfully vague answer."

"But it's an answer," she whispered.

He growled softly and lowered his mouth to her neck. She tilted her head back to give him access.

"Answer one more question for me, Ivy," he murmured, drawing a hand down to her bottom and pulling her close. "Truthfully."

"Mmmm . . . If I can . . ."

"What were you going to say to me when I returned to you that night two years ago?"

Her heart stilled, the emotions of their lovemaking still forefront in her thoughts as she considered the depth of what he asked. She knew what he wanted to hear from her, and although the pain of that night would always remain, she wouldn't lie to him now.

Grasping his cheeks lightly, she gazed into his eyes. "Even though we're not of the same class, and I knew my brother would fight against it, nothing mattered to me but you. I would have said yes."

She watched the turmoil cross his brow, sensed the same frustration in him that she felt in losing what could have been, the loneliness in years lost. And then he exhaled a long breath and rested his forehead against hers.

"Promise me," he maintained soberly seconds later, "that no matter what happens this night, you will remember what you just told me and what it means for us now."

"Why?" She tilted her head to the side with curiosity and leaned back. "What is it?"

"Just make me that promise," he insisted.

Smiling, she pacified him through a sigh. "I promise, Garrett. Now tell me what you're afraid is going to happen tonight?"

He smiled faintly in return and released her. "The problem is I'm not sure *what* will happen, but I need you to believe in me, Ivy. And trust me."

Her eyes narrowed teasingly as she placed her hands on her hips. "Trust you? You entered my bedchamber and took advantage of me, sir—"

He chuckled, and then in one quick action, wrapped a large palm around her neck, brought her face to his, and kissed her hard on the mouth.

"I need to leave," he whispered seconds later.

She nodded, reluctantly letting him go for a final time. "Will you arrive before the marquess? I'd rather not greet him alone."

He ran his fingers along her jaw as he murmured, "You won't greet him alone. That's a promise I will make to you."

And then before she could comment further, he was at the door to the passageway, glancing back once before he closed it softly behind him.

He only had crumbs left to eat, and little water, which he safeguarded with growing despair. The woman hadn't been to see him in a long time, or at least it seemed that way, since the drugs had slowly worn off to leave him with an awareness of how desperate his situation had become.

He couldn't see anything in such thick blackness, not even his wrist chained to the wall at his side. He could move from the cot, but only two or three feet, and he heard nothing. Absolutely nothing.

She kept him in some sort of dungeon, that much was clear, though he couldn't be certain how long he'd been here. Probably weeks, he thought. And as his head had cleared, he also realized his confinement had something to do with the Martello diamonds stolen two years ago.

Their loss had been partially his fault, he accepted that. But being held captive by a woman who told him nothing went far beyond all he could understand. He remembered following Benedict Sharon to Winter Garden, watching the man for days before deciding to confront him by surprise, but instead, finding the man in dinner clothes, sprawled out facedown on the floor of his library. And the next thing he remembered was waking up here with a splitting headache. The woman had arrived hours later to leave him the broth and bread, and when he was weakened and could no longer physically fight for his freedom, she began drugging him with laudanum.

But now something had changed. He could feel it, just as he could feel Ivy's presence. She was searching for him, and he felt sickened at the thought of her becoming involved in this—whatever it was.

Suddenly, Ian became aware of a very low vibration surrounding him, a deep hum, like a gushing of water or the thunder of horses in the far distance, though he still could hear nothing but the sound of his own breathing in the stale, foul air.

He sat up, glancing around into nothingness, his head spinning from such a quick movement on his part. And then he heard the click of the latch on the door and an odd rush of relief swept through him as he realized he hadn't been completely abandoned.

The door slowly opened and she stood there, a small lantern hanging at her side. For seconds she watched him, her body hooded and cloaked so he still couldn't see her face within the shadow.

"Who are you?" he croaked out, his throat dry and raspy, his eyes squinting even from the very dim lighting.

"You're awake," she said quietly. "That's good because I have news."

He got the sense she was young, or at least not old, though without seeing her features he couldn't know for sure. And although her English proved she came from good family, her voice could be anyone's.

"Have you come to release me?" he asked, trying to sound hopeful rather than as enraged as he felt.

"The Marquess of Rye and your sister are lovers. She is living in the Baron Rothebury's home, and he joins her at night. I've seen them."

She gave him time to absorb that news, and when the meaning of her words finally seeped into his muddled brain, he didn't know what to think, to feel—furious at his sister, baffled by the coincidence, agitated that he hadn't, and couldn't, protect her like he should. And who could know if it was true. But right now, he decided, the information wasn't nearly as important as the timing.

"Who are you?" he repeated gruffly. "And why are you telling me this?"

She took a step closer, clasping the lantern behind her with both hands so he couldn't see her face.

"I'm going to the ball, to surprise them all, and then I'm bringing her here."

His heart began to race. He swallowed the bile in his throat, and muttered through clenched teeth, "You have me, you don't need her. Leave Ivy out of this."

She chuckled, then replied, "She's worth more than you are."

He bolted, attempting to reach for her, but the chains gripped his hand. He roared with rage when he couldn't get quite close enough to break her neck, though his swift movement startled her enough that she stepped back to the safety of the doorway.

"There has been a change to the plan," she said seconds later, her tone growing distant, somber. "Nobody has found the diamonds because they haven't tried hard enough. But they are surely in the house. If your sister disappears, the generous marquess will tear the walls apart to find her. He will trade them for her, and I'll be gone before anyone knows what happened to either of you."

"I'll kill you," he seethed in a deadly breath.

She shook her head to whisper, "We met once, long ago, but you don't remember me, do you? You don't even know who I am."

Another loud shout of agony escaped his chest, and he yanked forward full force with the thick chain again, this time drawing blood from his wrist. But she only looked at him from the shadow of her hooded cloak.

"Men have died here before you, and after I leave, nobody will know this dungeon exists." Dropping her voice to a whisper of loneliness, she said, "I'm sorry, Ian. You shouldn't have been a part of this."

And then she was gone, leaving him with nothing but the blackness.

Crushed by a feeling of helplessness he could no longer control, Ian fell back on the cot, brought his hands to his face, and wept.

Chapter 17

It started snowing at four o'clock. By six, the Winter Masquerade was well under way, music playing, footmen in blood-red livery serving champagne and hors d'oeuvres to a growing crowd in the Rye estate's magnificent ballroom.

Ivy stood in the foyer with nervous anticipation. In every respect, she was the Marquess of Rye's chosen hostess, though to her great relief, Madeleine and Thomas, Lord and Lady Eastleigh, stood beside her. As the highest-ranking members of the aristocracy in Winter Garden, aside from the marquess, who had yet to make an appearance, they greeted the arriving guests with stately elegance, giving her moments here and there to move away and observe the growing crowd.

With her hair dressed in pearls, not a curl out of place, she wore the earrings Garrett had given her, stunning teardrop emeralds, as the only jewelry on her person. Her gown, made of the finest white silk, accented them beautifully, as tiny ribbons in yellow, blue, pale green, and pink, curled into the shape of roses, lined the white lace of her neckline and wide skirt.

Footmen stood on either side of the sparkling, stained-glass archway, handing out masks in black or white silk for those who hadn't brought their own. As yet, nobody had arrived who seemed out of place or reluctant to be inside the former Rothebury home, and Ivy had yet to notice anything odd. In that regard, she supposed it might only be the Marquess of Rye's arrival that would stun the crowd this night, and certainly the appearance by a man rumored to be either a rake or recluse would no doubt create a stir worth revisiting at tea for months to come. At the very least such a stir would make the Winter Masquerade a success, especially to those who chose to attend only for the resulting gossip.

Thomas and Madeleine made a striking pair, both dressed in deep blue, both foregoing masks, as did she, while making introductions. Madeleine's gown fit her perfectly in a shade that accented the unusual color of her blue eyes. Thomas, clearly proud to be her husband and escort, kept a hand at her lower back in a display of possessiveness.

Ivy envied them. They disagreed on occasion, but in a loving manner that showed the deep respect they had for each other. She felt the same kind of admiration for Garrett, she supposed, but not at such a deep level, as they still had so many questions unanswered between them. Her feelings for him had returned full force during the last few weeks, however, and it concerned her that when, or even if, he found the famous Martello diamonds, he would leave her with a kiss on the lips and a gentle good-bye. She still worried that his feelings for her were only a function of her usefulness, though recalling the events of just a few hours ago assuaged her. And he had given her a small fortune in emeralds, which of course meant something. Unless he stole them, she decided, grinning outwardly at his comment.

"Having a good time already?" Madeleine asked softly, her face close to Ivy's.

Ivy groaned, keeping the smile on her lips. "I admit I'll feel better when Garrett arrives."

Madeleine sighed. "Well, at least the gossip is about to flourish. Penelope Bennington-Jones and her daughters just arrived."

Ivy glanced toward the front doorway, noting Newbury taking pelisse-mantles from the three. She recognized Penelope at once as an older image of Hermione, large of stature, with broad hips and shoulders, having nearly the same homely features and prosaic expression. Penelope looked a bit flustered as she brushed fresh snow from her plaited blond hair, her gown a veritable plethora of bows, ribbons, and lace in every imaginable bright color, that fairly begged to be noticed. Hermione appeared less enthusiastic, her features somewhat dour as she cast her eyes to the ballroom with obvious apprehension. Tonight, she wore a gown of pale yellow and white lace that did nothing for her coloring but would, perhaps, allow her to blend into the background should that be her desire.

Yet it was Viola who stood out among the three. A

young woman of no more than eighteen, she'd been blessed with dark brown hair, hazel eyes, and rather angular features on an angelic face far prettier than her mother or sister's. She'd donned a gown of green-and-red-plaid and dressed her hair with a green satin ribbon that accentuated her coloring. She also seemed more intimidated than the other two, casting quick glances all around her and lightly furrowing her brows when she noticed the grandness that was now a fairly full ballroom of masked dancers.

Penelope strode toward them, her head high, a flat smile pasted on her rouge-painted lips.

"Good evening, Lord Eastleigh," she said with a quick curtsy, "you look well."

The earl offered her a slight bow. "As do you, Mrs. Bennington-Jones."

Penelope cleared her throat before acknowledging Ivy or Madeleine.

"Lady Eastleigh," she remarked, "it's always good to see you."

"And you as well, Penelope," she returned in a tone thickly accented. "I hope you and your daughters will come to tea sometime soon."

Penelope blinked, then seemed to gather her wits as she replied, "We should enjoy that, I think." Turning to her side, she presented her daughters. "Viola, Hermione, you remember Lord and Lady Eastleigh."

Both girls curtsied, Hermione looking bored, sullen, Viola curious as she kept glancing back to the ballroom.

"And you must be Lady Ivy, sister of the Earl of Stamford," Penelope asserted through a rush of air. "I remember you from years ago. You and your brother always playing at the lake."

That surprised her, more so because Penelope made it sound as if children playing outdoors at a lake was a highly peculiar event. Smiling, Ivy brushed over the comment, and answered simply, "It's a pleasure to make your acquaintance, Mrs. Bennington-Jones. I'm delighted you could attend tonight."

Penelope's brows rose and she looked her up and down while offering a slight curtsy. "Will your brother be here as well?"

She swallowed a choke in her throat. "Unfortunately, he's in Italy for the season, though we expect him back home in the spring."

"I see." She glanced around. "Then who is escorting you tonight, madam? Mr. Burke or the mysterious Marquess of Rye?"

Ivy detected a blunt shrewdness in the woman that made her all the more unappealing. Viola seemed to notice as she all but cowered from her mother's rather obnoxious questioning. Hermione simply looked at her, her pale eyes narrowed as she focused on her words.

Clasping her gloved hands together in front of her, Ivy replied matter-of-factly, "It's probably more accurate to call me Lord Rye's hostess for the evening, along with the gracious company of Lord and Lady Eastleigh. As for Mr. Burke . . ." She shrugged minutely. "I'm afraid I've no idea if he's coming at all."

Penelope stiffened and patted the uplifted plaits at the back of her head, probably just realizing there was no gossip to be had along that line.

"Well," she said with exasperation, "there are so many people we need to see tonight. If you'll excuse us, Lord Eastleigh, Lady Ivy."

Then without even a curtsy, she turned and hustled her daughters toward the footman handing masks to guests at the top of the ballroom stairs.

"Her manners are atrocious without the outward appearance that her manners are atrocious," Ivy observed just loud enough for Madeleine to hear. "I should say that's quite a talent."

Madeleine laughed. "I thought she was fairly well behaved today, actually."

"I don't trust her," Ivy asserted, more to herself.

Thomas leaned in to interject, "Are you sensing that as a woman or a seer?"

She gave him a wry smile. "Both, I think."

Thomas rubbed his wife's back. "Most of the guests have arrived. I'm going to walk around the outside of the house to look for anything suspicious."

"It's snowing, Eastleigh," Madeleine cautioned. "Take your coat."

"Of course," he growled with a grin. "Whatever did I do to survive before I married you, my lady?"

She sighed. "I've no idea, my darling, but do please go. You're wasting time, and Ivy and I must mingle."

He caressed her chin lightly with his thumb. "Stay alert." And then before she could offer a reply, he turned and walked to Newbury to request his coat, his limp pronounced from the effects of the cold.

"He adores you," Ivy said with an enviousness that surprised her.

Madeleine grinned, tilting her head to the side as she lifted the string of rubies at her neck. "He does, doesn't he?"

A footman approached them holding a tray of champagne, but while Madeleine took a glass, Ivy declined, intent on staying focused this night.

"Do you enjoy marriage, Madeleine?" she asked, hoping she sounded merely curious.

The Frenchwoman turned and smiled. "Of course. Some days I miss the independence I had before Eastleigh and I met, but it's usually a fleeting reflection. You'll feel the same after you've married."

She felt her pulse speed up, her stomach suddenly flutter with uncertainties. "I fear I'm rather too old for marriage."

"Nonsense," Madeleine scoffed. "I was nearly thirty when I married." Her eyes narrowed, and the side of her mouth curved up coyly. "Besides, I don't think Garrett will let you go so easily."

Ivy almost choked and wished at once she'd taken the proffered champagne. "I'm not so certain that's true. He's . . . obsessed with finding the Martello diamonds, and I fear that may be his only concern. I don't think he's truly considered marriage to anyone."

Madeleine's fine brows arched for a few seconds, then she lifted her own champagne, pausing before taking a sip. "You know, Ivy, before I fell in love with Eastleigh, I thought much the same."

Her mouth curved upward. "That he had an obsession greater than you?"

Madeleine pinched her lips together to keep from laughing. "No, I *was* his obsession." She took a sip from her glass. "I simply meant that I didn't see love when it stared at me directly, perhaps because I feared it." Her features grew woeful as she added, "Actually, it was poor Desdemona who opened my eyes and forced me to consider Eastleigh's real actions and feelings."

"Desdemona?"

"Surprising, is it not? Before she testified at the Rothebury inquiry and left for Northumberland she and I talked. She candidly informed me that Eastleigh loved me deeply but it was *I* who failed to notice what everybody else already knew, probably because I was quite afraid to witness it myself. Love changes people, and it's much easier to avoid it than to face it, especially when it hurts."

Ivy felt her mouth go dry, and she tried to free herself from the implication, from even considering the chance that after all this time his love for her could be rekindled. "I'm sure . . . I'm sure Garrett—"

"Is in love with you," Madeleine cut in with a low tone of assurance. "So am I and so is Eastleigh." She took a step closer, dropping her voice to add, "Perhaps it is not the diamonds but you who is truly his obsession. You are here, are you not?" She sighed, and glanced back to the front doors. "Sometimes, for all our intuitive thoughts, we ladies can be remarkably obtuse when it comes to the obvious, particularly when it involves the love of a man."

Ivy had absolutely no idea what to say, or even how to feel at such a casually spoken retort. She'd been taken unawares by something that to her meant everything, as if the world had suddenly been offered to her without her awareness of the facts, and all she had to do was grasp it. Yet just the idea that Garrett, through contact with the Marquess of Rye, might have been responsible for bringing her here, even if thoroughly unlikely, disturbed her immensely.

She had to think rationally, to contemplate a notion that had thus far not occurred to her; but considering it now was horribly inconvenient, to say the least. More than anything, however, she needed to see Garrett, to look into his eyes and feel for herself the truth of Madeleine's words.

"Lady Isadora has arrived," Madeleine said softly, "and she's bringing her niece, Lady Margaret of Brighton."

That alarming comment pulled her from her pensive thoughts. "Lady Margaret of Brighton is Lord Rye's betrothed."

Madeleine swiftly turned to look at her again, all humor faded. "He's not betrothed to anyone, as far as I'm aware."

Confused, she murmured, "I heard that from Garrett. The diamonds were stolen at their betrothal ball."

The Frenchwoman's mouth dropped open a little, and then she turned to watch the two of them enter the foyer. "She shouldn't be here. Something isn't right . . ."

Before Ivy could respond, Lady Isadora and Lady Margaret, both smiling, were strolling toward them, the elder white-haired and pink-cheeked, dressed in green and ivory, the younger, a pretty blond in becoming ringlets perhaps only twenty years of age, dressed in blue satin and frills. But where Isadora seemed merry at the thought of a ball, Margaret looked triumphant, keen of thought, and Ivy sensed a coldness in her from the moment their eyes met.

"Lady Eastleigh, how lovely to see you again," Lady Isadora declared, her voice sweetly soft.

Madeleine took one of the older woman's hands and dropped a kiss on each cheek. "I'm so glad you could attend tonight."

"As am I. How long has it been since the last Winter Masquerade? Three or four months, has it not?"

"Actually, it's been two years, my dear," Madeleine corrected her gently.

The elderly woman waved a wrinkled hand. "My goodness, I can't possibly keep up with the time."

Madeleine smiled, her attention straying to the younger woman. "And who is your lovely guest?"

"Hmm? Oh, yes, I brought . . . um . . ."

"Lady Margaret of Brighton," the woman interjected, moving in front of her aunt. "I am Lady

Isadora's niece." She turned steely eyes to Ivy, skimming her appearance from head to foot. "And you must be the seer."

She said the words as if they were scribbled in black ink upon Ivy's gown, and Ivy disliked her immediately. Thankfully, Madeleine cut in before she could comment.

"It's a pleasure to make your acquaintance, Lady Margaret," Madeleine replied smoothly in perfect form. "This is, indeed, Lady Ivy of Stamford."

Lady Isadora glanced at her. "Are you married to Lord Stamford?"

Ivy smiled at a woman clearly dear to all but who was slowly losing her mind to age. "No, in fact he's my brother, Lady Isadora."

"Seers have a difficult time finding husbands, I should think, Aunt," Margaret said with feigned sweetness. "How fortunate Lady Ivy has a brother to care for her needs in the coming years."

Beyond rude, the statement completely took her aback, though with it came a strong sense of foreboding, even alarm. In a flash of insight she realized Lady Margaret knew something, concealed vital information from all of them, and planned to use it this night.

Quickly, Madeleine seized the moment, giving the younger woman a hard stare as she said politely, "Perhaps you'd like some refreshment, Lady Margaret."

Margaret's lips curled upward. "Has Paul arrived?"

Ivy's brows rose. "Paul?"

The woman huffed with self-satisfaction. "My betrothed, the Marquess of Rye? You are staying in his home, are you not? Have you not seen him yet today?"

And then a coldness struck her, a maliciousness from the woman so intertwined with her personality it left Ivy too dumbfounded to speak.

His face, smiling as he danced . . . then distorted, dark, desperate, snowflakes beside him . . . needing her help . . . crying for her . . . tears falling on crystals . . .

A shiver of fear coursed through her.

She knows something about Ian . . .

Lady Isadora leaned forward, and in a low, conspiratorial voice disclosed, "He's not expecting us. She wants to surprise the marquess tonight."

"And I'm certain she shall," Madeleine acknowledged, casting her a fast, admonishing glance before moving forward to take both of the ladies by the arms. "But since he isn't here yet," she continued, leading them toward the stained-glass archway with a graceful air, "let me get you and your aunt masks and some of the marquess's marvelous champagne." Glancing back over her shoulder, her ice-blue eyes full of warning, she mouthed: *Find Eastleigh.*

Garrett had never been so tense in his life. Waiting to make his appearance as the now-infamous Marquess of Rye left his nerves raw, aggravating what little patience he had left—so much so, he'd downed two whiskeys at the inn before dressing for the event that would no doubt change the course of his future.

After making his way through the tunnel, he'd returned to the inn, bathed, shaved, and donned his finest evening dress, black on white silk, with a black-and-gray-striped cravat, made of a quality Ivy had never seen him wear before. Although a light snow continued to fall, it didn't feel all that cold, so he planned to walk to clear his head and allow some time to pass before what was soon to be his grand entrance.

He hadn't wanted to leave her side after making love this afternoon, especially without telling her who he was and how deeply he felt for her. But he had no choice. She would have to accept him as someone completely new to her, someone with enormous wealth and an inherited title for which most ladies in the land would swoon and trade their souls to acquire by marriage, and guarding his heart until he revealed everything tonight was his only self-defense. He expected her outrage at the revelation of his secrets, and he'd prepared himself for the worst of it. He simply had to trust that she would forgive him in the end.

Finally, he buttoned his finest wool coat, pulled on leather gloves, and stepped out into the stillness. The village seemed remarkably quiet, as did the inn, probably because nearly every resident of Winter Garden now danced in his ballroom and drank his expensive champagne. Gazing across the lake at his house, now lit up like a beacon, he braved the mild cold and began another trek along the forest path, attempting to piece together in his mind exactly how Ivy might react, and every ploy he could possibly use to convince her that nothing between them had ever been a lie. In the end, however, he fully realized there would be difficulties ahead this night, and he would face them, every one.

It took him almost fifteen minutes to reach the property. Thankfully, the snow melted on the ground as it touched it so that his shoes weren't wet and freezing his feet when he arrived. He saw almost nobody, but he could hear the orchestra playing, the rumble of talk and laughter from the ballroom, and it amused him that everybody inside awaited his arrival like the second coming of Christ. And the only thing he cared about was seeing Ivy.

He got his wish the moment he turned the corner to face the front of the house. She stood at the top of the stone steps, looking incredibly beautiful as the brightly lit torches on either side of the doors cast a glow upon her face and gown—a glorious angel in white surrounded by snowfall that sparkled like diamonds. The vision nearly took his breath away.

His heartbeat began to quicken as she suddenly noticed him in the distance. She lifted her skirts to carefully descend the steps, then fairly ran into his arms.

"Anxious for my arrival, my darling Lady Ivy?" he said through a chuckle as he held her tightly against him.

She threw her arms around his neck and hugged him close. "You've no idea," she replied breathlessly. "I'm so glad you're here."

He kissed her forehead lightly, then grasped her

waist and pushed her back far enough to gaze into her eyes. "What are you doing outside without a wrap?"

"Madeleine sent me to find Eastleigh," she answered at once. "I think . . . I think something's wrong, and so does she."

He sobered quickly, noting the conflict in her features. "What's happened?"

She shook her head a little to clear her thoughts. "I'm not sure anything's happened yet. The Marquess of Rye hasn't arrived, but his betrothed has, and she . . . she knows—"

"What did you say?" he cut in, his voice low and grave as he felt his blood turn to ice.

She frowned, tipping her head to the side, seemingly confused by his sudden shift in manner. "Lady Margaret of Brighton is here. She's the niece of Lady Isadora Birmingham and came as her guest. And Garrett, I think she knows something about Ian."

Stunned, he released her, taking a step back to stare at the house. "Jesus . . ." he whispered under his breath.

Ivy stepped so close to him her gown smothered his legs beneath his coat. "What is it?" she asked, her voice filled with apprehension.

He inhaled deeply and lowered his gaze to hers. She looked worried, confused, and with trepidation gnawing at him, he realized that everything he'd planned had been altered.

Margaret shouldn't be here, shouldn't even know

about the Rothebury house, or his whereabouts, unless she'd been involved with stealing the diamonds originally. There could be no other explanation. She knew Ian from the party long ago, and if she truly had an aunt from Winter Garden, it was possible she knew Benedict Sharon. And if all of this was true, there was every chance that she had played him for a fool.

"Garrett—"

"What did she say to you?" he asked, attempting to keep the rage and alarm from his voice.

She smirked. "What did she *say*? Not very much, but she was quite tactless."

He nodded, feeling a surge of relief as he realized Lady Margaret remained as conniving as ever, or she would have exposed him at once. That meant she was hiding something to reveal later.

"Why do you think she knows something about Ian?" he asked seconds later.

She shivered, and he reached out to wrap his arms around her once more.

"It was just . . . a feeling, a coldness I felt from her." She closed her eyes. "I saw his face again, Garrett, but he was . . . smiling, dancing. And then there was a blackness with . . . snowflakes all around"—she swallowed—"and I felt his fear."

After a long moment of silence, he murmured, "She shouldn't be here."

"That's what Madeleine said, and she was concerned, which is why she sent me to find Eastleigh." She paused, then asked in quiet anguish, "What is going *on*, Garrett?"

He groaned, catching the faintest scent of lilac in her hair, on her skin as he hugged her to lend her his warmth. "I'm not sure."

"Something is very wrong," she whispered. "I feel it in my bones."

Inhaling deeply, he held her close, afraid to let her go and suddenly wishing they could simply leave together and never look back. But reality faced them this night, and they needed each other more now than they ever did before.

With resolve, and knowing the time for truth had come, he cupped her chin and lifted her head a little so she could see his face. "It's cold, and you need to go inside. I'll find Lord Eastleigh."

She didn't like that at all. "No, you need to come with me, especially if Lady Margaret—"

"You have to trust me tonight, Ivy."

She gave him a wry smile. "We've discussed this already. You know I do."

He rubbed a gloved thumb along her cheek. "We'll confront Lady Margaret when I'm inside. But until then, remember that I know the Marquess of Rye, and I know he broke his betrothal nearly two years ago."

She pulled back a little, confused. "Then why is she here?" Irritation sliced through her words as she added, "I can't imagine that he still loves her."

He almost laughed. "I'm quite certain he never did."

"You don't know that." She glanced back to the house. "Then again, maybe that's why he hasn't yet ar-

rived. He knows she's here, and he's afraid of the en-
counter. I would be."

"Ivy . . ."

She looked at him again, and he gazed into her eyes,
glowing beautifully by torchlight, charged with wit and
uneasiness and a trace of good humor.

Quashing a quick jolt of nervousness, he dropped
his voice to a deep whisper to disclose, "He thought
she was annoying, yes. But the fact is, he broke his betrothal because he was then, and is now, passionately in
love with someone else."

A certain stillness enveloped them as they stood in
the faint, silent snowfall. Slowly, she scanned his face,
her features growing serious once more, her brows furrowed lightly as the truth behind his words lingered, as
if their meaning held something of intense value she
couldn't quite grasp.

Then he lowered his mouth to place a slow, burning
kiss upon her lips, to avoid the questions he knew she
had, to feel her just once more before the emotional
upheaval to come.

"Go inside, before you freeze," he whispered at
last, placing his palms on her upper arms as he gently
pushed her away. "I'll find Eastleigh, and then we'll
find you."

She sighed, slowly lifting her lashes to say huskily,
"What if we missed him, and he's already back in the
ballroom?"

He grinned. "Then you'll find him first."

"Garrett—"

"Go, Ivy," he insisted as he dropped his arms to release her. "I'll be there soon."

She paused for a few seconds, concern in her expression. Then, giving him a hesitant smile, she turned and walked quickly back to the warmth of the house.

Chapter 18

A blazing heat struck her as she entered the foyer, though Ivy hardly noticed with her excitement rising and her nerves on fire. Quickly, she fluffed her skirts and brushed snow from the lace on her sleeves, then walked to the glass archway to study the gathering of Winter Garden's finest for a minute or two, thinking, trying to reconcile her rising panic with the knowledge that everything in the ballroom looked perfect.

She couldn't find Eastleigh among the guests, though she spotted Madeleine at once, standing near the northern windows next to Lady Margaret, speaking to an older gentleman she didn't recognize, probably introducing them. Lady Isadora sat in a velveteen chair beside her, sipping champagne and smiling as she watched a flurry of colorful skirts twirling before her in time to a splendidly played waltz. Penelope and Catherine Mossley had retreated to the far northeast corner, their heads together as they talked in whispers, Viola standing beside her mother giggling at something two young men were saying to her. She could see neither Hermione nor Elizabeth, Catherine's granddaughter, whom she had met tonight for the first time, anywhere, though with their ordinary appearance and quiet manners, both girls probably blended into the crowd unnoticed by all.

Her first thought was to go directly to Margaret's side and question her incessantly until the woman disclosed exactly what she knew of Ian or his whereabouts. But she and Madeleine had planned a magnificent party, and as she accepted a white mask from the polished footman at her side, she tried to restrain herself from acting rashly, remembering that she'd been invited to the house and now chosen to be the marquess's hostess. That thought in mind, she tied the mask at the back of her head, kept her chin high, lifted her skirts, and began to descend the steps to the ballroom floor.

Ivy decided to play her part, as the only thing she could do, and so she immediately started circling the ballroom, chatting with various members of the local gentry and attempting to make them all feel welcome. The music played loudly, and the ballroom felt rather stuffy, but footmen passed among the guests, offering plates of delicious-smelling hors d'oeuvres and endless glasses of champagne, and from the laughter and crowded dance floor, she could only surmise that the Winter Masquerade would be considered a rousing success by all, regardless of whether the Marquess of Rye chose to attend his own event.

But beneath her refined appearance and underlying desire to learn the secrets of the house and its guests, something about Garrett's demeanor tonight plagued her and remained in the forefront of her mind. She sensed a shift in him, a marked increase in the intensity between them during their last exchange that left her on edge, as if he withheld some vital information she should know but didn't. And it involved the Marquess of Rye, the mysterious figure about whom everyone whispered and speculated yet who remained unknown to all but two people at the party—Garrett and Margaret. And Garrett had been as shocked as Madeleine to know that the woman was here.

But how this remarkable . . . coincidence had occurred she couldn't quite fathom. There was more to this event this evening than she understood, more than a night of hoping to learn how the house, and the residents of the town, related to her brother and the missing Martello diamonds.

At last she came upon Penelope and Catherine Mossley as they stood by the tall, north windows, each now slightly ajar, the fresh, cold breeze reviving her as she realized she'd need the air in any exchange she might have with Mrs. Bennington-Jones.

Catherine noticed her first and offered a smile and a light curtsy. Penelope curtsied as well, though the look in her eyes, even behind her mask, suggested both suspicion and a degree of annoyance at the interruption.

"Are you enjoying yourselves this evening?" she asked both ladies at once.

"Certainly, we are, Lady Ivy," Catherine Mossley said politely. "The house is exactly as I remember it."

"Indeed," Penelope agreed as she attempted to straighten her mask. "Though we've never been to the Winter Masquerade without the owner and host being present to receive us."

Ivy had to wonder if her comment directly reflected her disappointment in not meeting the marquess upon arrival or if she truly missed the excitement of having Lord Rothebury at her side in rapt attention. It didn't matter, unless the woman wanted to introduce her eligible daughters to a higher-ranking member of the gentry than those already in attendance. She decided that had to be the case, since the only possible way for Penelope Bennington-Jones to regain any kind of social standing in the community would be if Hermione or Viola married better than Desdemona had—a hope that at this point didn't seem at all likely.

"Are you expecting the marquess anytime soon?" Penelope asked, cutting into her thoughts.

She gave the woman a satisfactory smile. "Let's hope so, Mrs. Bennington-Jones."

Penelope's lips tightened to a flat line of annoyance from that nonanswer. Ivy carried on as if completely unaware of the woman's displeasure. "By the way, where is Hermione? She won't want to miss Lord Rye when he arrives."

Penelope's brows rose as she straightened her shoulders. "I'm certain she went to the ladies' withdrawing room with Elizabeth to freshen herself before the event. Hopefully, it won't be too long now."

Mrs. Mossley interjected, "You're certain he's coming, Lady Ivy?"

She lifted a shoulder negligibly. "He said so in his last correspondence with me, and I don't suppose he'd authorize such a wonderful party and not attend himself."

She watched Penelope smile genuinely for the first time. Obviously, such a fact had not occurred to her.

"That's exactly what I was thinking," Penelope fairly blurted. She turned to her youngest daughter, who stood with her back to her mother, conversing openly with a rather handsome young gentleman. "Viola, go and freshen yourself before Lord Rye arrives."

Viola twirled around at the sharp intrusion, her laughter fading as she quickly nodded and replied softly, "Yes, of course. Where is Hermione?"

Sternly, Penelope replied, "Probably doing what you should be doing. Now go, and make sure every hair is in place."

"Yes, ma'am," she muttered, offering a meek curtsy to Lady Ivy before brushing past them.

Penelope cleared her throat and straightened, interlocking her fingers in front of her enormous skirt. "Has Mr. Burke arrived?"

Ivy warmed inside from just the mention of his name. "He has. I'm sure he'll be in the ballroom momentarily."

"Perhaps he'll dance with Hermione," Catherine intimated, her eyes wide as she glanced from one to the other. "They are already acquainted, after all."

Penelope tipped her head down a fraction, giving the woman a hard stare. "I'm sure Elizabeth is better suited to dance with the likes of Mr. Burke."

Mrs. Mossley blinked. "Of course, you're right."

Evidently, Mrs. Bennington-Jones had decided no man without a proper title or sufficient income would do for her daughters, and Ivy had to bite her tongue on a rude retort, most notably that Mr. Burke needed no dancing partner but her. Thankfully, she was saved by the perfectly timed arrival of Hermione and Catherine Mossley's granddaughter, Elizabeth, who both appeared from within the crowd and sauntered to their sides.

"Viola said Lord Rye will be here soon," Elizabeth cut in excitedly, rudely failing to acknowledge their hostess.

Penelope sighed through her teeth. "Let us hope so," she directed to Lady Ivy.

Elizabeth, a tall, brown-haired, brown-eyed, ordinary-looking woman, so thin she seemed almost hidden inside the folds of her bright red ball gown, suddenly seemed to realize she stood among them.

"You're the famous seer," she said with seemingly sincere interest, her thick eyebrows raised so high they became obscured by her mask. "I've read of your pursuits in the London newspapers—"

"Ladies do *not* read newspapers," Penelope chided in a low breath of impatience.

Elizabeth, either from experience with Mrs. Bennington-Jones's nature or ignorance of the rebuke, ignored the comment altogether. Cocking her head to the side, she bluntly asked, "Did you ever find the famous Martello diamonds?"

That question rendered her speechless.

"The *Martello* diamonds?" Penelope repeated. "What are those?"

"She reads the London newspapers, Mother," Hermione cut in, her features controlled even as her voice remained cool.

Ivy couldn't decide if Hermione intended to denigrate her mother in front of others or side with her in belittling Elizabeth for pursuing something cultured ladies would never do. Hermione was indeed very clever, she decided at that moment, and frankly she found the interaction almost as fascinating as the new topic.

"The Martello diamonds were stolen two years ago, Mrs. Bennington-Jones," she asserted at last. "I was asked to help investigate their disappearance."

Penelope snorted. "That's ridiculous."

Ivy stifled her irritation again by smiling, then replied, "The Home Office didn't think so." She paused for effect, then added softly, "And neither did Lord Rye."

"Lord Rye?" That from Viola.

She nodded once to the girl. "He is the legal owner of the Martello diamonds."

"Good gracious," Catherine Mossley spat out in a fluster.

Penelope's mouth dropped open an inch, as did Viola's.

"That wasn't in the papers," Elizabeth muttered.

Ivy took note of every reaction, then gave an exaggerated sigh. "They were part of his grandmother's dowry when she married into his family. She was an Italian princess."

Viola whispered, "They must be priceless . . ."

Clasping her hands in front of her, she said, "Indeed, they're large blue diamonds, surrounded by rubies, set in a golden tiara."

Suddenly Penelope grinned in delight she couldn't hide, probably, Ivy mused, because she stood there proudly envisioning one of her daughters wearing the priceless diamond-and-ruby-covered tiara at her grand wedding to the marquess.

"No wonder they asked a seer to help," Catherine said as she shook her head in wonder.

"But it didn't work," Hermione countered seconds later, her voice low and thoughtful. "You never found the diamonds, did you, Lady Ivy?"

Startled by the directness of the question, Ivy looked at her, sensing more than a trace of malice from the girl, who now stared at her through narrowed eyes. With a shrug, she said forthrightly, "I suppose if one reads the London newspapers, Miss Bennington-Jones, one would know that's true."

Penelope gasped at the mere suggestion of one of her daughters doing such a thing. Ivy ignored the older woman as she gazed at Hermione closely, noting that she never flinched, though one corner of her mouth twitched very slightly into a near smile, as if acknowledging the fact that she'd met her match.

"I wonder what it must be like to wear such a tiara," Viola said wistfully.

"You feel exactly like a princess," came a voice from the crowd. "An *English* princess."

Ivy glanced over her shoulder to see Lady Margaret standing directly behind her, unnoticed until she spoke.

Margaret waited until she knew she had everyone's attention, then smiled with a deep satisfaction, and declared, "I've actually worn the Martello diamonds."

Everyone gaped at her. Ivy turned to study the woman squarely, as it became clear to her like a slap to the face that Margaret Dartmouth of Brighton knew something about the theft. Ian, Benedict Sharon, and the Martello diamonds, all remained missing, and Lady Margaret, who admitted to once wearing the precious jewels, presented herself here in Winter Garden tonight. Margaret didn't have the tiara, or the diamonds, or she wouldn't be here now. But the woman *knew* something, and it had to do with Ian and his involvement in informing Lord Rye of Benedict's plan to steal the diamonds. She felt the connection, the cold deception, to the core.

"How on earth were you so fortunate?" Elizabeth asked bluntly, eyeing the woman up and down.

Margaret smirked. "I am the Marquess of Rye's betrothed."

Catherine and Elizabeth said nothing to that remarkable news, apparently shocked into silence, though Viola sank into her stays with obvious disappointment, and Hermione chuckled lightly with a hand to her mouth. Penelope threw a quick, hard glare at her elder daughter, then turned eyes of pure distaste on Margaret.

"If you are the Marquess of Rye's betrothed," she articulated carefully, "then why is he not escorting you this evening?"

Margaret's shrewd eyes narrowed, and her lips thinned as if she had to control the desire to reveal an enormous secret. Suddenly Ivy wanted to applaud Penelope for her gauche breach of decorum in asking such a frank question.

"Lady Ivy, may I have a word?" Madeleine said, striding gracefully to her side, her husband following closely behind.

Ivy couldn't have been more grateful for the interruption. Brightly, she replied, "Of course, Lady Eastleigh. Please excuse me, ladies."

Without waiting for acknowledgment, she turned her back to the others as Madeleine drew to her side.

"He's here," she murmured, her mood more solemn than excited.

Ivy felt her heart began to race. "You saw him? Or were you introduced?"

Madeleine studied her for several seconds, then whispered, "Stay next to me. He'll come to us."

And then, very slowly, they all grew aware of a hush that enveloped the ballroom as the music came to a halt in midrefrain. Seconds later a low buzz of simultaneous conversation began as it became apparent to all that something spectacular was about to take place. The Marquess of Rye had arrived.

Her nerves sparked even as a cloud of uncertainty permeated her thoughts. Until this moment, she'd not given his physical appearance much thought, but now her curiosity left her nearly beside herself with wonder and anticipation. Only the countess's somewhat pensive demeanor gave her the slightest concern, but she tried to ignore the bit of apprehension that continued to nag her.

"Where's Garrett?" she whispered.

Madeleine had no time to answer. At just that moment, a footman at the top of the stairs banged a staff three times, drawing an immediate silence from the audience, who now stood staring at the staircase in rapt expectation.

"Ladies and gentlemen," he bellowed, "I present you Paul . . . Garrett . . . Faringdon-Burke, Baron Audley, Viscount Dunwich, Earl of Saulsbury, Marquess of Rye!"

Ivy stilled as a powerful wave of incredulity washed over her.

Paul Garrett Faringdon-Burke . . .

Paul Garrett Faringdon-Burke . . . Marquess of Rye . . .

His footsteps echoed on the foyer's marble floor as he came forward. And then he appeared, stopping at the top of the large staircase, his face covered by his black silk mask as his eyes scanned the crowd, his arms to his sides, his regal bearing exuding a marvelous physical strength, authority, and a grandeur likely never before witnessed in Winter Garden.

Paul Garrett Faringdon-Burke . . . Marquess of Rye . . .

"No . . ." she breathed, feeling the blood slowly drain from her face.

Madeleine grasped her hand and whispered, "Don't—move."

For a timeless moment nothing happened. And then he spotted her, their gazes locked, and a cold realization of a long and calculated deceit began to dawn.

She started trembling, shaking inside, and Madeleine squeezed her hand once in silent warning.

Shoulders rigid, he clasped his hands behind his back and slowly began to descend the steps, one by one, his gaze focused solely on her as his mere presence forced the gathering to part when he reached the ballroom floor.

A low murmur began to rise as he walked past bowing gentlemen and curtsying ladies, the confusion, the chatter from the crowd growing ever louder as he closed in on Ivy near the back, northern windows.

She heard a gasp from behind, then one of the ladies said, "Holy Mother of God, it's Mr. Burke . . ."

She couldn't speak.

No, he's Paul Garrett Faringdon-Burke . . . Marquess of Rye . . .

"And you didn't tell us, Lady Ivy?" someone else mumbled.

Through a growing blur of unreality, Ivy detected more whispers around her, Hermione snickering faintly, Lady Margaret's rustle of skirts, Viola and Penelope circling ever nearer, Madeleine clinging to her hand to keep her from running. But she never looked away from his large, approaching figure.

How could I not know?

Seconds later he stood before her, gazing down to her own masked face, his features unreadable beneath the black silk of his, and suddenly she felt a rising fury within like nothing she'd experienced before.

"Lady Ivy?" he acknowledged with a slight tip of his head.

The familiar sound of his resonant, baritone voice brought forth a rush of clarity, overpowering her with the fierce urge to slap him hard across the mouth as she stared into his eyes, to deliver a blow of humiliating pain like the one he'd inflicted upon her these last two years. As he inflicted even at this moment.

But they all stared at her—the best of Winter Garden society—and as a gently bred lady, the sister of the Earl of Stamford, and the hostess of this masquerade ball, she would never purposely give any of them the gossip of the ages. *That* was beneath her.

Drawing a shaky breath, forcing back tears of anguish and rage, and her own immeasurable confusion over each lie, each hidden truth, she pulled her hand from Madeleine's grasp and—inch by inch—raised it in elegant greeting.

She felt no hesitation from him as he reached for her, his warm, strong fingers that had stroked her so intimately now surrounding hers as a stranger of magnificent power. Then lifting her knuckles to his mouth and offering her an appropriate bow, she lowered her lashes and curtsied deeply, a shiver of heat pulsing through her as his lips lingered.

"My lord Rye," she murmured with a delicate air, "it is a pleasure to make your acquaintance."

She remained humbled before him for seconds, until at last he gently drew her to her feet.

Immediately, as if on cue, a cacophony stirred the mood as the orchestra began another waltz, as the noise of conversation grew louder still with the shuffling of bodies and a flurry of color, as servants returned to their duties and the champagne once more began to flow.

Ivy pulled her hand away just as Lady Margaret positioned herself between them.

"My lord, how nice to see you again," she said with a quick curtsy.

"Lady Margaret," he returned coldly, clasping his hands behind him once more as he looked her up and down. "What a surprise to find you at my Winter Masquerade."

Margaret didn't even flinch as her eyes remained sharply focused. "I thought perhaps we could share a word, my lord."

He looked at the woman who had once been his

betrothed, his features hard. "I'm certain a discussion between us will be quite revealing. You can be certain I'll find you later." He turned his attention back to Ivy. "But for now, I'd like to dance with the most beautiful lady at the ball this night. Would you honor me with a waltz?"

Margaret sucked in a sharp breath; Penelope groaned, probably because she hadn't even been given an introduction.

She scanned the immediate crowd, feeling disoriented, enraged, helpless.

"Lady Ivy?" he repeated, stepping closer to her.

She looked back into his eyes. He spoke with an authority she'd never heard from him before, as a high-ranking member of the nobility in full command, and were it not for the great shock of learning his true identity, she'd have been startled by his utterly majestic composure. To refuse him now would cause an embarrassment beyond decent protocol, for both of them. And he knew it.

"I'd be delighted, my lord," she said flatly, her wits returning, her courage finally reaching the level of her anger.

His lips twitched minutely, then he lifted his elbow, and she placed her gloved palm on his forearm as he led her to the center of the floor.

He took her quickly into his arms as he fell in time to the music. She followed his lead, both remaining silent for a moment, knowing every single eye in the ballroom was upon them.

"You're a marvelous dancer," she declared with only the slightest trace of sarcasm.

"As are you," he replied.

"You are also artfully deceitful, my lord," she whispered, keeping her focus on his chest.

He slowed their pace a little, and she could feel his gaze on her masked face.

With a yielding tenderness, he countered, "Only about my title, Ivy, nothing else."

She stiffened in his arms as he pulled her closer, and she glanced around to note that thankfully the party had resumed. They were scrutinized from afar, certainly, but they were only one of several dancing couples on the floor, and nobody could hear what they said to each other. That knowledge gave her fortitude.

Through a breath of undisguised sorrow, she whispered, "I can't even look at you . . ."

"And I can't take my eyes off you, my darling," he admitted seconds later, his tone threaded with meaning. "You are stunning to behold."

Her lashes fluttered upward at the gentleness he conveyed through his words, and as their eyes met, he offered her the warmth of the smile she'd seen only hours ago in the privacy of her bedchamber. The smile she knew.

"Did I tell you two years ago that I loved you?" he asked, his voice barely heard above the din.

She faltered, blinking quickly, shaking her head. "Don't ask me that now," she whispered, the grief within nearly overflowing.

He inhaled a full breath, moving away from the center of the floor, slowing their pace to nearly a standstill.

"Love never dies, Ivy, even if the mind forgets the feeling for a time." He placed his fingers under her chin and lifted her face to his. "I fell in love with you the moment we met. I don't remember that, but I *know* it, and I'm almost certain I told you because I understand myself well. I wouldn't have taken you to my bed without knowing I would marry you, and I wouldn't have asked you to marry me without realizing we were meant to be together."

Tears stung her eyes—from the heartache, the memory, the gripping awareness that they had lost two years that would never be returned to them. She tried to pull away from him, but he held her tightly at her waist, refusing to let her go.

"You've haunted my dreams since that night I made you mine," he continued with grave conviction. "You called to me, grieving for me in a way I couldn't comprehend but that I *felt*. And that's why I brought you here, to Winter Garden. I needed you to help me remember my past with you, what happened that week, and what we meant to each other. And today I discovered the final truth, a truth more priceless than any treasure."

She shook her head, her lips trembling, and he gently caressed them with his thumb.

"I love you, Ivy," he whispered in a husky timbre. "I've loved you all this time. And I know you wouldn't have accepted a proposal of marriage from me two years ago, as you knew me then, if you didn't love me, too."

Time seemed to cease for her as she stared into his eyes, so beautiful, so full of hope. And then she remembered her promise, and his meaning struck.

. . . nothing mattered to me but you. I would have said yes . . .

"You coerced me today," she whispered.

He jerked back a little as if startled. "No, Ivy," he insisted, his voice and manner intense. "I just had to know if you loved me, the man, before I told you who I am."

The man . . . As you knew me then . . .

"Why?" She shook herself free of his grip, pulling away slightly. "You've asked me to trust you repeatedly, and yet you've never trusted me."

"Ivy, that's not true—"

"I'm sorry, Lord Rye," she cut in, her voice quavering with inner strength even as she lowered her lashes. "I don't know you at all."

Before he could comment, she lifted her skirts and turned, moving quickly through the crowd and up the grand staircase.

Chapter 19

With crumbling poise, Ivy decided to retreat to her bedchamber, a place where she could think and not be seen, to clear her head and make decisions about her immediate future. To decide if she ever wanted to see him again.

Her first thought had been to leave the estate and never return. But running outside in a snowstorm without preparation would be senseless. She knew he wouldn't follow her; he would want to give her time to reconcile all that she knew of him now with all that she remembered of their week in London, all that she'd heard of the mysterious Marquess of Rye with the memory of how they'd spent their time together in Winter Garden. His declaration of love on the dance floor had been charming, witty, and laced with trepidation, but with each carefully chosen word she'd grown ever more furious—at the trickery, the deceit and lies.

Quickly, she made her way to the second landing and down the long, darkened hallway to her room without seeing a soul and hearing only the buzz of laughter, talk, and music from the ballroom below. She'd left the door to her bedchamber unlocked, and noted only vaguely that it stood ajar when she reached it.

She entered, shut it behind her, and leaned against the solid oak, closing her eyes and breathing deeply.

"How could I not know?" she whispered to herself as she finally considered how every single clue to his identity had been staring her in the face since the moment they met—his cultured manner, his endless income, his obsession with finding the Martello diamonds—*his* diamonds, above all things.

The urge to laugh bubbled up inside of her as she realized the depth of her ignorance. She understood now that he couldn't tell her who he was in London until he knew Ian wasn't responsible for the theft, until he knew she lacked any involvement as Ian's sister. It also explained exactly why two years ago he told her not to respond to his marriage proposal until he returned.

But he hadn't returned.

Suddenly tears held during all the months of loneliness welled up in her eyes, of the pain they shared that hadn't been discussed, the hopelessness she felt when her heart was breaking and he'd tossed her aside. She supposed she understood why he couldn't trust her with every detail when he couldn't even trust his own memory, though knowing he hadn't tried to speak to her still managed to bewilder and infuriate her. The fact remained that he should have told her before now. He should have prepared her for tonight.

Straightening, Ivy turned and wiped the tears from

her eyes. As desperately as she wanted to leave the Rye estate, she needed to remain for Ian. Finding him was her goal for the moment. After the secrets of this night, this house, were revealed, she would confront Garrett about every detail he'd kept from her. Until then, she intended to let him suffer with his worry.

With a fluff of her skirts, she turned and pulled the latch to open the door once more—and came face-to-face with Lady Margaret of Brighton.

Ivy groaned within, noticing at once that the lady carried two glasses of champagne, one for each of them, she supposed.

"I saw you come up here," Margaret said, a half smile on her lips. "I thought perhaps we could talk for a moment."

Ivy sighed. "Lady Margaret, I really need to return—"

"It's about your brother."

That interjection left her stunned.

Margaret handed her one of the glasses which she took without thought, then watched in silence as the woman stepped past her and into her private room, glancing around before exhaling with exaggeration. "You know, this should have been mine."

Ivy stiffened. "You said you wanted to talk about Ian?"

Margaret looked at her, then down to her glass. "I'm sorry, Lady Ivy, that was rude, I know. I think it—I think it's now obvious that Paul is quite in love with you."

Ivy had no idea what to say at the moment, and so she took a sip of champagne, an indulgence in which she rarely took part but needed this night to calm her nerves.

"He's really quite a gentleman," Margaret carried on, lifting her own glass to her lips. "He never touched me once with passion, never looked into my eyes as he did yours." She paused, then murmured, "And he never once kissed me."

A heady relief stirred within her, and she took another sip, a larger one as the warmth began to spread, stalling because she wasn't at all sure what Margaret wanted from her, why she was here, or even if she now spoke the truth.

Finally, she remarked, "I—I'm still not certain what this has to do with my brother, Lady Margaret."

The woman's eyes narrowed beneath her mask. "I was in love like you are once, kissed and seduced with passion I thought would never end."

She shook her head, taken aback and clearly not understanding. "With Ian?"

Margaret snickered, moving closer as she drank lightly from her glass. "I'm rather jealous, you know, of what you have with my former betrothed, but I never had, or wanted it, with Paul, or with Ian."

Ivy took a final long swallow of champagne, then walked to her vanity table, resting the glass on top. Looking at the lady through the mirror, she said, "I'm sorry, Margaret, but—"

"I was in love with Benedict Sharon."

Ivy pivoted around to stare at her, speechless.

Margaret laughed, a calculated, bitter laugh that permeated the room with a numbing coldness. "Surprised, aren't you?"

"Yes . . ." she whispered, her throat tight, mouth going dry. "You know what happened to him, don't you? Where he is?"

Margaret eyed her with calculation. Then in absolute contempt, she replied, "If I knew that, we'd be together. And we'd have the diamonds."

Ivy knew those words held some vital information, information she needed to tell Garrett. But she couldn't understand them. Suddenly she was desperate to get out, to escape. Her head hurt, and her body felt hot all over. Her heart began to race from a growing sense of danger, an unexpected, fearful anxiety that seemed to seep into her skin, making her dizzy as she realized nobody in the ballroom knew she and Lady Margaret were alone in her bedchamber.

"Where is Ian?" she asked breathlessly, attempting to focus as she reached behind her to clutch the edge of the vanity table.

Margaret shook her head. "He ruined everything for Benedict and me, you know. He made it so very difficult for us to get away and live together happily."

Confusion reeled within her. She didn't understand. "Where—where is . . . my brother?"

In a low breath of fury, Margaret spat, "I hope he's *dead*." With that, she threw her champagne glass hard at the mirror behind Ivy's head, shattering both with the violent force.

Ivy ducked, catching herself before she fell to the floor, fine crystal, glass and pale liquid spraying across her hair and back.

After smoothing her skirts, Lady Margaret turned and walked to the door, and without another word or glance over her shoulder, quickly quit the room.

Shaking violently, Ivy tried to stand. She tripped on her skirts and dropped to her knees, falling forward, her palms landing hard on shattered glass. Suddenly the room spun around her as she attempted to rise once more. But she couldn't. Something was wrong—with her feet, her . . . hands, the pain—

"What happened to you?"

A voice she knew came from the doorway. Helping her. A soothing voice. But she couldn't see, couldn't move.

I'm—bleeding . . .

And then she lay on her back, staring up at Hermione— or . . . Viola. Viola in a different—then mumbling, rushing water, Ian's face, Garrett—

Help—me!

She closed her eyes to the blackness.

Chapter 20

It took only minutes for Garrett to realize something was very wrong. He'd let Ivy leave the ballroom because he knew she needed time alone to consider all that had happened this evening, to grieve in private before he sat her down for a good, long discussion. But when he charged forward in search of Lady Margaret, unable to find her in the crowd, with nobody certain of her whereabouts, he began to worry.

He'd realized immediately that Margaret shouldn't be in Winter Garden, but he'd been more concerned with making his grand entrance and how Ivy would react than the meaning behind the lady's surprise return into his life. Now, with both of them absent from the ballroom, a certain alarm gnawed at his gut, and he decided it was time to take action.

He knew Ivy hadn't left the house by way of the main entrance; Newbury had strict orders to inform him if she walked through the front doors or ordered the carriage. So, after speaking briefly with Thomas and Madeleine, the three of them left the ballroom fairly unnoticed as the gathering carried on much as it did before his amusing and rather pompous introduction. Thomas left them to find Mrs. Thurman and direct her to engage the available staff for a quiet first-floor search, and then he and Madeleine climbed the center staircase to the upper floor, his first intent to go to Ivy's bedchamber, where he suspected she went after leaving the ball. His head ached tonight, and with each step he felt a sharp stab of pain to the beat of his thundering heart.

They traversed the long, dim hallway in silence, seeing nobody, though festive music could be heard from the ballroom below. They found her bedroom door ajar, and with a marked trepidation, he opened it.

"Jesus, what happened?" he whispered as he fairly ripped his mask from his face.

Madeleine brushed past him, then gasped, her mouth opening wide in horror.

He stared in shock at the scene before him, the broken mirror, the shattered crystal, excellent champagne dripping from the top of the vanity table to soak into the rug.

"There's blood here," he said, his voice catching with a suddenly overpowering sense of dread.

Removing her own mask, Madeleine knelt to look at it. "It's not much, Garrett. It looks—"

"Like she cut her herself on the glass," he interjected.

Madeleine glanced up to his face. "Or someone did. We don't know who was in here, and there are two champagne glasses."

He turned his attention back to the vanity, spying the second glass, mostly empty. In two steps he reached it, lifting it, smelling it.

"This isn't my champagne," he said. Then after taking a tiny sip, he clarified, "Something's been added."

Madeleine came to her feet, staring at him, her face pale. "You think she's been drugged?"

He shook his head, bile rising to the level of his panic. "I don't know." He ran his fingers through his hair, frustrated, uncertain what to do next.

Madeleine inhaled a deep breath. "Let's think rationally, Garrett. She's not in here, so she left. And if someone drugged her, she would have to be carried, *non*? And nobody could carry her that far without being noticed." Reaching out, she gingerly touched his arm. "That means she's here, and we'll find her."

He nodded once. Then abruptly he turned and walked into her withdrawing room, noting with some relief that the vanity chair remained snug against the wall, guarding the entrance from the tunnel. Whoever was here had left by the hallway door. Or more than one person was involved.

Garrett returned to the bedroom proper. "We need to search the rooms on this landing."

Madeleine nodded. "Should we send word to the authorities?"

"No," he replied at once. "At least not until we have a better idea what took place. Involving too many people before we're exactly aware of what is happening could cause complications too numerous to mention—"

"Pardon me, my lord?"

He and Madeleine turned to the doorway to see Newbury standing before them, his features wide with surprise as he took in the scene.

"What is it?" he grumbled.

Newbury gave him a slight bow, then said, "A package has arrived for you, my lord."

Garrett frowned and began to walk toward him. "A package? From whom?"

The butler shook his head. "I've no idea. There's no card," he remarked as he held out a small, square box for his view. "But I thought you should have it straightaway."

Garrett stared at it for a second or two, noting the golden wrapping paper held together by a scarlet bow. "Thank you, Newbury, that will be all," he said, taking it from the man's hand as he dismissed him.

"It looks like a present," Madeleine said, moving closer to inspect it.

"Yes," he agreed with unease as he hastily began to untie it. "An oddly timed present."

After dropping the ribbon to the floor with swift fingers, he fairly attacked the wrapping paper, tossing it aside as well. Then, without delay, he lifted the lid, took one look within, and felt his heart stop.

Madeleine gasped.

"Oh, God . . ." he breathed as his hands began to shake.

Inside, protected only by old, crumpled newspaper, rested the famous Martello tiara, its rubies sparkling, the gold shiny—and the three priceless blue diamonds missing from their settings.

"There's a note beneath it," Madeleine whispered.

Gingerly, he grasped the paper with two fingers, pulled it from the box, and began to read.

She's alive, and I'll trade her for the diamonds.
Find the diamonds . . .

She wasn't stupid, Margaret told herself as she gracefully lifted her skirts and retraced her steps to the foyer. Now that she'd scared Ian's sister into submission, she supposed Paul would be looking for her, for both of them, and she would be forced to confront him as he began to put the pieces together.

Although she'd been an unlikely suspect, it seemed odd to her now that he still didn't realize her involvement in stealing the Martello tiara two years ago. If he did, he surely would have sought her when he entered the ballroom. At least she needn't worry that she might be arrested, a horrible thought that made her shiver with revulsion. But he would confront her eventually, and to be prepared, she needed armor, something he wanted desperately. Benedict had told her everything about his house, its secrets, and she had a fairly good idea where he'd hidden the diamonds.

She needed to find them, and it was time for a thorough search, regardless of the fact that she wore her best ball gown. With what she would gain for the effort, she could buy a wardrobe of new and fabulous dresses. She knew the house, and had a very good idea of the mysteries it held. The diamonds were here, and so was the incredible tunnel system, not to mention the fascinating, medieval dungeon about which very few, if any, people other than she knew. That's where she would start.

As she reached the bottom of the stairs, she turned in the direction of the library, the room where Benedict had said his ancestors had carved out the first walled entrance, passing only one or two obscured faces along the way. It didn't matter who she said good evening to; she didn't know a soul in Winter Garden aside from Paul and Aunt Isadora, though it did seem to take her forever to reach the end of the long, dimly lit hallway. She paused only briefly to assure she wouldn't be noticed, then clicked the handle and stepped inside, thankful that she found herself alone. After closing the door softly behind her, she stood silently for a few seconds, listening to the din of ballroom music, then walked with caution to the bookcase.

Pain . . . diamonds, Garrett, Ian . . . Snowflakes falling, sparkling, jewels . . .
Garrett . . . Help me!
The pain in her head thudded her to partial aware-

ness, slowly, bringing with it a fear of something. Something urgent. She couldn't see, couldn't remember who she—where she . . .

What happened?

And then the smell struck her soundly. Putrid, rotting . . . the smell of death . . .

The cat . . . in the tunnel . . .

Garrett . . . please . . . find me . . . help me . . .

I'm . . . in the tunnel!

She tried to raise her eyelids but couldn't manage it. They weighed so much. She couldn't move, wanted to sleep, needed to sleep. But the pain made her feel so sick, kept her awake enough to sense an indescribable danger.

Something was wrong . . . the smell, so horrible. The silence, so terrifying. . . . Something . . . *is wrong . . .*

Ian's face, Garrett, fear . . . snowflakes . . . diamonds . . .

. . . find me!

She stood over her for a long time, watching Lady Ivy struggle with her dreams, nearly aware for a moment before drifting back to unconsciousness.

It didn't matter. She'd hidden her well, in a place no human should spend a moment, much less eternity. But her plan focused on nothing but the diamonds, and for that she kept the lady alive.

Time was getting short. He would be searching by now, had probably received the gift she left, and the note, and he would panic. He would search, but he'd never find this place. It hadn't been maintained for centuries, forgotten by all.

No, unless the Marquess of Rye paid her for her troubles, poor Lady Ivy would die here, and rot, just like her brother. Just like poor, foolish Benedict.

That thought made her smile, and without the slightest wavering in her decision, she closed the door to the chamber, locked it, and quietly left the dungeon.

Penelope was truly getting annoyed. She'd accepted an invitation to a magnificent ball, an invitation so grand it should—by itself—grant her presumed attendance at lesser social events in Winter Garden for a long time to come. And because of this presumption, she mingled proudly for the first hour or so without a care to the hard stares and snide tongues of those who couldn't believe she had the audacity to attend tonight's Winter Masquerade with her two daughters.

Learning that the secretive Marquess of Rye was none other than Mr. Garrett Burke the architect proved shocking at first. It had, however, taken her only a moment or two to realize with extreme satisfaction that he had been welcomed in her home on one occasion. And so she decided to use that detail as the night carried on, as she mingled with guests who once knew her personally and invited her to tea and dinner parties, but who now snubbed her as if she reeked.

Unfortunately, it so happened that events like this one, regardless of that fact that this was the first in two years to which she'd been invited, tended to spur the memory of what Hermione and Viola's older sibling had done. And bringing the . . . opium-smuggling incident and the baron's disgrace forefront in her mind incensed her. She'd chosen to forget about the horror of scandal as she readied herself for tonight's spectacular event, but now as she stood in the hot, loud ballroom, *still* unable to secure for her daughters a formal introduction to Lord Rye, her irritation had started to bubble to the surface like an acid stomach gone untreated.

True, Hermione had met him once, even if she didn't know his actual identity at the time, but Viola had not. And even if she never spoke it aloud, she realized her hope of a good marriage for Hermione was all but gone. The scandal had destroyed it, and soon her faithful middle girl would be on the shelf, likely to look forward to nothing more than taking care of family as she aged. But there lingered a hope that Viola, the prettier of the two, and the more innocent, could make a decent match and secure them all financially.

Penelope prided herself on her rationality. She understood how the world worked, and that Viola was little match, either socially or in appearance, for a man of such superb stature and title as the marquess. And after his somewhat grandiose entrance tonight, it had become painfully clear that the man had his eye set solely on Lady Ivy, a woman better suited to his class and needs as a gentleman. Still, she was a keen woman, and although there lingered a trace of hope that he might find her youngest daughter engaging, she'd been aware from the start that just being invited to one of Lord Rye's marvelous galas mattered most of all, for Viola and their future.

But the marquess had left his own party. And now she couldn't even find Hermione or Viola. Even that selfish and obtrusive Lady Margaret of Brighton had vanished, though the perfectly played music continued as the guests became intoxicated with drink and dance and laughter. Not so for her. She intended to work at this event, to introduce her available, marriageable daughters—who'd been unfortunately restrained by social castration for two long years—to Winter Garden's finest eligible gentlemen. But she couldn't very well accomplish her goal if her daughters weren't even in the ballroom.

So, in a huff, she went looking for Catherine, finding her friend in deep conversation with Lady Isadora, a woman who was slowly losing her mind to age and had no memory of the damage caused by Lord Rothebury or the scandal that enveloped her daughters. She only wished she could say the same for everybody else in the village. If that were the case both her daughters would now be married and she could spend the remainder of her days in peace and relative comfort.

As it was, they were running out of time. And so after learning that the two ladies hadn't seen her girls in at least thirty minutes, the three of them began their own quiet search.

*   *   *

Garrett and Madeleine left Ivy's bedchamber and began a sweeping search of the second floor, exploring each room rather than just calling her name from the doorway. If she'd been drugged, she could very well be unconscious, lying on or beside a bed or dressing table somewhere and unable to reply.

But as they met again at the top of the landing, neither of them had seen her or heard any noise that might be unusual for a house preoccupied with a masquerade ball.

"What next, the bottom floor?" Madeleine asked breathlessly, her tone overflowing with worry. "I can't imagine she'd enter the tunnel in a ball gown, and it's freezing outside."

Garrett gazed down at the small box in his hands, studying it as if it held some key to the sender he didn't quite perceive.

"Why give me this now?" he asked, thinking aloud.

Madeleine shook her head. "I don't know, but the timing does seem . . . odd, does it not?"

He felt the muscles in his shoulders tense as his stomach roiled with anxiety. "Someone has been holding my grandmother's tiara, without the diamonds, only to present it to me tonight." He turned and looked at the Frenchwoman. "Why tonight?"

Madeleine crossed her arms in front of her. "It's . . . the biggest event in Winter Garden. Someone wanted to surprise you, obviously."

"And that would make sense if a woman waltzed into the ballroom wearing it. Or even if it had been sent to Ivy for her to wear as my hostess. But that's not what occurred. It was sent in a package to be opened by me alone."

"Well," she replied, "if we had found it in Ivy's bedroom, I would think it's from whoever was drinking champagne, but the fact that it arrived separately could mean anything. Of course, the obvious answer is exactly what the note suggested, trading the diamonds for Ivy."

"Blackmail," he whispered. "But I don't *have* the diamonds . . ."

"And whoever possessed the tiara all these months would certainly know that," she added for him. "So why give it back to you?"

"Precisely my question," he said, his jaw tightening. "Why return the tiara when it alone is worth so much? The rubies are intact. They could be removed and sold, the gold melted down."

"Or the person could have blackmailed your family for the return of the tiara without the diamonds."

"Exactly." He studied the box for a moment, then lifted the lid to look down at his priceless treasure. "Extortion for money cannot be the reason it was returned to me."

"Perhaps this seems so confusing because there is more than one person involved," Madeleine speculated, lowering her gaze to the tiara again.

"There has to be," he conceded. "But it's more than that. When I was attacked in London two years ago, I saw the figure of a woman just as someone hit me from behind. There were two people involved at that time, and I assumed it was Ian and . . . I don't know. Some woman who knew one or both of us." He closed his eyes and rubbed his aching temples. "But what if these are *separate* events? Different people with different plans?"

She shook her head. "I don't understand."

He scrubbed a palm down his face, then glanced to the bottom of the stairs, ignoring the music, the laughter of the ignorant as most of his guests remained unaware of the maliciousness taking place this night.

"I've been thinking too symmetrically," he murmured seconds later. "Too . . . rationally."

"Garrett—"

"Why am I being told to find the diamonds now," he cut in, "after all this time in Winter Garden? What makes this . . . person think I can suddenly discover their whereabouts and exchange them for Ivy before . . . what? The crack of dawn?"

He realized he was being snide, and further perplexing her, but his frustration level had risen to match the gravity of the event—an event he wasn't sure he understood at all.

"It hardly seems likely that you could do such a thing," she remarked with an air of doubt. Thoughtfully, she asked, "So . . . you think receiving the tiara at the precise time you did isn't blackmail but . . . more of a message?"

Very slowly, Garrett shook his head. "No, not a message." He sneered. "It's a taunt."

Her brows rose, then, inhaling deeply, she asked, "But who on earth would taunt you? What would be the purpose?"

He gave her a sideways glance. "The only person who had the diamonds, as far as I'm aware, was Benedict Sharon."

Her mouth dropped open a little. "You think he's alive, hiding . . . somewhere in the house all this time?"

"No, that's impossible," he replied after a moment of careful speculation, replacing the lid on the box. "Even supposing he could live for months in this house without being noticed, he'd have no reason to stay here, especially if he had the diamonds. He'd more likely be on the Mediterranean shore basking in the sun and spending my wealth at his leisure."

Madeleine pulled back a little, her lips curving upward. "You don't think it's his ghost," she said rather than asked.

He snorted. "Absolutely not." Seconds later, he drew in a long full breath, and muttered, "But someone is playing me for a fool, ridiculing me from a position beyond my grasp, and being remarkably clever in the process."

"Lady Margaret?" Madeleine whispered.

He frowned. "She's clever, but she wouldn't return my tiara if she had it in her possession, whether the diamonds were missing or not, because I would then suspect her in the theft. She'd be better off selling the rubies."

"But she knows something," Madeleine warned, "or she wouldn't be here."

He nodded. "Indeed."

She waited, her eyes narrowed in contemplation, then muttered, "Can you think of anyone else who could possibly gain something from playing with you in such a dramatic fashion? It seems so . . . irrational."

He stared at her through narrowed eyes. "That's exactly what it is."

Irrational. Like a gentleman stricken with sudden impoverishment, or a woman scorned by a lover.

At that moment, Garrett decided he'd finally had enough—enough of the malevolent teasing, the secrets and lies. Enough of the fear and panic. This was *his* home, *his* party, and yet someone toyed with him over and over, probably watched him from afar, likely doing so since he'd purchased the property and arrived in Winter Garden. Someone knew the house inside and out, and even now sat waiting, mocking him into action.

Well, he would take action, take command, and to hell with the gossip should propriety be violated. Ivy was in this house, or very near it, whether awake and held against her will or incapacitated, and he would do everything in his power to find her, even if his actions caused scandal, or he had to tear apart his new home with his bare hands.

"So what do we do?" she asked, her quietly spoken words slicing into his thoughts.

With resolve, he shoved the box into Madeleine's hands. "Give this to Newbury and tell him to put it in the safe for now. He'll do it without question. Then find Lady Margaret. Stay close to her, but don't let her know you're suspicious of anything."

She nodded. "And you?"

With a half smile, he straightened his collar. "I'm going into the tunnel."

"Why?" she asked at once.

"Because there I can move freely, see and hear things from a different perspective. And if Ivy's inside, I'll find her."

"But . . . dressed like that? And alone? Garrett—"

"She should be my *wife*, Madeleine," he stressed, his voice filled with a bitterness he couldn't hide. "If not for this despicable deception, she would have been my wife for these last two years." He straightened, his own words filling him with an inner strength. "I *will* find her, regardless of who is hurt in the end. Just as you know Eastleigh would go to any lengths to find you if you were missing and in danger."

She sighed with clarity, admonishing in a near whisper, "Be careful."

He nodded once, then turned and headed back to Ivy's room.

Chapter 21

It was the smell that stirred her into final wakefulness, a stench more powerful than anything she could have imagined.

Ivy opened her eyes slowly, seeing nothing but utter blackness. Disoriented, she glanced around blindly as she reached out with her fingers, realizing immediately that she lay on a freezing stone floor, someplace void of all light and sound.

A sudden terror gripped her tightly, and she swallowed a scream. She tried to sit up, though it took great effort, her body aching with every minute movement, her head splitting from sharp, intense pain. The putrid smell of rotting flesh nauseated her, and she turned her head to the side, taking short breaths through her mouth to keep from losing her stomach. She managed to pull herself up onto one elbow as she fought to relax and think rationally, to calm her racing heart, to *remember*.

She'd been at the ball, and then—in her bedchamber, with Margaret. But Margaret left and then . . .

It hurt to think, and she shuddered from the dampness, the extreme cold. She needed to find a way out, to get away from the horrid smell. She still wore her ball gown, making movement difficult, though thankfully the layers would probably keep her from dying in such a frigid temperature.

But her head hurt too much to attempt to crawl, and so she drew herself up as she lay once more along the stone floor, clasping her hands together at her belly and doing her best to shield herself with her knees, wrapping a layer of her silk skirt around her shoulders and neck, purposely keeping her face to the wall in some measure of protectiveness.

She couldn't judge the time and so she could only pray that Garrett would already be looking for her by now. Forgiving him would take time and a lengthy discussion, but finding herself suddenly alone and afraid, it was his face she longed to see, his arms she longed to feel around her.

She loved him with every breath, and the thought that scared her most was that she'd never be able to tell him. Now, in the darkness, she would gather strength by keeping his face, his determination, at the forefront of her mind, trusting him.

I'm here, Garrett, my darling. Please, please find me . . .

He wasn't sure what he'd be looking for in the tunnel, but when he returned to Ivy's room and once again observed the mess of broken glass and spilled champagne, he felt a renewed sense of urgency. Quickly, he disregarded the scene and walked to the tunnel entrance, tossing the chair aside and clicking the latch to open the paneling.

Darkness loomed ahead, and he grabbed a spare oil lamp on Ivy's wardrobe closet, lit it, and then entered the chilly, musty passageway.

He knew his way without giving it much thought, and so he moved fairly quickly, deciding that since they'd found nothing on the second floor, he would take the stairs to the library entrance, then move toward the cellar. But as he approached the top of the steps, he paused, hearing faint strains of music from the ballroom coming from his immediate right and behind the wall.

Surprised, he lowered the lamp to the wooden floor, then placed his palms flat on the paneling, feeling the vibration of the music from the other side.

Hastily, he began to feel his way upward along the wall with his fingertips, moving quickly toward the top, searching for a now-familiar latching mechanism to slide the paneling. He found it almost at once, and with a click the lock gave way and he began to push the wall aside as he'd done in the wine cellar.

With little resistance it moved easily, and seconds later he peered into a shortened closet of sorts, a small room now vacant, but with a beam of light coming in through a tiny hole in the floor, no larger than the circumference of a lady's finger. Kneeling, he brushed traces of dust aside with his hand, then lowered his head and placed his eye directly on it.

There beneath him he could see nearly all of the foyer, Newbury handing a coat to a gentleman, two ladies standing at the top of the ballroom stairs as they talked and laughed and drank liberally from their champagne glasses.

Garrett sat back, his heart pounding in his chest as he glanced into the darkened passageway, feeling an odd combination of profound enlightenment coupled with overwhelming fury.

He'd never considered there could be tiny rooms throughout the house inside which a person could hide, spy on the family at dinner, dressing and bathing, even in bed, and yet still remain hidden even from the passageway. If there were other closets like this one throughout the house, and he had every reason to believe whoever built this one would have built others, then it would certainly be possible for someone to stay hidden for an indeterminate length of time, moving undetected, hiding or exiting when necessary, knowing exactly where the family and servants were at any given time.

Even now someone moved about his house freely, which explained how they'd been closed in the day they found the entrance to the wine cellar and the lock of hair on Ivy's bed. He and Ivy had no doubt been spied upon, listened to, perhaps even watched during their intimate encounters, and the knowledge made him sick with revulsion.

The orchestra began another well-played minuet, and Garrett stood, dusting himself off before exiting the closet space and pulling the paneling shut, his fear closing in on him as he realized Ivy could be lying unconscious in any such unknown room within the house. If he searched alone, it could take him days to find her, and he didn't have days. The only thing he could do was gather every servant on the property, light up the passageway like afternoon sunshine, and do a detailed search.

With renewed resolve, he picked up his own dim lamp and headed toward the stairs to the library.

Ian had grown despondent. His bread and water had been gone for a time, though he could never know how long without light. He'd been caged for weeks, drugged until only recently, and at last he'd regained most of his memory. Yet now, with full awareness of his plight, he decided he'd rather be drugged. At least then he wouldn't suffer the knowledge that he was going to die alone, chained to a wall in an unknown dungeon, without even his sister aware of what happened to him, much less the ability to tell her good-bye and that he loved her.

It was the thought of Ivy that kept him alert, he supposed, and the mere frustration of knowing he would no longer be near to protect her—assuming he was ever found at all. Then again, he'd not been a very good protector these last two years as he'd charged ahead on his miserable quest to return the Martello diamonds to its rightful owner, only to lose his own life in the end.

He wished he could know if there was truth behind the woman's claim that Rye and his sister were lovers, but as things stood now there wasn't much he could do about it anyway. The Marquess of Rye would make an excellent match for her, except for the tiny fact of her being a bastard child of the nefarious Baron Rothebury. And since Rye knew the full details, he doubted the man would marry his sister, though to give him credit, at least he hadn't spread the word and ruined her reputation as he had ruined her future by taking her as his lover.

But he'd never be able to help her now. His arm ached from being chained to the wall, held in the same position for so long. He no longer felt hunger, but thirst nearly overwhelmed him. And so he tried not to think about it.

I'm so sorry, Ivy . . . so sorry . . .

Be happy . . .

Ian closed his eyes. All he had left was sleep.

Ivy!

Her eyes fluttered open to the blackness, her pulse suddenly racing as she sat up abruptly, holding her nose from the lingering stench, trying to piece together the thoughts, the message, that had startled her awake.

She felt his presence, Ian's presence, in the dark with her, close by. Calling to her.

She finally felt alert enough to stand, but she was cautious in her attempt, gradually pushing herself onto her knees, then gingerly touching the wall for balance.

Its sturdiness surprised her, and it took her only seconds to realize she'd been left inside a thick stone structure, void of windows.

Clutching the cold wall, she slowly reached out and began to move, taking tiny steps as she followed the edge of the enclosure. Within moments she'd reached the corner, feeling suddenly fearful of what she couldn't see around her, near her, as she continued to slide her shoes along the stone floor.

Seconds later, she felt a difference at her fingertips, and then she touched wood—a wooden door.

Relieved, Ivy reached for the latch, but after several moments of skimming the door she realized the wooden slab was simply a flat surface, though she could tell from touch that it was very thick. She pressed her ear against it, hearing nothing but silence fused with the sound of her own beating heart.

She fought a quick prickling of tears but withheld them, knowing her best chance for escape required a stable mind, and she pressed on, determined to stay focused. Garrett would be looking for her by now, she could take comfort in that, though if *she* didn't know where she was, how could *he*? And *why* was she here?

Ivy decided her best approach was to continue following the wall, to learn what she could about the place of her entrapment. Once again she began to move, continuing at a markedly slow pace in fear of stepping onto the body of the dead animal—or whatever it was. The smell truly nauseated her, but she managed to avoid any disastrous effects by breathing through her mouth.

Her head still hurt, but the pain had lessened, clearing the fog that shadowed her memory.

Clinging to the stone wall as she crawled along, she focused on what she remembered last. She'd had a discussion with Lady Margaret, and then the woman had stormed from her bedchamber. She . . . fell—she remembered that, which explained why her hands were sore now. She'd cut them on glass. And then . . . she could swear she saw Hermione, but by then whatever drug she'd been given had taken effect and blurred her thinking so that—

She stuck her hand on something moist, startling her as she stopped moving in the black enclosure. And then she felt the tiny crawling on her skin and realized she'd struck a web of large proportion and released a host of spiders across the wall, the floor.

Ivy screamed. Terror enveloped her before she panicked, and she sprang away from the wall, shaking out her gown, her hair, feeling the creatures on her skin, the web on her face. In a frenzy she screamed again, and again, trembling with fear as she shook herself, brushed herself off the best she could, her breath coming fast and heavy and loud. She tried to get away, to move to the other side of whatever tomb they'd locked her in, but the blinding blackness left her confused about direction, where she'd been lying earlier, where the web was located. And the spiders—oh, God the spiders—

Suddenly her feet struck a solid mass, tripping her. She fell over, her knees landing on something soft, her palms on wet stones—the source of the smell.

She shivered, shaking her head, righting herself as she realized she sat on the torso of a human. Not a cat. A dead human. For a timeless moment, she thought she'd gone insane.

No, no, no, no, no. . . . Please, God, help me!

Through quick breaths and a racing heart, she squeezed her eyes shut, and ignoring all thoughts of what she was doing, she quickly crawled off the body, her shoe catching on clothing. She yanked her foot away hard and fast, hearing the clinking of metal buttons hitting rock but ignoring it as she moved forward on all fours, her hand outstretched until it touched the wall.

Then she curled herself into a ball, hugging her gown around her knees as she melded into the stone as much as she could, rocking back and forth as tears flowed down her cheeks.

Decaying flesh, spiders and webs, blackness, entombed for eternity . . .

Insanity.

"Garrett . . ." she whispered. "Find me . . ."

Garrett reached the bottom of the stairs just as he heard a click of the latch from the other side of the library entrance. He stilled, pulling back against the wall and dimming his lamp as the bookcase moved aside and light filtered in from the room.

He readied himself to grab whoever came through—then noticed Madeleine squeezing through the crack.

"What are you doing?" he whispered.

She sucked in a breath as she slapped her hand to her chest. "You startled me!"

"Sorry, " he said, moving into the light.

Quickly, she grabbed his arm. "Something's happened. I was just coming to look for you."

He allowed her to pull him through the tight opening, and she shut the bookcase behind him.

Garrett stared at the scene before him. Lady Margaret sat on the settee near the center of the room, holding a wet cloth to her forehead as she leaned back almost indelicately, her legs spread out, her gown in disarray, her free arm limp at her side, eyes half-shut.

Immediately, he walked toward her. "What happened to you?"

She said nothing at first, just blinked as she tried to focus on him. "Paul?"

He fought the urge to shake her. Instead, he turned to Madeleine who had brushed past him to sit beside the girl.

"I found her on the floor in here, unconscious," she said. "I don't know what happened."

Garrett stood erect in front of them, hands on hips. "Can you speak?"

"My head hurts," Margaret whispered.

He hoped so, but that wasn't the answer he wanted. "Where's Ivy?"

She shook her head. "I—I don't know."

"What were you doing in here?" Madeleine urged, patting the woman's hand in an attempt to comfort.

Margaret shook her head in tiny movements. "I can't remember."

Garrett groaned, his impatience teetering on violence. "We don't have time for this—"

The door to the library opened at precisely that moment, cutting him off. He turned just as Penelope entered, followed by Catherine Mossley, Lady Isadora, and, lastly, Hermione.

Penelope's eyes widened as she took in the scene. Then suddenly realizing she stood in the presence of the marquess, she made a vain attempt at curtsying. The others did the same.

"My lord, sorry to disturb you, but . . ."

He crossed his arms over his chest, brows furrowed. "But?"

She cleared her throat. "I'm looking for my daughter, Viola. She has disappeared."

"And I am looking for Lady Ivy," he replied with annoyance. "She, too, has disappeared."

"Perhaps they're together," Lady Isadora said brightly.

He grunted. "I doubt it. Now if you'll excuse us—"

"What did you put in my champagne?" Margaret asked in a low tremor of malice.

Garrett's head flipped around sharply. He stared at his former betrothed, who in turn tried to focus on Hermione.

"What did you say?" he murmured, watching her closely.

Margaret glanced up to his face. "She gave me

champagne, but it was clearly laced with something.
I remember now—it made me sleepy, which is why I
fell."

A tremor of rage cut through his chest as he turned
his focus to Hermione. She just looked at him, her features unreadable.

"Did you give champagne to Lady Ivy?" he asked as
he began to walk slowly toward her.

"I did not," she replied succinctly.

Penelope stepped in front of her daughter. "My lord,
this is ridiculous—"

"Be quiet, madam," he warned, his voice dark.
"Answer my question truthfully, Hermione."

Penelope's mouth popped open, and then she closed
it abruptly.

Hermione blinked, apparently taken aback by his
mood, the sudden tension filling the air. "If you're
asking me if I gave Lady Ivy champagne, the answer is
no, I did not."

"She gave it to me," Margaret snipped, her voice
carrying more strength as she tried to sit up.

Garrett fisted his hands tightly to keep himself com-
posed. "And did *you* give it to Lady Ivy, Margaret?"

Her lips curled in distaste. "Hermione suggested I
give her a glass of champagne after the obvious turmoil
you caused when you arrived." She lifted a shoulder
negligibly. "I simply followed her to her bedchamber
and had words with her."

His head reeled suddenly as he felt the air being
sucked from his chest.

"Did you argue with her?" Madeleine asked as she threw him a warning glance.

"Yes, but I left her there alone," she replied somewhat caustically. "I don't know where she is. If she's disappeared, it isn't of my doing."

Garrett's eyes narrowed. "What are you doing in Winter Garden?"

She smiled flatly. "I came to visit my aunt, who subsequently asked me to accompany her to the Winter Masquerade. There's nothing sinister in that, is there?"

He shook his head in disgust at the lie. Lady Margaret was clever and manipulative, and she clearly had more to tell him, but he believed her when she said she didn't know a thing about Ivy's disappearance. He had no reason to think she knew about the house, much less have the help she'd need to devise a scheme so rich in drama. He ignored her for now and turned back to confront Hermione.

"You drugged her, didn't you?" he maintained in a deadly tone of caution. "Why? Where is she?"

Penelope grabbed hold of her daughter's shoulders. "My lord, you can't possibly think—"

"Oh, yes I can," he cut in, "and I do. Where is she, Hermione?"

The woman didn't even flinch as she stared at him through narrowed eyes. "I don't know."

He didn't believe her, and it took all that was in him not to reach forward and break her neck.

"But you told Margaret to offer her champagne that would render her unconscious," he continued, attempting to put the pieces together even when they made no sense at all. "Did you take her through the passageway?"

Hermione didn't answer, just continued to stare at him with a growing contempt that seemed to radiate from her rigid form.

Garrett was sick to death of the evasiveness. "Where in Christ's name *is she*!" he bellowed in rage, clenching his fists at his sides.

Penelope gasped, as did Lady Catherine. Hermione never blinked.

"Maybe she's in the dungeon."

Very slowly, Garrett pivoted around, his head swimming, to stare at Lady Isadora, who'd spoken for the first time in a soft, wistful voice.

"What did you say?" he breathed.

The elderly lady smiled. "Well, it is a mystery, is it not? And what is a good mystery without someone locked in a dungeon?"

"What dungeon?" he repeated.

At last Hermione blurted, "She's insane."

He ignored that. "What dungeon, madam."

Lady Isadora shrugged. "I really don't know a thing about it."

Furious, Garrett turned to Madeleine, who shook her head, as perplexed as he.

"But Margaret does. She's the one who told me about it," Lady Isadora added.

He blinked. "Margaret? Your niece?"

"Of course."

Garrett looked back at his former betrothed as his heart started racing with the possibility. "Explain that to me," he ordered.

"She doesn't know what she's talking about," Margaret repeated, with a wave of a wrist.

Immediately, he strode to her side, surprising her so much that her eyes opened wide, and she flinched.

Placing both palms on the sides of her hips, he leaned forward so that his face nearly touched hers, trapping her against the settee.

"You will tell me what you know of the dungeon now," he whispered so that only she could hear, "or I will inform your parents of your various love affairs—"

She gasped, pulling back in utter shock.

"I will assure them," he continued, "that you are ruined, and this is why I broke our betrothal."

"But—but none of that is true," she seethed.

He lifted a shoulder in shrug. "I don't care."

She blinked as her face paled.

Smiling in immense satisfaction, he murmured, "Who do you think they'll believe?"

Seconds of silence lingered. And then tears welled up in her eyes, and she admitted softly, "All I know is that Benedict mentioned it, that it's attached to the tunnel in this house."

Stunned, he repeated, "Benedict Sharon?"

Glaring at him, her eyes misty and red, she whispered, "I loved him."

Abruptly, he stood, fairly gaping at her, trying to understand, to control his racing pulse. And then it hit him. "Our betrothal was a ruse from the beginning, wasn't it? You were involved in the theft. You helped him steal the Martello diamonds."

She said nothing, though her face turned an ugly shade of crimson.

He inhaled a staggered breath. "What happened to Ian?"

"I don't know," she spat.

"What *happened*, Margaret?"

And suddenly he knew. Taking a step or two away from her, his gaze traveled over the length of her, his mouth opened in a paralyzing shock. "You were the woman in the church, weren't you?" he asked in a raspy voice, his mouth dry. "The woman who watched in the corner while—then who hit me? Benedict?"

She snorted with fury. "My, you have it completely figured out, my lord."

Disgust permeated him to his bones. Suddenly questions about the theft, that night, everything, filled his mind. "Then where was Ian? Or did you and Benedict Sharon contact me, claiming to be him? You both set me up to die—"

"I did *not*," she interjected with closed teeth. "I didn't know he was going to hit you, or hurt you. It wasn't supposed to happen that way."

Now he understood, and a strange peace settled in. "But you took the money I'd brought in exchange for the diamonds. And then you left me for dead."

She said nothing, just turned and looked at her aunt, who'd gone so pale she looked as if she might crumble.

Seconds later, he murmured, "I don't have time for this."

Snidely, Madeleine said, "What do you know of Ivy, Margaret?"

Garrett answered for her. "She doesn't have any idea. She's not that smart."

Hermione snickered from behind him, and he turned to look her up and down. "But you do, don't you?"

She shook her head with feigned innocence. "Actually, I don't have any idea, my lord."

He looked at Catherine Mossley. "You've lived in this village all your life. Are you aware of a dungeon?"

She gaped at him, her skin as ashen as Lady Isadora's, seemingly lost in the confusion of the last few minutes. Finally, she said, "I—it's possible. This house has been here for nearly five hundred years, owned by . . . monks, originally, during the Black Death. I wouldn't be surprised if they'd had a dungeon built during that time. You'd have to ask Sarah Rodney to be sure."

"Where would an entrance be?" he probed her directly, knowing he didn't have time to hunt down the historian.

She pinched her brows together tightly. "I—I don't know, probably beneath the house, and near a water source."

Near a water source . . .

"The lake?" Madeleine asked as she stood.

He thought about that for a second or two, then enlightenment struck. "No, a well."

Chapter 22

The trip through the passageway seemed to take an extraordinary amount of time, he thought, and Garrett was nearly beside himself with impatience and worry.

A dungeon. God Almighty, who would put a person in a dungeon? The thought alone filled him with an indescribable terror, and to think Ivy had somehow been led to one, or carried and deposited inside, left him beyond horrified.

He led the way, followed by Madeleine. Although Lady Margaret had insisted on coming with them, he'd ordered her to stay, and he'd closed the tunnel entrance behind them to ensure her cooperation. She had no light and didn't have any idea where to look. He still had numerous questions that required answers from her, and he would get them. But first he would rescue Ivy from hell.

"Where are we going?" Madeleine asked from behind him, holding her skirts above her ankles as he rushed her along.

"To the main tunnel entrance," he replied over his shoulder. "Where's Eastleigh?"

"I don't know. I left him to search the bottom floor when we went to Ivy's room."

He didn't reply to that as he continued walking down the passageway. They'd curved around the bottom now and were nearing the entrance from the wine cellar.

"If Ivy is down here," Madeleine speculated, "wouldn't she have had to walk?"

"I'm not so sure," he said, slowing his pace as he came to the door. He handed her the lamp as he began looking for the door to the alcove. "If she was unconscious, she'd have had to be carried."

"Then a man is involved," she insisted. "That would be the only way she could be carried this distance."

"Or more than one woman." He found the latch and heard the click. "Be careful in here," he warned. "The well is to the left, and it's open; I don't know how sturdy the stairs are."

She nodded and returned the lamp. "You first."

With little effort and only the slightest creak the door opened. He held the lamp out to survey what he could see of the area, though the alcove appeared as black and empty as it had before.

He tried the top step, gradually lending his weight to it, and found it sturdy. Then, with a controlled haste, he descended the remainder of them and moved quickly toward the well. He could already hear the trickling of water again but nothing else.

"Ivy!" he shouted.

Nothing.

"There has to be a door somewhere," he said to Madeleine, as she walked to his side.

Immediately, they both began to search with the lamp held high, moving from the edge of the well until they'd made a circle of the alcove, finding only solid earthen walls.

"I don't see anything that could be a door," she muttered, her voice filled with a growing desperation.

Garrett felt panic rising to the surface once more. Stopping in the center of the small room, he closed his eyes to think.

"When Ivy and I were in here weeks ago, someone entered through the door at the top of the stairs." He raised his lashes and looked at her again. "Why?"

Madeleine very slowly shook her head. "Perhaps . . . she heard you?"

"Exactly, my thought."

He watched her forehead crease with her own stupefaction. "But if she did, why didn't she confront you?"

Garrett rubbed his eyes.

Think!

"If these are two separate events, then we can assume Margaret's plan of stealing the diamonds was rational."

"Rational?"

"It was stupid, yes," he replied, "and criminal. But it's not the work of an irrational mind."

Madeleine's mouth dropped open as realization struck. "So you think whoever came in here knew you were here and didn't confront you because . . . Why?"

"She enjoyed it," he answered simply. "Enjoyed our anxiety, our . . . getting caught."

"She?"

He turned and glanced back to the stairway. "I can't imagine a man would care about playing me for a fool, watching me from hidden enclosures, sending me a package containing my own tiara wrapped up in a pretty red bow." He shook his head. "No, this is the work of a woman."

Madeleine drew a deep breath. "And we know Hermione Bennington-Jones drugged Ivy. So she is likely—but could she carry her down here?"

"She's a large woman," he agreed, "but she would probably need help."

"From Viola?" Madeleine mused. "Or someone else? Elizabeth?"

Garrett glanced at the floor of the alcove, certain he was missing some vital piece of information, something he *knew* but couldn't quite—

His head shot up. "What was she doing in the passage space on this side of the wine cellar?"

Madeleine looked confused again.

He turned and once again studied the wooden staircase. "She didn't know Ivy and I would be down here; we entered through the tunnel in the forest. And if she only opened the door because she heard us, then she had to be between the wine cellar and this door, in the passageway that leads upstairs." He paused, then murmured, "But there would be no reason for her to be there, unless—"

"There's another door," Madeleine whispered.

"She didn't catch us," he breathed, "we caught her . . ."

Garrett reacted at once. He took the steps two at a time, entering the passageway and holding the lamp high.

"That's the wine cellar entrance," he said, pointing toward the floor paneling directly in front of him as Madeleine moved to his side, breathless. "The passageway to the library is to the left, so—"

He moved to his right about three feet to view the wall he and Ivy had noticed the day they'd entered.

"It doesn't look like an entrance to anything," Madeleine said from behind him.

"It doesn't have to," he maintained, passing her the lamp once again. "I found an entrance to a closet space in the wall inside the passageway earlier. This is exactly like it."

His fingers quickly skimmed the top of the wall, finding nothing. He then began to draw them down the sides, growing ever more discouraged with each passing inch, until he reached the floor. And then, on the left side, a foot from the bottom, he noticed a notch in the paneling, exactly like the one in which Ivy found the spider when they had discovered the first door upstairs.

His heart began to beat wildly in his chest; perspiration broke out on his neck and back as he stuck his finger inside. He heard the click and stood abruptly.

Palms on the wall, he pushed, and it rolled open to the side.

Madeleine sucked in a sharp breath of surprise.

Directly in front of them stood a massive iron door, with one small round window in the center and an iron bar across the front, secured with a large metal lock.

He peered into the window. "I can't see anything."

"Try the lock," she directed, holding the lamp up to give him a better view.

Wrapping his hand around it, he yanked hard, but it remained solidly bolted. Wiping his sleeve across his forehead, he said, "We need a key." Then in a fury, he leaned back and shoved his foot hard against the door once. Twice.

It didn't budge.

"*Goddammit!*"

Madeleine placed a palm on his arm in comfort. "Let's find Hermione or Catherine Mossley. Maybe they know something about a key. If they can't help, we'll get a locksmith."

He clenched his teeth, breathing hard, his muscles tight. "You go through the wine cellar entrance, I'll return through the passage to the library. We can find them faster if we separate."

She nodded as he fairly shoved her aside to unlatch the paneling near the floor.

"Just push the rack aside and move forward about five feet. You'll see the stairs that lead to the kitchen." He grabbed the lamp. "I'll meet you in the foyer, and if you see Viola or Penelope, bring them as well."

With that final order, he disappeared into the darkness.

Ivy opened her eyes abruptly. Something had jarred her awake, something beyond the blackness, a sound maybe, a noise that had penetrated the stone, though she couldn't know if it had merely been a dream. She shivered from the bitter coldness, huddling against the wall, forcing herself to focus on only Garrett.

He would find her. She had absolute faith that he loved her enough to trust that she would never leave the house, or him, without one last good-bye. She refused to consider anything else.

Wrapping a layer of her silk gown around her shoulders, she leaned her head against the wall and closed her eyes once more.

With extra care, she wrapped the package and tied it with another red ribbon, just like the one before it. Then she left her darkened closet space and entered the passageway, careful not to make a sound because she knew the marquess was inside the tunnel system, and she didn't want him catching her.

But she would go the other way to avoid him, to change her clothes in one of the unused bedchambers. They'd never know she was there, that she sometimes even slept between the sheets. Really, it amused her that she'd gotten away with so much, with so little help, for so long.

She quickly reached the hidden door and clicked the latch. Then after squeezing through the entrance, she dropped the package on the vanity and walked to the wardrobe where she'd left her gown. She donned it as fast as she could manage by herself, then slipped on her good leather shoes. That done, she checked her features in the mirror and, with a calculating smile on her lips, lifted the mask to her face and tied it behind her head.

After straightening her shoulders and smoothing her skirts, she retrieved the package and walked to the main door.

With a final glance into the room, she stepped into the deserted hallway and closed the door behind her.

Garrett reached the library entrance and stepped into the light, noting at once that everyone had left and feeling a sudden fierce anger at himself for not taking Hermione with them when they went to the well. But then after a bit of thought he wasn't so certain she knew very much. Either that, or she knew everything. She was very good at hiding information and not showing emotion on her face.

Swiftly, he walked to the open door, lowered the lamp to the floor at his side, and stepped into the hallway, moving as fast as he could to the foyer, thankful that the orchestra still played, keeping the majority of the guests ignorant and engaged.

He noticed Thomas first, his head above the others, standing next to Madeleine—and behind them both stood Hermione, Viola, and Penelope.

"Where were they?" he asked through a fast breath as he moved to Madeleine's side.

Penelope huffed. "How dare you speak to us—"

"Be quiet, Penelope," Thomas interjected, his voice pierced with irritation. "I noticed Viola coming down from the upstairs landing earlier, so I've been following her. When I spotted Maddy, she directed us here."

Madeleine gave her husband a quick smile. "I found Hermione on the ballroom steps just as I came in through the hallway from the kitchen, and she has something for you," she said. She crossed her arms over her chest and glared at Hermione. "Give it to him."

The blond woman's lips twitched beneath her mask. "I have a gift for you, my lord."

"A gift? What the devil is going on?" he asked in low rage.

Penelope flushed from the cursing, then wrapped an arm around Viola's shoulders in some measure of protection, her lips tight.

Hermione didn't falter as she brought her hands forward very gradually from behind her back, cradling another gold box in her palms.

A box like the other.

Garrett grabbed it and pulled the ribbon off in one hard tug. He dropped it to the floor and lifted the lid, at first seeing nothing but crumpled newspapers within.

With fast fingers he pulled everything out until he stared unbelieving at the contents.

"Holy Mother . . ."

"What is it?" That from Madeleine as she moved to his side.

The key.

"Oh, my God," she murmured. She looked up abruptly. "Where did you get this, Hermione?"

The woman shrugged, and pure hatred coursing through her voice spat, "I found it."

"*Found* it?" he repeated unbelievingly.

With a flicker of a caustic smile, she added, "It is addressed to you, my lord, is it not?"

"There's a note," Madeleine said, when he pulled the brass key from the box.

He grabbed it, opening it to read:

I want the diamonds. Find them, and I'll give you her location. Find them before she dies.

Garrett's mind had become a blur. The secrets, the taunting, the teasing, the novelty . . .

"It's a game," he whispered, dropping the empty box to the floor. "It's an insane, goddamned game." He choked down a cry of fear. "And someone is using Ivy's *life* as the pawn."

"But we know where she is," Madeleine encouraged him. "And now we have the key to release her."

Hermione paled, her lips parting just barely in acute surprise.

Garrett stepped so close to her she had to pull her head back to view him. But she never looked away.

"You were part of this blackmail scheme, weren't you?" he whispered gravely.

Penelope winced and brought a hand to her mouth, swooning and looking as if she might faint.

Hermione's gaze never wavered. "I was only a messenger."

He wanted to slap her. "A *messenger*? What the devil does that mean?"

She offered no reply.

"Let's get Ivy out of there, Garrett," Madeleine said, grasping his arm. "We'll discover truths later."

He looked up and stared hard at Hermione. "Watch them, Eastleigh. Don't let them leave."

"I think we'll all get some champagne and chat," he remarked coldly. He looked at Madeleine, and his features softened. "Be careful, sweetheart."

She touched her husband's cheek, then the two of them turned and raced toward the library.

Her plan had fallen apart. Hermione had been caught before she could hide the box, and now she was a suspect where she should be glowing with untold wealth from the sale of the diamonds that could have been hers.

She hadn't meant it to happen like this. She'd only wanted to kill her nemesis, the bastard Benedict, who'd confronted her in his home, ordering her out when he shouldn't have. But she'd also heard him mention the diamonds, and after she killed him, she wanted them. Benedict owed her that much, owed all of them that much, and she'd vowed to do whatever she could to find the precious stones for herself, even if she needed to resort to kidnapping and ransom.

Now, seemingly in an instant, it was finished. They'd stolen her only card to play, and soon Lady Ivy would be discovered, the diamonds, she supposed, never found.

Her plan had failed, and with it, so had the hope she'd held for those she loved. She had nothing left.

Standing at the shoreline, in a peaceful snowfall, she spread her hands wide. "I've truly failed them, Father," she whispered. "Forgive me."

And then, with silent tears, braving the cold, she stepped forward and slowly glided into the lake.

Chapter 23

Garrett had never been so worried in his life—worried for her, for them. As the time ticked by, he couldn't help but berate himself for allowing his deception to continue. If he had told her everything before the ball, maybe she wouldn't have run from him to find herself alone and in such a vulnerable position. He couldn't help but blame himself for her kidnapping. He should have gone after her at once. And what if they found her alive, and she never forgave him for his deceit? What if she never wanted to see or speak to him again? His panic from the thought took his breath and threatened to undo him, but he refused to allow it to stop him in his pursuit. Nothing mattered now but finding Ivy.

With Madeleine following closely behind him, he walked as fast as he could through the maze that would lead him to her. He'd considered going through the kitchen and the wine cellar, which would be faster, but he'd left the lamp in the library and he absolutely needed light.

He felt like crying, in sorrow, in rage—or better yet, killing someone with his hands—as he began to comprehend just how scared she must be alone in the darkness, with the rats and spiders. It was all he could do to keep himself together. He was all she had.

At last they reached the doorway to the dungeon. Breathless, covered with perspiration, his hands shaking, he lifted the key to the lock and shoved it inside.

Old and covered with rust and dirt, it took him several seconds to get the key to turn. And then he heard a click and relief washed over him.

"It works," he said, mouth dry, voice rough. A moment later the lock dropped off, and with little effort, he lifted the iron bar. With a long, loud creak, the door opened.

"Jesus," he whispered as the stench struck him hard.

"It smells like death," Madeleine stated through a cough.

"But it couldn't be Ivy," he said, more for his own reassurance, taking the lamp from her. "Leave the door open," he added as he took a step inside.

Garrett lifted the light as high he could to get his bearings. Directly in front of him, he noticed six stone steps that hugged the wall and curved to the stone floor, but nothing beyond that.

"I'm going down," he said over his shoulder. "Hand me the key in case I need it, then go and tell Newbury what's happened and have him send for a doctor."

"I should come with you—"

"No," he cut in sharply. "Nobody knows where this dungeon is except for you and me, and I don't want to risk us both getting locked in."

She was silent for a moment, then replied, "Use caution, Garrett. I'll be back."

He heard her footsteps disappear in the passageway as he began his descent into hell.

"Ivy!" he called out.

Nothing.

"*Ivy!*"

He heard nothing but silence—and a trace, a gentle trickling, of water.

"*Ivy!*"

Once he reached the bottom step, he began a cautious approach toward the center of the room, the lamp held high, the smell nearly intolerable. And then he saw a door—a large wooden door with a lock attached, and broken.

Swallowing hard, he moved quickly toward it, shoving the lock to the side with his foot as he pulled on the door. Remarkably heavy, it still managed to move for him, and he stepped into what truly had to be a dungeon, a stone floor, a few wooden beams, and undoubtedly soundproof. But aside from that it was empty.

Turning, he walked out and continued around the room until he found a second door, secured with a heavy metal lock. Trembling with apprehension, he passed the lamp to his left hand and tried it with the key. It clicked, then turned.

"*Ivy!*" he bellowed again.

This time he heard a thump. From . . . somewhere.

He set the lamp down, then pulled the lock from the latch, dropped it to the floor, and proceeded to shove the door hard with his foot.

It opened at once.

He grabbed the lamp and peered inside, shock and horror slicing through him as bile rose in his throat. He'd never seen anything like this in his life.

On a threadbare cot lay Ian Wentworth, Earl of Stamford, covered in filth and chained—*chained*—to the wall.

"Jesus, God," he mumbled, rushing forward. "Ian . . ."

He didn't move, but Garrett could see the quick rise and fall of his chest. He tried to shake him awake, but the man was pale, thin, and his eyes never fluttered. A man near death.

Garrett rubbed the sting from his eyes, then stood and walked back to the center of the dungeon, knowing there had to be another door. There had to be.

Suddenly he heard footsteps from above. For a second he thought to take cover, until he noticed the hem of Madeleine's skirt as she, Newbury, and two or three other men began descending the stairs. And he could see a light. Thank God, she had brought a lantern.

"Ivy's brother's in here," he shouted. "Get him out now. He's dying."

Suddenly he moved, a raw energy returning to overpower his fury. In mere seconds he found a third door, locked like the second, and with suddenly calm hands, he inserted the key, turned it, and shoved the door with his shoulder.

It opened at once, and he rushed inside, struck soundly by the smell that stopped him cold.

The smell of death. And then his gaze fell upon her, huddling on the floor against the far wall, and nothing else mattered.

"Ivy . . ." he whispered, his throat closing over with emotion.

She looked up, her eyes wide as she blinked from the light. Then she recognized him, and they filled with tears. Immediately, he moved to her side and lifted her into his arms as she started to cry.

"I knew you'd find me," she whispered, her voice husky, barely audible. "I knew you'd find me . . ."

He sat on the stone floor and held her for a moment or two, kissing her forehead, smoothing the hair from her face, feeling a renewed anger well up inside of him as he stared at the cobwebs, the decomposing body on the floor, inhaled the rankness in the cold air.

Seconds later, Madeleine stood in the doorway, looking flustered and concerned, her cheeks pink, stray curls out of place. She gaped as she took in her surroundings, then tipped her head toward the center of the dungeon floor. "Who is that?"

"I suspect it's Benedict Sharon," he replied.

"I *stepped* on him," Ivy murmured through a shudder. "Oh, God, please get me out of here."

"With pleasure—"

"Wait a minute," Madeleine cut in, moving forward, holding her own light up high as she gazed at the decomposing body.

Garrett stood, holding Ivy as she clung to him, her legs shaking as her feet finally touched the stone floor.

Madeleine walked toward the body, closing in on it as she lowered the lamp. With a satisfied twist of her lips, she glanced up and said, "See the sparkling?"

He took a step closer, holding Ivy's hand as he peered down to the lifeless form.

In a pool of dried, putrid blood, spread out from the chest of the decomposing body, Garrett's three priceless stones glittered brilliantly in the lamplight.

"The Martello diamonds," he whispered.

"He had them the entire time," Madeleine conjectured. "Apparently even died with them on his person. That's—utterly horrible."

"They—they look like they were in the pocket of his dress coat," Ivy said in a trembling voice. "When I tripped over him, my shoe caught, and I thought I heard metal buttons on the stone when I pulled free of him." She shivered. "Diamonds in snow . . . falling . . . tears falling on crystals . . ."

Garrett tipped his head to the side to look at her. "What does that mean?"

She swallowed hard. "I saw it in my dream, my vision. I—I think he died in here, Garrett, aware that he would never be found." Her voice dropped to a whisper of sorrow. "Just Benedict and the diamonds . . . stones that meant nothing to him in the end."

For seconds nobody said a word, the terror surely felt by the man enveloping them as the meaning of her words sank in. Then Garrett gathered his wits and hugged her tightly against him. "Let's get out of here."

At that moment Newbury appeared at the doorway. "My lord, the key to Lord Stamford's shackle was left on the table beside him, I suppose to be used by the person who kept him locked in here. We've taken him upstairs and called for a local doctor."

"You've—found my brother?" Ivy whispered with a heavy swallow. "He's been here in this . . . place the whole time?"

Giles nodded once. "Indeed, my lady, but he's—I'm sorry to say he's very near death."

"I have to see him," she said with newfound strength.

"I'll take you," Garrett insisted. "Can you walk?"

She tugged at his arm. "Yes. Please, Garrett, now."

Madeleine said, "You go. I'll collect the diamonds and arrange to have them cleaned and put in your safe."

Garrett turned to her and, with a hesitant smile said, "Thank you, Lady Eastleigh."

She offered him a delicate curtsy. "It's been quite an adventure, my lord Rye."

Then without another look at the hideous room of death, he and Ivy silently left the dungeon.

Chapter 24

I vy relaxed against the copper bathtub that had been filled to the brim with hot bubbly water. She'd already washed her hair and now simply wanted to sit and soak away the tension and horror of the last two days, relishing the low-burning fire in the grate at her side, the scent of lilacs, and the comfort of her bedchamber on the Rye estate.

She'd sat at Ian's bedside for hours following their rescue, and Garrett had stayed in the background, allowing her to cry and hug her brother and be there for him should he not recover. He'd been in dire need of liquids and she'd spoon-fed beef broth to him, occasionally talking to him and holding his hand, whether he knew she was there or not. By morning his color had returned, and by the following afternoon, he opened his eyes.

He would be very weak for a long time, but he would live, and they would eventually share their stories. But she wanted sleep first, then peace, then a long and frank discussion with Garrett. They hadn't said much to each other yet, but she had numerous questions, and she suspected he'd spent the last two days learning what he could about what happened—two years ago and the night of the Winter Masquerade.

Ivy inhaled deeply of the scent of lilacs, absorbing the warmth, her eyes closed. And when suddenly she heard the click of the latch to the passageway entrance from her withdrawing room, she didn't even lift a lash.

"Did you come to scrub my back?" she asked huskily.

He didn't reply for a moment, probably unsure what to say now that they were alone for the first time, and she snuggled farther down into the tub so that every part of her body below her neck remained hidden under bubbles.

Finally, he drew a deep breath and moved toward her. "If that's all you want from me, darling Ivy, I'll be happy to scrub your back," he murmured. "I just can't see you very well with all the bubbles."

She opened her eyes a crack, gazing at him as he lowered his large body onto the settee and stretched his legs out to rest them on the edge of the tub.

"That's the point of the bubbles," she replied slyly. "I think it's good to leave some things to the imagination, don't you?"

He gave her a sultry stare. "My imagination needs pampering."

"As does my body, and you shouldn't even be in here," she returned after a moment, closing her eyes again.

He exhaled a long sigh. "We need privacy to talk, Ivy."

Without pause, she stated, "Then you're very fortunate I locked the door to the hallway, my lord Rye."

"Indeed."

They lingered in silence for a long moment as she realized he needed to gather his thoughts. At last he removed his feet from the side of the tub and placed them flat on the floor, then leaned forward and rested his elbows on his knees, his hands clasped together in front of him.

"The Home Office is sending a man or two to look into the death of Benedict Sharon, and to investigate the house fully," he disclosed, his voice low and thoughtful.

She opened her eyes and looked at him. "What happened, Garrett? Who did this to us?"

"I've been trying to piece together the events," he began without hesitation, "and I'm not certain I know everything."

She sat up a little. "Then just tell me what you know."

He cocked his head to the side a little, his features growing soft, his gaze reflecting firelight. "I know I love you."

She sighed, her heart swelling with tenderness even as her mind fought the lingering anger within. "And you probably also know I'm furious with you."

Her somber tone penetrated the air around them, stifling the mood even more. For seconds he said nothing, then at last he murmured, "Your brother is doing better, I hear."

"I know," she replied softly. "You saved his life, Garrett."

He said nothing to that, just watched her. Then, looking down to his hands. he revealed, "A man walking his dog found the body of a woman floating in the lake this morning."

She gasped lightly and sat up a bit more. "Does anyone know who she is?"

His glanced up, focusing on her chest. "You're distracting me."

Her brows furrowed, and then she noticed the curve of his lips and crossed her arms over her breasts to shield them from his gaze. "Who is she?" she asked again.

Without hesitation, he replied, "Eastleigh seems to think it's Desdemona Winsett, Hermione's sister who was ruined by Baron Rothebury two years ago."

Her mouth dropped open a little. "I don't understand. I thought—I thought she'd moved to the north country."

He leaned back again, lacing his fingers together on his stomach. "Thomas and Madeleine confronted Hermione, and she acknowledged that her sister's husband was killed in a wartime accident, and then not long after her baby died from fever—two months after it was born. Apparently Desdemona had never really recovered from the loss, and blamed Rothebury for the loss of all she held dear in her life. She left Northumberland last year, returned to Winter Garden without anyone being aware of it, and began living in this house."

Now unconcerned by her nudity, Ivy sat up fully, leaning forward in rapt attention. "How could she *live* here without servants, or . . . staples? And nobody saw her?"

He shrugged a shoulder. "Hermione and Viola helped her, and since the house was vacant, she could move around at will, learn its secrets."

"She killed Benedict, didn't she?"

He nodded. "He found her and ordered her out. Of course she had nowhere to go. I suppose he posed a threat to her already fractured life."

"But how—how did he get in the dungeon?" she asked through a shiver.

"She dragged him in a sheet, with Hermione's help, just as she dragged you."

She frowned again, thinking. "I remember seeing Hermione in my bedchamber after Lady Margaret left, and—and I thought I also saw Viola in a different gown, but now I'm wondering—"

"I don't think it was Viola; I think it was Desdemona. They look very much alike."

She reclined against the tub again, rubbing bubbles up and down her arms, enjoying the fact that he studied the slow motion of her fingers.

Exhaling a breath through his teeth, he continued. "Ian, who felt responsible for the theft of the tiara, had been following Benedict since he left London. When he arrived here to confront the man, he found him dressed for dinner but lying unconscious on the floor of the library. Desdemona struck Ian from behind, and then, with Hermione's help, she was able to drag them both, one by one, through the passageway to the dungeon. When they discovered Ian had come for the Martello diamonds, and that Benedict had them when he lived in the house, they decided—or at least Desdemona decided—that the price for the diamonds would save her family from financial and social ruin."

"But you bought the house," she whispered.

He smirked. "I don't think she liked that very much, but she still had plenty of places to roam without being caught, and I only sent a minimal staff. She's the one who toyed with us, Ivy. She would purposely scratch the walls, left the lock of Ian's hair. She's the one who blackmailed you. She had the tiara that she recovered from Benedict—who had probably already removed the diamonds—and she found an opportunity to use it by sending it to me the night of the ball. But in the end, all she wanted was the diamonds. They, alone, were worth everything to her, and she knew I'd trade them for you."

Ivy shook her head in growing disbelief, in sorrow. "She never knew he had the jewels on his person when he died, and never thought to look."

"When she died, she was wearing the locket we found in the tunnel."

Ivy furrowed her brows. "How—How did she get the locket?"

"She lived here," he answered huskily, "even after

you and I were here together. And she knew every room and tunnel in the house."

Ivy closed her eyes. "Poor Desdemona. Ruined by a man who seduced her and wouldn't marry her, then resorting to crime to make amends to her family. It's awful."

"It happens too frequently," he agreed in a deep, quiet voice.

For a long moment she said nothing, then softly, she disclosed, "I was always glad you never got me with child two years ago, Garrett. The same could have happened to me."

"Look at me, Ivy," he insisted in whisper.

She raised her lashes to gaze into eyes of thoughtful devotion, the fullness of love.

"I intended to marry you, you know that."

"I do," she answered.

"And you would have said yes," he reminded her with a gentle eagerness he couldn't hide.

Ivy inhaled deeply and leaned her head back against the copper edge of the tub. "I would have then, yes, but—"

"Ivy . . ." he whispered with longing. "I'm so sorry for not telling you my identity two years ago, for not trusting you in Winter Garden, for keeping secrets. Regardless of circumstances, I should have been honest from the start. I *do* trust you that much. I only had to learn to trust myself, my instincts." Through a shaky exhale, he admitted, "I never want to lose you again. Please—" He swallowed hard. "Please say you'll marry me now?"

For a long, still moment, time seemed to stop. Ivy looked into his dark eyes, so full of hurt, of sorrow for years lost, of regret for things that couldn't be changed. Yet with all she now knew, the fact that the Marquess of Rye wanted to marry her despite knowing she and Ian were bastard children of the Baron Rothebury made her heart sing with pure joy. That was all the proof of love she needed. The secret he'd carried for two miserable years was where he'd held her trust in his hands.

"Ian needs me," she whispered, her lips cracking with a trace of a smile.

He knew he'd won. A visible relief poured over him, so powerful that for a moment she thought he might break down into tears. Then he scrubbed a palm down his face.

"Ian has consented to the match," he returned, his tone thick and choked. "I've already asked him."

She cocked her head to the side. "He's delirious and sick."

"He's *coherent* and *pleased*."

When she said nothing to that, he reached over and stuck his fingers in the water, then began caressing her arm with the back of his nails, up and down. "Ivy . . . ?"

"I refuse to succumb to another seduction tactic," she teased, as if completely unaffected.

Suddenly, he was on his knees, leaning over her, his palms on the edge of the tub.

"Garrett—"

His lips closed hard over hers, and without thought, she wrapped her wet arms around his neck and held him close, pulling him against her as his mouth teased hers to submission.

"I need to know," he said softly against her mouth, "if I told you I loved you two years ago."

She sighed against him. "Yes, you did."

"And what did you say?"

She pulled away from him a fraction and placed her forehead against his. "I told you then, as I'll tell you now: I knew I loved you the moment my fingers touched your lips when we were introduced. I loved you then, I love you now, and I will never, ever stop loving you."

He swallowed hard as he reached for her palm and brought it to his mouth. "I'm so sorry I hurt you, Ivy."

She inhaled a shaky breath. "And I'm so very thankful you came back to me."

Lady Ivy Wentworth married Paul Garrett Faringdon-Burke, Marquess of Rye, in a lavish ceremony in London, April 20, 1852. With her brother walking her down the aisle to give her to the groom, she proceeded without reservation, her heart filled with love, and the famous Martello tiara—diamonds intact—sparkling in all its radiance upon her head.